Hi Angelina,

Thank you

Even My Hair Is Mad

LISA K. STEPHENSON

Even My Hair Is Mad

ISBN:

978-1094740201
Printed in the U.S.A.

First Paperback Edition

Also by **Lisa K. Stephenson**

Late Bloomer
Covenant: The Sister Series Compilation
Borderline
Green Trees

www.lisakstore.com

Twitter: lisakstephenson

Instagram: @lisak.stephenson

To Jevasia,

The teenage girl in High School who never thought she was beautiful enough...

1

Forty-nine minutes later and there they were, unprepared. The audience members were now impatient, their long sighs and indistinct chatter resonating through the large auditorium. New York Fashion Week was proving itself to be the busiest time of year for Nova, who was responsible for selling out shows and packing auditoriums with critics, the general public, and the press. Overhearing the audience, the models began to grow nervous. With the lights low and everyone anxious, it was the perfect time for Nova to make an appearance.

Nova stepped swiftly from behind the curtain and walked towards the microphone, which was positioned in the center of the stage. She adjusted it accordingly and tapped the windscreen to ensure that she could be heard. She looked out into the audience; their intense stare made her nervous. Her palms began to sweat, her hair began to frizz, and she was starting to feel uncomfortable. Standing still, she cleared her throat and waited — waited for the words to make their way from her lips, to say something at all. But there was only silence. The murmurs had stopped at least, and the audience watched her, anticipating a word, a sentence—anything.

Nova stood frozen, panicking, as her eyes scanned the

room, her hands and legs beginning to shake. As she listened to her heart begin to race, she tapped the microphone once more, this time just to assure everyone that an update was coming soon, and she would be delivering some kind of news. The question was...*when?* Members of the media stood, whispering to their neighbors as they made their way past them and towards the exit, speaking into their tape recorders. The news was quickly going to pour out: "*Marian Doll, Fashion Designer Runway Show, Epic Fail*". Nova, realizing that this was all her fault, wanted to scream. She would be out of a job, forced to live on the street, and blackballed in the industry for sure; but she still remained standing. Her breathing now heavy as she shoved her hands into her pockets.

More people stood to take their leave, and Nova watched in horror as the once packed auditorium began to diminish in size. Nova ran off the stage. Grasping the curtains, she drew in a long breath before stepping back out to face the audience; but the room was now desolate. Moments later the sound of an alarm blared, the patrons who remained in the scanty auditorium startled by this, their heads motioning around the room unsure whether or not this was a part of the show or a harbinger of danger. Nova placed her hands firmly atop her ears, lowering her head in disappointment with her eyes closed.

Groaning, she turned to beat the little alarm on the nightstand, bringing on a sudden headache she prayed it would stop with little to no effort.

Living with her sister in a small town right near the water the sun was always shining, the birds were chirping, and just outside, the kids were heard playing and riding along the pier on their bicycles by the high-rise apartment complex nearest the beach in Oxnard, California. Nova's seven-year-old son Tucker was slowly getting acclimated, enjoying the sunshine and making new friends. Feeling a sense of joy, Nova outstretched her arms, welcoming the new day, but this brief moment of happiness was short-lived as the feeling of despair washed over her. The futon she occupied in the den was cozy and acceptable for now, until she was able to fend for herself again -- at least until she could come to terms with her newly estranged husband, Terry.

Nova, standing by the front door overlooking the water by

the beach as her sister made an appearance, entering from the living room.

"Good morning," Marian smiled. She was the eldest of the two, and an intern now to the highly respected fashion guru, Joanna Morris.

"Hey," Nova said solemnly, wearing a look of dread upon her face as she grows anxious about the marriage counseling session she had in just a few hours. Marian offering her a cup of chamomile tea, hoping it would calm her nerves.

"Don't let this get to you," she said. "Terry is just doing what most men do," she continued, taking a seat atop the futon after gently placing her cup of tea on the floor by her foot.

"I just don't understand why he's doing this," Nova replied. Startled by the ringing of her cell phone, she reluctantly turned to answer it.

"Hello?" she answered, her voice calm.

"Hello, may I please speak with a Nova Signature?" a woman's voice replied.

"This is she," said Nova.

"Thank you. My name is Angela Robinson and I am calling from Portfolio Recovery Services—"

Immediately, Nova hung up, embarrassed as her sister looked on; she knew it was just another bill collector calling to pester her about the outstanding debt she owed. Things were quickly falling apart, and if Terry left, she would no doubt be homeless.

"Why don't you just call dad?" Marian asked.

Nova shot her a loathsome look. "I don't have a dad and last time I checked, neither do you," she snapped before stepping out of the room and making her way upstairs to take a cold shower.

"It wasn't entirely his fault you know," Marian shouted up to her. She blew on her tea to cool it before taking a sip. Just then, Nova was heard shrieking in fear from upstairs. Marian jumped out of her seat, spilling the tea across her lap. She raced up the stairs and pounded furiously on the bathroom door.

"Nova!" she screeched, fearing the worst. "Nova open the door," she demanded, listening as the water continued to run, beating against the empty tub. The locks clicked and Nova stood before her, draped in a towel. Her eyes filled with tears as she removed her headscarf.

"My hair is falling out!" she cried, removing lumps of hair exposing the bald spots. Marian let out an exasperated sigh.

"Jesus Christ! I thought something happened to you," said an aggrieved Marian.

"I'm losing my hair! That is an emergency, I—I have a bald spot Marian. No...no, two large bald spots! There are patches on my head," Nova said, her voice elevated.

"Nova, that's because you're stressed. This Terry situation has you losing your mind. Maybe you can go see a dermatologist," Marian suggested before heading back downstairs. "I'm going to the warehouse."

Nova stood in front of the mirror staring at herself. She could not believe her reflection -- her hair was falling out, her eyes were puffy from lack of sleep and dehydration, and if things weren't bad enough, she was gaining weight in her mid-section. *What's happening to me?*

It had been four months since Nova and Terry decided to separate, but it wasn't truly over. She was angry and made the decision to leave based on predetermined emotions. Nova believed she was justified; but she still managed to convince herself that her decision to leave was selfish. *What about Tucker?* He needs his dad, but she was so infuriated with him that she packed one suitcase for the both of them and decided to make her way to her sister's home, where she was now beginning to feel like a burden.

The first time Nova left, Terry did not contact her for days, leaving her to wonder if he ever truly loved her at all. She was his wife for crying out loud and yet, he so casually allowed her to walk away. No fight, no question about it. Upon returning home to their two-bedroom apart in Burbank - after vacationing with her sister and friends - she walked in to find a half-naked woman lounging on her living room couch. It was devastating, to say the least, and yet neither of them seemed to care. When she confronted Terry, he stood listening to her rage, grinning whilst the woman stumbled her way through the door, never to be seen or heard from again—or so she thought.

Nova became pregnant at age seventeen and had been

quarreling with her now alienated father, pleading her case on why she shouldn't be tossed onto the streets like a wild animal. It was this moment when Nova realized her life was beginning to fall apart; but then, Terry proposed. It was not your average, well thought out proposal. It was a hood proposal, a sly, *let's just go on and get married* kind of thing, and Nova was so young and gullible. Of course, being in love, Nova hurriedly agreed. With her father now highly disappointed, he turned to Marian, praying she would never be as foolish -- and she wasn't. Marian went on to finish college, get a good job, and has now decided that she wants to follow in their father's footsteps of becoming an eminent fashion designer.

Nova constantly felt like the black sheep of the family and thought that maybe, just *maybe*, her love for Terry was simply stemming from daddy issues. Her father, Raymond Dash Signature, made a name for himself in the fashion industry, designing affluent handbags and watches. The Dash Signature Collection sold in places like Neiman Marcus, Barney's New York, Saks Fifth Avenue, and in its very own store on Fifth Avenue in New York. He even opened one right here in Los Angeles on Rodeo Drive.

But Nova wanted no affiliation with him or his riches; he did, after all, throw her out of their two-million-dollar estate when she was only seventeen and six weeks pregnant. He disowned her because he was afraid of what the world would think — he was ashamed. Nova had gone through a lot since then. She struggled to find peace within herself. She had to learn how to cope with her losses, and raise her son when she was only just a young woman herself.

Their mother had passed away when she was only eight years old and Marian was twelve; things were difficult for their father, trying to raise two girls whilst simultaneously submerged in his work, satiating his hunger for fame and riches. It was understandable, considering he was raised in poverty, just on the outskirts of Crenshaw. She used to call him Daddy Signature, but as the years pressed on, Nova despised him for allowing her to live impoverished, never once contacting her. Now, she was forcing herself to hold on to the one man who had become a hero in her eyes, no matter how toxic he'd proven himself to be.

Struggling to fit into her jeans, Nova sighed, wondering when it was she had gained all this extra weight. She was no doubt far heavier than she had been about two weeks ago. She was unable to button her pants, and the shirt sleeves of her button-down shirt were now too tight. At only twenty-four years old, she was losing her vitality. She had never exceeded 135 pounds, even after giving birth. So this was unfamiliar to her, not being able to comfortably slide into her own clothes. Not only was she losing her self-confidence, but she began to fear the way Terry would see her. What if he thought she was ugly? Why would he look to rekindle things? After all, if she was appearing to give up on life and no longer care, then why should he?

The pineapple hairstyle she routinely wore, accompanied by a pair of two-inch gold hoop earrings, was now impossible to achieve. The back of her hair was falling out and thinning; placing it into a ponytail now would only expose it.

With only thirty-five minutes remaining until she had to be at the therapist's office, Nova contemplated another idea—a low ponytail with a side sweep, to hide the hair that was going missing on the right side of her head. A naturalist for the past two years, this was the first time that Nova and her shoulder-length 4C hair was experiencing such trauma. Nova thought that swearing off perms and chemicals of any kind would be far more beneficial for promoting hair growth and length retention. But who knew a little stress would have her suffering from what looked to be the beginning stages of alopecia — although Nova prayed that this was not the case.

Walking downstairs feeling mildly satisfied by her appearance she clumsily tripped over the small outdoor step separating the glass building door from the gravel walkway. Outside the high-rise apartments she moved hastily, scurrying over to ask the neighbor to keep an eye on Tucker, who was playing in the front lawn. Maria Holland was a sweet, elderly woman who occupied the beach house next door; newly retired, she would come here whenever she needed to get away, and in only four months, proved herself to be trustworthy and a good friend to both Nova and Marian. Tucker was busy playing, and Nova decided against disturbing him while dialing for a taxi cab.

Seconds later, she was climbing into the back of the automobile. Fixing her cardigan, she wondered whether or not she was overdressed. Since Nova couldn't fit into her jeans, she decided on a pair of spandex slacks, a loose blouse, and flats.

The car ride was silent. She missed Terry; despite their weekly sessions, she was always heading home alone which, to her, was proving that their sessions were unsuccessful. What were they really accomplishing? She had no clue. Sometimes, it just felt like Terry was wasting time and although Nova wanted to increase their sessions, Terry objected, claiming that his work schedule would not permit more sessions than they already had planned.

Ten minutes later, she arrived at the commercial building in downtown Los Angeles. She paid her fare and proceeded to enter inside. In the lobby, Nova pressed the doorbell for her therapist's office. She stood, humming to herself as she waited for the door to ding and allow her access into the room.

There had been sixteen sessions, and Terry had already emotionally checked out; his responses were brief and, at times, rude -- but Nova didn't mind. She convinced herself that the most important thing was that he was showing up.

"Hi," the doctor said with a smile once Nova entered the office. He stood to greet her, Dr. Phillip Wallace. He was patient and kind. Nova liked that he was a man too; she felt that if there were any cryptic messages from Terry, he would decode them for her -- and he did. Terry was unable to get away with the use of slang or jargon unfamiliar to the average woman. It was great, to say the least. Taking a seat on the couch, a docile Nova and Dr. Wallace waited patiently for Terry to arrive, who by now, was ten minutes late. Nova planned on telling Terry that she was ready to return home. It was time.

The bell buzzed from inside the office and Nova's heart dropped. She had no idea why his presence made her so uneasy — the anticipation alone caused her to feel overwhelmed, but in a good way. She felt just as nervous as she had when they first met. She was never willing to admit it to him, but he still gave her butterflies whenever he spoke. She was still very much in love with Terry. He was all she had come to know for the past eight years and of course, they were married, so she wasn't ashamed of her unwillingness to let him go.

Terry walked into the office. He was wearing a jogger's suit and a Knicks Baseball Hat. He was tall and slender, dark-skinned and dangerously handsome. Nova began to feel insecure; he looked vibrant and well-rested — he looked *happy.* Meanwhile, Nova knew she looked the way she felt: desperate. Dr. Wallace instructed him to have a seat.

"It is always a pleasure to see you both!" he said light-heartedly. Nova nodded her head profusely before realizing that Terry did not greet her as he usually did. He used to give her a tight hug, a kiss on the cheek, and grab her hand as he sat down. Now, he was cold, standoffish, and refused to make eye contact with her. He appeared bothered to have to spend his Saturday afternoon in a therapist's office.

"So, why don't you both tell me what's been going on?" Dr. Wallace said politely.

Nova hesitated before responding. "Um... Tucker is doing well, and he's made some new friends since summer started," Nova began to chew the inside of her cheek, a terrible habit she displayed whenever she was tense. "I've also been looking for a job, as you mentioned during our last session that keeping busy would help me to focus less on our separation," Nova said.

Dr. Wallace nodded his head in agreement. "Yep, that's always good to hear. Terry, how about you? What's been going on?" he asked.

Terry turned to face Nova, finally making eye contact with her.

"I just had a baby."

"Oh boy," Dr. Wallace whispered nervously.

2

Four Months Ago

Spring break in Miami and it was for sure a celebratory moment for Marian. Playing along the beach was Marian, Nova, Heather and Roger, everyone excited now that Marian's final semester was coming to an end. Marian had returned to school deciding to acquire her Master's degree in Fashion Design. Lying on the sand, the sunglasses decorating her face and the sun hat large enough to protect her melanin, Nova turned to face her friends and sister deciding to raise a toast,

"Grab your margaritas," she said standing, swaying as she raised her glass, inebriated. The hot sand under her feet and the birds chirping in the distance. "To my beautiful sister, you are so smart and I am so proud of you for completing your degree and following your passion," Nova smiled. Heather and Roger looking on, squinting their eyes to watch as her body oscillate back and forth,

"Nova honey you're way too drunk, have a seat," said Heather. Additionally, Nova was there to celebrate her twenty-fourth birthday, which was a bittersweet feeling. Despite not necessarily being able to afford such a trip she desperately needed a break. Nova saved while working the night shift as a waitress before being terminated for her constant tardiness only days before their trip at a nearby restaurant in Burbank where she and her husband resided. Raising a seven-year-old, working nights, and living with her husband was no easy task, she was truly exhausted. Heather was judgmental, feeling as though Nova wasted her life, choosing to keep her baby at such a young age, deciding against going to college and she felt it was partially due to the anger she was feeling in regard to her father. Heather Hamilton was twenty-five, 5'5 with brunette hair extending to the center of her back. Born and raised in Miami, she and Marian had been friends for years having met as undergrads during her time at UCLA. It was different for her, she hoped to meet celebrities and of course their offspring and was elated when she met Marian learning later on that she was the daughter to Dash Signature himself.

Marian begged her new friend to keep her secret, she so desperately wanted a name for herself, and not to live in the shadow of her father, hence the reason she asked everyone she knew to address her as Marian Doll. Thinking the name had a nice ring to it, the name of the brand she would soon come to develop and as luck would have it, everyone she associated with was happy to oblige. When school officials called her name, calling to question the coincidence of her surname, she would merely brush it off, exclaiming there was no relation—a lie, but it worked and for this she was glad.

Inadvertently their father managed to keep them out of the public eye throughout their adolescence. He was not shameful in the least, but he was always so immersed with his work that the children spent their time with nannies—not him. Marian soon grew to resent him for having never truly raised them and once she became old enough to understand she did not mind that he was away. A rebellious high school teenager she was throwing school parties she knew he would not approve of, crashing his luxury cars and sneaking out at night to spend time with her boyfriend. But she grew tired of being recalcitrant, her father now bringing his work home, jealous of how much attention, time and love he had for the accessories he designed. She also one day wanted to feel that passionate about something, anything and so, she decided why not clothes? It was the one thing she had come to appreciate, from the different fabrics to the unlimited designs that she could create.

It was a world of endless bliss.

Marian and Nova were very close and nothing had changed between them. Even after Nova was forcefully removed from their home, Marian too wanted to leave; she could not believe her seventeen-year-old sister was being tossed from their mansion, by the hands of their own father. Witnessing this she decided shortly thereafter to remove herself, this also aiding in her reason to disassociate from his name. Nova now a Higgins and Marian a Doll, both women were living life on their terms, neither having spoken to their father in years.

As the sun began to set on day two of their excursion Marian and Nova lay next to one another basking in the beauty of the skyline. Admiring the red-orange sky with a cool breeze now whisking over them, her hair defying gravity as Nova felt the strands of her twist out respond slightly, she smiled, tilting her head back and closing her eyes.

"I'm always having the same dream Marian," Nova said, her voice just above a whisper.

"What kind of dream?" asked Marian turning her body to face her sister, bending her elbow and placing her hand along her head to hold it up.

"A dream that you're running your own fashion show during New York Fashion Week and I'm there, standing in front of the crowd and I freeze; not because I don't know what to say, but because I can't believe I'm there, can't believe you made it and I'm right there with you," she laughed.

"You're going to be everywhere with me, Bug," Marian smiled; taking her right pinky interlocking it with Nova's to perform their handshake. Heather and Roger standing to retire back to their suite. Tilting her neck back, Marian assured them she would soon be joining. Both Marian and Nova enjoyed watching the sun go down, looking to their left to see the beach emptied, although one couple remained, shouting at one another in the distance, but the ladies knew better than to interfere. Standing now, holding hands and walking along the beach they made their way to the hotel, upstairs into their suite.

On the seventh floor in the common room of the large suite contained double glass doors leading out to the patio, a sectional and winding staircase which led to the upstairs bedrooms where both Heather and Roger slept. Marian occupied the room furthest to the back while Nova slept in the room closest the kitchen. Each room occupied with its own chaise lounge, throw pillows, computer desk, and television. It was a moment to splurge, right there overlooking South Beach and taking into account that they were all alone and it felt great.

Nova made her way to the jacuzzi found just outside the common room before entering onto the patio. Heather and Roger were upstairs scrolling through their social media pages. Heather ran a travel blog where she posted videos and photos of herself trying new foods, tanning by the beach, diving from aircrafts, and climbing the stairs to view The Great Wall of China with her senior class in high school—a photo she refused to delete until she was one day able to return and take another.

Roger let out a large sigh, sitting up straight as he studied the incriminating photo he had now come across. Standing to his feet he raced next door into Heather's room, grabbing her by the arm,

"Are you seeing what I'm seeing?" he asked fighting the urge to laugh. Heather now turning to face him, curious as she grabbed his phone, burying it in her palm for a better view.

"Are you going to tell her?" she asked him. Roger Washington, a senior attending Morehouse College, he met Heather and Marian one day at a concert for their favorite punk rocker Billy Idol. Their connection instant and their friendship still strong, but nothing could have prepared them for this. Towering over his peers, Roger is a flamboyant, African-American gay man who enjoys long walks on the beach and of course the company of his girlfriends.

"I have no idea. Maybe we should just let them find out on their own," he said. Just then Marian entered, watching her friends look suspicious caused her eyebrows to raise.

"What's going on you guys?" She questioned. But her mind was truthfully on food and wanted to ask whether they would be interested in ordering room service. But it became obvious no one was going to be ordering any food that night. "Seriously, what's going on?" She asked again, this time sounding apprehensive. After a great shower and a wonderful day at the beach, the last thing she needed was to be playing a game of *guess what*. Roger handed her the cellular phone, tapping it when it fell asleep and the screen went black.

"Maybe we shouldn't tell Nova," Roger said as Marian took a long look at the screen. Laura, an apparent old friend of Roger's, kissing Terry in a photo, a recent photo posted right there on her social media account. She saved them the trouble of searching for his profile as there it was, a tag. Marian felt her heart fall to her feet; he was cheating. Immediately she made an executive decision handing Roger his phone,

"No one says anything. I'll try to handle this when I can—"

"Hey," Nova said interrupting them standing by the threshold of Heather's room at the top of the staircase. She was wrapping a towel around her dripping wet body. "I was thinking we could get some dinner; I am starved." She said smiling. But the looks on their faces were anything but pleasant. Deep down Marian was afraid. She knew how much Terry meant to her sister and was sure this news would devastate her. Only two days into their four-day trip, Marian contemplated now if she should in fact tell her sister the news, standing as she stared off into her sister's loving eyes.

"I have something to tell you," she said, struggling to hold back her tears. Heather and Roger both interrupting,

"No," they said in unison but Marian was not listening. Nova grew curious.

"What on earth is it, you guys are scaring me?" she said chuckling nervously. Marian then stretched her hand out, opening her palm, waiting for Roger to give her the phone. A few seconds later it was up, the photo that Marian was dreading, she turned the phone, handing it to her sister. Nova could not believe her eyes as she stood there speechless.

"No way!" she said obsessing now, scrolling further through Laura's social media profile, an Afro-Latina—instantly she felt insecure. "There's no fucking way! When was this taken?" she panicked. Unraveling now right before their eyes, everyone feeling pity.

"Hey, hey, we don't know anything and we're going to party, drink and, of course, we are going to get through this," Heather said, reassuring her, both Marian and Roger nodding their head in agreement. But Nova could not focus. She was gone now, mentally her mind escaped. The only thoughts consuming her was what was happening in her home, to her son, and that's when she snapped; realizing she had to leave. There was no way she was going to make it another two days. Terry, her husband, with another woman. Impossible, she thought. This was probably some sick joke, maybe they wanted her to find the photo, so, maybe the man in the photo was him. Her mind was in overdrive as she now threw articles of clothing into a suitcase.

Heather, Marian and Roger all stood downstairs in the foyer with their hands-on top of their heads, confused, shocked, and honestly saddened that poor Nova was going through this. There was nothing anyone could say; her mind was made up and she had to leave by any means necessary.

"I have to go," she now stood crying hauling the suitcase behind her. The room felt dark, she could not move, remembering the woman's, name she removed her cellular phone from her pocket—trembling now. Taking a seat, she scrolled through the timeline for a Laura Walters. Laura was beautiful. Coming across videos, she listened as he mimicked speaking Spanish alongside Laura, laughing, kissing, photos of them together at restaurants, and another photo of them both at what appeared to have been a company barbeque. Nova felt weak, lacking the strength to move, to stand or even speak, she simply slid into the sofa, curled into the fetal position and continued scrolling.

Marian stood around helpless to stop her, concluding that it best, she too leaves. Nova was not going to be the same for the remainder of the trip. Disappointed, as they were just hours away from her birthday. Nova began weeping, the sounds of her cries loud and haunting. Everyone rushing to her side, kneeling as they all tried giving her a hug, but she could not feel them. The story and the photos of them replaying through her mind in a circular motion like that of a picture carousel, terrified of the heartbreak journey on her road to redemption. It was beginning to feel like the worst day of her life and she thought nothing could ever take the place of her father tossing her out of her home seven years ago. But this was it, this was enough to send her to a dark place, and before she knew it, she was there.

Crying herself to sleep and waking up before dawn, Nova

watched her friends sleeping on the floor next to her. Their trip was, without a doubt over, and so, she stood, refusing to brush her teeth or comb her hair lifting her suitcase, tiptoeing out of the front door and making her way to the airport. It was her birthday today, turning twenty-four, but she wished she was just dead, feeling empty and wondering how she was going to continue loving her son. All she thought of walking through the airport after passing TSA was whether she could go on being a mother to him. Women fear to admit this to themselves, when their marriages or relationships become rocked with infidelity there are thoughts of abandoning their children, I mean hell, postpartum depression is all about regretting them anyway.

Nova knew this better than anyone because during her postpartum depression she struggled to bounce back, resenting Tucker for landing her in a position where her father abandoned her, her husband was barely home, and she could no longer enjoy her life. She drove herself crazy, quarreling excessively with Terry, refusing to make love, physically abusing him at times and contemplating suicide. But he stood by her side, helped her through the process assuring her that everything was going to be okay and that their marriage was going to last, he was the one for her, or so she thought.

The tears flowed freely down her cheeks, once she boarded the aircraft and decided to check her phone again, minutes before having to set it to airplane mode. Now then realizing the usual midnight *Happy Birthday* text was not received. She had no more tears left to cry after an hour of sobbing, the woman sitting next to her appearing to be uncomfortable. Nova lost her appetite, nothing tasted good, she was requesting multiple bottles of water and falling in and out of sleep throughout the five-hour trip.

Hours later she stood in the hallway, preparing to turn the key slowly to their two-bedroom home in Burbank—her hands shaking, her mouth dry, and a migraine beginning to set in. She could hear the television set blaring inside, obviously someone was home, her son speaking in the kitchen, requesting a sandwich and then she heard it, the sound of a woman,

"You want peanut butter?" the strange voice asked. Nova quickly turning the key, unlocking the door, pushing it open.

The three-piece sofa set just before her, occupied by Laura who was lying down preparing to rise, their eyes locking. Nova remained speechless, unable to move when Tucker came over to hug her.

"Mommy, your home!" he shouted, elated. Terry appearing from inside of the bedroom. They all stood face-to-face, then Laura began moving hastily, her hands blocking her face as if she was going to be hit, while simultaneously hopping around to put on her shoes. Nova stepped to the side, granting her access to the front door as she continued staring at Terry, her face unreadable—he grinned. Massaging the back of his head, he instructed Tucker to return to his bedroom.

"I honestly thought you were going to be gone longer," he said. That's it, that's what he said. He made no attempts to plead his case. He did not even try as he remained unremorseful.

"Why?" Nova asked, the tears now falling, but she refused to allow him to see her cry as she aggressively began wiping them from her face. Shouting now,

"Why?"

"Look, calm down, why don't you get some rest and you and I can talk about this when you're up and—and you're not emotional," he said sternly. Nova could not believe her ears! Was this her husband speaking? Plagued by the questions swarming her mind she had fallen to her knees, powerless, "I just want to know why," she sobbed. He felt nothing but annoyed.

"Get yourself together, I will take Tucker and we'll be back in a few," he said. Hysterically Nova stood, responding to him, her face now drenched in tears. He did not love her. This was evident, but when, when did this happen? Why was he doing this? She simply could not understand. They were married, she was his wife.

"Leave my son! You go!" she screeched and without hesitation or a second question Terry threw on his shoes and made his way past her, moving swiftly to the elevators. She stood in shock, her eyes widened, wondering to herself if he was really leaving, just like that. And yes, just like that, he was gone. Nova sent her son downstairs to play in the community playground as she sat inside crying until the sun went down.

Her phone buzzed uncontrollably—it was Marian begging her to respond. She couldn't reply, she simply laid there, motionless, as the night lights began seeping through the windows. Tucker was begging her for a bedtime story having returned once the street lights began to shine. Ignoring him for twenty minutes, she finally got a grip on herself, standing and taking the suitcase she had taken to Miami, emptying it, and taking it into her bedroom where she began tossing new clothes and undergarments inside. She then entered Tucker's room where she threw some clothes for him into the suitcase as well. He sat watching her, holding on tightly to his action figures, terrified of how sporadic she was behaving.

Nova grabbed her shoes, telling Tucker to get his on too. She dialed for a taxi and when one came, she thrust the suitcase onto the backseat. Driving along the interstate with Tucker secured next to her, she watched the view and the moonlight bouncing off of the river just under the Burbank bridge. Arriving outside of her sister's apartment she made her way inside, into her sister's waiting arms. Marian whispered to her, "Happy Birthday Bug. I love you."

Present Day
"Nova?" the doctor cried. Nova had spaced out for a moment, fluttering her eyes, Terry was watching her, waiting for a response. She was at first incredulous, seeking to learn the truth. Clearing her throat, wiping her sweaty palms along her pants, she whispered,
"Is it Laura?" Terry slowly sat down, nodding his head in agreement. Nova knew asking these questions would hurt her but demanded to know anyway. Maybe she was a masochist or maybe she felt that by hearing the truth, it would assist her in finally moving on. She had no real reason for asking these questions, but clarification was what she needed the most,
"So, you and I—"
"We can co-parent," he said, interrupting her. Nova shot him a hard look. Her voice breaking up,
"Doctor Wallace, this is not, um, this is not how we're supposed to end. We hired you so you could fix things," she cried, turning to face Terry and grabbing him by the hands,

"We can get through this. We are a family; you, me and Tucker. Why—why on earth are you doing this?" she begged. "I just want to come back home. I want us to fix things. The baby was a mistake, I'm sure," she said, sobbing hysterically now. Terry, taking a deep breath, could not believe what he was hearing. The more she spoke the more uncomfortable he became. Slowly removing his hands from her grip and making eye contact with Dr. Wallace, praying he would intervene, Terry stood, but Nova would not allow him to go. Her eyes filled with tears and she started gripping Terry by his pant leg, Doctor Wallace grabbed ahold of her.

Terry stepped slowly out of the room, bothered by the fact that she had grown to be so weak. The sounds of Nova's crying following him out of the room—her worse fear had come true.

3

Seven days after receiving the devastating news that her marriage was over, Nova has still sequestered herself and Marian has started feeling drained, realizing she can no longer emotionally and financially support Nova and her nephew. Knowing this, she called in the cavalry, their Aunt Alexandria. Their late mothers' sister, Alexandria Howard lived just up the coast in a beautiful three-bedroom house with a two-car garage. Alex was not much older than her nieces; the six-year gap between her and Nova and only two years older than Marian, made it somewhat easy for her to relate to their experiences and converse with them on a paralleled level. A blunt woman, Nova avoided speaking with Alex on such matters; she was oftentimes judgmental, and on more than one occasion, had proven herself to be quite antagonizing.

Listening to Alex's car pulling into the driveway, Marian took a long sigh as she stood in the kitchen preparing breakfast for herself and Tucker as she has the past few days. Nova, locking herself away in the den, did not emerge unless it was to use the bathroom or grab a piece of fruit—her crown beginning to tangle. Marian grew tired of watching her sulk, it was like, how could she not have seen this coming? And the thought of her willingness to take Terry back despite knowing he had now fathered a child made Marian question her sister's self-esteem.

Upon her return that first night their conversation was brief because, truthfully, Nova was frantic, snot running from her nose, her eyes swollen from crying. It was the hardest thing for Marian to have witnessed, but she did her best in consoling her. The limited information she received was enough for her to decipher from a logical standpoint, understanding that Terry simply no longer loved her. Maybe it was her lack of confidence in herself that pushed him away. Marian contemplated on dialing him, asking him to take Tucker for a few days, but she feared to upset her sister, Nova would no doubt become irate—at least that's what she assumed.

Lost in her thoughts, the knock on the door interrupting her; it was Alex, Marian stepped down to the foyer and unlocked the door to allow her access to the two-bedroom apartment. Once inside, Alex resisted the urge to interrogate her niece, instead, taking a look around and seeing how untidy the place was it was safe to say that Marian had her hands tied and was dealing with enough. Marian's aberrant behavior telling—she was cooking.

"Well hello there, strange how you no longer greet your guests. Is that a millennial thing?" Alex questioned, confused as to why Marian opened the door and did not greet her properly, feeling mildly disrespected. Marian had not noticed this, though, she was too busy trying to avoid burning the breakfast she was cooking.

"Auntie, I am so sorry. I just feel so flustered. With work, and interning, and now I have to go out of town for a while!" She said taking a deep breath as she continued to maneuver around the kitchen.

"I understand. What's been going on? You were pretty vague on the phone," Alex said, taking a seat now by the dining table. A gym fanatic—her style business casual, she wore slacks, a blouse, and a cardigan, her typical go-to look, accompanied by long braids and stud earrings; her nails and toes always polished.

"Well, Nova is devastated about her marriage ending. I guess Terry will be filing the divorce papers soon. She learned he had a baby with the woman she caught him with when she and I went to Miami," Marian said. Unremorsefully Alex responded,

"You mean she's wallowing in her own self-pity? What's new? Men cheat. She should be finding ways to keep busy, not sulking," Alex said. "And where is Tuck?" She asked looking around.

"Upstairs sleeping," answered Marian putting the finishing touches on breakfast. Do you want anything? Some tea maybe?" Alex nodding. As Marian continued moving about she asked, "So, um, do you mind taking her for a while?"

Alex shot her a questionable look, "Excuse me?" she asked chuckling. "You've got to be kidding. Has she not been working? I mean what am I missing here?"

This is what Marian feared, having to disclose the truth to her aunt who was in her own right successful and independent. A firm believer that every woman should have their own, and never be dependent on a man,

"Well, Terry took care of the finances—"

"Oh, dear God," Alex said interrupting her. "So, she was one of those *stay at home wives*," she mocked, her face reading disgust.

"Don't judge her auntie," Marian said, defending her sister. Their voices were now elevated.

"Oh, I'm judging. She didn't go to college, got pregnant and then became a stay-at-home mom? Who raised her? What ambition does she have?" Alex shouted. Neither women noticing that Nova now stood by the threshold, her arms folded, her hair tied, and her pajamas wrinkled—angered by their conversation, she turned to face Marian,

"Why is she here?" she asked, speaking about Alex. Alex responded,

"I'm here because apparently you have nowhere else to go. What is this I'm hearing Nova? You have no job, no money, no nothing. You were just what? Something for a man to stick his dick in whenever he got bored because he kept you locked in a house all day?" she asked, her tone condescending.

"I don't want to go anywhere with you!" Nova cried. "I will be homeless before I live with you, Marian what's going on?" she asked, turning to face her sister.

"I have to leave for a while and someone needs to look after you," Marian pleaded. "Please, I really need you two to get along, for me at least. Plus, Nova, this will be good for you," Alex rolled her eyes as the kettle started whistling. Nova, feeling defeated, grabbing for an apple from the fruit dish on the kitchen counter. She turned to Alex before exiting,

"You're single and miserable,"

"Whelp, welcome to the club," Alex snapped.

4C hair has the tightest
curls of all hair patterns,
with hairs forming
tight S's and Z's or coils.

That evening, Nova packed after a long morning and afternoon of quarreling with her aunt and sister; ultimately it was decided that it best to leave with Alex. Kissing her sister goodbye, she and Tucker climbed into the backseat of the Black 2013 Range Rover her aunt drives. An entertainment attorney Alexandria favored the finer things in life.

Arriving at Alex's home, Nova and Tucker stood just inside the doorway taking in the view of the beautiful house. The walls were all white, the marble tiles black and white, and the black and white paintings of African-American models with 4C natural hair all decorated the walls. Alexandria did more than embrace her culture, she lived and breathed it. Taking it all in, Nova's face suffused with color, she was impressed. This modernized house grandiose, her aunt recently purchased it two years ago, but Alex and Nova did not have the strongest relationship, both of them allowing their communication to lax once Nova began to envy her family for their success, while she had yet to find her calling.

Nova hated hearing that she was just a stay-at-home mom or a wife. She wanted to be more than that but had no idea where to start and now with her heart in shambles, she began feeling like the process would only, once again, be delayed. Taking a seat on the bottom of the steps, Alex told Tucker to head into the living room to watch television, she and his mother were to have a word. Tucker stood; looking up to Nova, awaiting her confirmation until she nodded her head and off he went. Nova stood with her hands behind her back, like a teenager preparing to be scolded.

"So—" Alex said with her hands pressed firmly together.

"I'm most likely getting a divorce and no, Auntie, I was not working, I do not have a dime to my name, and I feel terrible. If you want to gloat about that or call me a bum then please, go right ahead," Nova said as her eyes began to well. But Alex could not bring herself to admonish her, instead, she decided on another approach—uplifting her.

"You are a beautiful Black Woman; do you understand me? You are strong, you are intelligent and most importantly Nova, you're a mom. Tucker needs you now more than ever, he needs you to teach him how to be a better man, a wonderful man," Alex spoke watching the tears now falling from Nova's eyes melting her heart. She was innocent in all of this, just another woman who loved a man and things did not work out in the long run. "I won't allow this to defeat you, I won't allow him to win. You are my niece, we are family, and I am going to see you through this," she confirmed.

The next few days Alex aided Nova and Tucker in getting settled into their new home with her, and of course, their new life. Terry had not called, not even to check on Tucker which was now beginning to upset Nova, especially since he was asking for him daily. Nova was not ready to communicate with him, asking Alex to contact Terry and possibly set up a meeting between them. Things were going smoothly or, so she thought. Although Alex did not want to come off pushy, she was adamant about Nova finding a job of her own. She was giving her an allowance of three hundred dollars a week, but this was mainly for her to get to and from job interviews, purchase groceries so she can feed her son, and get him the supplies he needed for school.

Nova appreciated all that her aunt was doing for her and Tucker; slowly, she was learning to be patient with herself again. One month later with still no visits from Terry and no response to Alex's messages, Nova was now anxious. She was unsure of whether she should just bring Tucker to the home they used to occupy in Burbank or if she should just give Terry a call herself. Tucker was missing him terribly and despite her grieving she decided on calling. The phone rang out bringing her to voicemail, but she hung up telling her son to get dressed, they were going to see his father. An excited Tucker did as he was told.

Most of their days were spent inside. Nova felt bad for taking Tucker from Oxnard where he had made friends, forcing him now to make new friends. She hated doing this to him, they had become nomads. She rubbed his head as she sat in the back of the taxi cab. Tucker was smart for his age, unproblematic, a perfect mixture of both Nova and Terry—a handsome dark-skinned young man. Arriving at their old apartment complex, Nova scooted out of the cab, taking ahold of her son's hand. Standing outside, she took a long deep breath before walking up the stairs and knocking on the apartment door, apartment 2N. As she stood outside she could hear the baby crying, realizing now that Laura was pregnant that day she had scurried from the couch, at least five months. She had not said a word, only dressed and left, which had made it impossible for Nova to have noticed back then.

The locks began unclicking; Laura could be heard yelling at her newborn, shouting in Spanish, "Callete la Boca," which translates to *shut up* in English. Nova could not believe she was speaking to an infant that way, but it was not her business. The door finally opened and there they stood, face to face, Tucker had his arms wrapped around her torso. Clearing her throat Nova stood there, wondering if Laura was going to say anything, anything at all, but she didn't. Nova, taking a glimpse behind her, could see the moving boxes, which she questioned,

"Where the hell is Terry?" Nova asked. Laura stood there, her long brunette hair uncombed, her light-skin blushing red.

"He went out to get more boxes," she said softly.

"Where on earth is he going?" Nova asked. Laura took a long pause before answering,

"We're moving to New York," she said.

"New York?" Tucker questioned, his voice innocent. Nova quickly placing her hands over Tucker's ears, said,

"Listen, I need to speak with him. He never told me he was moving, that's—that's impossible. When on earth was this decided?" she asked fighting back tears, but she could feel her eyes beginning to well—feeling embarrassed. Licking her lips, knew she had to find out what was going on. She wanted to stay, she needed to see Terry. "Why is he moving to New York? What about his son?" Nova asked, her voice cracking.

"He told me he spoke to you and you knew he was taking Tucker," Laura said. Nova could not believe her ears, shouting, "What!"

"Look, maybe you can call him, but I have to get back to the baby," she said shutting the door. Nova looking down at her son as tears now fell from her eyes. Tucker tugging on her shirt, his voice was faint,

"Mommy don't cry." Nova stood trembling.

Nova and Tucker went outside and sat there, waiting. She decided to take a seat on the stoop leading up to the apartment complex once her tears had dried. She was not going anywhere, instructing Tucker to have a seat, she handed him her phone to play games long enough to keep him distracted as she thought about what she was going to say. She had no intention of arguing in front of her son, but at this point she didn't seem to have a choice. Terry was leaving, this was obvious, fearful now that her divorce may have the potential of getting very nasty.

Fifteen minutes later, Terry's red Toyota Corolla stopped in front of the complex. Tucker, leaping to his feet, tossing the phone in Nova's lap as he raced down the stone steps to greet his father who did not look too happy to see them. Getting out of the car, he forced a smile, Terry was in no mood to fight, his back seat filled with cardboard boxes. Nova now stood, her arms folded, watching as Tucker interrogated him as any child would do that haven't seen or heard from their parent for a while. Terry walking towards her simultaneously speaking to Tucker who missed his father, and this he could tell.

"This is what you do? You pack yourself up and move without even so much as a word?" she asked. An ecstatic Tucker interrupting Nova to speak to his father, however Terry found this to be rude, instructing his son to wait his turn to speak, advising that he and his mother were having a conversation.

"Look, I hired a lawyer and I was told not to have any contact with you until the divorce was finalized. We weren't sure what state of mind you were in and Laura was afraid for the safety of the baby. Alright? That's why I did not call. Plus, I know you needed time to get over things and move on," he said. Nova, once again, could not believe her ears!

"Are you kidding me? Your excuse for not calling your son was that you had no idea what state of mind I was in? That is complete bull-crap and you know it!" she screamed. Tucker looked at her, causing her to feel ashamed.

"What do you want me to say?" he asked. "The divorce papers were sent to Marian's house over two weeks ago. My attorneys' information is also in it, if you want to hire a lawyer you can, or you can just sign so this thing can be settled," he said.

"No, we're not speaking about the papers, you told Laura that Tucker is going to New York with you and that is a lie. You've never even spoken to me," she said using her hands for extra emphasis.

"Everything is outlined in the papers, if you have any questions, Nova, contact my lawyer," he said attempting to walk away after kissing Tucker on his forehead. Nova stood crying, tossing her hands in the air, Terry's back now to her, having walked past her lugging the boxes in his hands.

"Why on earth are you doing this? Why do you hate me so much?" she asked, speaking to his back. And just like that after climbing the stairs, he went inside, shutting the apartment door behind him. Nova stood outside dialing for a taxi, Tucker watching. She could not believe she was breaking down in front of him, her hands shaking—disheveled. As the cab driver pulled up under the palm tree, she climbed inside, instructing him to head over to Marian's house. Arriving at the apartment, she stood outside, removing the keys from her back pocket. Tucker was being such a good sport, she thanked him.

Inside, under her feet, she could see the stack of mail her neighbor was so kind to shove under the door, and there it was, the UPS envelope addressed to Nova. Telling Tucker, he could go outside, Nova shut the door behind him, sliding her back down the wall until she sat on the floor, ripping the envelope open and removing its contents. In it she found a business card, a letterhead and documents with *sign here* stickers annexed. Nova screaming loudly, gripping the forms—this was really happening, she was served with divorce papers, flipping through the packet, she could see where Terry had already penned his name. This was all becoming too much for Nova to process; she sat sobbing, realizing her emotions were all over the place; she could not get a grip of herself.

As she read through the forms, she noticed the letter to the rear, requesting full custody to Terry Patrick Higgins, causing her heart to skip a beat. The reasons citing her unfit due to a lack of financial stability. Rising from the floor in a state of panic she opened the door, locking it from the inside and slamming it closed. She ran down the stairs, calling to Tucker and phoning another taxi. Tucker approached her, sweating,

"Mommy, please can we move back here? I miss my friends!" he said in excitement. But Nova could not focus. Once the taxi pulled up she begged him to get inside, but Tucker refused. This was not the time! She was getting angrier by the second, shouting at him,

"I don't have time for this! Get inside the cab now!" Nova could not believe she had just raised her voice to her son, she was losing herself. But he listened, and as they scooted inside she apologized, watching him look through the window, choosing to ignore her.

Nova snapped when she arrived at Alex's house calling her name but she was not home. She never felt more scared in her life as she paced, kicking off her shoes. Tucker disappeared into the living room where he sat watching television. The room began to feel small, like the walls were closing in on her; her life was falling apart. Placing her hands atop her head and removing her headscarf, she noticed the strands of her hair falling out. Her breathing increased, she is so angry, but clueless on what to do. She marched upstairs, screaming to herself, entering into the master bathroom, slamming the drawers, searching for a pair of scissors.

Locating the large scissors, Nova stood above the bathroom vanity. The large bathroom ornate with porcelain tile, Nova rubbed her hands slowly across the smooth, tan counter before pulling her 4C hair, stretching it as she lifts the scissors chopping the first bulk. Nova watched her hair fall into the sink. She felt liberated as she took another bulk and began cutting some more. The sharp scissors snapping, her eyes widened as she cut, chuckling to herself, she realized she had made a mess. Taking a deep breath, she stood taking in her new look. She was bald, her head would need to be shaved for a clean-cut—but it was all gone. Nova examined her shoulder-length 4C hair, now merely strands located in the bathroom sink, and parts of her hair along the floor; her chest rising and falling in agony.

Rubbing her hands along her bald scalp, she began to sob, walking out of the bathroom and making her way back downstairs, pieces of her hair trailing behind her, leaving a mess along the carpets. Back downstairs she heard the keys jingle in the front door. Turning to face her was Alex. Immediately Nova burst into tears.

"Why on earth are you crying and what the hell did you do to yourself?" Shouted Alex.

"Terry wants full custody of Tucker, citing that I am financially unstable to raise a child and he's leaving to go to New York, he wants to take my son, making sure I won't ever see him again," she sobbed handing Alex the papers from the attorney. Her hands trembling, pacing sporadically. Nova spoke quickly, her mouth filled with saliva; she was so ugly when she cried. Alex skimming them quickly, scoffed as she made her way over to the bar to pour herself a glass of vodka over ice after placing her briefcase on the ground.

"Stop crying, this fool just wants to scare you. They think you aren't knowledgeable of the law and from what I can see here, you aren't. Terry is an idiot! He just neglected his son for a whole month which means he doesn't make his son a priority. You do. Not to mention all those intermittent visits he made with her while you were with Marion, he just wants to run off to New York with his new bimbo and elude child support payments by now deeming you unfit to parent," Alex said. "Sign the divorce papers, throw his ass on child support, and let him go live his happily ever fucking after," she continued while walking away, shouting as she stepped up the stairs, "you couldn't just wait five minutes before chopping off your hair? Jesus Christ, what am I supposed to tell your sister?" she bellowed, groaning in despair.

4

The summer was coming to a close, two days after her meltdown and a visit to the barber, Nova was given a dark Caesar and a line-up around the perimeter of her head. Tucker was not a fan of this, he and his mother now looking alike. After signing the divorce papers and placing the package in the mail using the return postage that was provided, Nova gathered the strength to have a conversation with her son, deciding they would spend the day together at a nearby park. A picnic would be fitting she thought, packing a basket filled with light refreshments—water, juice, sandwiches and some gummy bears, Tucker's favorite.

Wearing her flip flops and a sundress she walked along the grass holding the basket and Tucker's hand. Nova found a wonderful place for them to sit right in Hollywood Park under a row of palm trees. Although she was not culpable in this case she felt terrible for Tucker, he would now be growing without his dad around, it was confirmed that Terry was relocating to New York in only a few more weeks, he received an offer for a new job opportunity there. Nova was feeling betrayed, as though he had spent most of his childhood with her and now his adulthood years, the years which mattered he would be spending it elsewhere, a new job, new home, better life and she wasn't going to be a part of it. But Alex steadily reminded her of the one thing Terry had given her that he couldn't easily take away—and that was her son.

Nova stared into his eyes as she prepared herself to deliver the news, the same news she too was still processing so she was by no means expecting Tucker to understand, or fully comprehend what he was being told, she only hoped that he would appreciate the fact that he would now be privy to the reality of what was going on. Deciding to stall no more, Nova began,

"Tuck, I have something really important to tell you," she said placing her hand atop his as he took small bites into his sandwich. His eyes looking into hers, "mommy and daddy are no longer together. What that means is, you and I won't be living with daddy anymore. Daddy is moving to New York and of course you can visit him, spend time with your baby sister and spend the summers there," she continued fighting the urge to ball. She could see the pain in his eyes. He was confused for sure, but he also had questions, his eyebrows knitted, appearing a few times to want to interrupt.

"I will answer any questions you have," Nova said softly. Tucker now put his sandwich down on the plastic plate and then the plate on the poker dot blanket. He said nothing, he simply stood, Nova looking up to him, Tucker now falling into her arms to give her a hug, indicating he understood. Closing her eyes, Nova embraced this moment as she let a few more tears fall, promising him that they were going to be just fine.

The defining qualities of 4C hair:
hair dries out quickly,
or struggles to maintain moisture
more than other curl patterns.

Sitting on the sofa in the white themed living room having a cup of tea with Alex, Nova pondered her next course of action. She and Alex questioning her passions, desires, anything she felt she could be good at, but nothing came to mind. Nova was even considering going back to school as her sister did to finally get her bachelor's degree. With no husband to care for and the freedom now to do as she pleased she wondered if this was the best thing for her to do. She appreciated the allowance Alex was giving her, but she knew better than to believe that was any way to live.

She admired both Marian and Alex for having their own independence, working and focusing on their goals, this is what she too wanted for herself. Unfortunately, she lacked any real direction.

"Are you happy?" she asked Alex once their conversation had come to a standstill to spark back up the dialogue. Alex wondered for a moment, replying, yes.

"But how, you live in this huge house all alone?" Nova said.

"I'm happy because I don't allow materialistic things to be the source of my happiness. Also, I enjoy working hard, I like being put under pressure, it gives me a sense of purpose. I'm older than you are and so, I know that these days it's hard to find a good man. You know, if you're too successful then you're intimidating, if you aren't successful enough then you're a bum who can't offer anything but sex," she said. "So, because of that, I've pretty much just embraced my life and loneliness giving thanks that I am successful in my own right and happy because I found my purpose and I'm doing what I love," she continued.

"You don't want children?" Nova asked.

"One day," Alex replied.

"I felt like if I didn't have a man and a child by say, age twenty-one then I was falling behind and my life would lack meaning, lack depth. I never in a million years thought I would be a single mother," Nova said.

"Women do it every day," Alex said. Winding down now, Alex decided to turn in, she wanted to sleep and she had work in the morning. She promised Nova she would stop by the elementary school to get the registration papers for Tucker before heading to work the next morning, for this Nova was thankful. She did not drive and taxi fare was taking up much of her allowance which she didn't enjoy. In addition, Tucker was in need of new clothes and textbooks. Things were silent on

Terry's side, no word of the child custody arrangement and nothing had yet been mentioned in regard to their divorce. Nova was sure to update her address when she returned the forms to the attorney. She was beginning to feel sick, as though the world around her was no longer moving. It was a rather unsettling feeling. Realizing now that being alone was not what she needed, but who could she call? The last thing she wanted was to be reprimanded by her aunt for deciding to go out and leave her alone with Tucker, or inviting strangers to her home for a pow-wow; and so, she wandered the 3200 square foot home, feeling nostalgic she remembered her past.

> The defining qualities of 4C hair:
> Individuals can experience shrinkage,
> Sometimes up to 75%!

2007

Standing against the locker slamming it before the bell tolled—a harbinger bringing to them the news of first period. Nova and her friends stood gossiping. The public high school she attended was known for its sports and exemplary debate team, neither of which she wanted to participate. With Marian only days away from graduating with her Bachelor's Degree from UCLA Nova was beginning to feel the pressure at home. Wondering if she too wanted to go college, or simply get a job. She heard so many horror stories from graduates—those who rack up debt, unable to repay their student loans and end up with bad credit by the time they turn twenty-two—so much for congratulations. Although her father set up a trust fund for both her and her sister, she couldn't help but fear the worst.

A toxic individual she had come to be after the passing of their mother, never speaking or thinking optimistically but rather reliant on the negative aspect of things. She figured if she did not allow herself to become excited or have high expectations then she would not stand to be disappointed. This was true, at least at home. With her father seldom around both Marian and Nova had to raise themselves—never feeling comfortable enough to speak with their caretakers. They provided one another with pep talks and daily comfort; ironically it was due to their father's absence that they had grown closer.

High school was hard and as a teenager, no one had the patience to handle her emotions. Nova preferred having male associates, she just figured men were less judgmental than the females were—the cheerleaders, the dancers, and the posh groups and of course your typical mean girls. Men were simple, straightforward and didn't care whether or not her shirt didn't match her pants or her relaxed hair did not fit perfectly into a ponytail. But when Nova began liking one of the guys in her circle that's when she realized, they didn't care because she wasn't their type. The two female friends she did have were fair-skinned and the men gravitated to them like bees to honey.

It was hard to watch and a very confusing time in her life. She struggled with low self-esteem, but could not identify what it was she was feeling. Ashamed, unloved, the darkest woman of the trio and while her friends always received gifts for Valentine's Day or Christmas she was left standing by the locker receiving a high five from the male friends she had who called her their "sister." Although it was a term of endearment it was strictly platonic in nature.

Then one day she was asked on a date while standing by her locker removing her textbooks to head to fifth period. Shutting it she was startled to have seen a gentleman, who was a tad bit darker than she was, smiling—his teeth perfect and white.

"You're really pretty for a dark-skinned girl," he said. Her emotions now perturbed, but she was happy someone had approached her and he was staring into her eyes, basking in her beauty. She decided on responding,

"Thank you," Theodore Higgins, age sixteen, player on the high school basketball team and literally could date any girl in school, but he liked Nova. He would stand from afar admiring her beauty, never allowing himself to be caught up in the enmity pinning light-skinned women against darker-skinned women. He thought it was a compliment telling her she was beautiful for a dark-skinned girl due to the misconceptions of notions such as dark skin women are not beautiful, but Nova did not understand, nor did she care, a boy liked her and that's all that mattered.

Sitting in class she would overhear the conversations being

carried on by her peers,

"Don't nobody want no nappy-headed baby," the boys and girls would say, Nova feeling self-conscious knowing that without her relaxer, her 4C strands were extremely kinky and at times unmanageable. Oddly enough the comments came from darker-skinned men, it was like they were disgusted by her complexion, her hair, her hands, her existence, making her feel like an insect that needed to be squashed; she was not ravishing, she was repulsive—shortly she too came to believe this.

Dark skin babies were hideous she thought, realizing now that had to be the truth, using her friends as the examples, the men frolicked to them, showered them with gifts, they were asked on dates and given a choice in who would get their attention, meanwhile Nova had to take what she could get, be grateful that someone had even thought to look her way. Emotionally she felt abused, hearing the constant criticism but remained powerless to stop it. Weeks following, she began avoiding Terry deciding she would not date another dark skin man—there was no way she was going to have one of them black ugly babies. Her kids needed to have straight hair and be light-skinned, her kids needed to be beautiful.

Some days during physical education Nova would sit amongst her friends: Jamar, Tameka, Toussaint, Tony, and Eric. Both Tony and Eric were romantically involved but did not expose their relationship in fear of being ridiculed. Both Tameka and Jamar too were gay, but he and Tameka carried on a relationship in school to avoid any speculation—kissing one another on the lips must have been awkward for them. Also, at the time neither one of them were willing to accept their sexual preference. It was odd, but they were all dark-skinned, well, everyone except for Tony, Toussaint, and Eric. Jamar was smitten by Nova, staring at her in veneration; one day alluding to the fact that she was pretty only because her nose was smaller than that of the average black girl. Nova felt flattered when she should have felt insulted, but ignorance is bliss, she had not known any better, and perhaps neither did Jamar.

That evening Nova was ecstatic, being told her nose was small did something for her, that remark gave her a boost of confidence. Looking at herself in the mirror thinking, *wow, my nose is small, I don't look like those other dark-skinned girls, thank goodness.* Nova had now come to believe that since she couldn't change her complexion she should be grateful for having small features, at least that was acceptable, apparently. Day by day she would examine the fair-skinned women, the Hispanic women, noticing they had smaller feet, longer and softer hair, a smaller nose than that of the average dark-skinned girl, pursed lips and the men loved them—identifying this as the natural standard of beauty and Nova wanted to take part.

Subconsciously hiding her hands and wearing shoes now that only made her feet appear to be smaller, men shoe sizes was what she fancied. Her style changing to accommodate this, her jeans tighter, her shoes smaller and after an abundance of research Nova came across a safe skin lightening cream she ordered from the internet using her father's credit card; the small dose of hydroquinone said to aid in lightening her complexion both quickly and safely. She was excited about the improvements she was going to be making to her body and skin, she couldn't wait to see the results. Nova even began speaking more openly to her friends about the men she liked, realizing the dark-skinned men did not like her too much she found herself smitten by a light-skinned man named Willie. He was tall, athletic build and had a beautiful smile, he too was attracted to Nova once he was told she liked him from her friend Jamar—a mutual contact.

Willie and Nova began speaking, spending time together; he was walking her to the burger joint after school where students were known to hang out. But Nova soon realized he was just looking to have sex with her and she was not ready, telling him she was a virgin and disinterested in losing her virginity in high school. Immediately he ended things and stopped speaking to her, indistinctly she could hear him and his friends making snide inappropriate remarks about her during the day. From then on, she stayed to herself, beginning to use her cream once it arrived and now stealing her older sisters' clothes for a tighter fit, revealing her curvaceous body. Marian noticing the changes found Nova in the study attempting to do her homework but remained distracted by television and loud music.

"How can you concentrate?" Marian asked turning down the stereo. Nova turning to face her, noticing her sister was a tad bit lighter than she was, a caramel complexion. "Marian, did you ever get teased in high school for not being light-skinned?" Nova asked. Marian knitting her brows taking a seat in one of the leather barrel chairs. "Um, no," she said. "Why? Are the kids teasing you?" she questioned.

"To be honest, I'm not sure. I know most guys don't like me because I'm too dark, but, they're friends with me." Nova said apprehensively.

"You're too young to be dating anyways Nova, focus on your schoolwork, besides boys are really stupid," Marian said.

"That's what you say, but you lost your virginity to Eddie in high school Marian. He liked you and he was Hispanic," Nova said.

"I do not understand you, so, do you want to lose your virginity? You don't have to do the things I do or things I've done, you have to be your own self," her sister said. Nova decided it best not to respond, Marian sitting upright staring at her, feeling bad for her baby sister. "You're really pretty Nova, don't let a bunch of horny teenage boys make you feel like you aren't," she concluded, standing and walking away.

Nova became aggravated, the skin lightening cream she was using was not working, after a month of applying it she was still dark and still, no one wanted to date her. One morning Terry found his way back to her locker, putting his pride aside to speak to her again,

"Hey, did I do something? You just stopped speaking to me," he said. Nova stood rolling her eyes.

"I know, I had my reasons. I have to go to class," she said bypassing him. Squeezing the straps of his book bag Terry ran towards her, fighting his way through the thick crowd of students,

"Listen, I don't know what your problem is, but I really like you. Let me take you the burger place after school tomorrow," he said, practically begging—standing in front of homeroom now Nova took a long sigh before finally agreeing.

"Fine," she said turning the doorknob and walking inside the classroom.

The next day after school Nova waiting patiently by the front door for Terry to meet her, he was late. As she continued standing she noticed the wave of students before her, some of which were the children of celebrities, she knew because they were picked up in stretch limos and surrounded by agents. She was grateful no one knew of her lineage and she could be regarded as someone normal. Terry finally appeared wearing his basketball uniform, she was confused,

"Why did you change?" she asked; Terry out of breath from running.

"Please don't be upset but our coach just called for an emergency practice. Can you come with me there instead?" he asked kindly; Nova looking around thinking about it, *what kind of games was he playing at?* Reluctantly she agreed, moments later they were in the empty gymnasium waiting for his teammates and the coach. Nova took a seat along the bleachers, Terry sitting beside her.

"Why do you always look so angry?" he asked reclining now. Nova chuckled.

"I do not," she said.

"Yes, yes you do. Don't fall victim to that stigma that all Black woman are angry, boys like me, we want to talk to you guys, but man, I be so afraid sometimes," he admitted. "You should smile more. When you're with your friends you're usually smiling and you look really good," he said. Nova blushed.

"Stop complimenting me, you know it isn't true," she demanded. Sitting upright now, his hands between his thighs, staring into her eyes,

"Please don't punish me for being nice," he said. But Nova did not understand, Terry was mature for his age this was evident but she was still trying to figure out herself, find solace in who she was and at that time, all she could do was believe he was up to something, a nefarious plot to probably bed her and then speak about her to his friends. *After all, why would he even like me, no one else did,* she thought. Watching her deep in thought, he leaned in to give her a kiss on the lips, Nova pleasantly surprised by his decorum decided on reciprocating, it was her first kiss and it was satisfying. The doors slammed shut when a few other boys came moseying inside the gym. Nova and Terry pulling away from one another, Terry arose, standing, shaking off the jitters after leaning in and telling her to watch him play. Nova did as she was told.

5

Present Day

Up all night reminiscing on her past Nova felt frustrated, weeping silently in the back of the house nearest the laundry room where she sat after wandering the premises the night before. Alex awakened; deciding she was not going into work, instead she would take Nova and Tucker to do his back to school shopping. She entered into the room she had arranged for Nova to stay, but inside the room was empty, the bed had not been slept in.

"Nova!" she bellowed, stepping downstairs wearing her silk robe. A knock came to the door, it was Janise, the cleaning lady who arrives every morning at 7:15 a.m. Alex greeting her with a smile before walking away and allowing her to do her bidding. Downstairs she called again,

"Nova?" Nova hearing her name wiped her eyes, feeling fatigued now she managed to stand rubbing her head and making an appearance,

"Good morning," she said. Alex staring at her knew something was not right, taking her by the hand she walked her into the laundry room, shutting the door behind them, Alex now stood with her arms folded,

"Cry it out," she said sternly. Nova wanted to be strong, telling herself that her tears were dry and she was now moving on, but her heart would not allow such a thing, she stood before breaking down.

"I—know I should not be crying, I just can't understand and I'm so scared auntie," she bawled. Alex sympathized,

"I know you are, but you've been a great mother thus far and Tucker needs you to be strong. But when you're having moments like this, moments where, you just need to let it out, tell me and I will take care of him while you take care of you," she said. "I don't expect you to immediately bounce back; heading out and pounding the pavement to find work, or pretend to know what you're doing. This is foreign to you, so you need to adjust to living an independent lifestyle, it will take time Nova, don't rush your healing," Alex continued. Nova remained at a loss for words, standing as the tears continued to fall from her eyes. Alex exiting, locking the door to allow Nova her space she headed into the kitchen where she began preparing breakfast for Tucker.

Alex cooked breakfast, cleaned, showered and took Tucker to do his shopping, although Tucker inquired on his mother's whereabouts Alex was very vague, trying her best to make their time together filled with laughter and fun. Nova stayed back, two hours passed and there she lay restless in the laundry room until a faint knock came to the door, it was Janise asking if she could retrieve some additional cleaning supplies. Nova stood deciding that it was time to get up and face the day. Unlocking the doors, she assisted Janise and then made her way upstairs to find her cellular phone noticing Marian had tried contacting her. Laying across the queen mattress in the room offered to Nova just to the rear of the hallway she returned her sisters call who after two rings answered with glee,

"Miss you!" Marian screamed, her background filled with noise. Nova spoke solemnly,

"Hey there," she said.

"Whoa, don't you sound miserable. Things with auntie cannot possibly be that bad Nova," Marian said, her tone lowering in devastation. "I'm really sorry I had to leave, but I have some great news I think might cheer you up," she continued.

"No, auntie has been phenomenal. I just need some direction in my life Marian, I feel lost," Nova admitted. "Plus, Terry hasn't contacted Tucker at all, I mean at this point I don't even know if he still lives here."

"Listen, here's the good news, the designer I intern for, Joanna Morris is allowing me to take one person of my choice with her to Seattle to visit, we're meeting this up and coming designer stationed out there," Marian said with excitement. "Nova, the trip is all expenses paid and we get our own hotel for two days! Also, I've been doing some research and the time we will be out there, the rock band Triple Door and singer Somaya Richards are performing at The Gated Hall. I can get us the tickets and if you can ask auntie to keep Tuck for a few days I'll get your tickets and email you the confirmation." She continued.

"Um?" Nova said hesitantly.

"No—no way do you have to think twice about this. You are coming! I mean, I honestly don't even know why I asked," she said chuckling. "I should have the tickets emailed to you by tonight, we leave next Wednesday. I love you, gotta go!" Marian said racing off the phone before Nova could have a chance to decline her offer. Nova wondered now, what she would even wear, what she was going to tell her aunt and whether or not she would even allow her to leave., the last thing she wanted to do was burden her aunt with her own responsibilities. Before Nova had a moment to process her thoughts the front door slammed, Tucker's laughter resonating through the long corridor on the ground floor and the sounds of bags rustling could be heard as well. Nova decided to shower quickly hoping her aunt would be interested in fixing Tucker a snack. She did not take long bathing her naked body and moisturizing shortly afterward. Nova surfaced to find Alex, Tucker and a strange gentleman standing in the kitchen all conversing about comic books and games over miniature sandwiches and milk.

Nova walked behind Tucker rubbing the top of his head and kissing him on the cheek. The strange man introducing himself to be a man named Hunter who was 6'3, African-American, slender with a bald head and a very full beard, his

complexion dark and his eyes blue. Nova wondered if he were
wearing contacts, she also wondered what he was doing with her
aunt; he was obviously much younger than she was. Nova shot
her a questionable look.

"Nova, Hunter is a member of the church I attend. He's
such an amazing guy. I completely forgot that he and I had an
appointment today to go down to the bay to pick up some
supplies for the ministry," Alex said taking a deep breath. "But
I mean since you're all here, why don't I just run on ahead.
Hunter this is my niece Nova, and of course you've already met
this Power Ranger, Tuck," she said slowly backing out of the
kitchen. Somehow Nova felt her aunt did this on purpose, she
continued standing next to Tucker as she watched Alex grab a
hold of her Birkin bag and step swiftly through the front door.
Hunter then stood awkwardly, Nova speechless watching
Tucker finish his food,

"Um, maybe I should just go," Hunter stammered. Nova
nodding her head in agreement looking on as he nervously
extended his hand bidding both her and Tucker a farewell.
Nova looking down at Tucker now asked,

"Who was that guy?"

"Someone Auntie said you'd like," he said laughing. But
Nova did not find anything amusing, instead, she was quite
upset. The last thing she wanted to do was date, she was still
mourning the loss of her marriage and the ink on the divorce
papers weren't dry—figuratively speaking. Filled with
dissatisfaction, she walked to the foyer to retrieve the bag of
items her aunt purchased for Tucker.

Nova and Tucker sat in the living room going through the
clothes Alex purchased and surprisingly Nova was impressed
with her selection and choice of clothing. After a while Tucker
was no longer paying her any mind, taking her phone turning
on the camera settings where he asked his mother to pose for a
picture, a shy Nova refused,

"Tuck, no way, put that down, I need to see how these
sneakers look on your feet," she said smiling.

"Mom, just say something," he begged standing adjacent to
her holding the phone steady looking to record her. Nova gave
in,

"Okay fine, fine," she said sitting up straight fixing her

blouse. "Um, my name is Nova Higgins and I am twenty-four years old, my son is forcing me to speak to you right now even though he should be trying on clothes," she said laughing, fanning for him to stop. "Okay, see, I said something, now can you come and try on these sneakers?' she pleaded. Tucker saddened.

"Mom, that is so boring," he said tossing the phone atop the couch before walking over to her to retrieve his new shoes. Nova pressing her lips firmly against his cheeks,

"Tell you what, when you're done trying on your clothes, I'll let you record a video of me and I will take it seriously. Deal?" she asked extending her right pinky. Tucker smiled from ear to ear,

"Deal!" he said interlocking his pinky finger with hers as to solidify their agreement.

Forty-five minutes later Nova put away Tucker's clothes in his bedroom, hanging his uniforms and fitting his sneakers neatly inside the sliding closet. Tucker downstairs, Nova returned to make them both a glass of lemonade, making good on her promise she returned to the living room where Tucker was awaiting her patiently to begin recording his video. Nova sighed; annoyed that he had not forgotten their agreement by now.

"Are you ready," he said playfully. Nova turned to roll her eyes as she set the glasses down on coasters atop one the sections found on the stainless steel opaque black tempered glass Maldives coffee table.

"Why do you want to make this video?' she asked.

"Well, my friends from Oxnard would let me record them doing their bike tricks, saying one day they'd be on television. I like recording, and since I can't record them anymore for the T.V, I want to record you!" he said with a devilish grin on his face.

"What exactly am I supposed to talk about Tuck?" Nova now deciding she would take his request seriously, she felt bad after all, because he was yet again taken away from his friends.

"I don't know," he said laughing. "You can tell people the reason you look like me, you know, why you're bald?" he said playfully.

"Okay, no need to be smart aleck. I was going through something emotionally and decided to cut my hair, you obviously don't like it, which is okay, but please don't be rude Tuck," Nova said softly.

"Sorry, but please mommy, you can talk about anything," he said. Nova said yes, deciding to take a seat on the sectional, instructing Tucker to stand so he can record her speaking. As she sat, she wondered what she would possibly say and decided; maybe Tuck was right, maybe she could explain why she was bald, by now she found it a bit dramatic that she had gone so far as cutting her hair.

"Okay, so, I'm ready when you are," she said. Tucker moved hastily, standing in front of her, using his fingers as he count down to one,

"My name is Nova Higgins and I want to tell you why I'm bald. You see a few days ago I was an emotional wreck and cut off my hair. My hair is a she by the way and she got mad and began falling out and balding when we found that my husband was sleeping with another woman, so not only was I angry, my hair got pretty upset too—"

"Mom?" Tucker said sadly lowering the phone. Nova sat in a trance, placing her hand over her mouth realizing the things she had said,

"Oh my God, Tuck, I'm so sorry," she said, standing to console him but he pushed her way racing up the stairs, slamming his bedroom door. Nova sat on the sofa, collecting her thoughts she knew she had just made a terrible mistake, her son is way too young to understand the affairs of his parents. At that moment she realized she needed to put herself in a time out, she was feeling bitter. The front door then slammed, it was Alex returning walking past the living room not noticing Nova seated inside, her head hanging low. She bellowed from the kitchen, "Nova!"

"I'm in here," Nova responded, her voice faint. Seconds later Alex entered. "Why are you sitting in here alone? Where's Tucker?" she asked.

"He went upstairs and locked the door," she said. "He asked me to speak for a video he wanted to record and I accidentally mentioned the infidelity with his dad and he got so upset," she said. Alex taking a seat,

"Oh jeez and he was having such a good day," she said pouting. "Marian called, says she wants you to come to Seattle with her, I agree, you can use some time away," Alex told her.

"Marian had no right to ask you that. I mean, I don't want to keep dumping my child on you, that's not the kind of mother I am—" Alex interrupting her,

"Oh cut it out, I told you already take some time. Tucker and I will be fine. Go and have some fun, get your mind off of things," she said standing now to head upstairs.

The next morning during breakfast Tucker had a request, as they all sat amongst the large glass dining table he turned facing Alex to ask,

"May I have a camcorder?" Tucker had wonderful mannerisms, he spoke eloquently and both Nova and Marian had once taken notice to how tidy and unproblematic he was—this made Nova proud. As they all sat eating, Nova decided to respond,

"Tuck, I just want to say sorry about yesterday," she felt the need to lead with an apology because Tucker had not spoken to her for the remainder of the evening the night before, which did hurt her feelings, but Nova did not want to overwhelm him, rather felt it best to give him a little bit of space, also, she was not too sure of what she was going to say. But now sitting with Alex things felt a bit easier, placing her fork down and turning to face him, Tucker returned the stare.

"I was pretty vague when I was explaining the split between your father and I and for that too I am sorry. You are very young and I didn't want you to look at your father differently—"

Tucker lifted his right hand, placing it on his mother's thigh, he then told her,

"Mom, it's okay," Tucker knew she was nervous, he could hear it in her voice and he hated seeing his mother appear to be so unhinged. He understood fully what was happening and why. Tucker had previously met Laura and even spent an entire weekend with her and his father while his mother was away in Miami; she was introduced to him then. Watching his mother's reaction that day told him all he needed to know.

Tucker was shy at times, but not your typical introvert, he

enjoyed making friends and hanging out once he began taking an interest in recording. Nova was not privy to this she only simply watched him from afar during the summer, outside, riding his bicycle and running races with the young men who resided along the street. Nova lifted his hand, kissing the back of it gently as she ran her fingers through his small 4A type hair afro. Alex watching them, smiling.

"Tuck, I'll get you a camcorder," she said. Nova turning to her quickly as Tucker stood elatedly dancing.

"Thank you!" he repeated, stretching his arms around Alex's shoulders; but Nova was not happy.

"Tuck can you take your breakfast into the living room, I have to talk to auntie?" Nova asked. Tucker agreeing, "I'm finished, I can just throw it away," he replied clearing his dishes from the table and skipping to the living room, Nova, peeking her head out of the dining room to ensure he was no longer in view. Standing now with her arms crossed, Nova said,

"You cannot spoil him like that."

"I simply offered to buy him a camcorder, I don't see the big deal," Alex said, her tone monotonous.

"He's a child and I'm his mother, you can't just offer him things like that without consulting me first," Nova said.

"Nova, it's just a camcorder," Alex continued.

"No, it's a want and not a need, and can be considered affluent in nature. You can't just offer him things that I can't right now, things that are a want for him and not a need. I don't want him associating you as the person who fulfills his wants, or-or makes him happy," Nova cried. "I'm his mother and I can't afford to make him happy right now, I can't have you spoiling him."

"Okay, I get it, no need to get all emotional and repetitive. I don't have kids, you know so sometimes I tend not to understand. How about this, how about I give you the money and you buy him the camcorder, this way it can appear to be from you? Consider the money a gift from me," Alex said. Nova scoffed.

Over the next few days as Nova waited patiently for Wednesday to come around she did some online research on creating and running her very own YouTube channel, wondering if she could even foot the bill, the equipment alone would set her back at least a few hundred dollars—in which case she did not have. Thinking of something more practical she asked Alex about the possibility of working for her firm, only to receive news that the office was currently overstaffed and not hiring, plus she would need some kind of certification or degree to even get started.

Nova was feeling down, like she was constantly hitting a brick wall, with every search she inputted into Google she was coming up short; almost anything that would supply her with a lucrative income required an extensive amount of experience, a degree or as her aunt said, a certification. Nova wondered if going back to school was a good idea, especially now that she and Tucker are residing with Alex and she is realistically surviving on three-hundred dollars a week. Day in and day out she was beginning to question the choices she made in her life. Subconsciously regretting her decision to enter into motherhood at such an early stage, she was now a dependent with a child to a woman only six years her senior. Also, watching her sister flourish and work on achieving her goals was making her somewhat jealous.

By Tuesday Nova spent the morning preparing Tucker's school clothes, packing away his school supplies and thanking Alex frequently for getting him registered into school. She was also packing a tiny suitcase of her own, for her trip the next morning. Living every day with no goals and nothing to look forward to was now depressing her, but once again she feared this, knowing that such an increase in stress would only prove itself detrimental to her crown; now she wanted her hair back, she missed playing around in it and massaging her new growth.

The defining qualities of 4C hair:
Hair is prone to tangles and matting
if not properly cared for and
regularly detangled.

Wednesday afternoon Nova landed in Seattle, the August weather in the high seventies and the sun was shining. She waited patiently outside in front of baggage claim for Marian to pick her up, watching the black stretch limo approach the terminal and making its way to her caused her heart to sink. Afraid to climb inside she waited by the curb for some type of confirmation that the ride was in fact for her and then, Marian jumped out of the back seat—looking stunning. Nova could not react immediately feeling self-conscious about her new look. Marian stood looking at her,

"What the hell have you done to your crown Nova?" she hollered, the pedestrians turning to watch her as she made her way onto the sidewalk running her hands along Nova's scalp. "Auntie had one job, all she had to do was keep you sane until I returned home," Marian cried. Nova now feeling the need to interrupt her,

"Stop being so dramatic, I had one moment of weakness," she said rolling her eyes opening the limo door to toss her duffle bag on the seat. Marian turning away informing her to climb inside; driving along the highway Marian could not take her eyes off of her, their driver checking the rearview mirror profusely. "My hair was really upset with me, I started neglecting her and she got mad, she started falling out and so, I had to cut her. I mean on top of everything else, I was super stressed. Terry sent me papers saying he was filing for full custody, of course, I was losing my mind," she explained.

"You didn't tell me about Terry wanting full custody! I mean, Jesus, what's been happening out there?" Marian asked worriedly.

"Nothing, auntie sorted that out, but, I don't know, I feel kind of liberated now that my hair is gone. I can grow her from scratch," Nova said, although she wondered why she was lying, she was still feeling insecure.

"Nova your hair is your crown, all that work you put into growing your natural hair and now it's gone, you can't blame me for being a little upset with you for making such a rash decision," said Marian.

"Ugh, it will grow back," shouted Nova getting annoyed. Sensing this Marian decided to lighten the mood,

"Yes, seven years from now, you know our hair takes a pretty long time to grow," she said laughing.

"Speak for yourself miss low porosity, with protective styling and good products and upkeep I should have my crown back in about six months," Nova said confidently.

"Maybe you should document your hair journey this time. Since I've been working with Joanna we've met a lot of influencers who review hair products on YouTube and stuff and they make pretty good money," Marian said nonchalantly biting her fingernail.

"Right, but I bet they have an outgoing personality. The other day Tuck tried to record me and I was just an awkward mess; besides, who would really care about my hair strands? I do want to find something I'm good at though," Nova said as the limousine came to a screeching halt in front of the Kimpton Palladian Hotel.

Despite her disapproval Marian decided to keep quiet, no longer discussing her sister's hair strands. After checking in the two sisters made their way to the fifteenth floor entering into their suite. Nova could not believe her eyes the room was gorgeous,

"Jesus Marian who is this lady?" she asked referring to Joanna. The large suite contained two king mattresses, a patio, three racks of clothes, accessories meticulously laid out, shoes, a complete bar, chocolate and a sectional. Marian appearing to be accustomed to the luxury maneuvered rather comfortably inside.

"She is the creative director for House of Matty and she's also a celebrity stylist. Designers such as Clinton Price served as her apprentice and now me!" Marian said excitedly as Nova examined the room, examining the clothing which had been left behind.

"So what's with the wardrobe?" she asked.

"Joanna isn't meeting Posh until tomorrow afternoon, so things got switched up a bit and so, we can go out tonight. I heard there's this really nice nightclub not too far from here. Go take a shower and I'll be out here fishing for a new look for you considering now you have no hair," Marian smiled. Scoffing for having mentioned the hair again, but it was the truth, she had spent all night preparing an outfit for her sister to go perfectly with her crown and now, different arrangements had to be made. Nova agreed.

"I have to call to check on Tucker and auntie, can you give me a minute?" she then asked.

"Yea of course," Marian replied removing pieces of clothing from the hangers on the racks.

Two hours later both Marian and Nova were dressed. Marian twisting her braids into a high-top bun, wore a neutral colored jumpsuit with the sleeves rolled up loosely, a belt and a pair of nude four-inch heels. The silhouette fabric both lightweight and fabulous. Nova, wearing a little red dress stopping well above her knees, accompanied by a faux fur jacket and a pair of Givenchy black and white striped five-inch sandals along with mild accessories and her makeup natural with long lashes. Heading down to the limo Nova stepped confidently, it was the first time in months she was feeling so great, not realizing she was beginning to lose some weight considering she was barely eating and her diet was now terrible. But, she had no complaints, the women looked rich and off they went.

The nightclub only thirty-two minutes away was packed, but instantly a model who worked with Marian recognized her, allowing the bouncer to grant her and Nova access. The music blaring loudly and everyone inside was either inebriated and dancing the night away or standing along walls waiting for their alcohol to kick in. Things inside were great, Marian then spotted an empty VIP table motioning for Nova to walk alongside her until they made it to the other side, pushing their way through the crowd. The table desolate, to the rear of the club, and there they sat waiting for someone to come along and tell them they had to move. Nova drank, lip-synched, partied and allowed herself to feel free. Marian enjoyed watching her sister look so happy and insouciant, shouting in her ear over the loud music, Marian asked her,

"Do you want to come to the meeting with me tomorrow?" she asked screaming.

"Yeah sure!" said Nova, just then a young woman walked over accidentally bumping into her and spilling the contents of her cup along Nova's dress, thighs and shoes. She was feeling sticky now, she let out a shriek cry. The woman apologizing fretfully,

"Oh, dear God, I am so sorry! That was an accident, I promise it was," earnestly the girl said. Marian stepping over to her,

"It's alright," she shouted to the strange girl.

"No, no, please, let me buy you guys a bottle or something," the stranger continued. She truly felt bad, loving the dress Nova wore, she knew it had to be expensive. Turning to face her again she continued on apologizing before Nova finally said,

"It's okay, don't worry about it," screaming in her ear, struggling to be heard over the loud music. Nova took a seat to clean her dress, but realizing that was a fail, she decided to excuse herself while she made her way to the restroom. The young lady stood, her and Marian exchanging a few more words before she assured her, she would purchase them drinks, promising her swift return.

Nova walking back to their section placing her hands atop her forehead she was feeling dizzy, seconds later the strange girl returned, in her hand two martinis and a club soda, she began passing them to the ladies, retaining the soda for herself,

"Thank you. You don't drink?" asked Marian.

"No," the young woman said smiling as she moved her body to the sounds coming from the DJ.

"What's your name? You're really pretty by the way," Marian said as she continued shouting in her ear.

"Oh, sorry I didn't introduce myself, my name is Noel," she said. Marian extending her hand to greet her,

"That's a beautiful name, are you from here?" Marian asked.

"Yep, born and raised, but I so desperately want to go to New York, California even, anywhere by here," Noel said smiling shouting into Marian's ear. Nova overhearing them, the words New York making her unsettled, standing to her feet she dashed out of the corner, pushing her way through the crowd, running back outside, her fur coat left behind. Marian and Noel now looking around,

"I'm so sorry, I have to go check on my sister," Marian said putting the glass down and stepping urgently through the crowd, outside her sister was pacing, her hands wrapped around her upper arms.

"Hey, are you alright?" Marian asked nicely, she was worried.

"No!" shouted Nova as she turned around crying. "I just felt triggered, by her saying New York, I mean, it's like everyone just wants me to be okay and I'm not okay. I feel like I'm weak for wanting to mourn the loss of my marriage," she said crying, her mascara running. Marian listening on,

"Sweetie you're not weak," Marian said, sympathizing but she was also confused by her sister's abrupt change in mood.

"I am, because I don't feel happy. I don't want to smile, I feel like I'm trapped between wanting to move on and just being stuck. Marian, I lost my best friend, okay, that was eight years down the drain. Eight anniversaries, eight years' worth of birthday celebrations, family vacations, love, all gone, just like that, in the blink of an eye and it's not like he's dead. He is alive, making new memories with someone else, right at this moment," she sobbed, trembling. Marian could do nothing but hold her, standing under the shimmering street lights, it was just them.

"What can I do Bug? Tell me, I want to help, I'll do anything," Marian asked, she was truly concerned and meant every word.

"Just let me grieve," Nova said. Marian agreeing unsure of what her grieving would consist of, she decided now it was best to follow her sisters lead and not impose any new people or ideas on her at this time. she was going to be her shoulder, she was going to be whatever Nova needed to make it through this, that she swore to herself.

6

Returning to California Nova felt guilty, she sent text messages to her sister apologizing copiously. She was offered a free vacation and instead she spent all of her time sulking after returning to the hotel following their first night in Seattle. She ate, watched television and slept while Marian and Joanna attended meetings, fittings, and shows. Any free time Marian had she was with Nova listening to her complain and replay the events of her failed marriage over and again trying to make sense of the outcome. But try as they may nothing was making sense, from Terry's abrupt disinterest to her finding herself tugging on his pant leg begging him not to leave—learning of this upset Marian greatly.

During the flight Nova continued contemplating the idea of starting her own YouTube channel, avoiding mirrors now she was dreading her reflection, apologetic to her hair strands realizing that shaving her head was not the smartest idea.

Alex and Tucker were out at a fair, once Nova entered the house she went upstairs, undressed, showered and decided on a nap; again, she thought about Terry, her sadness aiding her into a deep slumber. Two hours came and went and as Nova opened her eyes, she continued on resting until she overheard the sound of iron clanking coming from the first floor. Standing to her feet she moseyed on downstairs believing the noises to be coming from her aunt, the house clothes she wore now hanging off of her since she had begun losing weight. Inside the kitchen she saw a man lying down under the kitchen sink, a toolbox to his left.

"Um, who are you?" Nova asked, gripping her cell phone in her hand. Just then Hunter popped out from under the sink, his clothes filthy.

"Oh hey, sorry, Alex just asked me to come by to unclog the sink," he said politely. "I hope I didn't disturb you," he continued. Assuming now this was just another one of her aunt's desperate attempts to get her to date again she said,

"Look, I don't know what my aunt is up to, but I just came out of a marriage. The ink on my divorce papers isn't even dry yet. I honestly need some time." She said speaking assertively. Hunter looking at her with a confused look on his face,

"I'm sorry, I just, I don't understand. I mean, did Alex say that to you, that she wanted us to date, you and I?" he asked timidly.

"Well no, but she thinks you're someone I would like according to my son," Nova said watching his facial expression change from bewildered to sad.

"I see, I am truly sorry," he said standing, dusting his hands. "I am honestly interested in dating Alex. I mean, it's a shame she can't see that," he continued. Nova stood watching him, her eyes widened,

"My aunt is old, you're my age," she said jokingly. But he was not feeling comical. Noticing this she decided to sound more empathetic, "Look, I'm really sorry. I mean have you tried telling her how you feel?"

"I have, which is why I'm so disappointed that she would think to pawn me off to you," he said, sounding angry now. Nova deciding it best to leave,

"Sorry about that, hopefully when she gets back you two get a chance to talk things through," she said, shortly after disappearing leaving Hunter along with his thoughts. He turned looking at the sink, wondering if he should finish the work he had started.

Returning to her quarters Nova felt terrible, staring at her cellular phone screen she did the unthinkable, she searched Terry and his new girlfriend Laura on social media. There she sat on the queen-sized mattress scrolling through posts, videos, photos of them and the new baby who they named, Tamara Lowe Higgins; pictures of a house they now occupied in Rockland County, New York. Nova filling with rage and envy, wondering why Terry still did not communicate with her when he was actually going to be leaving—according to those photos he was already gone.

Her heart was beating differently as she read through comments and seen that even Terry's mother approved of his new union, never once contacting her either. She spoke to how proud she was of her only son now becoming a homeowner; Nova could feel her heart shattering inside of her chest. Friends, coworkers, comrades all leaving comments, the same friends she was once introduced to and no one, not a single person inquired on her whereabouts or that of their son in any of the photos. It was like she was watching him live a whole new life in which she and Tucker never existed.

There, her last name printed following the name of a child she did not procreate. It was devastating and all along Laura's timeline was Terry advising Laura she should revise her surname to match his. He was happy, he was smiling and sadly, he was living his life without an ounce of remorse—this was evident. Nova thought of being devious, commenting ferociously but decided not to, she wanted to take the high road, she was going to continue mourning in peace, although she knew it was unfair she could only give thanks to the fact that she had such a strong support system. Both Alex and Marian helping her so tremendously, but despite all this she couldn't help but feel like a failure and as such delved deeper into Laura's page, curious now on why she was better.

Laura is an Afro-Latina, her dark skin complexion smooth, her mother from the Dominican Republic, her father from Trinidad. She was curvaceous, hair long extending down to the middle of her back. She writes in Spanish mostly, so Nova cannot translate what she has written, but she posted Terry many times over, them together, some photos Nova seeing again for the second time, realizing his affair began months before she actually confronted him.

Laura is a booking agent for The New York Yankees baseball player Emmanuel Scott, it was now that Nova began putting the pieces together. Born and raised in New York Laura was from Brooklyn Heights, she attended Brooklyn College where she earned her Bachelor's degree in media communications. She began her career in 2012 and since then slowly has begun making a name for herself, judging by the photos she had taken a trip out to California for an event where Emmanuel had an appearance and that's when it happened; she and Terry met and began dating.

It appears now that Laura used her connections to get Terry into the industry, Nova was never informed of what job he would now be working, but his employment status on social media now read *Sportscaster for The New York Yankees.*

Nova thought she was dreaming, living in a twilight zone, fueled now with anger, she was feeling many forms of aggression, disdain and confusion. Unable to control her emotions she wept, malevolent thoughts racing in and out of her mind, a headache coming to greet her as the veins in her head begin to pulsate and her hands grow sweaty. Nova shaking, as she continues to scroll, anxious and fearful of what she is to find next. She is wanting to do something, break something, rip something, yell, thinking of ways she could relinquish her rage she ran down to the garage where she stood in the center looking for things to throw. Within a matter of minutes Nova caught herself tossing buckets of paint along the walls, removing tools and slamming them on the floor, screaming with each toss and every slam. Engrossed in this tyrannical behavior she did not notice Hunter standing along the threshold of the garage door, walking inside, grabbing her as she sobbed, another paint can tossed midair before hitting the ground. Fighting him as she bawled, she could feel his arms tightening around her, clenching her hands together as he whispered in her ear,

"It's going to be okay." Falling to the floor slowly, Nova continued to cry, grabbing a hold of his biceps, squeezing them tightly.

Pulling up steadily into the cobblestone driveway were Alex, Tucker, her neighbor Ryan and his daughter Cassidy were returning from the carnival; the children racing out from the backseat to run about and play. A recently divorced Ryan enjoyed spending time with Alex, an older gentleman he was the social media marketing manager for her firm. A kind handsome man in his late forties, his complexion fair, his eyes a hazel brown and his body type athletic build with a clean haircut and full dark beard with some grey hair strands.

"Alex!" He shouted as he stretched feeling fatigued now, "These kids wearing me out," he laughed.

"You're telling me? I had no clue this is what you deal with on a daily basis," she chuckled reaching into the backseat to retrieve her handbag before slamming the doors shut. The sun was still shining and the weather felt perfect, walking to the front door overhearing the sobbing in her garage. Knitting her brows, both Alex and Ryan stood watching the door, listening keenly,

"Someone is definitely crying in there," he said, pointing to the garage door. Alex took a look around to make sure the children were not nearby before opening the door to find Nova sobbing in the arms of Hunter who sat shrugging his shoulders, unsure of what to do next. Alex handing her bag off to Ryan thanked Hunter before rubbing her hands along Nova's back preparing to get her to stand to her feet to be taken inside. Exiting, both Ryan and Hunter remained standing in the garage, awkwardly introducing themselves to one another.

Inside the living room, Nova was seated, having a hot cup of tea Alex prepared before also taking a seat, both Ryan and Hunter leaving to go to their respected homes. As Alex watched Nova she could see the sadness in her eyes, because of this she could not bring herself to be angry at the mess she created in the garage.

"What happened?" asked Alex. Nova feeling ashamed could not answer right away; instead she simply twirled her spoon in her tea. Alex asked again, "Nova, what happened? If you want to go to therapy, we can arrange that. But you have to let me know what I can do to help, this isn't healthy," Alex said. Just then Nova placed her tea on the coffee table, shooting to her feet she ran upstairs to fetch her cellular phone where she dialed Marian. Alex remained seated, bewildered now. Upstairs the phone rang, Marian answering on the second ring,

"Hey there!" she said sounding elated.

"Marian, can we put together a script for my YouTube channel?" Nova asked, realizing now she had just boarded the emotional rollercoaster. An hour ago she was weeping uncontrollably and now, she was speaking to her sister about the possibility of starting her own channel. An excited Marian said,

"Oh my God yes! So you're going to do the hair thing?" she questioned.

"Yes, I just have a lot I need to express. Marian, what should I call the channel?" Nova asked, sitting on the edge of the sofa which occupied the room. Both women growing thrilled at the thought, Alex now making her way inside taking a seat on the carpet. Nova decided to put her phone on speaker, "Marian, auntie is here," she said to her, a voice slightly elevated.

"Marian your sister is going crazy!" Alex shouted. Nova shaking her head profusely, disagreeing.

"No, no I am not. I just finally realized that I have to move on with my life and I need to do something that is going to make me happy. Marian!" she shouted as if to direct her next statement to her, "Terry has been cheating for months! I mean, probably since the beginning of the year and I had no clue. None whatsoever and this Laura woman, I mean she's successful and beautiful and what am I? Some housewife without a degree and, Grandma Higgins hasn't called at all, not even to speak with Tucker, nothing at all!" she said. Marian and Alex remained silent wondering how to react,

"Nova, if all of this is happening it's no coincidence; it's more than likely that Terry had moved on a long time ago. Maybe the only person who didn't know, was you," Marian said slowly, Alex nodding her head in agreement.

"You guys they haven't even called my son. Granted I may not matter, but, he hasn't even called our son," she said sobbing now, her eyes red from crying. Alex crawling on the ground, rubbing her knee, drawing a long breath as she tried consoling her; the room felt dark. Nova's liveliness now leaving her as she continues to grow envious of the wonderful life she envisions Terry now living. Marian trying quickly to uplift her spirits again,

"Hey, so I've thought of a name!" she said. Nova sniffling, uninterested now, but she decided on hearing it anyway,

"What is it?" Nova said.

"How about *The Nappy Crown?*" she said laughing hysterically. I mean, you do have 4C type hair and there are many women with your hair type who have no idea how to care for it," she continued.

"I like that," Alex said chiming in.

"Also, Nova there is a YouTube channel I absolutely love watching, the influencers channel is called *NappyFu TV*, I think you should definitely give her channel a watch and try to pick up some tips on delivery," Marian said,

"NappyFu? Wow, you millennials just never cease to amaze me," Alex said.

"Oh wait, I have another one! What about *Sistas Nappin'* or *Nappin' Sistas?*" Marian continued, laughing again.

"Look, it doesn't even sound like you're taking this seriously," Nova snapped.

"Seriously Bug, I'm the only one coming up with names," Marian replied.

"Listen, ladies, why don't we wrap this up? Nova, you get some rest, I'm going to get started on dinner and bring Tucker inside. Also, I'll get the camcorder tomorrow morning," Alex said standing now preparing to exit. "Marian, I love you," she continued.

"Love you too auntie" her voice bellowed from the speakers. Alex now left, both Marian and Nova remained on the phone.

"Nova please stay off of social media, I know that's where you had to have gotten all this information. I want you to start doing something that is going to make you happy. Anyways, I have to go, love you," Marian said.

"Love you too," Nova replied.

Finger Detangling:
You want to detangle your hair while
it is soaked with water and conditioner.
This makes it easier for your fingers

to glide through each section...

By Friday morning Nova stood pacing in the upstairs bedroom she occupied—walking back and forth watching her telephone on the bed; her hands on her hips. She was contemplating dialing Mrs. Higgins; she would pick up the phone and then set it back down, a routine she was performing for the past two hours. Finally, after convincing herself that speaking to Mrs. Higgins was solely for Tucker's sake and not her own, she picked up the phone, locating her contact, she pressed the phone icon to dial her. The phone rang and Nova could feel the sweat piling up atop her forehead.

"Hello," the elderly woman answered, her voice whimsical. Nova panicked, hanging up the phone as she sat on the edge of the bed beating her palm against her forehead. *Why am I so damn nervous?* She asked herself. Then the phone rang, it was Mrs. Higgins dialing her back, taking a deep breath Nova answered,

"Hello,"

"Hi, someone called me from this number," Mrs. Higgins said. Nova knitting her eyebrows, stuttering now she replied,

"Yes, um, it's me, Nova," Mrs. Higgins was elated, it was obvious she was smiling now, gleefully she said,

"Oh my beautiful darling, how have you been? Where is Tucker?" Nova could not understand, if she was so happy to hear from her, why hadn't she called in lieu of all that had transpired between her and Terry? But Nova knew better than to engage in such a sensitive topic over the phone. She requested that both her and Tucker pay Mrs. Higgins a visit, and to her delight, Mrs. Higgins very happily agreed.

Across town Nova and Tucker arrived at the small house in Vacaville, an hour outside of San Francisco where Terry was born and raised. The home his mother occupied was passed down to her from her mother and her mother before her, it was a generation home. Mrs. Higgins hoped to one day have a daughter she too could pass her home down too, but there was Terry and although she had an interest in giving him the home, he had other plans. Now, Mrs. Higgins toggled with the idea of leaving the home to baby Tamara.

Standing on the porch under the scorching hot sun, Nova

gripped Tucker's hand tightly, she was edgy.

"Mom, that hurts," he whined; Nova looking down on him apologizing, she had not heard or seen Mrs. Higgins in almost a year. Oddly enough this did not raise any question in her mind because Mrs. Higgins was not the kind to visit frequently or call often, and so, Nova was used to not hearing from her. But with her and Terry now pending their divorce she thought things should have been different. The elderly woman was heard on the other side of the door, Nova now knocking releasing her grip of Tucker's hand.

"Who is it?" Mrs. Higgin bellowed; her voice harmonious.

"Nova and Tucker," Nova said.

Mrs. Higgins voice grew in excitement, "Oh my goodness gracious," she said. "Tucker is that you?" she continued. Nova could hear her walking towards the front door, rushing almost. The locks on the door unlocking and there she stood. A sixty-five-year-old, 5'2 dark-skinned woman with wrinkles and a head filled with grey hair. Bending down to hug Tucker, he smiled. Nova getting a whiff of the saccharine perfume she wore.

The one floor, two bedrooms, one-bathroom home was exquisite; the wallpaper which hung from the walls appearing to never have aged a day. Nova took a look around remembering her teenage years when she resided there along with Terry, watching her stomach grow day by day. Pictures still hung of Terry's dad—Hudson Higgins, beside him a family photo of Tucker, Nova, Terry and Mrs. Higgins from that day in the hospital. Taking a long look at the smile swept across her teenage face holding her newborn standing beside the love of her life, Nova began feeling wistful.

7

2007

Nova was laughing so hard her cheeks began to hurt, the basketball players in The Burger Joint not too far from their high school were sitting in the booth enjoying their burgers and fries all while bullying Erwin Tanaka of the tenth grade. Erwin was Asian-American and although he was the smartest kid in his class, he wasn't able to solve

his biggest problem—being tormented by the upperclassmen jocks. He visited The Burger Joint in an effort to fit in, but his attempts did not go unnoticed, nor did they go unpunished,

"Look at this dweeb," Terry's friend Garth said. Terry and all five of his friends, including Nova all turning to face Erwin who stood by the counter placing his order with the cook, the diner was not that big, resembling a neighborhood pizza shop, there were only eight booths for seating, a counter with a few stools, a Pac-man gaming machine, and the seventies theme made it easy for the disco lights to occupy the ceilings without question or concern. It was definitely a teenage hangout spot, one everyone had come to favor, but it was an unspoken rule that only the jocks sat inside the booths and their girlfriends of course.

Nova felt special, both she and Terry were growing closer

by the day, by month three they were inseparable. Nova would go to his practices at the end of her last period, watching him play whilst she worked on her homework. Everyone respected her, she was dating a jock and while other girls envied her, some only wanted desperately to befriend her. Terry was mature, he always knew the right things to say, dressed very nicely and it didn't hurt that he was a gentleman—opening and closing doors, footing the bill every time they went on a date and never once did he pressure Nova for sex in return. He was patient and Nova appreciated him for this; the furthest they had gone with intimacy was kissing for long periods of time in his bedroom.

Terry held her hand when walking in the hallways, walked her to class, stood outside waiting for her after class and they helped one another with their homework. Terry was now ready to get his license; he was tired of having to take public transportation when taking Nova on a date, or having her meet him at their desired locations. Although Nova did not mind because she did not want Terry finding out where she lived or knowing who her father was. He was still oblivious to this; despite his inquisitive nature she would provide very vague responses in relation to her own family and their back story.

The loss of her mother taking a major toll on her family, they still had not recovered and although her father was always working anyway, something was making her feel uneasy in their home. Marian now preparing for graduation, Nova was not worried about her life or what direction she was looking to take, she only had one thing on her mind and that was Terry and their relationship. She began to prioritize him over everything else going on in her life: classes, family time, her sister and exploring colleges. She was always told; eleventh grade you look for colleges and twelfth grade you look for money. But Nova was not worried, she knew of her trust fund and the money her father had set aside for her and so, she simply thought it careless to fret over such trivial matters. Marian on the other hand, while attending high school searched tirelessly for a good school to attend, studious and named valedictorian her senior year, in turn, making them proud.

Terry did not mind that Nova was so detached from her

family, he welcomed her into his home with open arms, as did his mother and father. Nova was like the daughter they never had, especially to Mrs. Higgins who enjoyed spending quality time with her, planting in the garden and cooking dinner for both Terry and Hudson. Hudson Higgins was a very ill man having to suffer from type II diabetes and recovering from his heart replacement surgery. The pacemaker he received during surgery, uneasy to maintain, but Nova was always aiding him, taking him for walks around the neighborhood as he schooled her on the importance of being a good woman, or better known to him as a housewife.

Nova learned that much of Terry's values stemmed from that of his father, he did not believe that women should work; he stressed the importance of raising a family on one income and having a multitude of children. Something he and his wife failed to do, Mrs. Higgins having given birth to Terry when she was almost thirty-nine years old. Both Hudson and Mrs. Higgins were fifty-seven years old at this time, Mrs. Higgins wanting desperately to become a grandmother while Hudson began coming to terms with the fact that he may never meet his grandchild. Realizing the unpredictability of life, his thinking was different and so he told Nova, if she could, have a child young.

Nova attended home games with Mrs. Higgins and Hudson, pushing his wheelchair and cheering on her boyfriend, she was always supportive and did everything she could to show Terry and his parents that she saw a future with him and for that, she would be around forever. Mrs. Higgins adored her, her willingness to help, her charismatic personality and even when Terry went away for out of state games Nova was still sure to visit his parents, providing his father with his medication and sometimes even cook for the married couple. Terry did appreciate this, both of his parents speaking sense into him, encouraging their union.

By summer Nova and Terry had been dating for a few months and began making plans to take trips together to the San Francisco beach, Beverly Hills and one day New York. Terry was obsessed, praying one day he would be good enough to play for his favorite team: The New York Knicks. Terry wanted to provide for Nova and was sure he would be able to do so, once he was drafted into the NBA. Nova would listen to him daydream and fantasize about how wonderful their lives would be, the mansion he would purchase for his parents and the doctors he would hire to care for his father—,

"The absolute best," he would say.

Terry was confident, Nova loved this about him and before she knew it she was leaving clothing, toiletries and hair products at his house. She was slowly moving in and Terry allowed it, his parents did not mind, she was far from a burden to them and as long as Terry was happy, they too were happy.

Night after night Nova was growing paranoid when Terry was away at practice for extended periods of time, or out of town for games. She feared he would sleep with other women, seven months and she was still a virgin, despite intermittently waking up next to him in the mornings and falling asleep next to him at night. Terry did not rush her, he understood she would need time and although he, himself was once sexually active; he dared not impose that on Nova. It was important to him that she did not feel rushed, Nova did appreciate this, and as such she wanted to have sex. Her body had begun craving him, intimately. Terry was now driving, Nova did not think to get her license, she did not see the point, Terry had one and anywhere she had to go she would simply take public transportation. She was in love, constantly Terry was showing her that he was capable of taking care of her and most importantly, he was patient. At age seventeen she was smitten by his decorum—her first love.

A week before their last day of school and summer vacation began, Terry was asked to tour with the basketball team, visiting three cities in seven days. By the end of June Terry returned home and began preparing for his senior year. An exemplary basketball player, he applied to colleges early and quickly college acceptance letters began pouring in; but Terry was only interested in the schools willing to offer him a free education in exchange for his basketball skills—he did receive this. Terry was working a part-time job at Foot Locker, attending practices and still playing basketball, he was rarely home and now that he had free time began sifting through his mail. Accepted into three division one basketball schools he was ecstatic: University of Connecticut, Boston College and The University of Richmond. But his excitement transient upon realizing they were all out of state.

Once July came around he and Nova had a serious talk, sitting on the edge of his bed, cartoons blaring from the television set behind them. The large room he occupied big enough to fit a full-sized mattress, two nightstands, a wardrobe, a twin sofa and some additional bins he needed once Nova began bringing her things over.

"I checked my school acceptances today," he said.

Nova saw the letters coming for him, but of course she could not open them. Also, looking forward to her senior year she was hoping to find a job for the summer where she could begin saving money for the expenses that came with being a senior. Nova was envious of Terry, realizing now that he was not as consumed with their relationship as she was; she missed out on applying for early admissions and applying for work at the beginning of summer as he did. Now she was dreading her senior year, having to play catch up with college applications and now looking for a job in July when she technically could have been working since May—and then came the news as she sat on the edge of the bed watching Terry toss a baseball in the air, catching it.

"I might be leaving," Terry said, his eyes lowering in disappointment as he now sat upright, placing the ball down. "I have a really important decision to make and I don't know, maybe you can help."

"Leaving to go where?" Nova asked, devastatingly.

"I'm not sure yet, I've been accepted into some really good schools and, I guess once coach looks them over, he'll tell me where to go," he said. Nova turning away as her eyes began to well.

"So what happens now?" she asked.

"Well, now, we enjoy our summer and of course senior year, after that, I'm honestly not sure," he said.

"Can't I just come with you?" she asked. But Terry's facial expression did not look promising, he turned away, picking up his ball to begin resume tossing it,

"Um, I guess we'll see," he smiled kissing her on the forehead. Nova felt lost, like she had no guidance or direction, in just a few months she had become so dependent on her boyfriend that she lost her own identity.

The next day Nova decided it was best she went home. She wanted to give Terry some space, although he was apprehensive about her leaving, he told her he was going to just practice and work, promising date night for the following evening. Their 5,030 square foot Calabasas house occupied a land size of 45,579 acres. Sitting on approximately one-acre view lot of mountain and city views, the Spanish style home recently purchased by their father in 2005 was supposed to be a new beginning following the death of their mother in 1998. With four bedrooms and four and a half bathrooms, a huge gourmet kitchen with granite counters, custom cabinets with top of the line stainless steel appliances, including built-in wine refrigerators, cappuccino maker, soda drawer, warming drawer and three dishwashers.

Nova seldom saw her father or her sister, at night running into either of them used to cause her a fright. The home having beautiful arches and beamed ceilings, custom wood and stone floors, a huge family room with a fireplace and French doors to the fabulous backyard, and a formal dining room with French doors leading out to the quaint courtyard and all within a gated community. The house also contained an amazingly large center island and profound eating area, master suite with spectacular views and a master bath with custom stone, steam shower and large walk-in closets—three additional bedrooms with en-suite bathrooms and another family room. One of the guards was very kind, Ross Morgan, he was the one who helped Marian sneak away at night when she was just a rebellious teenager.

Inside were pearl backsplash, and farmhouse sink. Nova's bedroom contained the street view and a patio she would spend her time on whenever she was doing her homework taking in the wonderful breeze, the palm tree just outside providing her with shade. Stepping inside Nova tossed her backpack to the floor, in it were some of the clothes she packed to return home for a few days from Terrys', untying her shoelaces she heard the clacking of heels making its way towards her,

"Where've you been?" Alex asked; Nova let out an

exasperating sigh.

"With my boyfriend," she replied rolling her eyes. Standing now she held her shoes in her hand, lifting her backpack tossing one of the straps over her shoulders.

"I've been here an entire week and you mean to tell me you've been at your boyfriend's house, for a week?" she asked firmly, her hands atop her hips.

"I mean, why do you care? You're not my mom," Nova snapped.

"No, I'm not, but your father is worried about you girls and asked me to come by," Alex said.

"Worried? Daddy doesn't even remember he has kids, don't believe me? Ask his fans, hell, ask his employees. They don't know about us, we're one big secret. So, he isn't worried about us, he's worried about his image," Nova cried before racing past Alex, making her way up the winding staircase. Nova stayed in her room that afternoon thinking of removing all the clothes from their hangers and packing them away. She had an abundance of clothes, this was for sure, her father had fashion stylists, personal shoppers and designers all stopping by to provide them with garments and clean their wardrobes from time to time.

Despite this, Nova was not the most fashionable always favoring a pair of jeans and washed out t-shirt with converses, their father did not approve but he never quite spoke on this to his children. Aida, the woman who came by to do her hair would be there the end of the week, knowing this also upset Nova, her own hairstylist never bringing to the attention of her father that she was not present for her appointments. Her job was to wash and set Nova and Marian's hair every two weeks, clipping their dead ends every four weeks, and perming their hair every six weeks.

Nova sat pouting listening to the birds singing just outside her window. She began missing school now more than ever, laying across her bed with her hands tucked under her chin, her hair flowing freely down her back she thought of no one but Terry. It was his laugh, his touch, their late-night play fights that had her obsessing over him. Marian making her way past the bedroom door, walked backward-looking in on her sister,

"Oh wow, look who came home to join us," she said laughing. Marian was always quite chipper during her young adult years, and refreshingly mellow. Her monotone voice spoke the same despite her emotions or mood. But Nova was in no mood to make conversation, she was angry with her sister too, angry that she didn't think to locate her. Nova did not have a cellular phone at the time and so, she could have been lost, missing or worst, dead and literally no one would have noticed; she felt invisible. "Nova, why are being such a brat? Daddy was worried sick about you," she said.

"I've been gone every day for almost two months and you want me to be grateful that daddy called in the cavalry, who too have only noticed I've been gone a week?" Nova snarled. "Please stop trying to convince me that, that man gives one crap about me, he doesn't. Oh and tell me please when is the last time he's even been here? Probably too busy bedding a bunch of women in Paris—" Nova continued.

"That is enough," shouted Marian.

"No, he doesn't love us; he abhors the fact that he has children!" She yelled. "And as my sister, good gracious, I thought more of you; you weren't the slightest bit worried either. Here you are smiling and behaving so joyously. Where was anyone's concern for my safety or wellbeing?" Nova screamed.

"Your sister said that's enough!" Alex shouted making her entrance into the bedroom. "Why on earth are you so angry? You have a roof over your head and clothes on your back, you should be grateful," she said. Marian sat observing. "Supper will be ready shortly, shower and I will see you both downstairs in a few hours and Nova, as long as I am in this house, you will be too," Alex said before turning to leave. Nova scoffed, facing her sister now she said,

"Get out." Marian did as she was told.

Downstairs Alex and Marian sat amongst one another in the kitchen, Alex aiding the chef with preparing their meals. She and Marian spoke candidly about having to take accountability for not realizing Nova was not present in their home. Although Alex was only visiting she felt a keen responsibility for the girls, they were after all her sisters' children and she knew just how much they both meant to her.

"You both meant the world to your mother," she told Marian—Alex standing before her chopping the baby carrots using the chopping board, her apron now filthy from rubbing her hands in it after seasoning the chicken breasts.

"I know we did," Marian said grabbing an apple from the fruit bowl sinking her teeth in for a bite.

"We have to fix this," said Marian.

"How?"

"I honestly do not know, but I have to speak to Dash that is for sure," Alex said.

Marian chuckling, "Why does no one call my dad by his real name?" she said.

"That's a good question, I've just always heard your mother call him that so I assumed it was okay," Alex said laughing while pouring herself a glass of white wine. "Plus, that's the name he answers to, no? I don't think anyone calls him Raymond beside his mother and his clients all call him Signature if I am not mistaken," Alex continued, taking a sip now. Marian nodding her head in agreement, staring at the glass in her hand,

"Auntie you should let me have a sip, I turn twenty-one in just a few more weeks," she smiled.

"Over my dead body," Alex said grabbing a hold of the wine bottle walking it in the dining area with her, taking a seat as she now watched the chef maneuver around the kitchen—her boyfriend Terrance.

4C natural hair is fragile and
prone to breakage

By supper time Nova was feeling tense, she had taken a nap in her room and awoke to find the sun was beginning to set just over the horizon—a view she very much enjoyed. Stepping out onto the patio inside her bedroom she looked down to see her father's car parked just outside in the driveway. Her father drove a 2008 Pearl White Audi R8 with customized rims, poking her head just outside of her bedroom door, she crept slowly to the stairs banner where she peeked down listening for the sound of his voice, his baritone heard speaking to Alex,

"What do you mean?" he asked her. Both Alex and Raymond were seated along the dining table. Raymond was 5'11 with a pear shape and an increased amount of stored body fat, he despised the thought of exercising and ate poorly, until Alex suggesting hiring a personal chef with whom she fell in love with only three years prior. But Raymond did not care; a dark-skinned man with many riches, he had an abundance of problems but focusing on his physical attributes was not one of them. Raymond was often lethargic and experienced shortness of breath whenever he would walk for long distances or even try moving up and down the stairs, he was not obese but he was well out of shape for a man at only forty-seven years old.

"You called me because you noticed there was something strange going on with Nova, well, she feels you don't love her Dash," Alex said. Raymond scoffed.

"Nonsense, I provide, she has clothes, and we're rich! What more does she need?" he snarled.

"Love," said Alex. "Some attention from her father, Dash you're barely home and she knows that. She was gone for over a week and there was no worry or concern,"

"What do you mean? I called you, which meant I was concerned," he said interrupting her. Alex drew a long uncomfortable sigh,

"Whatever happened to you, huh? You think my sister would be proud of you now? Seeing you neglect your children," she said.

"I am not asking much of you, help the girl, talk to the girl, and keep her out of trouble. That is all," he said standing preparing to leave; Alex's eyes widened.

"You're not having dinner with us? Again?" she bellowed as he went out of sight exiting the dining room, disappearing down into the basement.

Upstairs Nova arose from the carpeted floors, racing back into her room locking the door behind her she grabbed a hold of her book bag stuffing clothes inside. She was going to stay with Terry, permanently, her decision now final and wherever he decided on going for school, she too would follow. Young minded she believed that what she and Terry had was love, their bond unbreakable and so why should she stay where she was not wanted, or-or even noticed? She thought. Slowly she was growing consumed with hated, tossing her backpack through the glass doors landing it onto the patio where she was going to shimmy down the iron bars just to the right of her home. Nova looked down at the long jump, her heart beating quickly, tossing her backpack once; this time onto the pavement just outside. Nova watched as the bag rolled past her father's vehicle, soon after she climbed over the ledge on the patio, gripping hold of the ladder, the flowers smacking her in the face, the thorns scratching her arms as she stepped downward.

The converse she wore causing her feet to hurt, once she reached close enough to the bottom where she simply let go and had fallen. Nova let out a shriek cry, but before she could recover she stood to her feet racing down the driveway towards the gates where the community guard stood watch. Nova was stealthy on her feet having successfully eluded him in the past; tonight, was no different. While Ross remained engrossed in his pornographic material in the security booth Nova felt lucky moving past him she ran down by the gates waiting patiently for a car to enter; a black Mercedes Benz approaching, tapping their code into the keypad she waited long enough for them to swerve up the winding hill before sliding her way past the steel gates.

Back home Marian was wrapping up her shower, throwing on some old house clothes and searching the ground floor to locate her father. She knew with the sun going down and his car outside that only meant one thing: he was either in his study in the basement or in the kitchen fetching food. But sadly enough that night he was doing neither, Dash decided to step out but he took another car from the basement leaving his Audi parked out front. This was not like him, Marian thought she knew her father's routine pretty well, but tonight he deviated, bringing her to wonder why,

"Auntie," her voice called walking into the dining room as Alex laid out their cutlery. "What's going on with daddy?" she asked. But Alex could not answer, she did not want to lie, because she honestly did not know and lying to Marian was like lying to her youngest sister for they both so heavily favored.

"Please go get Nova so we can have dinner," Alex told

Marian, watching the look on her face go from confused to sad. "We've been doing alright without Dash these past few days, I mean, he comes and goes and there doesn't seem to be much we can do—unfortunately. But, first thing in the morning I will be getting Nova a cellular phone because she cannot just keep vanishing without a trace of any kind," Marian decided it best not to respond as she turned walking back through the dining room and into the foyer, then up the winding stairs calling to her sister.

"Nova!" she bellowed, the high ceilings carrying her voice causing her to hear her echo. Walking past the first two bedrooms—her father's room which he always kept locked and his office. Marian stepped into her sister's room where she noticed the hangers on the floors and the mess she had made. Marian was not surprised to have found that her sister had once again run away, but she was disappointed that this time she did not think to confide in her first.

"Auntie!" Marian shouted returning to the dining room, "Nova is gone."

8

Alex grew immensely angry sitting at the dining room table, tapping her right foot atop the marbled titles, dialing her brother in law who refused to answer her calls or respond to her messages. Alex came to strongly impugn his parental skills, Nova despising her father, yet Dash remained nonchalant. Alex wondered why he was acting this way, but Dash was resentful towards his children, blaming them for the untimely death of his wife—despite knowing that it was the malignant illness that had taken her from him.

One hour later, their dinner mildly hot, Alex sat, Terrance preparing to leave, although his job was incomplete, but Alex could not keep him any longer. Even though they were romantically involved Alex did not allow this to interfere with her professionalism, remitting payment and a wonderful tip she thanked him for his services before rising to walk him out of the Spanish style mansion. Alex walked along downstairs, locating Marian sitting on the couch in the living room watching television, appalled she said,

"What on earth are you doing? Nova is gone, we have to find her," Alex screamed searching frantically for the remote to turn off the television, she was successful, but Marian did not take lightly to this,

"She ran away and came back, she will be back," she said extending her hand, her palm facing upward, thrusting it in the air to indicate her growing impatient, she was waiting for Alex to return what she had taken.

"Listen, I am the adult here—"

"No, you're not even thirty, you're not much older than us and I am not a child. Nova isn't going to listen to you, the exact same way she isn't going to listen to me. We're peers in her eyes, not adult figures, now please may I have the remote to finish my show? Also, the dinner is getting cold and I honestly don't see why you didn't allow Mr. Terrence to just serve us. No one else wants to be here auntie and we can't force them," Marian said. Alex took a seat tossing the remote onto the cushion beside her; Marian seated as well, both looking defeated.

"So what now?" Alex asked.

"We wait," Marian said switching on the television.

Retaining Moisture:
Even if you have low porosity hair,
4C hair needs to be kept moisturized.

Standing outside of Terry's home at 10:37 p.m. Nova could hear his parents inside speaking amongst one another just under the window. Nova was losing her poise as she stood with her book bag, the straps gripped tightly in her hand. Taking a deep breath she rang the doorbell, instantly regretting her decision. But her feet felt stuck to the ground, unable to move she remained standing, wishing her legs would cooperate and she could run away, but there she was, Mrs. Higgins opening the door allowing Nova space to enter inside.

"Well, hello there darling," she said leaning in to give Nova a hug and a kiss on the cheek. She did not think twice of her presence, Nova had been spending so much time with them she was now just a member of the family. "He's not here you know, gone to a party in the hills," she continued before heading back into the living room to take a seat next to Hudson who was seated in his wheelchair, a blanket covering him. Nova was unsure of what to do next, so she thanked Mrs. Higgins for the information she received and stepped lightly to the rear into Terry's bedroom where she searched for any clue of where exactly he had gone.

Nova did not fancy taking public transportation, especially late at night but she had no money and only a bus ticket she had since before school ended. Neither her nor Marian liked being picked up by their driver, Laverne and so, she received a bus pass, which at that moment she was all too grateful for. Checking Terry's laptop, she located a conversation between him and a girl named Kellyanne on Facebook in a small dialogue box, Kellyanne was telling him to meet her at a house party just above Lux Liv; a nightclub on the other side of town. Nova did not think twice, Googling the address she headed out, waiting down the road for the L87 bus to arrive after properly letting Mr. and Mrs. Higgins know she would return shortly.

The night was feeling chilly and with Nova alone on the other side of the tracks wandering aimlessly, she was scared. But there she stood in front of the crowded nightclub, where patrons were all waiting to get inside. The club occupied the bottom floor of a building, looking up Nova could see the lights from the apartment on the third floor. It was hard to hear whether or not music was playing due to the loud music coming from the night club but something inside told her Terry was there and so, she searched the building for a way inside without having to pass through Lux Liv—she wouldn't have been allowed inside anyway.

Standing outside for what felt like twenty minutes, a group of teenagers came racing out from an alley behind the building, they were laughing and having a great time. Nova only assumed she could enter through there and so she did. Waiting for them to clear the entrance she walked down the wheelchair-accessible ramp located on the side of the building, and entered in through the steel doors, down in the basement the pipes leaked and it reeked of something malodorous. Nova quickly covered her nose, opening yet another door exposing a staircase in the dilapidated hallway. Walking up the stairs she now heard the music blaring from apartment 3C; banging the door she waited for someone to approach.

The locks clicked on the other side and when the door opened Nova felt lost, the stygian room filled with inebriated teenagers all groping one another.

"Welcome baby!" a strange voice sang to her as she walked inside, holding onto her sweater tightly, her eyebrows knitted.

"Where's Terry," Nova shouted to him over the loud music.

"He's in the back baby!" He replied; shouting. Nova fought her way through the tough crowd, men pulling her in all sorts of directions trying to bend her over to dance for them, but she very politely declined. This was the first time Nova had ever been to a house party and was she was not impressed. The upperclassmen were behaving like animals, everyone shouting the obscenities from the music the DJ played and jumping on top of one another, Nova made it to the back of compact apartment. She was feeling claustrophobic. Banging on the bedroom door, she turned the doorknob entering inside where she found Terry passed out on the bed wearing only his boxers and a naked woman sleeping next to him—his arms around her torso.

Trembling, Nova took a deep breath before shaking him awake; she could not bring herself to look away. She continued on staring wiping the tears from her eyes intermittently. Terry grunting, his eyes fluttering open, he turned his body to face Nova, but did not believe it was her and so, he resumed sleeping, turning back over. The woman feeling a shift in his body now began to open her eyes, her bare breasts and vagina exposed; Nova tried her best not to look but could not keep her eyes off of her, she felt ashamed, jealous, angry—a surge of emotions, some of which she could not identify.

The girl, who Nova assumed to be Kellyanne began squirming trying her best to remove herself from Terry's grip, grunting now as he just did, pushing,

"Terry! Terry wake up," she said, her voice faint. Nova stepped back now, watching her fumble to stand to her feet,

"Did you guys have sex?" Nova asked her quickly before she could exit. The woman turning to her watching as Terry now sat upright, his heart racing,

"Nova!" He shouted, wiping his eyes so he could see clearly. The small room in the apartment dingy, smelling of marijuana, Nova took notice as she stood, careful not to touch anything with her arms folded. The tears now falling down her cheeks,

"Listen, I can explain," Terry said and Nova wanted that, she wanted an explanation; she wanted to know she meant something to him. The young lady now was gone,

"Okay, explain," Nova demanded. "You said you were to going to exercise and work today, not come to a house party and have sex!" she screamed, hitting him with one of the pillows from the ground, disgusted that she had touched the yellow stained cushion. "Ewe," she murmured. Terry rummaging around to find his clothes, locating his pants and the t-shirt he wore he asked Nova to come with him outside, but she refused, she was not leaving until she knew the truth, "You had sex didn't you?" she asked again, this time her tone increasing, She was unsure of what to do next, she was young and in love, and no matter what his answer was she knew she was going to tell herself it wasn't so, and pretend it never happened, but she wanted confirmation, she was in desperate need of it.

"No," Terry lied. A bald-faced lie right to her face, using his hands to assist in relaying his message, he spoke slowly, enunciating his words, "she's an old friend of mine and we literally just got high, we both were um, hot, and we undressed and fell asleep. That's it, Nova I swear," Terry stammered, his Adam's apple protruded and the large gulp he took heard from across the room. Nova continued standing with the tears falling from her eyes, Terry was feeling remorseful, regretting his decision, up until that night they were both virgins, Terry promising Nova he would wait for her. Nova was no fool, she knew he was lying, but she also knows she loved him too much to do anything about it or to reprimand him, and so, shrugging her shoulders while tasting her salted tears, she said,

"Okay."

Upstairs the bedrooms did not only exude elegance, but they created an inviting ambiance; especially Dash's bedroom and the one Alex were given for her temporary stay. The luxury Mediterranean style bedrooms all decorated with a rustic use of wide plank oak wood flooring, exposed wood beams and solid wood furniture. Additionally, a glass chandelier also added a nice touch along with the curtained back wall, narrow windows—minimizing sunlight and giving off exceptional visuals to the palm trees and high hills just outside. The use of barn sliding doors used to match the bedrooms rustic feels and dark brown color choice.

That night Alex could not sleep, the loud thunderstorms frightening her and the thought of Nova alone bringing about a cause for concern. Their relationship not always the best, but they were her nieces and she knew it was her job to assist their father in protecting them. The cool breeze making its way into her bedroom felt great, relaxing, sitting up she decided to make her way downstairs where she put on a pot of milk bringing it to a boil—warm milk with cinnamon was what she craved. Marian too could not sleep and decided on making her way down the stairs and into the kitchen where she was surprised to have seen the lights illuminating inside.

"Auntie?" she called quietly stepping into the kitchen.

"Yep," Alex replied, pouring her milk now, waiting for it to cool. "Just making some milk before bed," she continued. Marian taking a seat on the stool by the kitchen island, Alex leaning now with the cup in her hand, blowing her milk to cool it,

"He wasn't always like this, your father. I mean he was never this distant with you guys, as children you both meant more to him than anyone or anything I could have ever imagined. Then the work came, then the demands of life came, then his priorities got messed up." She said taking a sip now, Marian listening actively, intrigued by the story she was now hearing for the first time.

"When I was born, your mother hated me. She needed help with you and instead of helping, my parents were busy raising me, the baby. Her mother single, depressing, my birth taking a toll on her since my mother was so young and Ana's mother never anticipated our father cheating. Then as I got older and our dad managed to create an amicable blended family, later on, I was introduced to Dash. Ana was always the happiest when she was around him, I mean smiling from ear to ear, skin glowing," Alex said, her voice wistful.

"Hmm, I wonder how things would have been had she still

been around, I mean, I was only fourteen when she died and I was like a big sister to you both from then on, I just don't know what happened between us, with our family, with Dash. I get why Nova feels rejected, I do, but how on earth do we fix it?" Alex asked.

"She has to want it too auntie, we can't fight her. I mean she keeps running away, but daddy isn't the only one here, I'm here and now you're here too, she can talk to us, she's the one shutting us out," Marian griped. The thunder from outside clapping.

Retaining Moisture
The kinks and coils of 4C curls
prevent the distribution of sebum
(natural oils produced by your scalp)
throughout your hair

When Nova opened her eyes the next morning she awoke to find that Terry was not beside her, she assumed he had gone for a run since the gym clothes were gone. Indistinctly she could hear the murmurs coming from the kitchen. That morning Mr. and Mrs. Higgins decided on having a long conversation with their son. Hanging out late, having a live-in girlfriend all before the age of eighteen were proving itself to be worrisome. Mrs. Higgins had high hopes for her son and his father, Hudson was extremely proud of his son and all his hard work, especially now that he was being considered for division one colleges. Hudson sat in his wheelchair as his wife and Terry continued their conversation, nodding his head as she spoke.

"We don't want you making any mistakes and messing up your future Terry. We like Nova, but, we don't want you two to get so involved that ya'll become careless now," his mother said. Terry groaning, standing with his arms folded, rolling his eyes, he was annoyed, the last thing he wanted to do was stand for a lecture.

"I know mom, I know," he grumbled. Nova remained behind closed doors in his room, sitting upright in the bed. She and Terry did not have a chance to further discuss the events which had taken place the night before although she was still feeling uneasy. He was far too drunk and she desperately needed sleep, feeling fatigued from the long day she had—despite the nap she had taken hours earlier in the day. As she sat inside of the bedroom, alone, she toyed with the idea of going home; she was missing Marian. As the thoughts entered and exited her mind, in walked Terry, shutting the door behind him using the ball of his foot whilst holding a tray with a paper plate on top, in it, freshly made bacon, scrambled cheesy eggs with pancakes.

"That smells really good," she said smiling. Making herself comfortable once again, "Terry, we have to talk," Nova said helping him set the tray on the bed as he prepared himself to climb in,

"I guess this a morning for lectures," he said sarcastically. Nova knitting her brows,

"Surely you didn't think we weren't going to speak about last night," she said shocked.

"I thought we were moving on, you said okay, we didn't speak about it last night. It won't happen again," he said placing a piece of bacon in his mouth and slicing into the pancakes. Nova wondered if they were to share, realizing now he had only brought in one plate. Turning to face him, she sat with her legs crossed, watching him lick his fingers and devour the food, not once offering Nova a bite.

"Terry do you love me?" Nova asked. Terry taking a long gulp, slicing into another piece of the pancake after this time drenching it with maple syrup, Nova was growing impatient, "Hey, do you love me?" she asked again, this time louder.

"Look, we've only been dating like half a year or so.... I mean, I like you and I think we're great together, we have fun, we date, and we hang out. Love is a pretty strong word," Terry said. Nova was feeling forlorn, as though the Terry she had met a few months ago was no longer there, unlike her, he was no longer a virgin and so, *what would he want with me?* She thought.

"I just want to make you happy," Nova said. "I want us to make love, but, I feel like if we do then things won't be the same. I just want to know that you're going to be here forever and that it's just us. No more screw ups Terry," she said solemnly. Terry taking a huge sigh once again felt it only right to convince Nova that he was in agreement, hoping this would get her to quiet down and allow him to finish his meal in peace, kissing her on the lips he nodded his head in compliance, words never leaving his mouth. Deciding now things were settled, Terry reclined, his back to the headboard, turning on the television and finishing his breakfast.

Nova stood, realizing there was nothing going through her mind aside from the fact that she felt threatened by a woman she had never formally met. A woman who was lying naked next to the love of her life, the man she dreamed of one day walking down the aisle with and having his children. With that, she figured it was time, time to allow Terry the opportunity to take her virginity and make love to her body so they would become one. Terry paying her no mind thinking she was simply going to the restroom where she would wash up and prepare for the day, but there she stood, lifting her nightgown just above her head exposing her bare breasts and a pair of lavender underwear. Nova was shaking, Terry now turning to face her,

"Wait, what are you doing?" he asked.

"I want us to make love," Nova said, her hands wrapped around her upper body, concealing her breasts. Terry placed the food tray on the floor removed his t-shirt—hastily taking Nova by the hand.

"Can you turn off the television?" she asked him, her tone just above a whisper. Terry complied, after all, everything he needed to see was right there in front of him. Nova developed quickly, weighing only 120 pounds with a curvaceous body and size 36B breasts she was gorgeous. Quivering she laid in bed, placing the covers over her body, removing her underwear under the sheets, Terry also removing his pants and boxers. Nova was feeling terribly uncomfortable, her body shaking as she struggled to kiss him. But Terry was not gentle; he was kissing her quickly, simultaneously slobbering on her neck and lips—it was disgusting. Placing her hand on his chest Nova stopped him,

"Hey!" she shouted. "Go slow."

Speaking with excitement, Terry agreed promising to go slow as he continued on kissing her, sending his hands slowly between her legs, Nova gasped. Laying on his side, facing Nova who was laying on her back Terry began slowly massaging her clitoris, Nova moaning passionately, her eyes closed as Terry suckled on her neck. Abruptly stopping he shot his head up asking,

"Do you want to give me a blowjob?" he asked whilst kicking the sheet off of his thighs. A confused Nova sat upright, her hands still stretched across her upper body, stammering she replied,

"What—what, I don't even know how to do that, is that what you want? Maybe I can learn," she said innocently. But he was not really listening; Terry was erected; now just forcing her head down between his legs, but Nova resisted. "Terry, I said be gentle," Nova screeched.

"Oh my God, it's just a blowjob Nova, all the other girls are doing it!" he shouted. Nova scurried out of the bed, rushing to get dressed, her heart in pieces, Terry realizes he hurt her feelings stood to his feet consoling her,

"Babe, I am really sorry, I am very sorry. You're right, I need to go slow. I am sorry. I promise I will go slowly and I won't force you to do anything you don't want to do," he said. But Terry did not care about Nova and her feelings, he cared about his own needs and quickly realized had he not resolved things she would have left. With her breathing heavy and her eyes shifting, Nova complied. Removing her panties once again she climbed back into the bed, Terry climbing in behind her, Nova kissing him now, feeling a bit more relaxed as Terry continued massaging her clitoris.

Terry was far more experienced, despite the lies he told Nova about him too being a virgin, Terry had lost his virginity by the age of fourteen to a girl named Allison McGill, with whom Nova was familiar. As he maneuvered around her body, Nova could not help but think of the night before, thinking to herself that he had done this with another woman, he had given his love away despite promising that it would be for her and only her, but as he stimulated her clitoris slowly the thoughts began leaving her mind and all she could focus on was the immense pleasure she was feeling.

Terry then lowering his head under the covers, his face

disappearing while his legs continue to dangle just off the mattress, sucking on her clitoris Nova moaning in excitement,

"Be quiet Terry said, I don't want my parents to hear you," lifting his head he gave her a pillow, motioning for her to put it over her face as his head once again disappeared from sight. With her moans now muffled Nova groaned, clenching the sheets and feeling her thighs begin to shake she was getting ready to climax. Nova could feel her hair strands tugging on the sheets, constantly having to adjust it, to avoid feeling discomfort. With each stroke of his tongue, Nova came closer to having an orgasm, until there it was, that feeling causing her body to tense up, her thighs to grip the sides of his face and her back to arch while she tossed the pillow to the ground. The sensation leaving her body, Terry continued sucking on her clitoris aggressively; Nova taking her hands to push his head away, her mouth opened wide, gasping in pleasure.

Pulling the sheets back, Terry came face to face with her, kissing her on the lips while slowly inserting his penis inside of her, but Nova stopped him,

"Wait! Are you wearing a condom?" she asked, her hands on his chest pushing him away, Terry pushing down on her—their missionary position making it easy for him to do so,

"No," he said struggling to kiss her as she pushed him away, again.

"No, you need a condom," Nova pleaded. Angry now he shot her an objectionable look,

"We're going to be together forever right, so why does it matter? Don't you trust me?" he asked. Nova did not want to upset him and so she allowed him to continue, "Okay," she said raising one eyebrow and pursing her lips, although her face read assured, inside she was bawling. Terry stroked her long and hard, Nova gripping the sheets and scratching his back. Terry was in great shape and while she rubbed her hands along his biceps she felt turned on—he was perfect, in her arms he felt strong.

That week during his days off from work Nova and Terry watched television, had sex, ate and went on dates—some days it was the movies and other days it was out for dinner. Terry's mother did not mind Nova staying but began insisting that she get a job, but like his father, Terry would hear of no such thing.

Promising both his mother and Nova that he would be the only one working and therefore will handle their contribution to the bills—Mrs. Higgins reluctantly agreed.

9

A month later and Nova was beginning to feel like a burden, like all she had become good for was sex after work, and providing Terry with a late-night back rub or fixing his meals as his mother soon instructed, she do, in addition to doing his laundry. Whenever Nova would complain Mrs. Higgins never missed the opportunity to turn those moments into teachable ones. Standing inside the laundry mat not too far from their house in the shopping plaza, Nova could hear her voice speaking,

"A woman's place is in the house, raise the kids, take care of the home and make sure your man is okay," Mrs. Higgins would say. But as time pressed on things got easier, Nova was thankful for Mrs. Higgins; she was even beginning to teach her how to cook Terry's favorite meals to which he was happy. By fall surprisingly, Nova was beginning to love being a stay at home girlfriend, Terry looked at her differently; he looked at her with appreciation. Kissing her each morning before he left for work, and if she was napping when he returned home, kissing her lightly atop the forehead as she slept; never underestimating the chores she did throughout the house and that she too could be fatigued.

Solely due to her husband's ailments, Mrs. Higgins worked

a 9-5 down at a textile factory not too far from home. Terry maintained his employment down at a local Foot Locker leaving both Hudson and Nova home-based during the day. A young woman tasked with the responsibility of caring for an elderly man was the last thing she wanted to find herself doing— but she made good with it considering there was not much else for her to do. Along with caring for Hudson, cleaning, cooking and completing Terry's laundry Nova also began doing her own research on the division one colleges and universities Terry were to attend once their senior year was complete.

Nova began looking forward to this, so much so that she thought about changing her look, she wanted to blend in more as a college student, especially one that would be dating a basketball player. But Nova lacked the most important thing— her own goals. As she searched the internet day in and day out she had come to realize that she was growing all too comfortable with living in the shadow of a man. A man she was not sure was going to be here forever and then it dawned on her,

"What would I do without Terry?" she questioned. At that moment Nova thought long and hard about her own goals, her own enjoyment and surprisingly, she could think of nothing. Later that evening when Terry returned home from work he showered as Nova remained stationed in his bedroom scrolling through the web pages on his laptop reading articles about sororities and fraternities, the one thing she did hope to one day do, now she was beginning to contemplate attending an HBCU. Stepping back into their bedroom, a naked Terry asked her,

"So, how was your day?" removing a pair of boxers and a white t-shirt from his wardrobe. Shrugging her shoulders Nova drew a long sigh before responding,

"The same as it is every day," she replied, her tone melancholy. This did not make Terry happy, he couldn't help but feel guilty. Although he did not say it, Terry felt responsible for Nova having felt the need to reside with him, permanently. He felt his cheating caused this and he could see that her self-esteem lowered, she no longer looked him in the eyes, she was always concerned with his life and ways in which she would fit in, never making any plans of her own. In addition, Terry felt stifled.

"Look, I have a game tonight at the park, why don't you come along and bring a book or something so you don't get too bored," he happily suggested, hoping this would cheer them both up. Hopelessly Nova agreed, tapping her fingernails along the laptop keyboard, her eyes lowered—she was deep in thought. Terry moseyed on over to her, kissing her atop the forehead before heading into the kitchen for a snack.

Find a good moisture and a good sealant.
Oils like coconut oil and olive oil,
and creams like shea butter
are effective at sealing moisture
in your hair.

Marian felt alone, with Alex now gone and her father away on business she was feeling like the summer was passing her by and she had yet to do anything memorable. With the television no longer a form of adequate entertainment Marian decided on making her way into the kitchen to bake, Terrance was there seasoning chicken for the next day and meal prepping for her father. Terrance was handsome, young and still in culinary school. But Marian knew better than to stare too long, Alex and Terrance were an obvious item, their relationship appearing serious. As Terrance worked, Marian decided patiently to wait her turn to use the kitchen by grabbing a seat along the island atop one of the stools, inhaling the sweet smells of garlic and pepper. Terrance breaking the ice,

"So, how's your summer going?" he asked mincing the meat.

"Boring," replied Marian, her eyes rolling.

"Ha, sounds about right. I mean, why don't you find something you're passionate about? Like an internship or something?" he asked.

Marian thinking now, "You're right, I graduate in a few months and I have nothing lined up for myself. My aunt is graduating law school soon and you're a Chef, I mean sheesh, I should be doing something productive," she said aloud, having had an epiphany. Terrance grinning,

"I'm surprised neither you or Nova want to do the fashion thing, I mean, look at how well off your father is," he said extending his arms as to demonstrate the proximity of their home. Marian chuckling,

"I don't do fashion, I mean honestly, I hate it. It's just clothes, why should it ever be taken so seriously?" she scoffed tugging on the bottom of her shirt.

"Have to ask your father that one. Oh, I meant to ask you, and please, stop me if I'm being too forward, are you able to ask your sister if her boyfriend can get me a discount on those new Air Jordan 22's?" he asked bashfully. "They're dropping this September at his store in Vacaville. He and my sister had a falling out a little while back so, she can't ask him." Marian's eyes widened,

"Boyfriend?" she questioned.

"Oh, well yea," he replied, thinking if he had said too much. "You know what forget it, I never should have asked," Terrance laughed. But Marian was not amused, nor did she care that he now wished to change the subject or retract his request,

"What boyfriend?" she asked sternly. But Terrance was not going to reply, as a man he was not going to be labeled a snitch, it was clear Marian did not know to whom he spoke of and just like that he wrapped up, cleaned and very respectfully took his leave, leaving a bewildered Marian alone with her thoughts. Hopping from her seat Marian dialed Alex who unfortunately did not answer and so, she left her voicemail, praying she would call back. That evening Marian remained restless, feeling like she was growing closer to learning of her sister's whereabouts, and despite her never saying so, she was deeply worried for Nova and her safety. Realizing now that their father was not only absent, but uncaring Marian could not blame her sister for leaving. Things were no doubt worse now than it had been before she began college, but so wrapped up in her studies she never quite took the time to pay attention. Dash now belonged to the public, his image exceedingly more important than that of his children.

Moments later once Marian decided to clear her mind, preparing a batch of cookie dough, the house phone sang.

Forgetting she dialed Alex, Marian answered; unsure of whom she was speaking to,

"Hello, Signature residence," she said, her voice soft.

"Marian, it's me," Alex said, the sounds of wind gushing against the speakers. Propping the phone to her ear now, moving her hair strands.

"Auntie, I think Terrance knows where Nova is, but he didn't want to tell me, can you ask him?" she said. A shocked Alex responding angrily,

"What! He knows how long we've been speaking about her and he didn't mention anything. What makes you think that? What did he say?" she asked now, her tone panicked. But Marian was at ease, feeling better knowing that Nova was, in fact, okay, no longer questioning her decision to leave. Simultaneously Marian prepared her cookies.

"He was pretty nonchalant when he mentioned her, but he said her boyfriend works at the Foot Locker in Vacaville," Marian said. A perturbed Alex remained silent, Marian wondering what she was doing. Seconds later indistinctly she could hear Alex badgering Terrance who was now in her home, reclining and watching television. Marian continuing to listen, deciphering what she could, their words unkind as they slew insults to one another. Listening patiently Alex now returned,

"He said she's down by Vacaville. Get dressed, I'm coming to pick you up," Alex said before hanging up the phone. Marian stood, deep in thought, she wondered whether or not she wanted to interrupt her sister and the new life she was living, anything was better than residing with their father at this point. They were given everything, access to a world where there are no limits and yet, they were unhappy. Knowing this Marian could not bring herself to disrupt her sister, instead, she decided it best to leave her alone, promising to relay this message to their aunt upon her arrival. Marian resumed her bidding; cleaning now.

Driving along the interstate Alex decided against picking up Marian feeling like the trip there would be a waste of time. Vacaville was well out of the way for both of them, the travel at least two hours by car. She thought on her ride, feeling disappointed that she had let her sister down. This was not the way the children should be raised, feeling like pariahs and often times neglected. Dash seldom home and in just a few weeks Alex was capable of seeing this for herself, just how unhappy the girls were, but what could she do to fix it were the questions making their way in and out of her head.

Arriving in the small town Alex drove around mindlessly, clueless on where to go she made her way over to the plaza where the Foot Locker sign hung just above the building, circling around the premises before parking her car in the parking lot, she overheard some children playing in the courtyard adjacent to the building. Stepping ferociously, she could think of nothing but the anger she would feel once she laid eyes on Nova—after all she was not leaving until she found her. The destitute neighborhood bringing her chills although the weather breeze blew warm.

Standing by the metal gates Alex slid her hands across the chain links, her eyes frantically searching while the teenagers dribbled their basketballs and rocked to the Hip-Hop music booming from the portable sound system. They were taking pictures and conversing among one another, the sun beginning to set. Then, she saw her, Nova sitting on the bleachers, her hair uncombed and her jeans fitted wearing an oversized t-shirt and pair of converses, watching the men race their basketball up and down the court. Enraged now Alex banged her palms on the fence, startling those closest to her, but she did not care, she simply wondered how she could enter the park, all logic gone, feeling emotional now she looked around, but Nova remained distracted, still not noticing her.

"Nova!" Alex bellowed, Nova's head now turning, squinting her eyes to see clearly for she could not believe it was her aunt. The boys continued their basketball game, their sneakers heard screeching along the concrete, Nova now standing, stomping her way past the boys and girls who sat next to her. Jumping down from the third row. Nova hoped to make a run for it. Alex, noticing her attempt to elude her, ran across the yard, chasing Nova for what felt like five minutes along the uncut grass, out of breath she coughed before finally, the oversized shirt flowing in the winds aided Alex in grabbing her before tackling Nova to the ground.

"What the fuck!" Yelled Alex, her legs apart as she climbed

on top of Nova pinning her to the ground, their breathing heavy,

"Get off of me!" Nova cried.

"No, why the fuck are you running?" Alex shouted, she was livid now, not only because she was forced to make her way to that side of town but because Nova had the audacity to run away from her. "I don't even like using profanity, but Jesus Christ, what has gotten into you?" she continued. But Nova remained silent, feeling nauseous now, her feet fluttering as she begged once again for Alex to climb off of her, closing her eyes tightly, inhaling and exhaling deeply, gagging whilst praying the nausea would go away, Nova fought the vomit that was making its way up from the back of her throat, her eyes widened, finally spewing,

Quickly, Alex slid off to the side, her face reading disgust, turning Nova who now faced the grass, hurling, her vomit-filled with chunks of oatmeal, her breathing stagnant.

"Well, that's what you get for running from me," Alex sniped still struggling to catch her breath. Night beginning to come down, but with only a few more minutes of waiting, Alex got to her feet, extending her hand to assist Nova in standing. "You know what happens now right?" Alex asked as they both began walking back to the courtyard where the boys and girls were looking to retreat. Terry standing with a basketball in his hand roaming aimlessly for his girlfriend.

"Hey," she called to him, waving her hand; Terry looking over to see both Alex and Nova approaching him, wondering why they had been covered in grass and the woman standing next to her furious.

"Who are you?" questioned Alex.

"Um, Terry," he replied, Alex looking to Nova who was too ashamed to make eye contact, kept her head low. Alex was not impressed, she had no desire to exchange words with Terry, the reality being, she looked down on him, he was not worthy to be with her niece and not only because of his socioeconomic status, but because he did not appear to her as a stand-up guy and Alex knew better. At such a tender age Nova would only be heading down a road of heartbreak with a man like Terry. He was cocky, sometimes interrupting her as she spoke questioning why he did not contact her parents, and never once catering to Nova or caring of her wellbeing. Alex wondered when he was going to show any sign of concern for the fact that Nova was covered in grass stains and reeked of vomit.

Snapping her fingers Alex instructed the teenagers to follow behind her as she made her way back to her vehicle. The black 2006 Lexus IS she drove parked just on the other side of the basketball court. Terry eyeing her up and down, taken aback by her beauty but he dared not speak climbing into the backseat as Nova stepped lightly into the passenger's seat feeling embarrassed. The ten-minute car ride back to Terry's house, silent. Arriving in front of the small house, the lawn un-kept, Alex stepped out of her car, slamming the doors shut as she made her way up the driveway walking steadily behind Nova and Terry watching him turn the key to his home, once inside, he called,

"Mom!" Alex and Nova walking in behind him, Nova moving swiftly to the back bedroom to gather her belongings while Terry make his way into the kitchen washing his hands before preparing himself a sandwich. Alex remained standing by the front door, trying carefully for her garments to not touch along anything. Their home filthy in her eyes, noticing the black gum stains on the carpet, the scratches and skid marks along the walls and that unpleasant smell coming from the bathroom just next to the entrance. Just then, Mrs. Higgins appeared, the elderly woman smiling before introducing herself,

"Hello beautiful," she said extending her hand to greet Alex. But Alex did not reciprocate, angry at her for allowing Nova to remain in her home for months without contacting her parents.

"Please, I am here for my niece, the one you were harboring for the past two months without thinking to call her father," Alex snapped. Terry now interrupting,

"Watch how you speak to my mother please, we don't know you," he said. Alex turned to face him,

"Excuse me?" she questioned. Mrs. Higgins pushing her son away,

"Ma'am, I didn't catch your name," she said removing the

smile from her face. Alex raising one eyebrow stood with her arms folded.

"Alexandria is my name," she replied.

"Dearest Alexandria, you look young, not much older than my son here, now I don't know what's truly going on, I can only assume you are here for Nova. While I do remain oblivious to the reason for Nova deciding to come here and reside with my family and I, I will say this, a thank you would be far more appreciated. She is fed, she is clothed, she is alive and she is well, meanwhile, two months later is when her family, I suppose come to collect her. I believe my young girl your anger or misunderstanding is misdirected," Mrs. Higgins said speaking slowly. Seconds later Nova emerged. Holding in her hand two duffle bags and on her back, a book bag—her clothes unchanged.

Alex deciding it best not to respond simply turned to walk away, Nova exchanging her goodbyes and kisses with Terry who remained eager to return to the kitchen. Walking outside Nova felt incomplete, like something had just been taken from her, with the night now upon them it was evident that Nova would be receiving an ear full upon her arrival home. Two hours and thirty-two minutes later Nova could feel her heart racing as they drove up the hill making their way to the Spanish style mansion overlooking the hilltop. Inside the stygian foyer, Nova struggling to navigate her way inside, Alex walking in behind her carefully searching for the light switch, mumbling obscenities. Overhearing the commotion downstairs Marian made her way to the staircase banner, flipping on the light switch from the top of the stairs where she stood overlooking them.

"Well, well, look who it is," she teased.

"Shut up," Nova snapped.

"Enough, Nova please go get cleaned up and return downstairs so we can have a conversation," Alex instructed. Nova did as she was told. Making her way up the stairs, moving past Marian who regarded her as filth,

"Ew, you smell gross," she cried careful not to let Nova touch her. But Nova knew not to take her words personal. As she prepared for her shower, she began feeling nauseous again; racing into the bathroom inside of her bedroom, shutting the door behind her, Nova fell to her knees, vomiting.

One hour and fifteen minutes later Marian and Alex were seated downstairs, Marian fidgeting, resisting the urge to have some more of the cookies she baked which were now in the fridge inside of a Tupperware container. Nova did not appear, losing track of time and feeling rather fatigued she was fast asleep in her queen-sized bed dreaming of the day she and Terry would run off together. It was in that moment Alex began to realize that perhaps Dash enlisting her help was not something she could manage. Too craven to make her way upstairs to fetch Nova, Alex peacefully decided it best to return home, advising Marian to please keep a watchful eye on her younger sister, Marian agreeing, although she had no intention of following through.

10

Present Day...

Nova remains standing, her eyes appearing lost, almost frightening as Mrs. Higgins stood, wondering if she should continue calling to her,

"Nova, darling?" she questioned, her tone soothing. Immediately her eyes began to flutter, Nova was now out of her trance, Tucker staring daringly into her eyes, looking up wondering where his mother had gone. Nova regained her composure, nodding her head as if to agree with all that Mrs. Higgins had been saying to her up until that point. She hated feeling like she was being disrespectful, but she was just in desperate need of some clarification or to awaken from this nightmare she was in. An elated Tucker greeting his grandmother with joy, it had been a while since they'd last spoken. Nova decided to take a seat on one of the wooden chairs surrounding the oak dining table.

"Nova, what on earth happened?" she asked. Nova shook her head in disbelief,

"I—I honestly don't know Mrs. Higgins," she replied innocently. Finally admitting to herself and her mother-in-law, "I did try; however, my dogged pursuit did not seem to pay off. I mean for the sake of my son, I had to, plus I was embarrassed to even tell you that Terry and I had separated, so I mean imagine my surprise that you knew this whole time and said nothing," she said. Tucker looking on, making Mrs. Higgins uncomfortable, and so, she instructed him to play outside, leaving the adults to conversate. Mrs. Higgins felt a mix of emotions, on one hand feeling disloyal to her son given the information she had been told and, on another hand, feeling sympathetic for the young woman. Nova did not appear to be culpable of the events which had taken place. Bringing the kettle to a boil Mrs. Higgins pouring herself and Nova a glass of tea, uneasily she said,

"I was told that you cheated on Terry and ran off with another man," her tone grim. Changing rather quickly as her lips now pursed. Nova could not believe her ears, the look of shame and disgust plastered across her face. Terry had told many lies, he was probably a compulsive liar, but never did she imagine he would speak ill of her for his own namesake. Nova toggled with the idea of whether or not she should even proceed with defending itself. The look on Mrs. Higgins face was telling, a look reading, *you are not a good woman, mother or person, my son would not lie.* Taking a seat and clearing her throat while dipping her tea bag in and out of the steaming water was hypnotizing to Nova. She too decided to follow suit.

Mrs. Higgins was growing impatient, having already drawn her own conclusions. But dearest Nova did not need to know that,

"Is what he said true?" she asked, raising the teacup to her chapped lips, sucking her teeth upon realizing the water had not yet cooled, her tongue burning.

"No, what he said is not true at all," Nova finally spoke, a weight lifting from her shoulders. The knitting of Mrs. Higgins brows meant she did not believe, Nova preparing herself now to be castigated.

"I see no reason for my son to lie Nova. He was very adamant about this, emotional too. Now, I would understand I mean, you and my son were both quite young when you got pregnant and wedded. This—this type of thing is common. But we mustn't lie," she said stirring the contents of her cup. Nova remained appalled. Admitting to herself there would be no convincing of Mrs. Higgins otherwise, her son, a cherub in her eyes and Nova, the unvirtuous. Mrs. Higgins could see the pain in Nova's eyes, despite what she had chosen to believe, she could not bear knowing that she had come to despise her and her hate unsuitable. She now only wanted the utmost best for her son after all she was led to believe he endured. And what mother would not?

"Please understand me Nova, if what you are saying is true then I owe you an apology to which I am not above providing. However, Terry is my son, I watched him throw away an opportunity of a lifetime to remain here with you, with his son. I just don't understand why he would throw away such a sacrifice if it was not deemed necessary," she said. Nova shaking her head now, happy that she was not alone in questioning his actions,

"Mrs. Higgins, me too, I swear I don't know and I have never done anything to hurt Terry. Terry was having an affair and I wanted to forgive him, but he wanted to be with someone else," Nova said, now struggling to speak through her tears. Mrs. Higgins extending her hand, placing it atop Nova's,

"Dry your tears, he is my son and I will always love him and if what you're saying is true then, of course, his deeds will not go unpunished," she said nodding her head in confirmation. Although Mrs. Higgins still remained a skeptic, Nova could feel she had done the right thing today, calling and dropping by. Moments later she raised her teacup taking a long sip of the Green Tea Mrs. Higgins provided her. Nova spent hours with Mrs. Higgins, laughing, reminiscing on the old days when she resided with them and speaking now to her current living situation. Mrs. Higgins no longer feeling proud of her son, rather strongly disappointed in him, both as a man and father, abandoning his son, possibly lying and hurting the one woman who Mrs. Higgins knew would have done absolutely anything for him. But she too felt partly responsible. Knowing that her son was merely a boy when she and her now late husband encouraged Terry to be wedded, remain at home, work and care for a young boy on his own with little to no support from either of them. Hudson shortly become bed-bound making it almost impossible to assist Terry and care for his wellbeing. But now is a new beginning for both Mrs. Higgins and Nova, their relationship starting anew, Mrs. Higgins, now only prayed that Nova would find the strength to become something great in life.

Nova decided to allow Tucker the chance to remain with his grandmother for the duration of the weekend, promising her return on Sunday. Learning of the truth did not sit well with her as she traveled back to her aunt's estate, weeping in the backseat of the taxi cab. Turning the lock on the door inside, Nova ran to her room like that of a teenager where she buried her head into her pillow sobbing until the sun went down. Startling her came the sound of the television in the living room blaring now that evening was upon them. Standing, straightening her clothing she stepped lightly down the stairs. Nova was terribly missing her hair now, her head feeling light— almost too light.

"Hunter?" she called to him from the middle of the staircase, bending to see who was in the living room, Hunter turning to face her, struggling to pry his eyes away from the television screen.

"Hey there!" he bellowed, motioning for her to join him. Hunter was still hopeful that he and Alex would make a wonderful couple one day, as such he remained her handyman, completing work around the house, this time, installing her sixty-five-inch flat screen television to the living room wall. Inside, Nova lifted her head slightly to see the television and the soccer game showing from the screen, careful not to trip over the tools Hunter had lying around. His face glowing, he was proud of himself and the work he accomplished.

"This looks so nice!" he said proudly. Nova remained standing next to him, her arms folded, at this point she would appreciate a little bit of a heads up from her aunt whenever Hunter or Ryan would be making their way by. Nova did not return his excitement, instead, she sat, plopping herself on the sofa. Taking a look back at her, realizing how sad she was Hunter turned the volume down,

"Alright, why the long face?" he asked. Nova could tell he genuinely wanted to help, the look in his eyes said so. But Nova was growing tired of having to explain herself, relive those hurtful moments and receive a plethora of opinions that did nothing to make her feel better. After all, no one was answering the one question she so desperately needed an answer to, *why did Terry leave?*

"Look, I know we aren't friends or anything so, maybe you don't feel comfortable telling me your business. But I'd sure like to try and help, you know maybe offer you some advice from a man's perspective," he said gathering his tools. Nova now sitting upright.

"What makes you think I need advice about a man?" she scoffed. Rolling his eyes,

"You're sulking and have been since the day I met you, of course it's about a man," Hunter replied, carefully though, as he no intention of getting too far ahead of himself.

"Okay," Nova said shrugging her shoulders, "since you're a man, why would a man leave a woman after sacrificing so much to be with her, marriage, a child?" she asked.

"Well, first and foremost, it depends on the man," Hunter said before taking a deep breath, his response guileless. But Nova was prepared, now deeply immersed in their conversation,

"Go on," she said almost begging.

"You seem pretty young. Besides, how old were you guys when you first got together and had a baby?" he replied, Nova sucking her teeth, growing restless of this repetitive theory, this pointless blather becoming devastatingly draining. "Seventeen. What does that have to do with anything?" she asked.

"Everything. He was young and to be honest Nova, maybe the only reason this guy was around as long as he was, was because of the baby," Hunter said with a shrug to his shoulders. "Most guys at that age are still experimenting, figuring out their lives, they aren't thinking about babies and happily ever after," he continued, grinning now. "I mean, I find it kind of odd that no one really warned you about that," he continued.

Reclining in her chair, she whispered, "Auntie did." Nova's eyes lowering in shame.

If you wear a protective style,
don't forget to moisturize regularly!

2007

By morning Nova did not hear any commotion which was abnormal in their day to day, she wondered where Marian had gone before noticing the bags and suitcases all piled on top of one another downstairs by the front door. Making her way downstairs, wearing her cotton pajamas, she noticed the front door lock opened, lifting the hatch she looked outside, the California sun burning her eyes, Nova placed her hand across her forehead just above her eyes to aid her vision. The uproar going on across the street heard from a distance, standing in front of a U-Haul truck was Marian, Myesha Henry and two men wearing uniforms. Nova waited patiently inside when behind her the sound of her fathers' voice caused her to twitch.

"These idiots," he muffled.

"Daddy?" Nova turned quickly watching her father look down on his Cartier watch, cleaning the face with his yellow handkerchief. Taking a deep breath Nova turned, she wanted to hug him, scream at him, leap into his arms, she wanted to do it all, but then she remembered that was not possible. Her father would never allow for such displays of affection—too stoic.

"Where have you been girl?" he questioned. Nova unsure of how to respond. She feared to tell the truth, his reaction may be far too unpleasant.

"With a female friend of mine," she stuttered, her eyes widened, her father always striking fear in her. Although he was never abusive, it was his tone, his demeanor which made him intimidating.

"You stay here or I will hire security to accompany you everywhere you go," he said moving past her, stepping outside speaking explicitly to the movers, his assistant and Marian who was now racing back towards the front door.

"Hey, you're up!" she shouted. Nova wondered why Marian was surprised by this, after-all Nova believed it to be morning.

"What time is it?" Nova asked apprehensively.

"Dude, it's almost 1 o'clock," Marian replied, lifting her duffle bags.

"In the afternoon?" Nova asked to clarify, shocked.

"Duh, why on earth are you so tired?" she replied. But

Nova did not have an answer, rather she too was wondering why she had awoken so late in the day. Deciding to wonder no more she grew curious as to where Marian was heading, noticing she was picking up the bags, walking them to and from the truck.

"What on earth is all of this?" Nova asked.

"Daddy is leaving for Paris in two days for a month, so Myesha has him bringing some of his things to a villa nearest the airport and then from there his stuff will be shipped," Marian advised her. But Nova did not listen, she was beginning to feel lightheaded,

"Okay, I'm going to lay down," she said.

"Ugh, you could at least help," Marian shouted from the bottom of the stairs. Inside of her room, Nova slammed the door behind her, crawling her way back onto her mattress where she closed her eyes, falling into a deep slumber.

Hours later Nova was awakened by the ruckus heard downstairs. The loud music blaring, giving her a migraine. "Jesus," she said to herself, tossing the sheets aside to stand. Feeling bloated and hungry, Nova was growing agitated, stomping her way down the stairs to find Marian and a group of her friends from school all huddled in the living room playing Grand Theft Auto while the radio played. They were alone, again, nothing new as Nova would have imagined. In the kitchen, she searched for food, anything other than the nutritional meals Terrance made. She wanted junk, some chips, dip, maybe even cookies. It annoyed her that their home was so isolated. Missing Terry now, their late-night walks to the corner store for Doritos and ice cream.

Marian and her friends all jamming to the music, passing around a joint and drinking alcohol. The smoke from the living room thick, standing by the living room threshold Nova began coughing, bringing attention to her as everyone turned to face her only momentarily. The punk rock students all soon after paying her no mind. Marian shot to her feet, inebriated she stumbled her way to Nova,

"Dude, you're still here?" she questioned, laughing hysterically. A confused Nova replied,

"Why wouldn't I be here?" she asked. Marian continued laughing,

"Every time you disappear for more than two hours, you've run away!" she shouted. Nova heard enough, she did not like seeing Marian this way, completely impaired, her words slurred, her hair uncombed, she looked unhinged. Just then Nova noticed the box of pizza on the mantle—pepperoni. Pushing her sister off to the side she made her way into the living room, to her right two students were kissing, Nova felt repulsed. Grabbing one of the boxes where six slices remained, she scurried out of the room and into the kitchen where she sat atop the island stool, having a glass of orange juice and the pizza she was lucky enough to locate, downing all six slices in a matter of minutes.

By morning before the sun could greet them the maids and Terrance arrived. Terrance feeling lucky to still have a job, Alex was quite displeased with him but knew he needed the experience and of course, the money. Marian had fallen asleep in the living room, curled into the fetal position on top of the sectional she slept peacefully. Empty beer cans, pizza boxes, cigarette ashes and vomit all around her. Both Miss. Mallory and Miss. Denise enraged. Having worked with Dash for over twenty-two years they had never been exposed to such filth. Also, sisters, they were known and appreciated by Dash for both their punctuality and diligence. Nova was excited to hear Marian get scolded, both Denise and Mallory had been working with Dash long enough to provide a verbal lashing here and there when needed when it came to the girls. Their Nigerian accents bringing her joy as she stands by the banister overhearing them awake Marian questioning her and her reckless behavior.

"This is unacceptable Marian," Miss Denise said, hovering just above her looking to help her stand so she could walk to her bedroom. As their voices drew nearer Nova ran back to her room where she shut the door behind her, but her excitement short-lived as her nausea returned forcing her into the bathroom where she began to hurl, vomiting all the food she had eaten the night before. Nova now growing worried. Waiting patiently until Miss Denise was heard placing Marian to bed, Nova called to her. The fifty-two-year-old 5'4 stocky build woman with a short afro and thin mustache came marching down the hall.

"Aww good morning beautiful, why aren't you asleep?" she asked nicely. Nova lowering her eyes,

"Miss Denise, she whispered, um, I keep vomiting and feeling really nauseous, do you think we can go to the doctor?" Nova asked, her voice tender. Raising her right eyebrow Miss Denise knew better.

"Ha, Doctor? No, you have sex?" she asked. A stunned Nova retracting her head in shock,

"Um, sex?" she repeated, unsure of whether or not she should tell the truth. And she did, nodding.

"Hmm, you maybe need a pregnancy test," Miss Denise said, her hands now just above her hip. "I will go get one, you stay here and try to keep calm. When was your last period?" she then turned to ask just before making her way out of the bedroom.

"I honestly can't remember," Nova said disheartened. Miss Denise now taking pity on a young Nova advised her to continue to rest. Nova did as she was told sitting on the edge of her bed, biting her nails before standing to face the mirror in her room. Examining her body, primarily her lower abdomen. She wondered if indeed she was pregnant, what would she do? How would her father feel? Besides, what could she possibly do with a baby, she too was a baby? Two hours came and went, and Marian was now awake, showering, Nova could hear her in her bedroom slamming the closet doors and speaking ignorantly on the phone with her friend. But Nova remained inside of her room, despite her stomach now growling and she could smell the fresh scent of scrambled eggs and pancakes that Terrance was preparing.

A knock came to the door, it was Miss Denise, holding in her right hand a bag from the drug store, inside, a box containing two pregnancy tests. Miss Denise instructed Nova on how to use it, then left her alone to continue her work—she had now fallen behind schedule. Nova remained standing, staring mindlessly at the pregnancy test wondering if this was a road she was willing to travel, replaying the nights her and Terry made love over and again in her mind. *Could I really have been that careless?* She thought. With her eyes fluttering and her hands shaking there was nothing left to do, but to take it, heading into the bathroom, sliding down her pajama pants and panties she sat on the toilet seat placing the pee stick directly between her legs—peeing now.

For the first time Nova paid extra attention to the sound of her urine, praying it was not so, praying she was not with child, her petite body trembling as she removed the stick, placing the cap back on; waiting now. Frightened by the abrupt knock to the door Nova stood, wondering if Miss Denise had returned; but instead, it was Marian, playfully requesting her attendance for breakfast. Nova hated that her sister was always so quirky, it seemed for Marian life never threw her a curveball and there was never a dull moment. With the room feeling dismal Nova ignored her, surprised now that the allotted time had passed and she was to learn her fate. Looking down at the test reading positive her gait clumsy, Nova cautioning herself to remain standing as Marian knocked again, this time aggressive.

"Open the door!" she cried, worried her sister had once again fled from their home. It was all too easy for Nova to leave which only made her family paranoid. Nova could not believe it, but despite her bewilderment and need for loneliness while she wallows in her sadness she knew that would not be a healthy thing to do and so, she stepped out of the bathroom, onto the carpeted bedroom floors where she made her way to the bedroom door, opening it. Things were moving slowly, her eyes lowered, immediately Marian could sense something was not right,

"Nova, are you okay?" she lovingly asked.

"Marian, I'm pregnant," Nova replied with tears falling from her eyes. Marian closing the door behind her in an attempt to be discreet, fearing anyone would hear them. She was speechless and for the first time calm. Marian had no idea what to do next, let alone say to her baby sister, no one could have predicted this, but they were only being naïve as Nova had spent many days away from home which only meant her actions were unaccounted for. Marian now realizing this said,

"We have to tell auntie." But Nova would hear of no such thing, shaking her head in anguish, pleading,

"Oh my God, no, they can't know," she said referring to both her father and her aunt who would no doubt be disappointed.

"We can't just keep this to ourselves, we have to tell someone," Marian begged, tossing her hands in the air. "What's the worst that can happen? Let's at least tell auntie," she continued. Nova now grew angry,

"Why can't I just get an abortion? You're old enough to take me. Or—or we can tell Miss Denise, she's the one who got me the test," Nova suggested.

"No, she will tell daddy, she's obligated to do so. Listen, I know this is a lot to digest right now, but we should tell auntie, I promise you Nova she will know what to do," said Marian before taking her leave to head into her bedroom where she dialed Alex.

Across town Alex was hitting the books. Law school proving itself to be rather arduous, with only four hours of sleep, three cups of coffee and morning sex she was feeling jittery; her eyes closing periodically. The one-bedroom apartment she resided in with her boyfriend Terrance was cozy. But she remained thankful having never left the neighborhood where she grew up she was determined to one day make a difference in the world. Studying criminal law before learning just how truly vain she would become later transitioning into entertainment law when learning of the lucrative income. Life then became about affluent homes, cars and Birkin bags. Looking down as her cellular phone rang she noticed it was Marian, but she could not bring herself to answer. She was studying and before she could take on the responsibility of raising a teenager and young adult she preferred to work on her assignments. Turning the phone on silent and turning it on its face was when she realized that she was truly not cut out for parenting. This prompted her to take a moment to retrieve her birth control from the medicine cabinet in the bathroom, filling a small glass with water before taking a long sip ingesting the tiny brown pill.

Inside of Marian's bedroom, Nova stood panicked, periodically begging her sister to bring her to the abortion clinic. Nova adamant about not being a teenage mother, because her life would be ruined, this much she knew, but not telling Terry was beginning to weigh on her.

"Should I tell Terry about the baby?" she asked Marian

who sat on the floor, her cellular phone next to her, waiting patiently for Alex to return her call. Marian did not have the answers; rather, she knew Nova would not like her answers. To her they were children and Marian knew when the day came to have children it would be with someone special. Deep down she was furious with Nova, only seventeen with a baby. Although her mind could not fully comprehend the nature of this situation, she simply knew it was bad; society teaching her as much. Miss Denise made her way upstairs knocking along the bedroom doors, locating both Marian and Nova, the looks on their faces distressed, imminently she knew.

Miss Denise decided it best not to question the young girls, only requesting their attendance for breakfast. She prided herself on being an honest, Christian woman and the last thing she needed was to be interrogated by her boss of his daughter's affairs and having to lie. Purchasing the young girl a pregnancy test was the furthest she was willing to go, although only afterward had she realized that even that too, was going too far. But the damage was already done. Marian and Nova both quietly standing, pacing behind her as they all entered into the kitchen; Miss Denise thanking Terrance for his patience.

The morning tense and still no word from Alex, Marian calling once again, this time leaving a voicemail to stress the urgency of their situation. Nova leaving them, returning upstairs, she was aggravated, dressing as she prepared to make her way to Terry's, feeling like she had to break the news, even if he did not take it well. She was going to tell him about the baby and then allow nature to take its course—whatever that meant. Marian hated leaving Nova alone and with only a few more weeks until classes began she was dreading having to return to campus. Distracted by the television Marian did not realize that Nova had gone.

By the afternoon Nova was standing outside banging on the front door to Terry's home, his mother answering within a matter of minutes. Mrs. Higgins was cleaning, wearing a pair of yellow latex gloves and holding onto a can of Ajax, she was surprised and yet relieved to see Nova. Nova was quite the helper to them, aiding her with caring for Hudson and now that he was growing sicker, Mrs. Higgins could use a helping hand, a break and so she greeted Nova with kindness. Nova could not understand why Mrs. Higgins was being so polite after the unpleasant altercation she had with Alex. But she decided not to question it, instead she stepped inside, her hands shaking as she asked for Terry, but Mrs. Higgins was unsure of where her son had gone, only assuming he was out playing basketball considering how nice the weather had been. Hearing this helped to ease Nova's tension only slightly. Because although she was ready to disclose the news, she was not ready to receive a response or even see the reaction she would receive if not positive.

Nova thanked Mrs. Higgins for the information she provided, temporarily bidding her farewell, Mrs. Higgins now feeling stressed as she watched Nova leave. Nova decided it best to walk to the playground, taking the time to think and believing the exercise to do her good. She was feeling anxious walking along the pavement, kicking the empty soda bottles, while eluding the sticks of gum on the ground. Her thoughts plentiful, wondering what kind of mother she would be, how much her life would change and whether or not she was ready.

Indistinctly listening to the shouting of the young men and women on the basketball court Nova pressed her hands firmly against the chain links seconds later, her eyes searching frantically for Terry who she prayed was there. Spotting him wearing a pair of black Nike shorts and sneakers with a plain white t-shirt Nova thanked the heavens before watching a girl on the bleachers shout his name in excitement. The woman familiar, Nova squinting her eyes hoping to get a better look; it was the girl from the party. Seeing her now fully clothed, Nova felt insecure, she was beautiful. Her skin caramel, her hair long and soft-tossed into a messy ponytail. But Nova did not want to jump to conclusions.

On the basketball court she stood, her arms folded, Terry preparing to take a three-point shot across the yard—spotting her, his balance impaired as the ball fell from his hands. The boys around him shouting, watching both Nova and the young girl on the bleachers, confused on what to do next. Nova watched as he made his way over to the bleachers whispering in the young girl's ear, their eyes locking as Nova now walked towards her. She had no idea what she was going to do or should do, she remained naïve, watching the young girl stand to walk away. In front of Terry, Nova began to question him,

"What the hell was that about?" she asked, her arms folded. Nova was hurting, her heart in her ankles. Nova was not at all confrontational, but at that moment she was ready to behave belligerently. Terry shrugging his shoulders replied,

"I have no idea what you're talking about. What are you doing here?" he asked her. His friends looking on annoyed, deciding to resume their game after shouting vulgarities at him. Nova appalled.

"What do you mean what am I doing here? That's not a nice way to greet me," she replied.

"Well, you just interrupted my game; I mean what do you want me to say? I thought you were going to stay home," he said tossing the ball in the air and catching it with his hands while speaking to her. Terry was not listening and Nova knew he was disinterested. Feeling like she was going to lose him, Nova said it, she blurted it out, in hopes that he would cradle her, love her forever and stop cheating,

"I'm pregnant."

The sound of the ball stopped, Terry now gripping it tightly, silence falling upon them, the screeching of the sneakers from the boys playing and shouting now deafening.

"Um, what?" Terry asked; the look on his face enraged. Nova now afraid to repeat herself, and so, she didn't, she knew he heard her the first time and so she remained standing; Terry placing his hands on his head in agony. "Jesus Christ," he then proclaimed. "Are you sure? Did you take a test? Have—have you gone to the doctor? When did you find out?" he questioned, panicked.

"Yes, I took a test and no, I haven't been to the doctor yet. I found out this morning," Nova confirmed.

"So, what happens now? I can't be a father right now Nova. You have to get an abortion," he said, tossing the ball to the ground. Nova could not believe her ears, although she too was not thinking of keeping the baby, she wanted Terry to at least try and convince her otherwise, she thought he loved her after all.

"You don't want a baby with me is what you're saying,"

111

Nova asked quickly fighting the tears that were now welling in her eyes. Sucking his teeth and drawing a long breath Terry replied,

"Nova I leave in one year, by the time you're ready to give birth I'll be on a plane somewhere going away for school. I'm sure you don't want to have to go at that alone," he sympathized.

Heartbroken, Nova reluctantly concurred.

11

Night came quickly as Terry continued his game, but he could not focus, this was obvious—his friends begging him to leave because mentally he was gone. Nova remained seated on the bleachers, waiting for him to finish so they could go home, his home. Now that Terry wanted her to have an abortion, Nova felt compelled to keep her child, deciding to break the news in front of his parents, hoping now they would convince him it was a good idea to stay around. Nova was being selfish, this much she knew, but her whole life now felt like it revolved around Terry and she could not imagine what it would be like not having him.

She was prepared for the hard times, the disloyalty and the seldom disinterest, as long as he remained an integral part of her, nothing and no one else mattered. Terry made her feel safe, at times wanted—more so than unwanted. She knew their relationship was not ideal but who else was going to protect her like he did? Cuddle her at night? Love her? She could single-handedly think of no one, she simply decided to tolerate as much as she could just as long as Terry continues to choose her in the end. Wrapping up their game, Nova felt relieved, she and Terry were finally leaving, the walk home unbearable as neither one of them spoke a word. Terry pondering his next course of action before making his way inside the pitch-black house, Nova steadily behind him; inside of his bedroom dropping his bags, before heading into the shower. Nova missed his bedroom although she had not been gone long. Removing her pants and shirt then climbing under the covers where she patiently awaited him. Once out of the shower Nova watched as Terry completed his brief nightly routine, climbing into bed, he turned to face her,

"So I thought about it, maybe you should keep the baby," he said calmly. Nova's face lighting up with glee, she was feeling a mix of emotions, but one thing was for sure, she was feeling relaxed. "I mean, I would still have to go away Nova. But, maybe you can come and once I make it in the NBA we will be rich anyway so, maybe having a baby isn't completely a bad thing," Terry concluded. His tone apprehensive but his words hopeful as he himself could not believe what he was saying, dreading the thought of having to admit to his parents that he was now having a child. But one thing is for sure, he was not going to give up his dream, he had no intentions of doing so.

"So you're still going to leave?" Nova asked. "I don't mind coming with you, just have to figure out where we're going," she continued, smiling, her hands pressed firmly against his thighs. Terry felt trapped, like now he was going to be with Nova no matter what, but he was not thoughtless, nor was he cruel, knowing she did not want to lose him and some part of him was happy she felt this way. Nova and Terry made love that night.

In the morning Alex opened her eyes to greet Terrance as they both lie awake watching the sunrise through her bedroom window. Alex was always an early morning riser and a night owl, that day she couldn't help but feel grateful. With her accelerated program coming to an end, she was only a few months away from graduation. Twenty-three years old, she was to begin working for Hayman and Lawrence PLLC, as a public defender shortly thereafter. Watching Terrance dress to make his way over to the Signature house she smiled. He was ambitious and far too kind, but always feeling insecure because Alex did not want anyone to know of their relationship, she feared it would ruin his position as Dash would not approve. He was protective, especially of Alex, because he knew just how much his wife loved Alex, as a baby she would raise Alex as though she too were a child of their own right alongside Marian.

Turning to check her cellular phone Alex noticed the eleven missed calls from Marian, some work emails and additional calls to which she all ignored. Checking her voicemail, she listened as a devastated Marian wept—a first for her as she was typically jubilant. Listening on, Alex heard it; Nova was pregnant and once again gone from their house. Alex had had enough, she was not going to continue to allow her nieces to stress her, livid now she arose from the full-sized mattress, racing into the bathroom where she showered quickly preparing herself for the day.

Alex had a strong feeling of where Nova could be and so, she drove along the interstate, speeding almost until she reached the small house in Vacaville, banging on the front door, shouting for Nova. Unbeknownst to her, Nova and Terry were both still fast asleep. Mrs. Higgins opening the door to greet her wearing her night robe while wiping the corners of her eyes. Yawning she said, "How can I help you?" Alex trying to retain her composure,

"Where is Nova?" she asked.

"Well considering the fact that you're here, maybe she's with Terry in his room," Mrs. Higgins replied. Alex then began to push her way inside, "Hey! This is my home, I did not invite you in here," Mrs. Higgins shouted. Alex now turning to face her,

"My niece is pregnant," she said watching the facial expression on the old woman change, going from distraught to defensive in a matter of seconds.

"Terry is not a fool! He has a full scholarship for basketball to three colleges. He is not that silly," she said again.

"Oh yes he is!" screamed Alex. "And quite frankly, you allowed this to happen, you have two teenagers in your house unsupervised, it was completely irresponsible of you."

"Watch how you speak to me, you have no idea what goes on in my home!" shouted Mrs. Higgins.

"Sex, sex between teenagers, that's what goes on in your home! How on earth did you let this happen? They are children!" Alex shouted feeling guilty for raising her voice to her elder. She could not believe how angry she was, because Nova was not her child and yet, she felt as upset as any parent would have been. Nova was throwing away her life and all for a man, were the thoughts plaguing her. She almost felt it to be impossible.

Awakening to the banging of his bedroom door—the invidious remarks overhead in the hallway hard to ignore. Terry and Nova moving with haste, dressing, Alex heard shouting on the opposite of the door to Mrs. Higgins who was trying to defend her son. Nova apologized to Terry, feeling like she would be exiled from his home due to Alex's antics. A furious Alex continued to bang the door, Terry turning the lock, opening it, he wondered why his mother allowed Alex to enter their home in the first place. The tiny hallway now filled with two screaming women, a weeping Nova and an aggravated Terry.

"Stop it!" he yelled; Mrs. Higgins stepping to him, slapping him across the face, surprising both Alex and Nova.

"What about your career?" she exclaimed. Alex made her way over to Nova casually dressed, her hair in braids which swung from side to side—Nova looking on, undecided on whether or not to speak.

"Look, Nova and I are going to be fine. We talked about it and we're keeping the baby. Mom, I'm still going to college, Nova just may come with me," Terry said. Alex now interrupting him,

"What? Are you crazy? Terry, you don't want a kid right now, okay. Both of you are children and you're both underestimating the responsibilities that come with having a child. Who is going to work? Nova, you have to go to school. Have you even begun applying to colleges? I mean there is no way that either of you have thought this through," she said. Mrs. Higgins nodded. But Alex was still unforgiving of the old woman; angry that she was so lax with the children in her home doing as they pleased.

"Nova we're leaving and let me make myself clear, you sneak out again I will have Dash hire every security agency within a ten-mile radius to keep you locked in that bedroom until you are old and gray, do you hear me?" Alex screamed;

both Mrs. Higgins and Terry exchanging a befuddled look. *"Dash?"* Mrs. Higgins mouthed to him. Ignoring her, Terry trailing behind them as they made their way towards the door, "Nova, we will figure this out," he said to her, watching she and Alex take their leave, a sad Nova remaining silent. Inside of their home Mrs. Higgins disclosed the information to her husband, who was now bed-bound, shortly thereafter requesting that his son join him in their bedroom. Mrs. Higgins furious but she was not one to scold her son, she felt guilty even smacking him. He was her only child and no matter what he did, she was going to remain by his side and support him, this she also told her husband who despite her claims could not bring himself on board with the idea. Hudson was living vicariously through his son up until then, he was unable to join the NBA having to care for his sickly mother and although he wanted children at a young age, he did not want children before becoming financially equipped to manage them and his wife.

An old school soul, Hudson spent the morning discussing with Terry the outcome of his decision and its consequences. But Terry remained unmoved thinking only of the fact that he was going to do all that he had been taught leading up to that point. He was going to be a responsible man and raise his child while providing for his girlfriend. Hudson did find this admirable, but also foolish.

"You won't want to go away when the baby comes. Graduate, get yourself a good job, marry the girl and live your life," Hudson advised his son for reasons unknown. A confused Terry feeling discouraged wondering if his father had given up hope in him, disappointed.

"Dad, I'm going to college," Terry scoffed.

"You won't last in there," snarled Hudson. "Not if you choose to keep this baby. You'll get distracted, you have to keep your head in the game, how can you do that with a screaming baby and a needy girlfriend?" Listening to his father speak upset Terry, Nova had been nothing but kind to him, caring and yet this is how he truly felt about her. Learning this, Hudson now began to loathe Nova feeling like she was causing his son to give up on his dream, sucking the life from him, as many women do. Angrily he turned away, his back now to

Terry as he stood walking out of the bedroom, his mother just in the kitchen humming a church hymnal as she prepared breakfast. Terry determined now to prove him wrong.

The Signature house felt gloomy. Sitting on the bottom of the staircase Marian watched as her sister and Alex entered inside. Nova resisting the urge to attack her, she knew Marian was going to tell their aunt, but she was angry that Marian did not wait until they were both together to do it or at least allow her time to tell Terry first. Downstairs in the foyer, just on the opposite side of the front door, Marian, Alex and Nova all stood, no one speaking a word for minutes.

"So—"

"...I don't know what to say," Both Nova and Alex simultaneously speaking. Marian rolling her eyes,

"Look, you're the perfect happy sister, why don't you mind your business, huh? You were so quick to call auntie—"

"Nova are you going insane? I told you I was going to call auntie and you were okay with it after a while," Marian replied.

"No! I wanted to tell Terry first and you just couldn't wait!" Nova screamed.

"Both of you shut up! We are going to the abortion clinic tomorrow. The last thing I need is for Dash to return to find you pregnant!" said Alex. Nova exhaling in frustration,

"Oh, who is going to tell daddy? It seems like you both just can't wait to get me in trouble," Nova said, realizing just how foolish she sounded once the words left her mouth. Marian heard enough.

"Fine, do what you want," she said.

"No, no one is going to just do what they want here. Nova I know things with your father feels a bit strained but you can always come to me or go to your sister, you don't have to find comfort in a man all the time, or run away to be with him. Terry is young, he has scholarships to colleges, and he does not want to be a father right now. I can promise you that despite anything he says. Hell, we're all young, why are you trying to destroy your life and become some baby momma or a trailing girlfriend for this boy? Is it really even worth it?" Alex said.

"Auntie, you're just lonely so of course I don't expect you to understand," Nova snapped. Alex scoffed. Reminding herself that Nova was still a child and of course immature.

"Lonely?" she questioned sarcastically knowing that Nova was not privy to her affairs with Terrance.

"Yes, you went off to law school because you were bored and lonely! Why do you even care so much? You're not our mother and our own father doesn't give a damn whether we stay or go, die or live. What's here huh, just a huge empty house when Marian is gone. I see cooks, hairdressers, stylists all come and go, but where's my damn father? That's right nowhere. I come home every day to a house full of strangers and you wonder why I'm so unhappy or why I found comfort in Terry?" Nova screamed stomping her way upstairs past Marian who remained seated.

"Maybe we can get her a dog?"

"Marian stop being such a smart ass," Alex said.

Shampoo Mindfully:
Yes, you still need to shampoo
regularly to keep your scalp and
hair clean, but you can lengthen
the time between washes to
2,3 or even 4 weeks.

Present Day...
Hunter stood watching over Nova as she stared off into space, lost. Snapping his fingers hoping she would come back to reality,

"Hey! Are you okay?" he asked modestly. Nova nodding her head,

"Yea, yes, I'm fine. Thanks," she said. Hunter suggested therapy for Nova she was clearly not in her right state of mind and although he did not know her too well, wanted the best for her considering her relation to Alex—a woman he had come to respect and adore. But Nova would hear of no such thing, wondering if Hunter could assist her with putting together the recording equipment she was going to purchase for her son. Nova raced upstairs, plopping herself on the soft mattress inside of her bedroom where she began jotting notes in a notepad, a name for her YouTube channel leaving her rather irritated.

Nova felt discouraged after hours passed and she was still feeling clueless, as such she scoped out the competition, looking how to narrow down her niche, did she want to blog? Record videos or just have a social media account where she would post updates about her hair growth and the reasons behind her drastic new look? It was all beginning to feel overwhelming, a little too overwhelming. But Nova did not want to quit she needed to prove to herself that she could do something outside of being a wife and mother. Then she realized exactly what she was missing, she needed inspiration.

That evening Nova asked Alex to call Hunter so they can all head out for a night on the town, she wanted to get out of the house and of course finally, have some fun. Alex quickly obliged as she enjoyed nights out and a weekend without Tucker was just what she too now needed. After spending the majority of her day on social media and watching a bulk of YouTube videos, Nova had a pretty good idea of what exactly she was going to go for in her series. However, she remained skeptical wondering who would even watch her? Why would anyone care that she got her heart ripped from her chest and decided to shave her naturally healthy growing hair? She was no different than any other woman who had ever been lied to, cheated on and left, but she wants to be different, how, is the question?

"There's a strip of bars and a nightclub not too far from here," said Alex blending herself a cocktail to pre-game before heading out. Nova did not care where they went, as long as she was out of the house and could see in the flesh all that she had been reading about online.

"Do you think that dark-skinned men don't date dark-skinned women?" she asked Alex. Alex taken aback by her questions, finding it to be quite random responded by saying,

"Well, I'm not sure," But that was not the answer Nova was hoping to hear.

"Well, you dated Terrance and he was medium complexion and you're dark-skinned, Ryan is medium complexion who you seem very cozy with and Hunter is dark-skinned and in love with you but you don't seem to want to give him the time of day," explained Nova.

"Whoa, Ryan and I are friends," replied Alex. "As far as

Hunter, I just think he's too young, inexperienced. Ryan is a divorcee with a kid, which to me, equals experience. I don't have to teach him how to be with a woman, he already has that down."

"...and yet, he's divorced. I don't see the correlation," Nova chuckled.

"Nova, where is this coming from?" Alex asked as she now grew impatient.

"I mean, I read a lot of these stories online where dark-skinned men don't find dark-skinned women attractive. It's like, when they reach a certain level in life then they just abandon the kinky coils for the straight and curly. I think about Laura every single day. I think about how Terry transitioned from loving husband when my hair was permed to nonchalant and emotionally abusive once I did my big chop the first time around and decided to no longer put chemicals in my hair. Something that minuscule altered his whole personality. Now, he has a career and the woman he's with is an Afro Latina whose hair doesn't defy gravity as mine does," said Nova.

"I see," responded Alex just as Hunter made an appearance. "Hunter, what's your take on this?" asked Alex taking a sip of her margarita. Alex was particular, sipping her drinks in accordance with its respected glass.

"I'm not really sure what I walked in on," he said bashfully.

"Dark-skinned men and women not being attracted to one another—well, to specify, dark-skinned men not wanting to date and marry dark-skinned women with kinky hair, that's it in a nutshell," she said laughing.

"Everyone has a preference. Personally, I love my Ethiopian Queens. But, a large percentage of them don't find themselves attracted to me," he said.

"...and there you have it," said Nova; rising from her seat, taking a sip from Alex's glass before making her way upstairs to get dressed for the evening. Hunter and Alex exchanging a look before dismissing herself.

That evening Nova remained focused, hoping to catch the gist of her niche, and as the night pressed on, she did; taking into account that a lot of Black men and women were in interracial relationships—bummed that she did not bring along a microphone for interviews. She was intrigued now, just wondering why. She remained grateful that within only a matter of minutes she was no longer plodding, rather her mind was racing with ideas, information and bursting with knowledge on a new topic she hoped to incorporate into her show.

Sitting around at the bar Nova took a long look around her, examining the men and women in the room, feeling a bit of culture shock realizing the neighborhood was predominantly Caucasian and yet a lot of African American men were walking around with Caucasian women on their arms. Nova did not want to discriminate or be seen as racist, she simply wondered why her skin and her hair was not good enough—if ever that were the case. Alex and Hunter were off, dancing the night away, their eyes glowing in the dark as the 90's pop music blared from the speakers. But not long after Nova felt a tap on her shoulders, twirling in her seat to greet a new face, Charles Leewood. Charles is a personal celebrity chef and restaurant critic. Nova smiled greeting him once he offered to buy her another drink, a tequila sunrise is what she was having, therefore requesting the same drink once again. Exchanging their acquaintances Nova could not help but notice just how handsome he is—Hazel brown eyes, dark-skinned with a thick beard and an athletic build.

Subconsciously Nova began comparing Charles to Terry, something she was no doubt kicking herself for, she could not deny that Charles was far more handsome, however, she did not like the fact that he spoke with a slight lisp. Inevitably she figured this would be a turn-off, but as the night began to wind down and the alcohol made its way into her veins she was finding him to be quite humorous. Alex glancing her every now and again to ensure she remained safe as she and Hunter indulged in some comic relief sitting amongst a few of the bandmates who were to perform live before the venue closed its doors.

By 3 a.m. Nova, Charles, Hunter, and Alex were standing outside along the sidewalk waiting for a cab, Charles speaking to Nova, providing her his contact information so that she may call him in her free time. He was interested, finding Nova to be immensely attractive but no matter how attracted she found herself to him, she was convinced that he all men were dogs and would eventually cheat or leave you for a White woman. And so, she shoved his business card in her back pocket as she made her way towards the Uber taxi that Alex and Hunter were sitting to the rear of waiting patiently for her to climb inside.

That night Nova could not sleep, Hunter passed out in the sofa and Alex tucked away beneath her silk sheets, the night was still. In the kitchen, Nova enjoyed a nice cup of hot cocoa, although the California weather was anything but chilly, the central airs in the house-made inside feel cool and cozy. With the use of her cellular phone, Nova continued reading, locating articles on interracial relationships, heading onto social media outlets such as Instagram and Facebook—where she resisted the urge to cyberstalk her ex-lover and his new beau. She was astonished to find that although Black men and women did date within their race, it was becoming quite seldom, not only that but a lot of women were being cheated on, left and sadly enough taken for granted in their relationships.

Nova now beginning to feel crazy, locating links to other articles outlining mental disorders and checklists for symptoms she was now checking off for Terry, wondering, how could she have missed the signs? Sipping her hot cocoa and rubbing her hands along her bald scalp. She was also researching new hair products to use, when it dawned on her, a name. pulling out one of the drawers from the kitchen island, Nova found blank sheets of paper and a lead pencil where she began jotting down notes, thinking; *The Mental Breakdown of the Black Woman*— too serious and demeaning she thought, scribbling out this suggestion. *Why Men Don't Love Black Women*—too subjective, she thought. *The African American Woman's Hair Strands*—my God, no, she thought, crossing out the name. Placing her hands under her chin, she pondered,

"How can I incorporate my hair and my frustrations?" she asked herself aloud. A few moments later Nova remembered why she cut her hair in the first place, she was angry, she was hurt and her hair was hurt, her crown began to fall out, shedding, as a result of her stress and so, she wrote, *Even My Hair is Mad*. Smiling to herself, she said, "This is it." Seconds later her cellular phone dinged, it was Terry.

12

Nova remained in bed that morning far later than she typically had. Saturday and with Tucker away, she was able to get some rest. However, she awoke, staring at her cellular phone, the message from Terry vague—but still a form of communication she was otherwise elated to have received.

"You still have things in the apartment, the landlord wants it moved or it will be junked," the message read. But Nova was confused, why was she receiving a message now? Terry was long gone, when did he give up the apartment? Were all the questions she was asking herself. She knew the remainder of her things were still inside of the apartment but it was not much which is why she never fussed; especially knowing that Laura was living there once Nova moved in with her sister. Taking a long sigh before turning over to face the notepad she spent the morning scribbling on, she decided to send a text to her aunt, asking if she would be so kind as to bring her over to the apartment to retrieve her things, Alex quickly obliged.

Once the afternoon came around and Hunter departed after breakfast, Nova and Alex pulled up to the apartment in Burbank. Nova was unprepared for what she was soon to face. She still had not formulated a reply to Terry but felt she should carefully consider her words, deep down inside she hoped they would have some dialogue that could possibly lead to her receiving closure. The apartment door unlocked, on the other side was desolate, there was no furniture, the carpet uncleaned, the kitchen sink filled with dirty dishes and the wire hangers fallen along the floors. As Alex and Nova stepped inside, Alex was confused, feeling like there was nothing but junk which remained.

"So you basically have nothing?" Alex asked. Nova shaking her head in disbelief, feeling like there was absolutely no point of her returning there. Walking in the bathroom she removed some of her old toiletries and inside of the bedroom was a small box packed and labeled with her name on it. Opening it, she found a few articles of clothing, some shoes and hair products tossed inside as though it were insignificant garbage. Feeling embarrassed, she feared her aunt would be judgmental, and although Alex did not say so, her face read otherwise.

"Yep, so you're judging me," Nova said chuckling nervously.

"No judgment, just a bit perturbed," responded Alex.

"Perturbed?" Nova questioned, unwilling to admit that she did not know the definition of the word. She assumed it to mean something awful.

"Well, sure, I mean you came into this relationship with nothing and you're leaving with nothing." Alex said lifting a garment from the box in repugnance, "You don't even need this stuff; you may as well leave it and buy new things."

"Wow," Nova said.

"Look, all I'm saying is, you have to be somewhat independent. Have a separate bank account he doesn't know about, I mean shit, have something for yourself!" Alex said, her tone critical. Standing now, her feelings hurt; Nova feeling the need to defend herself, she was feeling attacked as Alex was being condescending. Nova knew this was going to happen, which is why she was apprehensive about residing with Alex in the first place.

"You know when you finally stop being such a hard ass and allow yourself to fall in love, all of that independent babble will go right out of the window. You don't know what it's like, besides, I wasn't just some baby momma, I was his wife." Nova sniped.

"Wife, baby momma, doesn't matter, have something for you! Something to fall back on. And Nova, when do you plan on filing the child support paperwork?" Alex asked, her hands now on her hip, she was careful not to allow her body or clothing to touch anything around her. With one eyebrow raised, she stood waiting for a response, growing impatient.

"Soon..." Nova said, but she was unsure.

"You sound hesitant, what's the issue?"

"Well, I mean I didn't know things were final. I just, well, I kind of hoped that maybe—"

"Maybe what! Maybe he would come around? Are you that desperate? Monday morning, I am taking you downtown to begin filing the paperwork, you have got to be kidding me. You stay home all day, remaining what? A hopeful? That's your full-time job?" Alex quarreled. Nova now weeping, her eyes burning as the tears flooded her face,

"Why are you like this? Why can't you just understand that what I am going through takes time? Sorry, I am not perfect, I didn't go to law school, I don't make six figures and I'm not some fashion student. I am just me. But one thing is for sure, I was a great wife and I am a good mom. I—I just don't know what happened. Jesus, I wish someone would just cut me some slack. I am still learning, why am I not allowed to make mistakes? Oh, because my mistakes are publicized because I have to live like a nomad and be content with an allowance from my aunt, who secretly looks down on me," she cried before pushing her way past Alex and walking outside, her breathing heavy.

Alex was not sympathetic and after realizing there was nothing there for Nova, she made her way outside to vocalize this. Alex was not unfamiliar to heartbreak; she just took the time to learn from her mistakes, her first love Terrance ending things, leaving her abruptly for another woman, only opened her eyes to the cruelty of men. From then on, she swore to know better and despite her warnings to her Nova, she did not take heed during her teenage years and now, she was suffering the consequences. Alex only hoped that as time passed Nova would allow herself to heal.

Nova felt compelled to say goodbye to their Burbank apartment, coming to the realization that this was as close to closure as she was going to come. However, she hated herself for thinking more of the text message, wondering if Terry secretly did miss her, otherwise why would he contact her about things remaining in the apartment? Things he knew were junk after-all. Nova knew better than to bring this speculation to her aunt and so, she didn't, deciding it best to keep her thoughts to herself. Terry did not ask about their son, but then Nova also wondered if perhaps Tucker had spoken to his father by way of Mrs. Higgins. So many thoughts were consuming her, positive ones, also the hope that Mrs. Higgins had a long talk with her son, helping him to see the error of his ways and maybe, just maybe that was also the reason for his sudden urge to communicate. But was her overthinking just too far-fetched? She hoped not.

Alex had errands to run and decided to take Nova along for the drive, but she was itching, feeling too uneasy, now that the text message was just sitting there, the thread staring at her, taunting her almost to issue a reply. To simply tell Terry that she loves him and will do anything to make it work. Maybe he also wanted her to make the first move, maybe he was shy and knew he wanted to come home but could not find the words. As Nova pondered these possibilities her phone rang, it was Marian calling to facetime.

"Hello," she answered. Alex reaching her destination climbed out of the driver's seat while leaving the air conditioner to run as she made her way into the boutique to purchase a cashmere blouse. Nova opting to wait in the car, where she and Marian began to converse,

"Marian, Terry text me," Nova said trying to conceal her happiness.

"What!" shouted Marian. She had no intention of speaking with her sister about Terry for she hoped to have news of Nova progressing and not regressing.

"Well, he simply told me there were things in the old apartment for me to retrieve," Nova admitted. Marian waiting for the remainder of the story,

"Okay, and?" she then asked.

"Well, do you think maybe it means something?" Nova asked her, listening to the words leave her mouth, making her recognize just how sad and desperate she sounds. Her eyes lowering, Marian replied,

"Maybe you should ask auntie to find you a good counselor Nova. And no, I am not trying to ridicule you, I truly want the best for you and want you to grow from this. Have you thought of a name for the show?" Marian asked, changing the subject onto something more positive. But Nova could not focus on that, she was focused on the text message and the hidden meaning behind it. Sadly, no one wanted to help her decipher it, and this was making her frustrated.

"I don't want to talk about the show Marian," Nova snapped. Marian drawing a long sigh.

"Don't let Terry and his obvious hovering distract you for what's most important Nova. If Terry was truly sorry he would say so, if he missed you, he would say so and most importantly if he wanted to work on things with you, he would say so. I hate to be the bearer of bad news, but it just sounds to me like you're holding onto some shred of hope that, that text message is supposed to mean more than it does. You're my sister and I love you, I want to be here for you, but Nova you have to meet us all halfway. Terry is gone, begin focusing on you," Marian said—Nova now gripping the phone tightly, fighting the urge to wail, gulping, as she grew angry now, choosing to no longer speak to Marian, ending their call.

Returning to her vehicle Alex could see the pain in Nova's eyes. Slamming the car door and preparing to take off she hated seeing that Nova could allow one person to ruin her day, her mood. Everything about her vivacious personality was being sucked away from her,

"You should go on date with Charles tonight," said Alex driving along the interstate; Nova knitting her brows, as she had completely forgotten about Charles, but she could not deny that she was now giving it some thought. "I read a book once called *Love Smart, Love Independently* by Lisa K. Stephenson and she said, 'if you're going to be stupid, you have got to be tough'. Do you know what that means?" asked Alex.

"That once again you're going to tell me I lack independence and how much of a bum I am? People fail to understand that it is always easy to tell someone to do something hard," cried Nova as the winds from their drive blew gently across her face.

"No, that's not what that means. I know you probably think you can't speak to me about what you're going through, but the truth is you can. However, don't be so weak about it. Admit the fact that while you were with Terry you gave him all of your power, remained in a relationship with a guy who despite everything I told you as a teenager was not ready at that time to be a parent. Admit that you were foolish because it's okay to be a fool for a man, but if you're going to be irresponsible Nova, get a backbone and be strong now that you're facing the consequences of your own stupidity," Alex said. Nova remained quiet, allowing the words to resonate with her. Arriving home after texting Charles while Alex ran her errands, a disenthralled Nova, smiling. She was also missing Tucker, deciding to give him a call. The sound of his innocent voice warming her heart and she was happy to hear that he was having fun with his grandmother.

All the while Nova thought she was slowly beginning to care less about the message she received from Terry, inside their home sitting on the edge of her bed, watching as her phone dinged and Charles respond timely to her messages, agreeing to a date later on that evening, but unfortunately, this wasn't enough. Nova was furious, hurt, thinking of whether or not to reply to Terry and speak her mind—he was deserving of that much. After all he put her through. Ignoring Charles now she retrieved the phone from her bed, typing away in fury, speaking obscenities, her message now the length of her middle finger and on she went; calling Terry out of his name, cursing his new relationship, infuriated that he would lie to his mother, therefore calling him a coward.

Nova paced, pondering whether or not she should hit send, praying even that someone, anyone would walk into her room and stop her from making such an unhealthy decision, but there was something inside of her, burning, wanting temporary relief that only an act like this could provide. She was being too nice, too lenient and too calm, bottling her emotions while Terry simply went on about his life, happy and in love, raising his new daughter while she pick fights with family members over whether or not they can gift her son a camcorder. It was all eating away at her, like a parasite preying on her flesh—only this impacting her heartstrings. Yanking them, tearing her down emotionally, and then she did it, she hit send. Seconds later she wailed, hating herself for now turning from angry to paranoid, awaiting his response, each time her phone dinged she felt a mix of emotions—dread, fear and possible happiness from finally getting the attention she wanted so badly, even if it was negative.

The time now read 4:43 p.m. and Nova would soon be heading out on a date, Charles scheduled to arrive by 6:30 p.m. to pick her up. Nova waited a few minutes longer before deciding to head into the shower. Downstairs Alex was doing some self-reflecting of her own, feeling in the mood for some companionship she contacted Ryan asking for him to come over. The second she asked, she wondered her reasons for feeling an attraction towards Ryan and not Hunter with whom she was beginning to spend much of her time. Feeling a bit bewildered about which of them to date, she feared there may have been some truth to what Nova was speaking. But as she poured herself a glass of water and prepared a bagel with crème cheese she began feeling as though she should relinquish some control and allow a man to date her wholeheartedly. The question being, who?

As Alex began weighing the pros and cons of which man she would allow to sweep her off her feet, Nova contemplated on which dress would show the most cleavage. Although she was not interested in having a one night stand she still wanted to look and feel her best, exuding confidence. By 6 p.m. she decided on the low V-cut, all-black bodycon dress, sulking by the fact that she was wearing clothes from her last relationship, bringing her to once again check her phone which had now been happening once every eight minutes or so. After two hours passed and he did not respond Nova felt sad. But she could not admit to herself the real reason. Dressing and applying her makeup felt strenuous, but she did it anyway. Charles was punctual arriving just minutes before his scheduled time, dialing Nova to let her know of his arrival. Stepping downstairs wearing a pair heels, a dress, large hoop earrings and

130

her hair perfectly oiled, Nova looked stunning. She couldn't remember the last time she dressed to impress. Alex and Ryan were seen snuggled in the living room watching a television show enjoying a bowl of popcorn, Nova calling to her aunt, letting her know she was now leaving. Alex waving her goodbye,

"Be safe!" she shouted. "Oh and send me a pin of your location!" Nova smiling agreed before closing the door behind her. Outside Charles stood, leaning against the passenger door side, opening the door for Nova, greeting her with a benevolent smile—one in which she reciprocated, thanking him for his chivalry. Driving down the driveway in his 2015 convertible Mustang, Nova felt like a girl from the movies.

"Where are we going?" she asked. One hand on the steering wheel, the other navigating the stereo, Charles replied,

"Back to my condo, I cooked up a very beautiful Italian dinner by candlelight," he said reaching for her hand, kissing the back of it gently. But Nova was not flattered,

"Oh, wow," she said patronizingly, sensing this Charles asked,

"Is that too simple for you?"

"Well no, but I thought we would at least go out considering it's the first date, not that you'd just be taking me back to your place," she scoffed.

"Well, excuse me, I mean, you contacted me in the middle of the day to tell me you wanted to be taken out, I simply did the best I could given the short notice. Plus, I am a celebrity chef," he said growing slightly annoyed, removing his hand from hers.

"If that's the case you could have rescheduled me, and you being a celebrity chef isn't my concern, I am not a celebrity," she said. Charles remained quiet, afraid he would say something rude, and so, he continued driving. Nova now playing with the thread unwinding from her purse as she too sat in silence taking in the views of downtown Los Angeles. Nova wondered if she was being crude, but she had no genuine interest in Charles, he was only here to past the time and take her mind off of the fact that Terry did not respond to her rant from earlier that afternoon, amongst other things. She resisted the urge to check her phone again and to curse him out for not replying, a part of her felt it was within her right to speak to him so callously—he was no stranger, he was the father of her child. But of course that did not pan out, once Nova and Charles arrived at the two-point-three million-dollar condo atop the San Diego hills.

Nova was beginning to feel anxious—self-conscious, reminded of her childhood home nearby; she began twisting the straps of her purse. Noticing, Charles gently placed his hand atop hers, waiting for his sensor to allow the garage door to open,

"It's going to be alright," he reassured her.

Upstairs Nova felt chilly, the air conditioning on high as she watched Charles turn the lock, holding the door, allowing her to walk inside first. Nova remained standing by the front door, taking it all in; the corner unit bathed in natural light from the extensive windows and open concept space. The modern cabinetry in the kitchen flawless appearing to have never been used, Nova wondering whether or not he truly resided there, or if the space was simply rented. In addition, were the granite countertops rich with a custom backsplash, high-end stainless-steel appliances, and a custom island. Walking in further, Nova noticed the frosted sliding doors leading into the fully enclosed master bedroom with a built-in walk-in closet. Removing her shoes to walk along the carpet, she could feel the plush carpeting under her painted toes, the master bedroom featuring dual sinks and a step-in shower. Charles then interrupting her,

"Darling, dinner will be served shortly," he called, now draped in a black apron, black slacks and a white V-neck t-shirt. Charles knew his way around the kitchen having graduated with a Bachelors of Arts Degree in culinary arts and then going on to work as an apprentice for the prestigious chef, Martin Delarosa. Spending most of his adult years in Spain, Charles returned with a knack for good taste, beginning his career as a food critic who was sure to speak his mind, no matter how harsh the truth, until eventually he decided to also work as a personal chef, working for musicians mainly who resided in the Los Angeles, California area. A bit pompous, but undoubtedly a ladies man considering he enjoyed enticing the taste buds of the women he found painstakingly beautiful.

The table set for two, candles burning, the lights turned

down low and a pot stew placed in the oven to simmer. Pouring a glass of 1996 Margaux into a large wine glass handing it over to Nova who stood outside on the balcony overlooking the beautiful scenery,

"So, the chicken is just cooking down a bit, I like when it's extra juicy," he said licking his lips seductively. Taking small sips of her wine, Nova continued looking up at the night sky, lost almost as she found herself staring off into space, something she had come to do quite often, but this time her mind did not wander. Charles worried that his attempts to make light of their evening was proving itself to be rather unsuccessful, "Why don't you tell me some more about yourself," he asked kindly. Nova turning to face him now,

"I am the soon to be ex-wife of a cheater, I have no college degree and I am now looking to finally find myself, if that makes sense," she said, taking another sip. Charles smirking, he could not think of a response, he was grateful for her honesty, but without any compassion for herself, she sounded cold. Looking down, Nova now felt like a failure as if the weekly allowance she received only limited her. Although that wasn't enough to cause this feeling, she was now feeling it more so than ever, dreadful that she would never be able to give her child a good, fulfilled life.

"You seem a bit distant," he said.

"I apologize, my mind just doesn't seem to be here these days, with all that that's transpired," she said quickly.

"Completely understood, however, just for tonight, allow yourself to let go, allow yourself to feel," Charles said gliding his hand along her forearm gently—tickling her almost. Nova laughed. Noticing her vulnerability, he decided on going a step further, removing the glass from her hand, placing both his and hers on the glass mantle just outside on the balcony, a bewildered Nova looking to him, Charles then turning her to face the mountain view massaging her shoulders. His hands firm, just as Nova needed, his breathing faint as her head began to fall—relaxed now, she turned to kiss him gently, their lips met and Nova could feel her clitoris begin to pulsate, but Charles knew better, stopping himself. Staring into her eyes, he said,

"I think the proper thing to do is have a meal first," he

smiled; embarrassed, Nova giggled, plopping her head onto his chest while wrapping her arms around his torso—his muscular forearms wrapped tightly around her for comfort, genuinely feeling elated for the first time in months. As their night progressed Nova enjoyed Charles's company, he was attentive, communicative and humorous. Once Nova disclosed her plans to create her very own YouTube channel, Charles offered to connect her with some friends of his from the industry who were professionals in videography. Sitting along the glass dining room table, Nova could feel the cool breeze gliding across her arms causing them to get goosebumps, Charles quickly arose, offering her a cashmere blanket or his suit jacket for warmth. To the blanket Nova obliged.

Two hours later their three-course meal was complete. The pair conversing of work and college days for Charles. Charles making his signature pastry for dessert to which Nova immensely enjoyed. Standing in the kitchen, a blanket wrapped loosely around her, Nova enjoyed a third glass of wine as she conversed with Charles whilst he cleaned.

"So no children?" she asked, wondering why she had not asked this earlier.

"Nope, just your average workaholic, book worm and socialite," Charles replied, his hands covered in soap. Nova nodding her head in complete disbelief,

"But you're a grown man, do you not want children?" she then asked. Charles laughing,

"Eh, fifty-two isn't too bad, of course, I want children, but I don't see the need to rush. I have my whole life ahead of me. Why not enjoy all the wonderful things I've come to acquire? I know you have a son, you've mentioned him briefly, which is fine with me. I don't want you thinking that because you have a son, I'd be turned off or disinterested in pursuing you further," he said. Although Nova was thinking along those lines she was too ashamed to admit it. In only a few hours Charles began to grow on her, unsure if it was alcohol but suddenly Nova felt lustful as though she would take Charles back to his master bedroom and make love to him. But she feared this would be too advancing and he would be turned off by her forwardness leaving her to remain stationed, sipping her wine slowly.

Nova never imagined herself dating an older gentleman but

something about Charles gave her chills now that she was able to overlook his slight lisp and focus on his endearing personality. Completing the dishes Charles dried his hands, scratching his left palm before grabbing a glass and refilling his drink, an inebriated Nova said, "Itchy palm, money maybe?"

"Superstitious much?" Charles said smiling as he walked Nova into the living room where they sat along the beige Artemest Carpanelli theater sofa. Taking a seat Nova gasped, startling Charles, "Oh my goodness, this sofa feels divine," she said lowering her eyes in satisfaction. "Where on earth is this from?" she asked. Proudly Charles began by replying,

"This is a one of a kind Artemest. My wi—," abruptly he stopped, mid-sentence, catching a hold of himself, turning to face Nova, the look in his eyes suspicious, "Sorry about that, what I meant to say is my designer, I hired, she uh, she was able to get this imported for me a few years back," nervously, Charles decided on changing the subject before taking a seat next to Nova who was now looking at him strangely. Taking the remote to the electric fireplace, turning it on, Charles rested his arm around Nova's shoulders as she fell into his chest, watching the electric fireplace shine brightly before her.

Nova's mind raced with an abundance of emotions, she was fearful, but yet intrigued wondering why she was finding Charles to be so trustworthy after only knowing him for such a short period of time. She wondered if maybe she was just looking to fill a void, looking for someone new to care for her, never having to penny-pinch or look forward to ending her week with a handout from her aunt in the amount of three hundred dollars. Nova knew that once school began again, taking taxi cabs to and from school for Tucker each day would quickly eat away at such a minor stipend. But what did she know? Rising, she looked Charles in the eyes, kissing him again, their kiss passionate lasting for what felt like minutes until the sound of his iPhone bellowed from the across the room.

Deciding to ignore the sound of his phone Charles and Nova continued their kissing, caressing one another as Nova removed the blanket, parting her legs to climb atop him; her hands gripping the sides of his cheeks and his hands gliding along the top of her head where one inch of hair now stood heavily moisturized. Their groping loud, the iPhone blaring once again, annoyed, Nova insisted that Charles answer, agreeing he arose, tossing her playfully aside, racing into the kitchen where he retrieved his phone, retiring into his master bedroom sliding the doors shut behind him.

Inside the room Charles answered while Nova remained oblivious sitting in silence watching as the stone look finish electric fireplace provide its rustic charm, the inner glowing logs and glowing embers creating a very realistic effect. Answering the phone to a woman Charles deciding to take his conversation into the master bathroom where he was sure Nova could not overhear him and he was right.

"Hey babe," he said calmly. The woman on the other line infuriated as she spoke,

"You haven't called all evening, where on earth have you been?" she asked.

"I—uh—I just made some plans with a client, babe, I should be home in the morning, you know how these Hollywood clients are, super demanding. It's a dinner party I'm hosting for Robert McCain down in Beverly Hills," Charles lied. He was quick on his feet, impulsive and articulate. His understanding wife simply responded okay. Ending his call, Charles turned his phone on silent, removing even the vibration effect, placing the phone on top of the nightstand face down before returning to the kitchen where he grabbed another bottle of wine from the cupboard. Nova felt it would be intrusive of her to question who was calling him so late and so decided against it. Happy to receive another bottle of wine despite already feeling lightheaded, Nova toasted Charles and their newfound romance.

13

Undressing as she caressed Charles's abdominals Nova felt like she was rushing, slowly regretting her decision to taking things this far, but with Charles feeling fully erected she could not stop now—at least that's what she told herself. That night as the shades were turned down and a very athletic Charles lifted Nova carrying her into his bedroom, their lovemaking was fascinating. Never having made love to anyone outside of Terry, Nova felt blissful, coupled with both confusion and fear. She worried she would be unable to please him, but slowly Charles made her feel confident, whispering sweet nothings in her ear as he stroked her ever so gently. That night Nova experienced her first orgasmic pleasure by way of penetration leaving her essentially satisfied and enthralled.

The sun was beginning to rise, the birds singing their sweet song just outside of the bedroom window as the automatic shades raised slowly as if to indicate the morning's arrival. Nova stretched, opening her eyes to find her naked body wrapped nicely under the silky white sheets, her makeup smearing the pillowcases and parts of the covers, embarrassed she lowered her head, turning the pillowcases over praying Charles would not take notice, and then the phone rang. As Charles slept

Nova pretended to drown out the sound of his iPhone bellowing through the nightstand drawer, unaware that before drifting off into a deep slumber Charles had hidden it there. Turning on the ringer, inadvertently, the upbeat sounds of the Apex iPhone ringtone crying now, Nova could no longer ignore it as a sleeping Charles snored, his upper body naked, his right arm stretched out to cradle Nova. Extending her torso Nova moved meticulously, careful not to awaken him as she pulled out the top drawer from the wooden nightstand ornate with a large lamp and decorative ecru colored lamp shade.

The phone ringing concluded, Nova thanking God as once the drawer opened the noise would only grow louder, peeping now the caller ID and wallpaper, Nova sprung to her feet; there they were, missed calls, concerned text messages all from a contact that read *wife* followed the emoji of a red-stained lip. The wallpaper a photo of Charles, a woman and three children all were appearing to be under the age of ten. Ripping the covers from him to wrap her naked body, Nova moved quickly into the kitchen, enraged—her emotions now clouding her logic as she searched frantically for a pot, realizing the cupboards to all be empty, the only silverware and China were those used from the night before and a few papers located in the top drawer in the island that had the words *sold* written across the top. Shuffling through the papers Nova learned the million-dollar condo was only recently purchased by her newfound lover and his darling wife, Margaret Leewood only two days prior.

Disgusted Nova stomped her way past a sleeping Charles into the master bedroom where she located a small basin just behind the toilet seat, the smile across her face cynical. Returning to the kitchen she let the hot water run, waiting patiently for the steam to rise, filling the basin with the water before making her way back into the bedroom, pulling her clothes close to her with her toes, losing her balance silently as the water slowly began spilling over, Nova tossed the water onto him, his response delayed, until the loud shriek frightened her, preparing herself to run away, tossing the basin onto the bed hitting him on the torso, he cried,

"Ow!"

Nova grabbed her clothes, sprinting towards the front door,

a large grin wiped across her face, running down the end of the hall, the silk sheet still wrapped steadily around her. Waiting by the elevators an angry Charles appeared, just then the elevator door dinged, inside were two couples, a child and a building associate wearing her uniform. Charles growled,

"Bitch, I know where you live!" he shouted refusing to attack her in front of the child and the strangers she now stood amongst, all looking at them with fear in their eyes wondering why they were creating such ruckus. The elevator doors closing.

"Fuck!" Charles screeched kicking his foot in the air, his fists balled in anguish, his pants drenched and his face stinging from the burns. Downstairs in the lobby, Nova stood, locating a restroom where she raced inside to change her clothes, her heart beating rapidly as she feared to see Charles and thinking of the damage he would inflict upon her—woman or no. Wiggling her way back into the little black dress and strapped sandals she marched back out into the lobby where she stepped outside hailing down a taxi cab remaining close to the concierge, paranoid of Charles coming down at any moment. That was the last time she would ever see him again.

Arriving home Nova took a long breath handing the cab driver forty-seven dollars to cover the cost of the trip. Slamming the door, she moseyed inside where she could hear Alex snickering from the kitchen. She was preparing breakfast for both her and Ryan while blending her lunch and dinner, the smoothie diet she was going to begin compliments of Ryan and his added suggestions. Nova looking as tired as she felt, a bit of her tension had been released however, she was no doubt glowing.

"If it isn't the morning bird," Alex teased, handing Nova an apple and preparing to pour her a glass of orange juice motioning for her to take a seat next to Ryan. Nova tossing her sandals by the kitchen threshold could not wait to take a bite, her migraine beginning to kick in.

"Auntie! I can't even begin to tell you about my morning from hell," Nova said taking a bite into her apple before laying her head on the counter looking over at Ryan who seemed unbothered by her presence. It was something about him that she could not bring herself to approve of. Appearing to have a

God complex as he sat there, reading through the newspaper while Alex slaved over the stove to prepare him breakfast and yet, he had done nothing around the house to assist her in any way since Nova's arrival. With breakfast now ready, Alex simultaneously serving them both, Alex replied,

"Yes, Nova," hoping to pry her eyes away from Ryan whom she noticed Nova was staring. Instantly, Nova was reminded of her grim morning, deciding now to continue,

"I am so pissed! That son of a bitch, Charles, he's married! I mean, wife, children, full family, married!" she said, the tone in her voice slightly rose. Alex immediately, turning to face her,

"Wait, did you have sex with him?" she asked, her curiosity at its peak. But Nova quickly felt the need to defend herself,

"Oh whoa, that was before learning he is married! That moron took us back to some condo he and his wife just bought and forgot to hide his phone or at least change the name of his wife in his contacts and his phone wallpaper!" Nova was growing angry all over again.

"Nova please calm down,"

"Absolutely not, I feel so tainted, that man is despicable," Nova said. Seconds later her phone dinged, it was a text message from Charles, who was surprisingly apologetic; as Nova removed the phone from her purse she remembered the text Terry never responded to, a part of her now feeling sad. "Oh great, now this jerk is texting me."

"Well, why not answer him and tell him you know that he's married and that you aren't interested," said Alex.

"No way am I telling that bozo he's married, he should know he's married and should be ashamed of himself. I'm blocking him,"

Folding the newspaper, Ryan decided on interrupting, telling Nova, "Sorry that happened to you, but truly all men are not the same," he said. But Ryan was the last person Nova wanted to hear from, although she was truly unsure of why she disliked him, she only knew that in comparison to Hunter, Ryan was coming up short. But it was not just him making her angry, it was the pain she was feeling from not only being ignored by a man she was still in love with but constantly rejected to now having been bamboozled by a complete stranger.

"No, you're wrong; all you men are the same, liars, cheaters, Jesus Christ,"

"Nova relax," Alex said.

"No, they're literally all the same, Ryan why don't you enlighten us on why you got divorced? The truth, please if you may," Nova said turning to face him,

"Nova that's enough," Alex sniped.

"No, tell my aunt, or why don't my aunt explain to you why she's even into you. What do you do for her? Meanwhile, Hunter is here fixing drains, putting up television sets and all you're doing is laying the pipe, in the bedroom," Nova screamed. Alex banging her hand atop the white marble countertops, shouting to her,

"Nova! Let's get one thing straight okay, just because a man, any man, is so-called nice or a good guy doing good deeds does not mean that I am obligated as a woman to reciprocate those feelings. A man shouldn't be praised for being respectful or kind to a woman, this should be a standard practice, you would do well to remember that. Otherwise, you'll fall for every Tom, Dick, and Harry who offers to cook you a hot meal in exchange for sex. Ryan, let's go," Alex heard enough, embarrassed as well by Nova's antics. She grabbed the dishes now filled with scrambled eggs, bacon and sliced strawberries carrying them into the living room where she and Ryan would enjoy their meals. But Nova was not through,

"But Hunter is not just being respectful, you're leading him on by having him do things for you that he should otherwise be doing for a woman who actually wants to be with him," Nova whispered before realizing she was speaking to herself as the room was now cleared of both Alex and Ryan.

That afternoon Nova showered, brushed the one inch of hair she had grown from her scalp and proceeded to play on her cellular phone while texting Marian hoping for an update on when she was to return home. But Marian remained imprecise in her response which only irritated Nova making it almost impossible for her to respond or having any reason to. Nova began missing Tucker, she gave Mrs. Higgins a call asking when would be a good time to pick him up, the benevolent woman advised Nova that anytime would be fine, as such, Nova wearing a PINK sweatsuit she was surprised still fit her, made her way downstairs to locate Alex who was in the living room cleaning. Ryan had gone.

Taking a deep breath Nova walked over to her aunt, her face innocent, batting her lashes she smiled,

"Are you still mad at me?" Alex refusing to make eye contact simply continued her dusting, although she was not angry with Nova, only slightly frustrated.

"You and I both know you could have handled yourself way better in there this morning than you did Nova," Alex said. Rolling her eyes, Nova reluctantly agreed, feeling like a brat almost,

"Yea, I get it, but auntie, I just don't get what you see in that guy. He seems so uptight like he wouldn't protect you if it came down to it," Nova said.

"You're judging a book by its cover," Alex said.

"Aren't you doing the same? Ryan is lighter-skinned, he's easier on the eyes, but he's clearly a pretty-man, not even a pretty-boy considering he's outgrown that phase of his life. But Hunter is way more hands-on with you and he isn't afraid to show you how much he cares," Nova pleaded.

"Hunter and I are friends, Ryan and I are dating and that is that," Alex said. "Now, you came in here with those puppy dog eyes, so what do you need?"

"Do you mind taking me to pick up Tucker from his grandmother's house," Nova asked, smiling.

"Of course I'll take you. You know what would be the ultimate achievement for you aside from shaving your head? Getting your license!" Alex emphasized, laughing, but Nova was not amused. As Alex drove she could recall the time she would come to this part of town whenever she was tasked with the responsibility of fetching a rebellious Nova. Reminding her playfully along the way, but Nova wanted desperately now to forget those times, finding them to now be the worst days of her life, outside of her son, Nova was truly living in regret. She was putting the best face forward but inside she was feeling lost, her self-esteem low and the emotional roller-coaster she officially boarded on Friday was now providing itself to be mentally exhausting. However, she was grateful for Mrs. Higgins, happy that she had agreed to take Tucker for a few days, although she missed her son, the couple days off did her some good—she was able to enjoy an orgasm and a great meal.

Outside of the one-story house, Nova stood preparing herself to knock, until she heard her name bellow from inside, it was Tucker alerting his grandmother of her arrival. "Mom is here," he shouted ecstatically. Nova remained standing, listening as Mrs. Higgins made her way to the door, unlocking it, Tucker raced outside, hugging her,

"Hey mommy!" he shouted. His backpack readied on his back, holding in his hand a bag from *Best Buy.* A curious Nova bending down as Alex stepped out of the car, greeting Mrs. Higgins, they were still not too fond of one another, but Mrs. Higgins was impressed to see how much she had grown.

"Tuck honey, what is this?" Nova asked opening the bag,

"It's my camcorder!" Tucker shouted his missing front teeth palpable. Immediately Nova stood staring at Mrs. Higgins, "Why did you buy this for him?" Nova asked her, Tucker looking up to her, his eyes darting back and forth between them, Alex finding it best to interrupt, grabbing Nova by the arm. But Nova was not willing to listen, she was emotional. She wanted to be the one to surprise Tucker with a camcorder. Alex wanted to give Nova the money but after thinking some more, Nova eventually decided it would be have been best that she save the money on her own, having done so week by week she almost had enough. Nova began feeling like a failure, losing track of time, Tucker now tugging at her garments,

"Mom, it wasn't from grandma, it was from daddy, may I please have my recorder back?" Tucker begged. Nova's eyes widened in disbelief,

"What do you mean? Did you see your father?" she asked, her hands lowered, Tucker grabbing the box from her, placing it back into the blue bag,

"Yes," he said, returning back to his grandmother where he gave her hug, Mrs. Higgins reciprocating the act, deciding it best she not get involved. But Nova was losing focus, grabbing Tucker by the arm, turning him to face her,

"As in he flew into town and you saw him?" Nova asked aggressively, witnessing this Alex grabbed her once again, this time squeezing her a bit as if to indicate their urgency to leave.

"Well, yea, we went to the park where he said he grew up playing basketball. He also said he used to bring me there as a kid before we moved when I was a baby and we played catch," Tucker said, his expression exhilarating. Nova fighting the urge to cry, turned away facing Alex who immediately consoled her, her bottom lip beginning to quiver, whispering she said,

"Please don't let this break you," But it was too late, Nova was drenched in tears.

"Auntie he came and said nothing to me about that, he saw our son and said nothing to me besides telling me to get my things," Nova whimpered, Tucker, tugging on the back of her cardigan as Mrs. Higgins looked on, bewildered,

"Is everything alright?" she then asked, Nova quickly turning to walk away, wiping her tears instructing Tucker to bid his grandmother a farewell—oblivious to the fact that he had already done so, before climbing into the backseat. Her hands trembling. Nova took several deep breaths before reaching into her back pocket, retrieving her cellular phone; she unlocked it, scrolling for his name, opening the message thread where she began typing as quickly as she could, infuriated, sending Terry a few unpleasant words. After hitting send, she sat in the passenger's seat, Alex climbing inside as Tucker spoke to his mother, his excitement, unlike anything she had witnessed. Her mind was gone.

Avoid shampoos which contain sulfates
or any of these other harmful ingredients,
and opt for a mild, sulfate-free shampoo.

2007

That night Nova lay awake caressing her lower abdomen, feeling for the first time just how stiff it was, her eyes beginning to water as she wondered what would happen if she were to abort her child, whether or not Terry would still love her.

The next morning Miss Mallory and Miss Denise arrived ready to begin their work as the sun began to rise, Terrance arrived shortly thereafter after getting little to no sleep the night before having to listen to Alex complain the entire night over the foolish decisions her niece was making. Although Terrance was disinterested, he knew that in order to have sex he would simply have to listen, smile and nod, periodically reflecting her emotions to show that he was, in fact listening although he could not recollect anything they had discussed. Personally, he hated the fact that Alex had been taking on the responsibility of overseeing a young adult and a teenager, two children who were not hers to deal with, in addition to that, Alex had her own set of responsibilities to tend to and unbeknownst to her, Terrance wanted a child. However, he chose to keep this detail to himself knowing that Alex would never be receptive to such an idea at this stage in her life.

By noon their home was in an uproar, a complete catastrophe with Dash preparing for his leave to Paris; his name resonating all throughout the house and his assistant taking calls while demanding the attendance of both Marian and Nova to join Dash in the parlor for lunch. Nova was nervous, Alex had yet to arrive and even though she was against getting an abortion a strange part of her felt safer knowing she was there, if the news just so happened to slip from anyone around them. This was odd, considering how much Nova loathed Alex and her authoritarian style of pseudo-parenting.

Downstairs in the parlor Nova began to sweat although the house was quite cool, staring into her father's intimidating eyes made things uncomfortable and despite her many attempts to avoid speaking with him, he continuously made it his duty to inquire about her future plans,

"Nova, what college are you thinking of? Same as Marian?" he asked grunting. Nova could not remember the last time they had all sat to enjoy a meal together, this must have been when her mother was still alive. This was not a first for Dash, hoping to get closer to his daughters only hours away from his departure but typically this was done with a fitting or a visit from one of his celebrity friends where they would all gather to discuss the industry politics, hoping this would teach his daughters the lessons he dreaded having to. Dash secretly wished his children would follow in his footsteps but he knew better than to coerce them, he only took pride in knowing that they had ambition and would undoubtedly be great one day on their own, no matter which field that chose to venture in.

Dash respects a person with integrity, and a strong work

ethic, always hoping that was what his children would take away from his absence, but this was the furthest thing from the truth, they did not see Dash as the hard worker he labeled himself to be, but rather a man who despised the fact that he had children. While his intentions were always good, his execution needed consistent guidance, even in his old age. Dash hoped his sister in law would convey this message to the best of her ability; but little did he know despite her many efforts, she remained unsuccessful in her attempts.

Nova did not respond, rather she instructed Terrance to refill her glass of water after having taken a large gulp from the 8-ounce glass. Dash was not in tune with his children, unable to sense their discomfort and nervousness, watching as Miss Denise and Miss Mallory enter and exit around them carrying their buckets of water and mops returning them to their quarters. As the stylists now began pouring into the parlor to request Dash in his master suite, Nova felt relieved, as though she could breathe again and then, she let out a large sigh. But her relief was short-lived once Dash arose, calling to her to join him in the room,

"Nova, come along," he said. Her eyes widened, Marian looking around bewildered, thinking of a filibuster,

"Daddy, Nova and I are going out in a few," she quickly said. But Dash would hear of no such thing,

"Nova, come along," he repeated, this time growing slightly impatient with his children. A moment of silence fell upon the room as Miss Denise re-entered, looking just beyond Terrance who remained standing at the end of the large table, his hands clenched behind his back awaiting further instructions after refilling Nova's glass. Marian watching Nova step slowly behind her father heading upstairs into the master bedroom where Arlene, an Indian-American fashion stylist, friend to Dash awaited them patiently. Her teeth crooked, she stood with her hair in a messy bun, behind her a rack filled with clothing for both a man and a woman, a surprised Nova, looking around the master suite large enough to fit the California king mattress, two wardrobes, a sofa and the walk-in closet and bathroom Dash so frequently spent much, if not all of his time whenever he was home and not in his study. Arlene raising her hands,

"Fancy girl," she said to Nova, her face gleaming, her

personality witty and expressive. "We have some looks pulled for you darling Nova, little Nova, fancy girl," she said again. But Nova was not following.

"Hi Arlene," she said nervously watching Dash get his measurements taken from a tailor adjacent to them.

"You're going to Paris baby, oh dear Dash you didn't tell the baby she is going to Paris? Oh, come, come, now," Arlene said facing him—her hands on Nova's jawline tenderly. Nova remained quiet; her facial expression unreadable, typically such news would have brought her an immense amount of joy, but that day was not the case. With her heart beating rapidly and the sweat building atop her forehead, Nova could not allow herself to feel anything outside of fear. Arlene began removing size 26-27 waist pants and size small tops for a petite Nova. Arlene stood with a bobby pin between her lips, measuring tape around her neck and a good eye on Nova trying to depict which fashion pieces would match perfectly with her father and his signature periwinkle and mauve look.

Arlene then stepped over to Nova wrapping her measuring tape around her chest to catch her measurements before making her way down to her torso, where Nova flinched, Arlene smiling,

"No need to worry Nova baby," Arlene said, Dash watching them.

"Why aren't you happy?" he asked her looking to light a cigar as the tailor now measured his inseams. But Nova could not be happy,

"I am dad," she lied, her eyes beginning to well. In that moment Nova was experiencing a different kind of fear, one she could not place into words, she was trembling, her eyes darting back and forth between that of Arlene and her father. With her arms extended and Arlene reaching her midsection she gasped,

"Nova baby, you're quite stiff here," she said, her index finger poking Nova in the abdomen, turning to Dash, laughing, but Dash was not amused. Nova continued standing, her breathing heavy as Arlene joked, "You gained weight baby? No—no baby," she said laughing, but Nova remained confused, Dash raising his right eyebrow, unsure of what exactly he had just heard. Nova was now beginning to feel nauseous, angry that her body chose now to react this way, she gagged. Arlene stepping backward, away from her, "Nova baby you alright?" she asked, meticulously stepping back towards Nova to measure her hips. Nova continued to gag, placing her hands firmly across her mouth as she continued standing, praying she would be given more time to make it into her bathroom, but faith would not have it that way. Closing her eyes, Nova began to spew vomit from her mouth; all that she had eaten for both breakfast and lunch was now sitting on top of Arlene's head, seeping its way between her hair strands. The vomit also making its way down to the carpet—a malodorous hitting her nostrils. Dash and his tailor both looking on in horror; Arlene now too beginning to gag as she ran into the master bathroom, locking herself inside, shouting obscenities in her native language.

"You caught a Bug?" Dash shouted, appalled that she was sick pushing his way from the tailor towards the bedroom door in anger. Nova removed herself from the suite, running into her room, shutting the bathroom door behind her as she kneeled over the toilet relinquishing the remainder of vomit that was needed. Dash heard shouting to Terrance accusing him of cooking food that made his daughter sick, Marian racing upstairs after hearing the uproar, placing her hands on the threshold of her father's door, her and the tailor making eye contact once she noticed the pool of vomit on the carpet. Downstairs, Dash was scolding Terrance who remained standing speechless, fearful that he would lose his job, moments later Dash was heard yelling to him,

"You're fired!" Marian entering into Nova's room, banging on her bathroom door,

"Nova, Nova!" she bellowed. Nova emerging, her eyes wet from crying listening to the turmoil taking place downstairs and Terrance pleading for his employment. Nova and Marian exchanging a sad look,

"We have to tell daddy the truth," Marian said to her sister, but Nova refused.

"No, we don't know if that was the baby or if it was the food," Nova said; Marian raising her head, looking at Nova, her eyes reading shameful.

"Don't do that, this is auntie's boyfriend, he needs to make ends meet, Nova," Marian pleaded. Nova began to cry, and remained unable to process the fact that her aunt was dating the cook.

"I'm so afraid Marian, I'm so afraid of him," she cried, the tears falling freely from her eyes as she lowered her head into her sisters' bosom.

"You're his daughter, what's the worst he can do? Be angry with you? Yell? Nova, we have to face this, and of course, I'm going to be there when you tell him, I won't let him do anything to you," Marian assured her younger sister. But Nova was trembling, her heart filled with distrust as she held onto Marian's forearm squeezing it. "Nova, I know daddy can be very unapproachable, but look on the bright side, he's ready to fire a man, lose a cook, lose a friend all because he believes he could have brought you harm, he loves you, he loves us, maybe he just has a tough time articulating it with words," Marian said holding onto Nova's cheeks, careful to look her in the eyes. "I love you and I promise, whatever he does to you, he has to do it to me too," she continued, "but we can't let this happen to Terrance." With her head down Nova nodded, overhearing Terrance continue to plead his case to their father downstairs. Grabbing Nova by the hand, Marian began walking, Nova feeling like she was taking a long walk down the corridor on her way to the electric chair, a surge of goosebumps racing up her arms.

Marian had one strategy, to remain guileless, speaking the truth as quickly as she could, and then assuring her father of their plans shortly thereafter, avoiding him anytime to process the news. In the kitchen a saddened Terrance was boxing his supplies, Dash retiring to his study down in the basement, Marian and Nova hesitant to make their way to him, whispering Terrance said,

"Please—"

"Yes, we know," replied Marian motioning for his patience. "We're going now." Nova and Terrance exchanging a look of doubt before watching as Dash reemerged, his assistant speaking to him. The pair walking along the downstairs foyer nonchalantly as though the events from earlier that afternoon did not transpire or a disheartened Terrance was not there packing his belongings. Marian disliking the fact that Dash was advising his assistant that they were now in need of a cook she blurted,

"Nova's pregnant!" Nova clenching her hands, Marian let out a shriek cry, the expression on Dash's face reading unpleasant, his brows knitted, his lips pursed.

"What?" He hollered. The walls felt like they were rumbling, the ceilings lowering, Nova felt the room closing in on her as she looked up to her father, everyone around them stationed. Miss Denise choosing to speak,

"Mr. Dash sir, please, she is only a child," she said knowing that the look on his face could only mean one thing. Terrance felt relieved now, waiting patiently for the moment to ask for his job back, he did not care that Nova had been so reckless to have gotten pregnant by the age of seventeen, he was selfish, thinking of nothing but his future with Alex and knowing that a woman like her, would need a man capable of taking care of her. The room dreary, Dash remained standing, his eyes fixed on a timid Nova who stood behind her sister in hiding. Nova now tugging at her sister, praying she would complete her statement, telling their father of the plans she had for the baby. Realizing now that she truly did not want to be a mother, especially if it meant losing her father completely, to which his eyes told a tale.

Dash remained standing, his assistant Myesha motioning for the girls to return upstairs. Working with Dash for the past four years taught her a many of things, his silence was not to be taken lightly. He was pondering after all, but an ineffable Dash was a man to fear. With only seconds passing feeling like minutes he uttered the words that sent a sharp chill down the spines of everyone in the room,

"Get out of my house." He said to Nova. Marian quickly panicking, screaming to her father,

"Daddy no!" the room in an uproar now, everyone speaking in her defense, Miss Mallory and Miss Denise remaining firm in their positions, willing too to risk their wages for a silent Nova who could not believe her ears. Inside she was panicking, wondering if his words rang true, wondering if perhaps she was only hearing things, there is no way her father would disown her, he was not that cruel, she thought. Marian gripping her hand, once the women all bellowed on the top of their lungs for Dash to reconsider, but this only infuriated him further. No one was to question his decisions; he was not weak and a plethora of women were not going to change his mind.

Walking towards Marian he shoved her to the ground, grabbing ahold of Nova who now screamed for her sister, dragging her as she fell to the floor, Dash was taking Nova to the doorway where he intended on leaving her outside. The women all screaming as Terrance stood texting Alex, outlining to her the details of what he so happened to witness, his words verbose; his fingers typing quickly for he knew better than to intervene. Receiving his messages Alex made her way from campus, climbing into her car where she rolled out of the parking lot in transit to their Spanish style mansion. The afternoon now filled with anguish as Dash tugged on a delicate Nova. Myesha, Arlene, Marian, Miss Mallory, and Miss Denise all standing, watching in horror, but Marian could not watch her sister continue to cry, struggling to break free from his ironclad grip. Marian ran to her father, punching his back, shouting for him to let go of her sister, immediately he turned,

"You want to go to?" He screamed to her, startled, fearful that he would hit her Marian stopped, blocking her face, just then, Arlene grabbing a hold of the young woman pulling her back, listening and watching as Nova kicked and screamed her way out of the house when Dash thrust her onto the front yard, slamming the door in her face. Nova overhearing Marian weeping inside,

"You can't kick her out!" she cried, sobbing loudly. "We were going to fix it." She wailed, the sound of her voice aggravating him.

"Who are we?" Dash grumbled listening as Nova banged on the front door from the outside, her feet bare, and the hot sun from the concrete burning her.

"Daddy!" she cried. Both Miss Mallory and Miss Denise silently crying by the parlor doors, Terrance watching in shock praying for Alex's arrival. Dash stood just in front of the glass doors, clamoring,

"Anybody who allows this girl back into my house will be

terminated, as for you," he said pointing to Marian, "If you want to follow her and fail then fine by me, but not a dime of my money will go into you any further. She is not your sister, she's too impetuous and needs discipline," he concluded disappearing down to the basement, walking past Terrance, their eyes locking momentarily—Terrance resisting to urge to ask on the status of his employment.

"She's your daughter," Marian wept. Her hands gripping the arms of Arlene who now slid to the floor holding her, her blouse wet from Marians tears. Nova found shade under a palm tree just outside the premises, looking up to the balcony of her bedroom she noticed the doors slamming shut, unable to make out who it was that closed it. Sitting with her knees to her chest, Nova dried her eyes, she had no money and no shoes, which meant she was not going anywhere. But she remained hopeful that Marian would soon open the doors and she would walk inside to her father smiling, telling her how apologetic he was for overreacting. Nova had never been scolded, by either of her parents; this was the first time her father had even gotten upset with her.

Nova had to think about her decisions, regretting them all now that she was stuck sitting under a palm tree outside. Knowing now that her father was merely disappointed, but yet she remained optimistic, watching now as Alex turned the corner coming up the mountain, her tires screeching along the dry pavement. Watching Nova under the tree brought tears to her eyes, enraged by the fact that she was sitting there, appearing to be destitute. Slamming the car door shut Alex ran to her, examining her face noticing the small scratches along her neck,

"Jesus, did Dash do this?" Alex whimpered. But Nova did not feel the scratches so she did not know they were present. Nodding, an infuriated Alex tried to remain calm. "Get in the car," Alex said to her, Nova standing, tiptoeing to the vehicle in an effort to ease the discomfort felt under her feet. Alex behind her sticking the key in the ignition to turn on the air conditioning. Slamming the door Alex stood in the foyer, looking around, making eye contact with Terrance who sat on one of the island stools. Marian next to him, climbing off, and running towards Alex to give her a hug. Marian wasting no time to fill Alex in on the details of what transpired that afternoon; also, inquiring on the whereabouts of Nova. Learning she was in the car, Marian slid her feet into a pair of slippers and bringing along Nova's, making her way outside to join her.

Alex was feeling far too angry to engage anyone as she searched the mansion looking for her malicious brother in law who she managed to locate in his office, sipping a glass of bourbon neat. Banging the door behind her, Alex walked to him,

"Dash what the fuck!" she hollered, Terrance and the others overhearing them.

"Alex you better watch your Goddamn mouth. I'm old enough to be your father," replied Dash, his tone eerily calm.

"I don't' care, you can't exile your own daughter, what would she think huh, what would Anastasia think?" Alex said pacing. Dash shot her a quick and loathsome look,

"Don't you dare mention her name! Don't you dare!" Dash said, his fists balled, his eyes beginning to well, "I never want to see that girl again and that's that. She wants to go live an impecunious life, then so be it. I have worked my ass off to give her a good life. Good school, good food, good clothes, a good childhood. We all lost Ana that day, we all did, but she, she cannot ruin me. Now you can either keep her or leave her, but I never want to see her again," Dash said.

"Dash my God, she is your daughter, your—your flesh and blood, she's young, she made a mistake," Alex begged.

"She spent the summer wrapped up in some boy—that wasn't a mistake, that was whoring,"

"You're despicable,"

"You feel so bad, then you keep her. I lost Ana because of her, Ana wasn't the same after she gave birth to Nova and now, she does this, after all I've done?"

"Don't! You don't get to blame Nova for Ana's decisions Dash, you don't get to do that, she is young and if anyone should be held accountable here it is you. Think about how neglectful you've been—"

"Neglect? You don't know shit about neglect. Now leave me alone." Dash demanded, reclining in his presidents' chair—feeling saddened. Finally, Alex said,

"I'll get some of her things and take her home with me," with a resigned sigh, Alex exited his chambers.

14

Present Day...

Arriving home Nova was staring off into space, Tucker calling to her, shaking her before making his way inside, Alex kindly telling him to get washed up for supper, leaving her to tend to Nova. Nova now numb feeling as though her mind was turning against her, her new nemesis—the thoughts from her past haunting. Alex remained quiet, caressing her arms, the gesture only to bring her comfort. Nova smiling now,

"I don't want to be this weak, I have to be strong for my son auntie, but I don't know how," she said, the tears now flowing from her eyes. But Alex was beginning to understand just how sad she felt. Feeling now that Nova did not deserve the ill-treatment she was receiving, wondering if she was simply down on her luck. Alex could do nothing but reassure her of the brighter, happier days to come. With her eyes red from crying Nova sniffled, the sharp pains felt in her eyes bringing her to rub them profusely.

An elated Tucker was heard in the basement setting up his camcorder, to Nova's surprise Hunter was there along with him, turning to face Alex, who immediately knew what she was thinking decided to defend herself,

"He volunteered to fix the water heater okay," Alex said looking at Nova, her voice just above a whisper. Nova did not bother to reply, running upstairs where she rummaged through Tucker's wardrobe looking for his uniform to starch and iron as the school year was vastly approaching—September 2nd. With August now winding down and Tucker growing acclimated to their living situation, Nova began thinking of ways she could begin earning an income. The internet browser on her phone now open, she searched options for working without a degree or certification, the results discouraging her. Nova had no talents, no real goals and at age Twenty-four was just beginning to see how important it was to have had some kind of a backup plan.

Nova spent the remainder of her day in the bedroom, Hunter making an appearance at the bedroom door once he was preparing himself to head home, Nova greeting him with a smile. Although neither of them verbalized it, they each felt pity for the other for a different set of reasons, which only began bringing them closer together, but for them both the reasons remained unknown. Nova just felt a connection to Hunter, like he was truly interested in learning what was plaguing her and willing to assist her in finding a solution—plus it did not hurt that he could offer her advice from a man's point of view. Feeling desperate she was still seeking validation and a benevolent Hunter did not mind providing it.

Laughing, eating popcorn and conversing in detail for the first time since Nova's arrival, Hunter and Nova spoke candidly about her relationship, their ideal love and expectations from both men and women. Nova felt confused, as though she had been living in a twilight zone, uneducated about the signs that she should have been wise enough to never have ignored. She also felt bamboozled, as though loving Terry for the length of time that she did only proved itself to be futile. Overlooking his mistakes in the beginning stages of their relationships were also things mentioned by Hunter, but Nova could not agree in the moment, feeling as though her forgiving nature was purely due in part to the fact that she viewed herself as a mild and compassionate individual, but as Hunter advised her on how she too contributed to the demise of her relationship she had no choice but to listen as he made a lucid argument to support his theory. Stating to her, "Terry only continued to cheat because he knew he would have been forgiven after the first time and there were no consequences."

Nova remained optimistic and her heart hopeful, it was not the easiest thing discussing her past relationship risking receiving such advice from someone who quite easily can be considered bias toward her gender. But Hunter was fair, his advice pure of heart and with each revelation, Nova pondered the thought of contacting Terry once again, this time for confirmation, closure. However, she felt ashamed, deciding it best to wait until she was alone to reach out. Even though his company was for sure needed Nova wanted to be alone but remained too polite to request it. Hunter continued speaking, self-disclosing, telling Nova now he and Tucker had so much in common due to his own personal experiences.

A disinterested Nova by 2 a.m. no longer cared for their exchange in dialogue; she was now buried in her phone opening the thread to prepare a message to Terry, what began as a message of uninterrupted rage, quickly turned into a heartfelt message ending with the words, "*I truly miss you.*" Hitting the send button sent Nova's heart down to her ankles as she nervously awaited his reply, but only figuratively. Hunter now noticing the lack of attention Nova was giving him arose turning to leave, Nova waving him goodbye as he disappeared into the stygian hallway. Closing the door behind him, turning down the lights she watched her phone now. Nova sunk into her bed, thinking she may be a masochist, she wondered if she approached Terry nicely, he would reciprocate her gestures, but why after all he had done was she still not ready to let go? Closing her eyes, her cellular phone dinged causing the room to illuminate. Immediately she sat upright, her eyes closed tightly, her palms sweating and her heart beating rapidly, turning the phone over she read the message preview from a phone number unfamiliar to her, it read,

"*Maybe we should talk,*" a confused Nova wondered if Terry was replying to her message from a different number or if this was an entirely different person. Trying not to remain desperate she waited a few minutes before replying, "*Terry?*" she wrote. With no time wasted another message came in,

Nova quickly reading it, " *Yes, tomorrow at three, Foot Locker parking lot,*" it said. Her lips now curled into a smile Nova's imagination went wild, thinking how lucky she was and how happy she would soon be, she basked in the joy of knowing that Terry did miss her too and maybe additional time was really all they needed to put the past behind them. Nova was ready to give up, feeling like she had given dating a try and things did not pan out well, afterward searching for a job or a career in which case learning maybe she was only good at two things—wife and mother, both of which was alright by her.

That night Nova slept with a smile plastered to her face, her night tranquil as she dreamed a many of things, her big wedding, the food she would have catered, the new home they would purchase now that Terry had a better job, which only meant better pay and of course, benefits. With their divorce not yet final Nova remained clinging onto one last shred of hope.

Downstairs Alex found herself awake heading into the kitchen for a snack where she heard tapping along her back door, frightening her. Realizing the tapping would not cease she stepped cautiously towards it unlocking the door and opening it to expose on the other side Hunter drenched in sweat as though he had just finished running around the neighborhood, something he practiced whenever he could not sleep. Panting he made his way inside pushing past Alex who was shocked by his presence,

"Is everything okay?" She asked him, fixing her robe to hide her negligee. Hunter now making his way to the refrigerator, Alex shutting the door, turning around,

"I just want to talk to you," he said. "Alex, I've been doing a lot of thinking and—and I just want to know where do I stand with you?" he asked taking a large gulp of the Poland Spring water; Alex's eyes lowering in pity, taking a seat on the island stool, her silk robe causing her to slide.

"I'm not sure what you mean," she said deciding to act aloof, given she needed more time to devise an appropriate response. An impassioned Hunter telling her,

"I just know you feel something for me, I mean, how could you not? I'm here all the time, we go to church together—well, we used to before your niece came—I mean, I'm grown and if what I'm feeling isn't how you feel, then I deserve to know," he said sadly. Alex thinking fast,

"I like you as a friend Hunter." She nodded watching as his facial expression changed. Hunter decided not to reply, turned and walked away, shutting the door behind him. The conversation with Nova earlier that day did something to him, he could hear in her voice whenever he would mention Alex how skeptical Nova was, and of course she would know more than he, taking all things into consideration his overthinking getting the best of him that night. Determining once and for all he was in need of the truth, four years chasing the same woman, hoping she would notice him and now he knew, it was all only a waste of time. Walking home Hunter feeling it was time to sequester himself.

The next morning came quickly, but Nova barely slept awakened at 9 a.m. from her own excitement she headed downstairs to fix breakfast for herself, Alex and Tucker. But there was a familiar face to greet her,

"Hey there," his voice said. Nova surprised to see him maneuvering his way around the kitchen, prepping the eggs by cracking them into a bowl for whipping. Nova was not impressed,

"I take it you spent the night," she snarled.

"Ha, I know you don't fancy me too much, but I was hoping we'd uh, get a chance to chat," Ryan said. Nova did not want to have a conversation with Ryan, him being the furthest thing from her mind. She declined to answer him, grabbing a fruit from the glass bowl and skipping her way back upstairs to locate Tucker who she was happy to find was still fast asleep. Nova was missing her tall hair strands, the pineapple afro, her twist outs and her braided Mohawks all complimenting her oval-shaped head perfectly. Now, although her head is small the one-inch hair only proves itself difficult to accessorize lowering her confidence slightly.

The one thing Nova was grateful for was the fact that she was now three pounds lighter and could fit perfectly into her jeans—the fitted type to compliment the little curves she did have. Envious of Marian for her voluptuous body, Nova sometimes hating the fact that she was not as beautiful as her eldest sister, her confidence still in shambles and her low self-esteem palpable, she tried to make it work. Standing in front of the long body mirror, Nova removed clothes pressing them along her skin to determine which top to wear, thinking to herself, "*What would Marian wear?*" However, too ashamed to dial her sister to speak on her inexplicable joy Nova took to an application on her cellular phone scrolling through potential looks that would assist her in accomplishing one goal for that day: operation make Terry fond of her again.

By half past noon Nova could hear the excitement going on downstairs. Alex and Ryan overheard debating over politics, while Tucker requested assistance with setting up his new camcorder. Nova remained in her room, deciding against joining them, feeling inundated by her emotions, angry at a simple device, only because she did not have the purchasing power she so strongly desired. She was preparing herself, her soliloquy spanning well over an hour as she asked and answered the questions she was preparing for Terry. She needed closure and along with that remained willing to reopen her heart if assured he would never abandon her and Tucker again. Removing her wedding band from the drawer in the nightstand where she buried it under her undergarments, Nova slid the ring back onto her finger standing as the time now read 11:42 a.m. and she needed to shower before heading out to catch the bus.

One thing Nova always could appreciate growing up in California is the warm, amicable weather, the view of the palm trees and the kind people who would greet her when walking along the sidewalks or standing at the bus stop. Across town, Nova made her way into the park occupying a park bench watching the boys from the neighborhood all engage in a game of street ball, reminding her of her teenage years—reading her watch, the time now 2:52 p.m. she was early. As her mind began to wander, Nova envisioned a nice dinner along the pier with just her and Terry, figuring out their plans for raising their children together and the conversation she would have to have with Laura, breaking her heart once she would learn that Terry was in fact still in love with his estranged wife. Nova chuckling to herself, her beautiful smile gleaming as her lips expand from ear to ear, never taking notice of the few gentlemen stopping to stare at her wondering if she possessed a mental disability.

The boys continued their game, Nova staring down at her watch fifteen minutes later wondering now why Terry was late and did not think to contact her, only as a courtesy. Just beyond the gated park, their car doors slammed, Laura and Terry spotting Nova almost immediately with eyes fixated on the team playing. Laura smirking, happy to see a bald Nova, thinking of how unattractive she now looked—her jealousy merely fueled as her own insecurities began to show; locking her arms into his, Terry turned to face her, bewildered by her abrupt clinginess. As their footsteps grew louder approaching Nova she turned, noticing Laura first through her peripheral vision, her facial expression reading resentment. Getting to her feet she quarreled,

"What is she doing here?" she asked, her voice slightly elevated. Both Terry and Laura exchanging a questionable look, Laura then deciding to speak first,

"Look, we're trying to be friendly, but Nova, you have to stop this," she said turning to face Terry nodding as if to seek his approval for speaking so rigidly. Nova was furious, although her embarrassment overshadowed her rage, she remained standing, determined to defend herself,

"What are you talking about?" she questioned coming face to face with Laura, Terry now placing his hands between them, deciding it best to reply,

"Nova we aren't together anymore so you can't text or—or call me in the middle of the night while I'm home with my girlfriend and my kid. Laura was nice enough to write you back asking for us to meet today, but this can't continue to happen. Now we've postponed the child custody hearing because we know you just need some time and of course, Tucker needs his mother. But we have to be platonic and try our best to get along for his sake." Terry concluded. Nova could feel nothing as she stood listening to the words leave his mouth. Feeling lightheaded, she remained stationed, her eyes lowered and her hands trembling as she shoved them into the front pockets of her jeans preparing to take her leave. It was the end, this she now knew and instead of allowing herself to relapse she was only going to make a conscious effort to let go.

The air blowing against her scalp telling her now that it was time to leave, but before she could go, there was one more thing, "Buy Tucker a cellular phone so he can contact you. Um, you won't hear from me again," Nova said assertively. Terry and Laura exchanging looks, a look of relief spread across their face, Terry nodding, but by then Nova was now across the yard making her way to the bus stop where she walked on the sidewalk crying simultaneously promising herself that this will be the last time she shed another tear for Terry.

With the late afternoon buses running terribly, every forty-five minutes to an hour Nova walked, kicking up dust with her feet, she walked to the next stop deciding to halt only when a bus would arrive, before she knew it she was standing in front of the office building just across the street shocked to find Hunter packing his trunk with supplies, she called to him, waving her hands in the air as if to signal an S.O.S. The cars driving down the four-lane road relentless in their pursuit; a careful Nova waiting until the coast is clear making her way over to him.

"Wow, what are you doing here?" she asked smiling, happy to see a familiar face. Hunter extending his arms to give her a hug to which she reciprocated.

"Me? What brings you on this side of town? I work for one of the companies in this building. Information technologist," he said lifting his bag of wires and USB's. Nova lied, telling him that she was only there to visit the Foot Locker where she was hoping to find a pair of sneakers for Tucker. Hunter, questioning her no further politely offering her a ride home, Nova quickly accepted, her feet throbbing and the night beginning to fall.

Pulling into the driveway, Nova thanked Hunter before requesting that he come inside—truthfully, she wanted to speak to him. Nova planned to tell the story of all that transpired that afternoon by way of a hypothetical, *what if.* This way she could avoid looking both desperate and foolish but still receive the advice she was so badly seeking. But to her surprise Hunter very nicely declined, Nova could tell something was wrong, remained seated in the passenger seat of the Black Honda Accord,

"Alright, what's wrong?" she asked him, but Hunter was

not going to disclose his emotions fearing it would make him look feeble.

"Nothing at all," he said, slurring his words as if to indicate that he was tired and ready to head home. Nova could take a hint, reaching out to give him a hug and a kiss on the cheek, thanking him, she opened the door and walked inside. The sounds of laughter and the television blaring heard from the doorway, peeking her head into the den just to the rear of the house nearest the laundry room it was Alex, Ryan, and Tucker all engaged in a family fun game called Twister. Alex struggling to maintain her balance underneath Ryan as Tucker laughed hysterically spinning the needle on the color board. Nova chuckling by the threshold, her arms folded watching the smiles on their faces, her heart feeling warm—she was finally home and she was content.

That night Nova helped Tucker prepare for bed, both in the small bedroom to the rear of the upstairs hallway, Nova removed pajamas, watched as he cleaned his teeth, brushed his hair and when he climbed into bed she tucked him in nicely under the Superman blanket.

"How are you feeling?" she asked him, sitting just by the edge of the bed nearest to him, his head lying flat against the pillow.

"I'm okay," he replied. "Mom, can you tell me about the time you and daddy went to the basketball court with me? He told me to ask you about it the last time I saw him," he said innocently. Nova took a long sigh, toggling with her brain on whether or not she would leave or deflect, almost immediately deciding on the latter,

"Well, your daddy says he's going to get you a new phone Tuck, so when he does, you can text him and call him anytime you want," she said watching as his eyes widened in delight. Tucker was definitely someone who enjoyed technology,

"No way!" he said. "A Phone? For Me?" he asked. Nova nodded,

"Yep, it will be all yours. Now, go to bed, I love you," she said kissing him atop the forehead making her way towards the hallway, turning off the lights before shutting the door behind her. Downstairs Ryan and Alex were in the kitchen mellowing out to the smooth sounds of jazz while prepping their meals for the upcoming work week. Nova in need of an alcoholic beverage to quench her thirst poured herself a glass of vodka from the bar inside of the living room before making her way to join them.

"Long day?" Ryan smirked. Nova paying him no mind, turning to Alex responding,

"Yes," But Alex was not amused by her impoliteness.

"Nova, please stop being so rude, Ryan is trying," Alex told her. Nova now feeling compelled to face him,

"Yes," she said raising her glass as if to indicate a toast. But Ryan was not her issue, men—men, in general, were now her issue, slowly deciding maybe it best to swear off of them. "Auntie, how do you get over an ex?" Nova asked her, nervously Alex turning to face Ryan before responding, but he instructed her to respond as he too grew curious of the answer.

"Um, I think time. I typically just bury myself in work and then when I get a chance to I try to date. But I haven't had many exes, there was only Terrance and Gabe," she said with a shrug to the shoulder grabbing Nova's glass taking a sip of its contents.

"Work?" Nova asked confirming,

"Yes, Nova, this thing called work," Alex said raising one eyebrow.

"I know you've always thought I was just such a bum," Nova said sighing. A peaceful Alex deciding to retire assuming that Nova was again climbing aboard her emotional rollercoaster, in which case she did not want to participate. Learning the hard way that love truly never dies, Alex opted in for a more suitable tactic to Nova's devastation; later on, aiding in her job search.

By the first week of September Nova was beginning to submit applications and Alex speaking to the partners at her firm on her behalf now that there were openings for a receptionist, but Nova quickly declined their offers citing her displeasure towards the scanty wages they were offering. The longer Nova resided with Alex the more impatient Alex became learning that Nova was still as immature as she was seven years ago.

The night before Tucker's first day back to school Nova

grew restless, unable to sleep she walked around the house, heading into the kitchen where she brought a pot of water to a boil. Looking around she thought about the camcorder, toying around with the idea of recording herself, venting her frustrations. Upstairs she walked into the room where a sleeping Tucker lie, caressing his face, she watched him peacefully, sliding the recorder from under his arms. Nova could not believe he was sleeping with it, making her sad, realizing now just how much Tucker was missing his father.

Returning to her quarters, the camcorder in one hand, a cup of tea in the other, Nova began writing, the pen getting away from her, staring now at three pages of her thoughts, before making her way down to the basement where she found a tripod, positioning the camcorder on top of it before searching the room for a place to sit. With no idea what she was doing she moseyed around the room, the floors chilly as she continued thinking of a way to approach her non-existent audience. Through her writing Nova found relief, she was able to express herself without being judged or feeling like a hopeless romantic still in love with a man who wanted nothing to do with her. This is not loving, she thought. Not self-love, not love for Terry, just unloving and self-abuse. Nova was blaming Terry for her bipolar moments but later came to realize the only issue was her and that she was the one in control of her actions. Still, Terry did not get Tucker a cellular phone, nor was he contributing financially towards Tucker for his back to school expenses which was now weighing heavily on her shoulders.

Having only six hundred and thirty-two dollars to her name Nova took a seat atop the wooden panel believing now to be a good time to relinquish her frustrations. Behind her, a wall filled with tools, and a dimly lit light, she emptied the space creating enough room for her to be seen with little to no other distractions around her. Afraid Alex would be angry, she removed only a few tools, leaving the wall bare only nearest to the left.

The tea now cool Nova took a long gulp, placing the mug next to her, the papers shuffling around in her hands, she sat looking forward into the camcorder lens,

"Hey everyone, my name is Nova Hi—" she said charismatically apprehensive, stopping, wondering if *Higgins* should be stripped from her stage name, quickly she felt discouraged; again, feeling as though she needed to solve another piece to the puzzle before getting started. Nova was not creative nor was she imaginative, envisioning herself as merely a free-thinker and completely free-spirited, just going with the flow of things, relying heavily on those around her for survivorship. But on her own now, Nova is quickly learning that there is someone dependent on her and with Terry now out of the picture, she can no longer find excuses and remain lackadaisical. Standing, she located a pencil scribbling atop the college ruled paper a new name, one that she felt to be memorable.

The door slamming just above her causing her to jump slightly, it was Tucker rubbing his eyes, draped in a pair of plaid pajamas, his hair freshly cut. His eyes wandering the room,

"Mommy, do you have my camera?" he asked her. Nova shifting herself towards him, nodding before removing the camcorder from its position. Handing it off to him she asked that he awaits her until she could reposition the tools where she had taken them from the back wall. Walking Tucker back to his bed, camcorder in hand, Nova looked down at her son, his innocence loveable. Upstairs, kissing Tucker on the forehead, Nova whispered to her now sleeping child, "Everything is going to be just fine,"

The next morning their home was in disarray; Alex and Ryan up early, dressing for work, Nova preparing Tucker for his first day in a new school whilst finally deciding it was time she begin working on her channel. The feeling both nerve-racking and exciting, she could not wait to speak her truth, especially after experiencing a one-night stand with a married man. By 7:08 a.m. they were all off, Nova waving them goodbye from the driveway watching Hunter go for his morning run just across the street. Ryan's daughter, Cassidy climbing into the backseat of Alex's car just before pulling off appearing to be one happy family.

Watching the truck disappear from view Nova bellowed to Hunter, hearing her only slightly, he turned, the sweat dripping from his body as the humid hot air beat against his chest.

"Come over when you're done!" she screamed. Removing his headphones, Hunter squinting, jogging in place, waiting for Nova to repeat her statement, and she did. Hearing her now loud and clear he nodded, pacing now across the street looking both ways for oncoming traffic. Nova skipping back inside, turning the lock behind her. Home alone she could not decide whether or not to cook breakfast, dance merrily along the ground floor, rummage through Alex's closet or finally devote her time to making her video. So many thoughts racing through her mind, a procrastinator she is.

Later that afternoon a faint knock came to the door, it was Hunter stopping by with a bag of chips and dipping sauce— Nova's favorite, she wondered how he knew. But he did not, they simply learned this was something they had in common, taking a moment to chuckle over the coincidence, Nova invited Hunter inside filling him in on her daily plans and the content she was working on. Snacking and listening to music down in the basement once Nova returned with the camcorder placing it steadily on the tripod, she removed the tools once again as she mentioned to Hunter her dilemma,

"I need a stage name," she told him. Immediately sending him into deep thought,

"Hmm, that's tough. Why not stick with Higgins or go with your maiden name?" he asked, the chips crunching along his teeth.

"I want no affiliation with Terry and my father practically disowned me when I was a teen, so I don't have any real reason to associate myself with him or his brand," she said.

"Brand?" questioned Hunter.

"Yes, my father is Dash Signature," she continued, plopping the tools into a box next to the table furthest the rear of the room. Hunter remained stationed, his hands lifted from the bag of chips and his eyes widened,

"As in the rich fashion designer guy?" he mumbled. Nova mindlessly nodding, yes. Hunter remained perturbed, unsure of what to say or do next, his neck extending as he took a new look around the room, his thoughts consuming him, learning now that their family were affluent, he had a plethora of questions,

"Wait so, Alex is rich, you-you guys are like multi-millionaires? This is a middle-class neighborhood, what on earth is Alex doing here? Why aren't you guys all living in some million-dollar estate?" he questioned. But Nova did not answer; rather she focused her attention on more pressing matters, a stage name.

"Hey, I don't want to talk about my father, can we focus on the name, please?" she asked.

"I would love to, but please Nova give me something, that's like telling someone you're related to that billionaire talk show host Ophelia and expecting them to continue being nonchalant about it. I mean, how is Alex your aunt? Is she your father's sister? I mean, why is she not just as well off?" he asked innocently, folding the chips and placing the lid back atop the dipping sauce. Releasing a large sigh, Nova decided to invite Hunter into her personal life, outlining to him the incident which took place years ago in their home.

"...and Alex is my father's sister in law, she's my mother's sister, they have the same father, different mother, that's why she's not much older than Marian and I. I guess none of the men in my family can be regarded as quality individuals, may be safe to say they were all womanizers and so I was only destined to procreate with one myself," she said growing anxious now to begin her segment. "Do you have any more questions for me or can we start?" she said impatiently, her hands placed firmly atop her hips.

Dusting his hands Hunter got to his feet, feeling energetic and highly ecstatic about working with Nova now on her project.

"Okay first things first, we have to get you a better background, you know something without nails and hanging tools," Hunter smiled. "Ah, what about your bedroom upstairs? We can position you in front of the bathroom and have the background taken out of focus, with you sitting at a vanity or something? What do you think?" he asked. Nova shrugging her shoulders reluctantly agreeing, she was feeling apprehensive about the idea of sitting at a vanity or in front of a bathroom, but who was she to complain? Clearly her ideas were no better. "Also, do you want to maybe add some of that color stuff to your face, like you know, to give you a glow?

Not—not to say you aren't glowing already, I mean, you know an extra glow," stuttered Hunter.

"Makeup?" Nova questioned.

"Yes!" he shouted happily.

But Nova did not take lightly to his suggestion, her self-esteem having already taken a plunge; she was ready to save face, pretending as though she was confident in her natural form, when in reality she was feeling far less sexually appealing and timid.

"I'm not looking to impress a bunch of sexually challenged men who otherwise can't get a nut off so they have to scope out pretty women on YouTube and beat their jacks off—" she replied angrily, sensing this, Hunter very politely interceded,

"Whoa, hey, calm down, it's not about that. I just think more women, who I am guessing is your target audience here, will be more inclined to watch your video if you look groomed and—and vibrant and happy. Your message is one thing, but your tone, visibility and delivery are all other aspects that you should take heavily into consideration, besides, what are your focal topics?" he asked.

"Hunter you're making this so complicated for me, and you're sucking the fun out of it. I have to have a glam team to tell women about why my hair fell out and I now despise men? It shouldn't be this complicated," Nova complained.

"It's only a complication if you choose to see it that way. I think this channel can be great, I know you're unhappy with my kind right now, which is understandable and who knows maybe there's a lot of other women who too, are unhappy and can relate to you on some level. I think right now is a good time to get out there and show women your vulnerable side, this damaged version of yourself—"

"Oh Jesus Christ, now I'm ugly and damaged?" Nova asked sarcastically. Hunter growing nervous, retracting his statements, stammering now that he was growing to find Nova attractive and hated the idea of displeasing her. Quickly he explained himself, but Nova was no longer feeling excited about her journey to becoming a YouTuber, she was feeling pitiful, her head hanging low now that she began thinking of all the work that would have to go into such a task.

"Let's just forget it," she said rising to her feet to remove the camcorder from the tripod. A disappointed Hunter turning to face her,

"Oh goodness, you can't be this hopeless and no, that was not me trying to insult you. I just genuinely believe in you and it's sad that you don't believe in yourself. Why are you letting him win?" Hunter asked. Nova confused turning to face him, her face readable, "He wins, every time you give up and choose to use the excuse of your last relationship as a reason to not better yourself, wallow, refuse to grow and become a stellar individual. I'm not here to preach to you, but you're so passionate and intelligent and—and patient, none of those good qualities should go to waste Nova all because the wrong man couldn't love you correctly," he said. Looking up to face him, Nova felt an abrupt burst of energy, feeling happier and far more intrigued, she grabbed the camcorder, racing through the basement doors, hopping sideways along the hallway, shouting to Hunter to join her. Amped, she ran upstairs to her bedroom where she searched frantically for a wonderful outfit to wear and locating her hair products to moisturize the one-inch of hair that had grown from her scalp. Hunter loving every moment.

While Nova showered, dressed and applied her makeup with the bathroom door opened slightly, Hunter prepared her stage. Deciding the ornate queen mattress and her plain back wall to be a far better view for audiences; the ivory chesterfield upholstered headboard, white sheets and the city shadow dark gray colored walls all appearing dynamically to Hunter. Thirty-five minutes later Nova emerged, draped in a red blouse and a pair of home shorts, her large hoop earrings hanging from her earlobes, her face naturally heightened using a light foundation, blush and false lashes with a black liner for her waterline bringing her eyes to pop. Looking around Nova did not question Hunter's decision, simply climbing atop the mattress; she stretched her arms, swinging her neck from side to side,

"Oh, we need a name!" she bellowed. Hunter stopping behind the camcorder, preparing himself to hit the "on" button,

"What is this first episode going to be about? Maybe this should be an intro episode, and your name can simply be Nova, later on, you add something else, he suggested, running fresh out of ideas.

"I am going to talk about what it means to have mad hair," Nova chuckled, her smile causing Hunter to blush, taken aback momentarily by her astonishing beauty. Both laughing, Hunter agreed, Nova getting comfortable, sitting Indian Style, behind the lens, Hunter counting down using his fingers, *5, 4, 3, 2, 1,*

"Hello there beauties and brawns with your barrettes and brushes, my name is Nova! That's it, just Nova, welcome to my channel. I am new to this platform and before we begin diving into why my hair is mad aka bald, I want to invite you all to like and subscribe by pressing the button below," Nova remained smiling, rubbing her hands along her scalp for extra emphasis with every mention of her hair—Hunter watching her intently. A jubilant Nova emulating the behaviors seen on other YouTube channels from the competition videos she watched a few days ago. Listening to herself, she was proud,

Spanning well over forty-five minutes Nova spoke, her words resonating, sending chills down her spine as she talked candidly about her failed marriage, the insight she received from Hunter in relation to men, which he found intriguing as she tied their conversation into her advice piece. Nova made it clear that she was far from perfect and that her 'Even My Hair Is Mad' journey was going to document every inch of her life as she overcomes her pain, re-grow her hair strands and make a better effort in selecting the right man to stand alongside her. Feeling confident with her message she closed,

"Okay, beauties and brawns, that's all I have for you today. Don't forget to like and subscribe and hit that little bell right below the video to receive notifications whenever a video is posted. If you need additional information on any of the products I mentioned that I will begin using in my hair for growth, length retention and shine then please check the description box below. Also, remember ladies, don't let him drive your hair mad!" Nova said smiling, Hunter counting down once again, turning down the red light. An ecstatic Nova could not contain herself, stepping in the bed, jumping down into his arms, wrapping her legs around his torso, kissing him passionately on the lips. Shocked, Hunter did nothing but catch her, cradling her as he reciprocated; their hug tight and warm.

"What did you think?" she asked excitedly climbing down from his hips. Hunter did not imagine he would come to find Nova attractive, but he did now and there was no hiding it, blushing, he said,
"It was really great." Happy to hear of his validation Nova returned to the bathroom where she cleaned her face free from the makeup, asking Hunter if he would do the editing to which he very happily agreed. But Nova did not think about the fact that Hunter would need to take the camcorder, bringing her to worry over what she was going to tell Tucker. Too excited, however, she did not ponder this long, allowing Hunter to in fact take the recorder along with him. Having reached a conclusion, she headed downstairs where she made her way into the kitchen after grabbing the mail. Tossing the letters along the countertop, she sent Hunter off with a tight hug and a kiss on the cheek, turning to begin preparing dinner before everyone would return home.

Moments later after placing the seasoned chicken in the oven to bake and bring the potatoes to a boil, Nova sorted through the mail, one of which addressed to her from the City Courts. The letter promptly outlining her attendance for a Child Custody hearing set to take place one month from today. Nova remained standing, a tear falling from her eye.

"He lied," she said whispering to herself.

15

2007

The apartment small, Nova wandered aimlessly around the one-bedroom Alex and Terrance occupied wondering where exactly she was to sleep, but before she could ask Alex was pulling out the sofa bed removing blankets and pillows from a storage closet nearest the bathroom. Alex had no intention of having Nova sleep on the pullout, she knew she was pregnant and although she had no plans of keeping the baby, she did not want her feeling such discomfort. As an unexpected guest, Nova was not expected to do much, Alex now beginning to clean as she awaits Terrance since leaving the Dash house.

Nova felt worrisome, sitting on the love seat located just under the window, their apartment on the first floor so the children playing outside could be heard distinctly. Alex distracting her, calling to her as she stood with her hands inserted into a pair of yellow latex cleaning gloves, Windex and paper towel in her hands,

"Have you called Planned Parenthood to make the appointment?" she asked, the look on Nova's face scaring her,

"Um, no, not yet, I mean, I was kind of hoping I would get to speak to Terry first, I mean this is a decision concerning us both," Nova said. Not be considered petulant but Alex was beginning to feel her patience thinning the more time she spent with Nova, growing angrier with her as they would converse,

"Don't tell me what I think you're trying to tell me," Alex sniped.

"Auntie I am confused, okay, Terry says he wants the baby—"

"Let me stop you right there," Alex said interrupting her, removing her gloves and placing the cleaning supplies down on the carpet, "I cannot afford another mouth to feed on my salary alone. I work as a law clerk for crying out loud and Terrance, Terrance barely makes any money as a new chef. Look, when Terry goes away for school Nova who is going to stay here and raise your baby? Feed and clothe your baby? I mean, who? Are you going to drop out of school to raise this kid!" Alex exclaimed.

Noticing how upset she was becoming Nova tried to placate Alex by expanding on her statement, "Look, I know and I hear you, I don't have a concrete answer for you, but I don't intend on burdening you with this responsibility if I do plan to keep the baby, the burden will be mine and Terry's to carry, not yours," she said. Alex realizing she was merely speaking on deaf ears continued her bidding; she was not going to allow Nova and her irresponsible ways to upset her any longer.

As the evening fell upon them Alex became worried, she had not seen or heard from Terrance all evening and she was now preparing dinner and wondered if he had eaten. Dialing him but having received no answer she could not focus, Nova seeing this questioned her aunt, but before Alex could respond to any of her inquiries, Terrance was turning the key, racing to the doorway Alex expanding her arms to hug him, kissing him profusely on the cheeks,

"Where on earth have you been?" she asked. Stepping past her Terrance remained vague in his response,

"I need to take a shower," he answered, a scornful look wiped across his face. Nova seated on the pull-out bed, watching him make his way past her, his eyes burning through her as if to indicate his level of contempt. Alex thinking it best not to follow him, wishing Nova was more tractable, fearing that she would leave if Alex were not watching. With her and

Terrance sleeping in the living room on the pull-out bed the chances of Nova eluding them was far less. Listening to the water run in the bathroom, Nova interrogated Alex, hoping to gain some insight into the dynamics of her relationship. But Alex was in no mood to converse; she was concerned for Terrance and bothered by the fact that he was not showing any interest in confiding in her. Alex dismissing her fears of Nova leaving dried her hands and made her way into the steaming bathroom where Terrance stood in the bathtub, his chest taking on the beating water.

"Babe," Alex said apprehensively.

"Yep," Terrance replied.

"What's wrong?"

"I lost my job baby, I mean, they could have said something and neither of them, none of them said anything to him,"

"Baby they're children, they don't know any better,"

'See, this is why I was not going to have this discussion with you, you're biased and I know they're your nieces, but Alex, they're not your responsibility. If their own father barely wants anything to do with them, why can't you just leave them be? Live your life and not get involved in their affairs?"

"My involvement had nothing to do with you losing your job, I think you're just angry," she scoffed.

"Of course I am angry! I need to provide for you and how am I supposed to do that now? I needed this job, for the money, the experience and you know how hard it is out here to find work as a new chef," he said, squeezing the water from his washcloth, the sounds of water slapping along the tub floor.

"What do you want me to do?" Alex asked taking a large sigh.

"Send her back to her father, stop playing mom and let us figure out our lives, together," Terrance said. Nova just outside overhearing them, grabbing her backpack and the duffle bag Alex packed she scurried outside, unintentionally leaving the door partially unlocked. Unfamiliar with this neighborhood Nova was unsure of where to go, where to catch the bus or even where to begin walking in direction to Terry's house. Walking along outside, the night pitch black Nova located a pay phone just outside of the seven eleven, dialing Terry's home phone just when his mother answered, her voice calm. Nova very politely explaining that she needed a place to stay, Mrs. Higgins did not hesitate; inviting Nova to return to her home, only, Nova did not know how to get there. Hearing this, Mrs. Higgins suggested a taxi, offering to cover the fare once Nova was to arrive, for this she was grateful. Hanging up the phone, Nova stepped to the curve where she pointed her finger, praying for a taxi to pull over, afraid she was, not knowing how they were to be identified considering she had never taken one before she simply hoped for the best. Naïve, the dangers of the world unfamiliar to her, she waited for someone to speak; the Native American man pulling over, driving an all-black Lincoln,

"Where you headed?" he asked. Nova regurgitating the address before climbing into the back seat, sinking herself into the chair, driving along the highway she fought to remain awake.

Inside the apartment Alex was hysterical, she and Terrance engaged in their most explosive argument yet. Feeling like he was to blame for Nova disappearing once again,

"Let her be with her boyfriend Alex!" he shouted. "She does not want to be here." Although it pained her to listen she decided maybe it was best that she did. Nova felt reluctant to receiving any of the help she was offered and Alex wanted so badly to rescue her from herself. But she feared it was too late and Nova would, in fact, be throwing her life away. Shutting the door, Alex turned the lock, facing Terrance who was now folding the bed back into the sofa, afterward cradling a sad Alex, burying her head into his chest, kissing her forehead softly.

Outside of the Higgins residence, Nova begged the cab driver to await her while she retrieved the fare from a kind Mrs. Higgins who after a few knocks appeared holding a few twenty-dollar bills in her hand. Looking down to examine Nova, she smelled of the inside of a hospital, the cab driver honking his horn impatiently. Mrs. Higgins walking down the dirt lawn wearing her bed slippers stopping to give him forty-three dollars, thanking him as Nova made her way inside.

"Is Terry home?" Nova asked her, Mrs. Higgins nodding

her head, yes, pointing in the direction of his bedroom where Nova noticed the light illuminating from under her bedroom door. "Thank you," she said softly. Mrs. Higgins hugging her, retreating shortly into her bedroom where she locked the door. Nova stood in the hallway knocking on Terry's bedroom door, the music from his stereo increasing, the sounds of cartoons blaring from his television screen. She knocked again.

"Mom I'm going to sleep!" he yelled.

"It's me," said Nova hoping he would recognize her voice. And he did, shooting to his feet, he sprinted to the door, which was only a few feet away from his bed, opening it, he tugged on Nova bringing her inside. Terry wasted no time undressing her, the young boy horny, but Nova could not keep up, she wanted to have a conversation.

"Wait," she said in between kisses but Terry was not listening as he continued to slob her lips, undressing her aggressively. Finally, after little resistance, Nova gave in, dropping her bags, listening as Terry whispered in her ear how much he missed her, but there was a feeling to the pit of Nova's stomach which left her doubtful, fighting to raise her head so the tears would not escape. Nova did not move, rather she lie still allowing Terry to take complete advantage of her, licking her lips as his body thrust up and down, her mind wandering off so as to ease the discomfort. Once he concluded, a smiling Terry turning to face her, laughing, their naked bodies under the cotton sheets,

"Are you alright?" he asked.

"No," said Nova.

"Okay, I'm sorry, I mean, is it about the baby? Are you still pregnant?" Terry asked growing curious.

"Yes," Nova whispered.

"Okay, good, I'm going to be rich Nova, we aren't going to have to worry about anything. Let's just get married and have our baby and you can just stay here with us," he smiled. Surprised, Nova could not believe her ears,

"You mean it? Like a real marriage?" she exclaimed with joy. Grabbing the sides of her face, Terry looking into her eyes said, "Yes, a real marriage. We can do it this weekend." Elated, Nova pressed her face firmly against his, kissing him, Terry

177

gliding his hands along her chest past her breasts, feeling for the stiffness of her abdomen to which he smiled before sliding his body down between her legs to perform oral sex.

Days later Nova was happy, she was watching her stomach grow and listening to Mrs. Higgins tell her stories of her pregnancy and how much of a blissful time it was. By now Nova and Terry were advising both Mr. and Mrs. Higgins of their planned nuptials, Mr. Higgins requesting he and his son remain in the bedroom for a talk, one that Nova was not asked to be present for.

A bed bound Mr. Higgins was not pleased, the expression on his face telling his son as much.

After much thought Hudson now reconsidering his initial demands of Terry, "No son, she isn't the one, I want the best for you boy. You have to go to school, get an education, head out there on the basketball court, don't be here with no baby and no woman," he grumbled, the Parkinson's making his hands shake. Terry stood, looking down on his father, angry that he could spew so much anger towards Nova, she was always quite helpful to him. His arms folded, he continued listening, "Dem girls only see you have ambition and want to strip it away from you, boy, you get that girl ah abortion and take your ass down to one of them division one schools and play for your daddy," he continued.

"I love her dad, she's kind, forgiving, she-she loves me," Terry said.

"All dem women gonna love you when you got that ball in your hand son, it ain't about no love with no girl while you still young. Plus, this is California, you ain't getting no marriage certificate without consent, and we ain't consenting," he mumbled.

"Mommy will," Terry said and I did my research. Nova and I, we have to go to counseling, speak to a judge and bring along our birth papers. Nova will get hers tomorrow and we will be married soon, perhaps not tomorrow like I would have liked, but soon," Terry sniped.

"You disobey me and become a bum you ain't staying in my house, you gonna go out there and be a man, raise your seed and take care of your damn woman," Mr. Higgins said, but Terry remained unfazed, confident that his mother would never allow such a thing.

"If you say so," he snapped. Mr. Higgins was shouting obscenities before telling Terry to leave, opening the door to exit, both Nova and Mrs. Higgins overhearing the angry old man.

"Is everything alright?" Mrs. Higgins asked, concerned. Terry nodding, taking Nova by the hand, walking outside shutting the door behind him, a curious Nova wondering where they were headed, but Terry just needed some air as he told her.

> If your hair gets dirty more often,
> alternate shampoo with co-wash or
> follow shampoo with an apple cider
> vinegar rinse. Wash your hair in
> sections to avoid tangles.

Present Day...

A bewildered Nova remained standing by the kitchen island reading through a letter that within a matter of minutes was able to pilfer her joy. A staggering revelation making her baleful, a feeling she had yet to experience despite all that she had endured. Before today, never finding a reason to despise anyone, only merely pitying those who behaved unkindly or those who were unjust in their actions—Terry now becoming one of these people. The self-doubt lingering, Nova now wondering if her demands to Terry were too excessive leading him to take such drastic measures expeditiously, or whether or not she was fit to be a good mother, however, she was not communicating with him, she only suggested a cellular phone for their child, no money for clothes or food, she was lenient and amicable, or so she thought. The transient moment for happiness earlier that morning gone, her eyes beginning to water, the time passing her by and the smell of chicken burning, the doors unlocking as the sounds of joy and happiness resonate through the halls and the foyer leading up to the stairs into the bedroom. Alex and Tucker were home, but their meal cooked to a crisp. Alex smelling the burning meat, racing into the kitchen, a mindless Nova staring off into space as Alex reached for the oven mittens opening its door, steam spewing from inside allowing smoke to fill the room, she bellowed,

"Nova!" Hearing her name, the world resumed again, a frightened Nova falling to the floor, the letter gliding past her, standing to turn on the water from the pipes as Alex lift the pan tossing it and the burnt chicken into the sink, the sizzling causing the smoke detectors to blare.

"Are you alright? What's going on?" asked Alex fanning the detectors hoping to quiet them. Nova remained silent, creeping slowly towards the island, bending to retrieve the fallen letter handing it to her aunt who after a quick glance could not find herself remorseful or concerned, "You were home all day, why haven't you been down to the courthouse to start the child support paperwork? You can't wait on me to do everything with you or for you, I am already overexerting myself," Alex complained. Silent, Nova turned to walk away leaving the note and its contents in the kitchen, Alex calling to Tucker advising they were going to order in that night, elated, Tucker replied with glee, but it was not long after he was making his way down to the kitchen infuriated, his eyes crying as he inquired on the whereabouts of his camcorder to which Nova deliberately ignored him.

"Nova, have you seen his camcorder?" Alex asked, her eyes lowered, her hands massaging her temple to ease her oncoming migraine. She was beginning to feel like a parent raising two children—one teenager and the other a child. Nova now interrupting them,

"Tucker the recorder is with Hunter, mommy borrowed it. Auntie, I am going to the court tomorrow and if you want money for the pizza or whatever you plan to order I will give it to you. No more freeloading, I don't want any more handouts," Nova demanded. She was feeling dignified in her approach, high-minded because she was no longer going to allow herself to remain a leech. Although she was pulling her weight in other areas, such as grocery and laundry, along with cleaning, she knew she had to do more especially with all that Alex had sacrificed for her up until now. Without speaking a word Alex nodded, she was no doubt feeling relieved. Unhappy with the fact that his mother had taken something which belonged to him Tucker spent the remainder of the evening locked away, coming down only once the food arrived and having to clear his dishes. Nova did not mind this as his absence gave her more time with her thoughts—everyone sequestered.

The next day Nova watched as Alex and Tucker took off down the road, Hunter going for his morning run, a few hours later knocking at their front door, a smile wiped across his face. Nova tucking in her lips, apprehensive about what she was thinking to request of him,

"Hey, do you mind taking me down to the courthouse? I would like to put my now estranged husband on child support," she asked him swaying the front door back and forth. Hunter looking at her with question,

"I think you can just apply for that online—"

Knitting her eyebrows Nova invited Hunter inside. That afternoon Nova and Hunter discussed the editing of her video which Hunter spent his evening the day before completing, assisting Nova to upload and add her tags and search engine optimization. He also walked her through completing the child support application to which Nova was all too grateful. Looking into his eyes as they sat around the coffee table discussing Nova's next big show she leaned in to kiss him, Hunter reciprocating this act, his penis pulsating, he arose quickly, stammering,

"I—thi—think I should leave," Nova standing pulling her sleeves down from her shirt covering her hands nervously, looking up to him as he moved swiftly past her out of the front door. Nova falling to her knees searching YouTube for her channel, there she was, her video uploaded—*Even My Hair Is Mad TV*, the lighting perfect, the background out of focus as they had previously discussed; it was seamless. She smiled before getting to her feet where she would now dress and head out into the world in search for employment.

16

2008

Seven months pregnant a high school senior Nova was beginning to feel uneasy. Her body now heavier than she had ever imagined and Terry showing her little to no attention whenever they were in school or when she awaited him afterward to head home—Nova was feeling unconfident. With her birthday only days away she began dreading the fact that she would be home, struggling to sleep or struggling to maneuver due to her ever-growing abdomen. Mrs. Higgins was far too excited, waiting on Nova hand and foot, ensuring that she wanted for nothing, however Nova still felt displeased. Her hormones getting the best of her as she would awaken in the middle of the night crying for reasons unknown, this only aggravating Terry and now he began second-guessing whether or not Nova should travel with him out of state for school; believing her presence to only be a distraction.

The protruded round stomach in front of her making it impossible for her to wear comfortable clothing, her jeans often unbuttoned, her blouses two sizes too big and her shoes oftentimes unbuckled or untied because she could no longer see her feet. But until Jamar came around to assist her, Nova had no other choice than to hope for the best and walk meticulously down the halls and staircases. Although appearing to be supportive, her friends judged her heavily whenever she were not around them, convinced that Nova would be no more than a baby mother to Terry who ultimately would leave her for someone of greater intelligence and determination. Nova heard the rumors, even mentioned them to her doctor during her visits, the ones Mrs. Higgins would accompany her on because Terry had practice or needed sleep.

With no word from Alex, Marian or her father Nova grew saddened, drowning herself daily in a river of tears. One night an inebriated Terry came staggering inside, demanding that they wed on her birthday. By December Terry turned eighteen choosing to party with his friends, leaving a then five-month pregnant Nova home with television and leftovers and a coughing Hudson, who from what Nova could tell was nearing death's door. Mrs. Higgins averring that Nova's baby would be a reincarnation of the old man, this statement often making things awkward as she could not fathom such a thing.

On February eleventh, her eighteenth birthday Nova was excited to do something new and exhilarating, hurrying home from school, her waddle making it harder for her to walk and somewhat impossible to fit inside of the car Terry was gifted for his birthday from his mother. The 1996 Toyota Camry bought second-hand from a neighbor was confined, even for Terry at times who stood at 6'5, having to push his chair as far as it could extend. Terry no longer working deciding it best to focus primarily on school, his parents supplying them with the items needed for their soon to be bundle of joy, Terry and Nova discussing names on their way home,

"Something with a *T*," he said, steering the vehicle, periodically turning to face her, But Nova no longer made eye contact, feeling filled with self-doubt, overweight and unhappy in her changing body. "Baby, today is your birthday, cheer up!" Terry said taking her by the hand, but Nova resisted, pulling her hand back, placing it firmly atop her lap.

"What are we doing today?" she asked.

"Can't do much, I'm not working," admitted Terry, this upsetting Nova as she felt she deserved something. They were no longer dating, no longer hanging out after school, she was barely seeing him, Terry now always with his friends, returning home when the sun went down, sexing her body and shortly afterward it was morning again—their mundane routine depressing.

"We don't have to spend money, we can go to the park or something," she pleaded, Terry facing her once more, feigning empathy in an effort to get her to change the subject or at least demand something more practical. But Nova was now privy to his tricks, the kind he would use to gaslight her, she was not going to change her mind this time, she wanted to do something, anything but remain home staring at four walls and a broken television set or online browsing for baby clothes they couldn't afford.

"I understand you're upset, but why didn't you just go out with your friends?" he asked repulsively. "You shouldn't just rely on me for making sure you have a good time on your birthday." Caressing her stomach Nova reclined in her seat, closing her eyes, regretful of her decisions. Although the ride was not long, Nova no longer could travel the distance between home and school, her feet swollen and the warm weather causing them to hurt too much.

"Fine, just take me home I'll go to sleep. You're going to play basketball I suppose?" she said sarcastically. Terry nodding in excitement, "I can't go with you?" she then asked, waiting patiently for his response, but he only scoffed, making it apparent his answer. Deciding to push the issue no further Nova simply climbed out of the passenger seat on her own once they arrived at his home, Terry no longer assisting her to get out of the vehicle; grabbing her book bag Nova turned to make her way inside to the smell of something putrid. Off in the distance, Mrs. Higgins heard sobbing. Mr. Higgins had died.

By the second week of March Nova was feeling stressed, with only four more weeks until her due date by way of vaginal delivery she was growing anxious and nervous. Since the death of his father Terry was different, he was far more attentive, spent most if not all of his time at home and every day after school he and Nova would get food, have a date evening or head out shopping for clothing for their unborn son. Mrs.

Higgins began sharing with Terry her speculation that their unborn could be a reincarnated version of Hudson, which Terry often entertained the idea of leaving Nova to question his mental aptitude. Was he simply agreeing because he too was mourning the loss of his father? Or did he actually believe this to be true? Either way, Nova was not pleased to hear of these things.

With her due date nearing Nova and Terry were beginning to feel a lot closer to one another and now that they were both the legal age to marry, decided it was time. Planning weeks ahead, Terry obtained their marriage certificate and on the first day of Spring in 2008, Nova and Terry headed down to the nearest courthouse after school, driven by Terry's teammate Jonathan who would act as their witness. Inside, the couple stood, exchanging their vows, Nova's growing baby bump parting them as they recited their nuptials draped in casual clothing and book bags lying at their feet. Listening as the words *I do* trickle from her lips, Nova felt the chills down her arm, the look in Terry's eyes warm, the tiny room making their moment both intimate and engaging. It was worth it, and with a pair of Sterling Silver bands costing them both roughly about one hundred dollars each, they placed their rings on its respected fingers. Terry's friend teasing him once he and Nova were instructed to kiss, making their marital status an official one.

Filled with Joy a pregnant Nova twirled out of the room, down the corridor, her flat shoes squeaking on the ground, her hair flowing freely inside. At that moment, Nova regarded that day as the best day of her life.

Avoid Over styling:
Styling products will dry out
your hair, build upon your scalp,
weigh down your hair and much more...

Present Day... One Month Later
In the driver's seat of Hunter's car Nova pulled the gear shifting it into drive, fearful she would forget her left from her right or the gas from the brake, she crept down the driveway turning the wheel methodically, one hand over the other under Hunter's

pristine direction. Hunter sitting upright, alert, his heart beating quickly, he feared for his life deciding today of all days he would volunteer in teaching Nova how to drive. *This is it, the moment she is going to kill us both*, he thought. His face unable to mask his dread, taking large gulps, shouting to her frequently, their car ride filled with displeasure, bellowing and a brief moment of Hunter covering his eyes when Nova turned onto the wrong lane directly facing oncoming traffic, the other drivers honking belligerently,

"Um—maybe, I should drive," Hunter suggested nervously once Nova swerved out of the way, cutting off another individual who was quick enough to move into the adjacent lane. Knowing how eager Nova was to learn he felt sorrowful, but he could not save her floundering driving, she needed lessons and proper training in which he alone could not provide. Pulling over Nova batting her lashes while pouting her lips,

"No, please," she begged, extending her torso kissing him gently on the lips. Nova unsure of her feelings for Hunter, she found him attractive enough but was feeling too uncertain of her past to consider anything serious with him and so, she only regarded him as a good friend with whom every so often she would exchange a sweet kiss—this, Hunter did not mind.

"Nova you're way too lousy at driving, swerving in and out of lanes, cutting people off, we could get into a serious accident if you don't start taking this a bit more seriously," Hunter pleaded, he did not want to take this opportunity of learning away from her, he knew she was trying, and although things were far from perfect he was happy that he could be there to aid her along. Nodding with excitement, agreeing wholeheartedly Nova shifted the gears once more, checking her blind spot and adjacent mirrors to any and all oncoming traffic before pulling out to resume her training; Hunter smiling, still feeling apprehensive but at least he was not sweating from his heightened anxiety as much as before.

Inching slowly Nova returned Hunter's vehicle into his driveway where they both remained seated,

"Do you ever think about going back to Michigan?" she asked him, laying her head on the headrest concurrently turning the ignition key to silent the engine. Hunter's movements symmetric to her own, his hands folded in his lap, nodding his head no. "But, you're alone here right? I mean, you came here for work, but was it really worth it? Seven months and you're now an avid churchgoing single bachelor in his early twenties," she said smiling. Nova did learn as much during their late-night talks and moments of reason where Hunter disclosed information to Nova relative to the male psyche. Thinking, Hunter did not truly understand if he were being insulted or if Nova was simply looking to acquire additional insight pertaining to him,

"I mean, I'm not sure what you're asking or telling me. For the most part I am content, I meet women and I date here and there," he said solemnly. "Correction, I was meeting women and dating here and there, until I met Alex and um, I guess at that point I wanted more, but the feelings weren't reciprocated so, time to move on," he said. Nova remained staring in his eyes, the California sun beaming through the car window causing her upper arm to feel warm.

"How do you feel about women and dating now?" she asked him, innocently.

"I think now I'd like to settle down and meet someone special," he replied. Feeling perplexed Nova feared leading Hunter on, he could quite possibly only be a rebound and for this she chose to tread lightly, politely taking her leave and returning to her home where she began preparing for the court hearing the next day. Terry was in town, Mrs. Higgins informing Nova of this as they were regularly speaking regarding Tucker—Nova now happier than she was a month ago and her crown thanking her for it. Inside of her bedroom she stretched her hair, noticing a remarkable three-inch growth, her hair now four inches, sitting atop her head heavily moisturized.

During the first weeks of her video going live Nova would check in constantly, making sure her video was generating views and by week five she only saw a measly eighty-seven views with zero commentators leaving her to believe no one made it past five minutes. By now as she ran her fingers through her tight coils, she pondered ways in which she could increase engagement and what exactly it would all mean for her anyway.

But unfortunately, nothing was coming to mind and she was feeling less interested in her YouTube channel and more worried about her hearing.

Concerned, Nova made her way down the hallway into Alex's room in the morning, 6 a.m. and Alex was up toppling her clothing bin in search of a sweater for it was said that the weather will be unkind to them today,

"Today's the big day huh?" Alex asked her, noticing her niece standing by the threshold through her peripheral vision. Nova nodding. "It's going to be okay; you've sent the list with all the pertinent documents; you have the receipts I gave you, proof of mailing and my pay stubs along with the letter I wrote. Things are going to be just fine. After all this is just the pre-trial, so I know it may be hard but try to be as amicable and calm as you can to avoid this going to an actual trial. Mediation may be best," Alex said, her hands now pressed tightly against her shoulders, shaking her playfully, smiling. Nova wondering why of all days Alex was so giddy,

"Auntie, why are you so happy?" she asked jokingly. Although Alex wanted badly to tell Nova her good news, she did not feel the timing to be appropriate enough, deciding to excuse herself and make her way down into the kitchen where she began preparing her Keurig machine to dispense her morning dose of coffee.

Downtown Nova struggled to make her way into the courthouse, the lines long and an unsuspecting Nova pushed by a rather tall gentleman just outside, he turned to face her, apologetic and charming, taking her by the hand avoiding what could have been a nasty tumble down the stone steps. Walking vigorously past him Nova made her way down the hall into the small room, resembling nothing like what she typically would see on television. The judge's bench, hard chairs and small court benches all unoccupied. Patiently she waited.

Fifteen minutes later the doors to the rear swung open, it was Terry, he came alone, he and Nova exchanging a nervous look. Terry pinning his lips together as he made his way closer to the bench, his arms folded before taking a seat and slapping the manila envelope on the table. Nova fighting to remain quiet, their hearing set to begin in only three minutes, she was feeling worried. As the judge entered the room grew still, the floors creaking and the light from the outside shining in but nothing could prepare Nova for the news she were to receive only shortly after a brief introduction. Revealed to be only a pendente lite or better known as a pending litigation hearing. Nova and her evidence was not considered and their case would be taken to trial, learning now that Terry was seeking to take Tucker out of California permanently, allowing Nova only periodic, supervised visitation.

The judge spoke callously, with no regard to her feelings, Nova feeling sick to her stomach hearing that they would have to soon return to heavily discuss the facts of their case, Nova also remanded to find work and a steady paying income otherwise she would be deemed unstable to afford raising child. It was no matter that Alex's earning was that of six figures, her life-changing could alter Tucker's wellbeing at any moment leaving Nova no choice but to fend for herself in an effort to keep her son. Listening keenly Terry found this news to be rather satisfying, Nova fighting tears, never given a chance to speak her side of the story. It was a grim feeling, like everyone were against her, even the strange woman in the black robe deciding the fate of her child with no regard for how she, Nova were feeling as a mother. The banging of the gavel meant freedom, but not quite. Instantly Nova shot through the double brown doors locating the nearest ladies' room where she ran inside the stall hurling.

Outside the mild vertigo bringing her to sidestep almost bumping into those around her, the gentleman from earlier that day standing in front of her, briefcase in hand smoking a cigarette, watching her closely on her phone dialing a taxi cab. The strange man walking over to Nova, putting out the butt of his cigarette under the chestnut-colored size thirteen oxford dress shoes.

"Donavan," he said to her, his right hand extended, the other holding firm the handle of his leather briefcase. The navy-blue three-piece suite he wore making her hot. With the 92 degree weather sun blaring down on them, Nova took a step back finding shade, her hand above her eyes to get a better view of him, he was not her type, fair-skinned with a goatee, only a few inches taller than her, which made him short in her eyes and therefore instantly unattractive. But her mind could not process this, yet, feeling heavily discontented. She is looking beyond him where the patrons were climbing in and out of vehicles, her taxi having yet to arrive. "Sorry, I guess you're having a bad day," he said turning to face her, retracting his hand—both hands now gripping the handle of his briefcase. He was smitten by Nova, instantly attracted to her, there was a stillness about her, but little did he know this was only a reflection of her current invulnerability.

"I don't know you and I don't mean to be curt, but I really am not in the mood for conversation right now," she said stepping down the stairs into the hot sun where she hissed, once again taking her hand for shade. Donavan walking behind her,

"I completely understand, I um, I watched you leave your hearing in quite a rush. I honestly don't mean you any harm, but I will beat myself up if I didn't at least attempt to speak with you in an effort to ask you out sometime. This place is less than ideal for picking up a date, but um, you're beautiful and—" Nova rolling her eyes, stepping down further trying to avoid the garrulous stranger. Taking the hint now Donavan retreated, walking over to the other side of the courthouse, entering into the parking lot where he climbed into his vehicle shortly thereafter—Nova's taxi finally arriving, honking to her.

Home now Nova cried, weeping uncontrollably as she sat along the stairs, tossing to the ground the papers and the documents she thought would be enough to earn her a victory— but such was not the case. Her mascara running, she sniffled moments later, standing to her feet, heading into her bedroom where the tripod still remained standing only this time in the corner. With her bed unmade, Nova dragging it towards the center of her room, the natural light seeping inside, she removed the camcorder from Tucker's bedroom, turning it on, placing it on the tripod, now hopping up on the bed. Her clothes wrinkled from her travels, her eyes red from crying, her makeup partially gone, she spoke. With each word Nova felt liberated, she was only seeking to speak her sad, pathetic truth, no intention of ever playing it for the world to see, but the venting was needed as she was losing a war she worked so diligently to avoid.

"I wish I could go back, I wish I would have listened to the people around me, my aunt, the cleaning women who were overseeing my sister and I, hell, even my so-called friends, I just—I just wish I could return back to a time where things were easy." She wept. "How can a man leave a woman and then continue to beat her while she's down, use the justice system to take away her child, after he made the decision to leave!?" her questions rhetorical as she waved her hands in frustration. "I don't bother him, he hasn't bought a shirt for my son, or-or even a pair of shoes, oh, but to win his favor he got him an unnecessary gadget which has nothing to do with his wellbeing, Terry, have you bought food for our son? Clothing for school or even supplies? No! You haven't," she screamed to the camcorder speaking as though it were, in fact, her now estranged husband.

"I stayed with him, I was with you Terry when you flunked out of college, lost your scholarship and had to work a job you hated even though I volunteered to find work to help us to make enough money to move out of your mother's house and what do you do? You abandon me the moment you find a career, get a new car, and move into a house and for who? And for what? A Dark-Skinned Becky!" she shouted, climbing to her feet on the bed, but Nova standing at only 5'2 still remained partially in view of the lens, her bare feet stepping onto the mattress, leaving temporary indentations while tossing around her hands and her voice cracking.

"You cheated, you criticized me when no one was looking, all because you were insecure, you broke me down to nothing, you played on my insecurities and pretended to love me so that I could be there until you were ready to move on, until your sorry narcissistic ass found a new source of supply, yep, I read that shit somewhere, you are a narcissistic bastard and what happened huh? You turned on me the second I cut my hair and decided to embrace my natural roots. Calling me names, teasing me when my hair was short and calling it jokes, your cruelty masked by clownery and all along I thought it was love! That wasn't love! That was emotional and mental abuse. But as a black woman I endured it because I kept feeling like I couldn't do any better, like there was no one else who could possibly love me and my roots, the way I thought you loved me. But nope I was heavily mistaken!" she continued, shouting now, plopping back into the bed, her legs crossed.

"I wish I was stronger back then I would have left your sorry ass right where I met you; I would have left you at hello, fuck! I wouldn't even have said hello! You weren't worth it then, the headaches, and being thrown out of my house because I was afraid of losing you. I am grateful for my son, but men like you, men who cheat and take advantage of kind-hearted women like me are despicable and should be eradicated." Nova catching her breath sobbed, her head bowed, the red light shining on her.

"I'm so angry with myself for letting you do this to me," she whispered, her tears falling onto the sheet. "Allowing you to break me and my crown, allowing you to watch me wither away to nothing due to your constant badgering and my lack of self-love and thorough understanding of what I was or who I was at that time. I loved you more than I loved myself and instead of returning the love, you abandoned me, punished me for it, left me because you thought you could do so much better. Why is the dark-skinned woman with the long curly hair better than me? How can she be better than me? You would joke about wanting to date a Latina and I would always just brush you off, they aren't the problem with men like you Terry, shallowness, selfishness, and self-hate is the problem with men like you. I have to be strong for my son—our son although it pains me to say it. But I have to be strong for him, because I can't resent you for the sake of him and I would never do to you what you are looking to do to me—strip me of my parental rights for a young man I dedicated my life to raising. I won't let you win," she concluded, her chin held high, her eyes puffy and her hands placed firmly on the sheets.

Nova rose to turn off the camcorder, feeling better now. After a nap Nova opened her eyes, watching the clock she knew Tucker would be leaving school shortly to make his way down the block to Alex's office to await her. But Nova deciding today will be a good day, grabbed a hold of her cardigan, dialing a taxi, heading to the elementary school where she stood outside waiting patiently for her son. Hearing the bell toll, other parents gathering around her, Nova watching as the school children ran across the playground, Tucker along with several other children and a strange man with his back turned to exit the building. Nova walking over to them, hoping to introduce herself to the person who appeared to be her child's instructor,

"Hi," she said politely. Donavan turning to face her, his eyes widened, Tucker racing past him, squeezing his mother around her torso,

"Hey mommy," he said happily, Nova mindlessly removing his backpack, her eyes fixed on Donavan who was now dressed casually.

"Two times in one day must be fate," he said smiling. Nervous, Nova extending her hand to make his acquaintance.

"That or you're just following me" she chuckled. Tucker watching the exchange between them,

"Mommy, this is Mr. Donavan, my teacher," he said joyfully, looking up at Nova, squinting from the scorching sun.

"Tucker is definitely a bright star in class. Tucker, do you mind giving your mother and I a quick moment to speak?" Donavan asked him. Tucker obliged racing off to play with his friends, Nova stood, arms folded, a smile wiped across her face.

"Hmm, so you're a mommy?" he asked her bashfully.

"I am," she said nodding. "Children?" she asked.

"Hmm, nope, I mean I consider myself to be fairly young, as are you, I mean—"

Interrupting him, "Why do you do that?" she asked laughing, "Do you just not know when to stop talking?"

"Ha! I teach second grade, I think I'll let you answer that for yourself besides, I feel it may be just my nerves, you're really beautiful and um, I don't know, it's a guy thing, you know, cut me some slack," he said. Nova could see how charming he was, deciding to give him her phone number with the children now beginning to disappear from the playground and Tucker would soon become restless. For this Donavan was happy, he remained standing watching her and Tucker walk away, his backpack hanging from her shoulders and with Tucker growing day by day he was now almost the same height as his mother.

Nova deciding to take Tucker for ice cream that day, both walking along the streets taking in the view of the healthy growing palm trees and beautiful weather now that the rain cleared just on the outskirts of the neighborhood; Nova having a long talk with her son.

That evening returning home with his mother Tucker searched frantically for his camcorder, pondering over when he would actually be able to use it. With Nova and Alex immersed in their own conversation on the ground floor, Tucker retrieving his recorder from his mother's bedroom returning to his room beginning his homework in only a matter of minutes. Distracted, he removed the camcorder, using it like an airplane, buzzing around the room making noises, his finger inadvertently pressing the playback button; he listened to the words coming from an unknown source. Confused, he turned his head quickly, thinking his mother was speaking from the bedroom door, but she was not there. Looking down now he could see her video on the recorder—the one recorded from earlier that day.

Taking a seat Tucker did not care for the contents he was witnessing, only angry that his mother was finding more usage in his gadget than he was and so, he stomped to her bedroom, grabbing ahold of her laptop, opening it and connecting the USB port in an attempt to transfer the files. Technology savvy, Tucker toggled with the idea of simply deleting the video but did not want to risk upsetting his mother. Noticing the open YouTube tab on her browser, he chuckled at the idea of his mother having a YouTube channel, thinking of her as being too old for such antics. To make light of the situation, Tucker decided on uploading her new video, searching tirelessly on how to do so, as he was unfamiliar with the site in this capacity.

A thinker he is, loading the video only moments after learning how, his laugh sinister thinking his mother would be ridiculed for having uploaded a video to what he deemed to be a platform for children and adolescents. Without confirmation, Tucker closed the laptop shut, deleting the video afterward from his camcorder, returning to the center of his bed, he continued working on his homework, the camcorder safely by his side.

17

Days past since Nova and Donavan exchanged their contact information and since then have not stopped communicating. Nova feeling guilty for misjudging him, but at that moment when he first introduced himself she was not receptive of anyone. Alex seldom home now spending most of her time with Ryan, by the weekend Tucker was ready for play, finding a multitude of ways to keep busy and looking to make new friends in the neighborhood; for this Nova was glad, he was beginning to open up. Thinking of her next trial date, Nova spent more time online searching for work, completing applications, responding to emails and even asking Donavan if there were any way he too could seek to assist.

While Nova remained in her quarters scrolling through job sites a loud shriek was heard from the bottom of the stairs, Alex calling to her, startling Tucker too who was in the living room watching cartoons.

"Nova, come here!" she screamed. Although high-pitched, Nova could not determine her tone, she only concluded she had done something once again to upset her aunt. Emerging after removing the laptop from her lap, she peaked her head out, walking tirelessly to the staircase banner,

"What did I do now?"

"You're viral!" Shouted Alex happily. But Nova remained unmoved,

"What on earth are you talking about?" she asked.

"Your YouTube video is viral, I mean, Cassidy was on her dad's phone playing a game and a snippet of a video from you came up, I heard your voice and when I looked at the phone, it was you, you're trending on Twitter, hashtag, even my hair mad!" Alex said shouting and laughing. Nova finally realizing this could be true, stepped swiftly down the stairs, thinking her first video could have done it, she was now buzzing, people were talking and her channel name, now a hashtag, *how bizarre*, she thought. Grabbing the phone from Alex, her facial expression immediately changes, a still photo of her speaking, her mascara running, the bags under her eyes profound, her face caught off-guard, with her tongue sticking out of her mouth slightly, she was no doubt midsentence when the screenshot was taken and transformed into a meme. Gasping in horror, Nova stood, fighting the urge to scream.

"Oh my God," she cried, searching the house for Tucker who had now disappeared from view. A confused Alex wondered why Nova was not celebrating, deciding to pay her no mind Alex taking a seat at the bottom of the stairs scrolled through the social media channels, women from multiple urban areas all commenting, agreeing and encouraging a tearful Nova. The hashtag going around Twitter with women voicing their concerns for the next generation of men and dating; claiming Nova to be the new voice of the relationship revolution. Alex could not believe her eyes, it was all happening so fast, her video moving people to sympathize with her, her tears, her vulnerability, her message to a past suitor all enough to create a community of supporters.

"Auntie, please don't watch that video!" an indignant Nova said, returning back to the foyer after searching for Tucker but not having any luck finding him. But it was too late, Alex did, in fact, watch the video and she found herself terribly moved and, proud. "I–I was crying...I don't even know how that was uploaded, Tucker must have done that, but I can't understand why. I mean...I–I just wanted to get some things off of my chest because I was so angry that day, but this, I mean I didn't want this, the world is so cruel, Auntie," Nova cried, her breathing heavy, palms sweating and her brows knit. Alex standing to console her,

"Hey, relax, I'm sure it will blow over in a day and where there is positive, there will be negative, ignore the negative commenters Nova and focus on the good things people are saying A lot of women found your words to be highly relatable and some women have reposted the video, like it, and a few are asking you questions, I think this is a good time to try something new and just embrace this first good thing that's happening for you," Alex said calmly. Nova feeling like her aunt had a good point, decided to do as she was told, heading back upstairs she kneeled, returning to her channel dashboard to find there were now over two-thousand subscribers and over four hundred comments along with a multitude of page views. The video having no caption, no links, no title and no description—it was just her, all her, in her purest form ranting for all of thirty-two minutes and fourteen seconds.

Apprehensively Nova prepared herself for the worst, taking a moment to scroll through her comments section,

"You're so brave, lol a dark-skinned Becky? Totally funny,"

"My baby father did this too, but you will get through it, we're women it's what we do,"

"Bald and ugly oh my goodness,"

"Love this and your last video, we need the hair tips, crown is growing sis,"

"Thank you for this! I feel like as women we aren't allowed to feel when men do these things to us, we simply have to take it and move on, no emotions and put a smile on for the children,"

"New sub here,"

"I think the video needs better lighting and for sure you could use some foundation,"

"I've watched this a good six times, so true,"

That night Nova remained awake, missing dinner and never leaving her room, the laptop tucked firmly between her legs as she read comments, created a twitter page where she followed the hashtag and read the commenters speaking to and about her. Questions filling her social media profiles and some women outraged by her loose interpretation of Afro-Latina women—offended. Nova wanting badly to reply and apologize, but she was too afraid to respond or acknowledge anyone. She anticipated such a positive response but did not expect it this soon, this quickly.

By midnight she reached more than fifteen thousand views and the comments continued pouring in. Alone in the dark, the house quiet, Nova remained seated upright, the laptop illuminated. Her fingers tired from scrolling, refreshing the screen and her eyes burning from reading. Her phone singing, it was Marian, answering she said,

"Nova, what on earth happened? Are you alright? What—what is this? Do you know you have a meme of your crying trending all over Twitter?" Marian asked. Nova said nothing, her silence misguided, she could not speak because she could not decipher what she was feeling or even why. She was not happy, she was not sad, rather, bewildered.

"Um, I have no idea what this is or-or even how to handle it. I just um—I am just taking it all in I guess," She said eerily calm. This worrying her sister, "People are so mean Marian, they're criticizing my hair and my—my clothes, my face," she continued. Marian empathizing,

"Oh Nova, you can't focus on the crude things people are saying, I mean, my co-workers watched the video and they love it, so many people love what you were saying and a lot of women finding that you spoke things that were on their heart. If people get past the physical the video is really heartfelt," Marian said.

"There's an ugly photo of me, transformed into a meme that says, *the face you make when you're struggling to stay a HEAD of it all...*"

"Nova please don't depress yourself over something that could single-handedly be a great opportunity. There are people who spend years uploading videos on YouTube and never catch a break as big as this for themselves. I should be home in a few weeks, we should have lunch or-or dinner, whichever you prefer," Marian said smiling on the other line. Nova closing her eyes, tilting her head back to meditate, agreeing with her sister before ending their call. Still, she could not put into words the way she was feeling, only learning now that she was not going to sleep, her anxiety will not allow her to.

The next morning Nova awoke to her laptop, having barely slept, she secretly prayed no one would still be speaking about her. Her phone filled with messages, voicemails and her email piling up, things were happening too fast, she remained unprepared, feeling like she could no longer show her face now that the expectations of her were so high. Too worried to brush her teeth or get out of bed, Nova remained seated scrolling through social media platforms, trembling now as she found old high school photos of herself taken from Facebook making its way to other platforms, her *fans* wanting more. An online community developed with women and men conversing over her statements, picking them apart and now calling themselves, *Nova's Crowns.* Astonished by the fast development, Nova remained quiet, Tucker knocking on the door hoping his mother were awake so he may apologize.

Nova was not angry, only nonchalant, she could not fathom what was taking place, hoping that things would blow over, she would return to her regular, pathetic life and no one would notice. Opening the door for her son, she hugged him, with Tucker growing daily he was not much shorter than her now. His angelic voice speaking quickly, shuddering, trying to gauge how much trouble he was now in, but there was no need for a scolding. Nova knew as much.

That evening Nova met with Hunter who called numerous times to meet with her, ignoring the emails and requests she was getting from all over social media—Nova was feeling slightly overwhelmed. Their long stroll in the park magical, laughing, reminiscing and Nova feeling like her and Hunter could speak about literally anything. He was growing on her, romantically but she was afraid of this; afraid that one day she would have to allow herself to be vulnerable again and although today is not that day a part of her felt troubled.

"Hunter, I just want us to be on the same page about some things," she said to him as the sun began to set just behind them over the horizon. Their neighbors all returning home from work and the children racing inside to prepare for supper. Confused, Hunter stood patiently waiting on Nova to complete the thought, "Well, I'm not looking for anything serious or romantic right now—"

"You mean with me? You're not looking for anything serious or romantic with me?" he confirmed. His arms folded, occasionally swatting away the pesky insects. Nova drawing a long sigh nodding her head, no.

"I like you, just not to be romantically involved with you right now. I just don't want to feel any pressure for a relationship, you won't have any from me and vice-versa," she said hoping to clarify. Hunter did not understand as he was carefully planning a date night with Nova to which he did not disclose but only hoped to surprise her. However, he felt discouraged, thinking perhaps he should shy away from her until the time was right. Nova did not like hearing this, rather she felt selfish, thinking now to tell him what he wanted to hear if it meant keeping him in her life a tad bit longer. But Nova knew better, hugging him tightly they parted ways, Nova heading back to her residence whilst Hunter kept on walking, his hands now in his pocket kicking up the small rocks on the ground.

Inside their home, Nova could hear the conversation taking place in the kitchen, Alex, Ryan, and an unfamiliar voice, but she sounded pleasant enough. Walking to the rear, entering, Nova took a look around to see the woman sitting on the island stand, her hair long and her business suit heavily starched.

"You must be Nova," she said extending her right hand to greet Nova, the cookie crumbs from the snacks Alex was serving falling from her lapel. Reluctantly Nova reciprocated, taking a seat next to her, staring at Alex wondering who would provide her the insight she needed on who this woman is.

"Well, my name is Agatha Marshall and I work for a public relations firm not too far from here, actually your aunt and I are in the buildings adjacent to one another. So moving on, I caught wind of this special video online that you posted that seems to have the cyber community in a bit of a frenzy. I wanted to possibly get with you to discuss some options, your intentions and of course explain a bit more what I can do or offer you in this case," she said smiling, Alex and Ryan both deeply invested in their conversation, something about the way she spoke was making Nova frustrated.

"Auntie, can I speak to you for a moment?" Nova demanded stepping over into the laundry room not too far from them. Ryan and Agatha conversing,
"Nova, what is it?" Alex asked.
"Who is that lady and why is she here? Did you bring her here?" Nova questioned. Alex could not comprehend why Nova was behaving so incensed, she simply wanted to aid her in building and developing what she now believed to be an absolute gold mine. But it was not Alex or Agatha who were troubling Nova, it was Hunter, it was feeling like she had made the worst possible mistake for choosing not to remain selfish and now, she was feeling uneasy. Her lips pursed Alex could see her niece was in no mood for the formalities or conversation and so, she turned, thinking it best to ask Agatha to visit another day. Shortly, Nova grabbed a hold of her wrist, shaking her head, no, stepped past Alex returning to the kitchen where she and Agatha were left to further discuss their plans and Nova's future.

> Detangle: this is extra important for 4C
> girls because the tight curl pattern
> of your hair can cause hairs to curl
> and coil around each other,
> causing tangles.

2008

With only one more month until graduation and a very pregnant Nova dragging her feet to class, she was slowly beginning to worry that her water would break in Geometry or English, this feeling completely unpleasant. By now Nova was not speaking to anyone, feeling like a loner and a young girl with no experience, or love in the world, only that of Terry who she managed to convince herself would remain by her side through it all and why wouldn't she? Terry ensured to convince her as much.

Three times a week after school Nova waddled down to the gymnasium to find Terry playing basketball with his friends and classmates, honing in on his skills, ecstatic for graduation and now learning that he would be attending The University of

Connecticut where he would receive a full scholarship for playing the sport. Nova was proud of her husband now, feeling like he was no doubt going to conquer the world, but a part of her still felt incomplete, fearing she would go into labor earlier than anticipated and missing the chance to complete her exams or worse, not graduating. Speaking with counselors Nova was given the opportunity to test earlier than her peers and because she would most likely miss graduation day did not have to bear the cost of those expenses—for this Terry was glad. He could use that money to purchase things for the baby, but he himself would not dare miss graduation day. Not quite ready to make such a sacrifice as he was regarded Mr. Popularity and, in the yearbook, voted most likely to succeed.

Nova feeling overshadowed, overweight, and saddened only wished Terry would find more ways to be inclusive of her and not have her feeling eclipsed. Noticing that the only time he would do something to make her smile was when she complained, then his transient benevolent gestures would cease leaving her to feel the need to complain once again. After practice Terry made his way over to her, ball in hand, Nova and Terry still had not thought of a name for his son, knowing he was having a boy made Terry all the more confident when bragging to his friends.

"I think I have a good name," he said drenched in sweat, wiping his face using a towel he retrieved from his gym bag. Nova looking into his brown eyes, fascinated by his beauty, she was feeling horny.

"Can we just go home?" she asked him. Terry returning her lustful state, immediately obliged. Back home Terry fixed himself a sandwich. Nova as well before heading into the bedroom where he sat upright in the bed, watching her play games on a cellular phone taking small bites while chewing, Terry decided to touch back on his initial statement,

"Hey, I have a good name," he said.

"What is it?" Nova replied.

"Adam," Terry said. Nova turning her chin up in disgust, "That's a white name, something black please," she stated. Terry scoffed,

"Well, that's a racist thing to say," he said.

"No, but I mean you and I are both dark, he's going to be

dark, which means he'll be teased and the last thing we should do is name him something white because we think something black is to ghetto," she said. "Let's be realistic."

"I wish you wouldn't think like that; my friend is black and his name is Chase. So is Jeremy and Jack, they're all black, but don't you think those are white names?" he asked feeling a bit annoyed.

"Right, and aren't they expected to speak proper or—,"

"Nova be quiet, you're not making any sense and you sound super arrogant. I will think of a name, but it won't be too black or too white, hopefully it's just right," he said hoping to appease her. Terry knew a pregnant Nova had a short fuse and was always quite emotional. He only regarded her comments as a hormonal reaction, bringing him to finish his sandwich, removing the dish from her lap, placing it on the nightstand Terry kissing her gently. Nova enjoying this very much, her body reactive, in between her thighs now a soaking wet. Her large stomach making it hard for Terry to kiss her facing forward, so he took to his side, laying Nova too on hers, both climbing under the sheet, Terry inserting his penis into her vagina once Nova removed her panties and Terry forcing his boxers down his thighs.

One week later sitting in American Literature listening to her teacher speak about the Revolutionary Period Nova heard a loud gush hit the floor, her pants soaking wet, the students around her repulsed, moving their chairs and desks away from her swiftly. Their instructor turning to face her, a frightened look wiped across her face,

"Oh my God," she murmured. "Nova, don't panic sweetheart your water just broke that's all, this is good, means you're going into labor," her teacher said politely. Embarrassed, Nova remained seated, she could feel nothing, only looking down on her round stomach thinking of all the things her and Terry still needed but were waiting to buy when his paycheck came along now that he began working again. *This is bad*, she kept thinking while looking around on the faces of her peers. She hated that all eyes were on her and the whispers growing louder, their principal making his way inside to assist her. All she could think of were her grades, failing her classes or worst, not having a high school diploma. Although her exams were taken, she still needed to attend classes to pass them, but little did Nova know her teachers had no intention on failing her, she was attentive, cooperative and an *A*-plus student, also despite her pregnancy, hormones and fatigue she attended school every single day.

The principal walking Nova down the hall, her shoulders back, he instructed her to breathe, the assistant principal next to him, instructing him to go on to call the ambulance while she sits and tend to Nova just outside the principal's office. The hallways desolate, Nova wondered if anyone had called Terry,

"Mrs. Moore can you page Terry on the loudspeakers please?" she asked heavily breathing intermittently. Mrs. Moore nodding, advising Nova that Terry had been called and is on his way from class and that the ambulance would be arriving shortly. Holding her hand tightly, Nova felt a moment of relief and then it came, the sharpest, tightest, most painful cramp she had ever felt in her life, she wailed but this was not contractions as she was taught that those would not come so soon after her water breaking, a worried Nova turning to face Mrs. Moore, tears falling from her eyes. The ambulance now arriving, students, teachers and other administrators looking on from the inside of their classrooms while the EMT made their way inside.

At the hospital the process felt long and grueling, the doctors immediately finding Nova a room, Terry by her side, having driven behind the ambulance because he was in the restroom when being paged from the loudspeakers and could not hear his name called. Both the young parents were all too nervous, unsteady as the doctors spoke, advising Nova that the pain she felt earlier was not a contraction but a common labor symptom. She was advised her labor would begin within the next six to twelve hours and until then a watchful eye would be kept on her. Kissing her hands, Terry aided Nova in undressing, she was going to be a mother soon, her heart racing with inexplicable joy.

Twenty-two hours later Nova held a sleeping baby in her arms, turning her head to face Terry who remained hovering over them, Mrs. Higgins also present, she wondered what they would name the baby,

"What was daddy's middle name?" asked Terry, ashamed for having not known this himself. Mrs. Higgins replying,

"Oh, uh, Tucker." She said. Nova and Terry exchanging a look, agreeing silently, Terry smiled, looking down on his face, he said,

"Hey, baby Tucker." The room filled with happiness as the nurse entered, Mrs. Higgins asking if she may take a photo of her new little family. The nurse obliged. Nova, Tucker, Terry and Mrs. Higgins gathering together by Nova's bed, Tucker fast asleep,

"Smile," the nurse said and just like that a photo was taken, Mrs. Higgins eager to develop it, promising to place it conspicuously in her home.

18

Present day

Four days since going viral Nova was now sitting in a studio, a crew of unfamiliar faces surrounding her, well, all except for Donavan who decided to accompany her. Agatha working diligently to help Nova reach an even larger platform. The small studio in Los Angeles hills held lights, backdrops, camcorders, and two clothing racks requested by Agatha from clothing brands and business owners now looking to market their brand through Nova.

Agatha was working hard, having lost sleep for the past three days, she now had a focus and she loved having a focus, a larger platform for Nova meant a larger return on her investment. While Nova was instructed to try on the clothing sent to her by brand officials, videographers spent time preparing for her show: *Even My Hair Is Mad TV.* Simultaneously dragged, nipped and tucked, assistants and interns for Agatha were shoving tablets and phones in her face, asking for her insight and approval for logo designs, unaware of whether she could refuse Nova simply agreed, telling the assistants and interns, yes, although this remained untrue.

"I have no idea what this stuff means," she mouthed to

Donavan who was now standing across the room helping a photographer pull down an appropriate backdrop. Nova felt like she was being commercialized, but with no attorney present she wondered if she were making the right decisions by remaining there and so, she requested a moment. Shouting, that everyone stops working and allow her some time to process her thoughts—the room quiet. Donavan stepping over the backdrops making his way to her, trying to calm her,

"Hey, it's alright, you want to go get some fresh air?" he asked concerned. Nova obliged him, moving stiffly in the clothes she was given to wear, once outside she dialed Alex who answered almost immediately,

"Auntie, I have no idea what's going on here, I mean, how am I protected legally? Who are all of these people? And when you said Agatha was coming to pick me up you never mentioned that we would be doing all of this," Nova said, her tone distressed. Donavan standing beside her, watching her facial expressions.

"Nova, Agatha is a professional and all she's trying to do now is brand you. This is a photoshoot, to pretty much get some new pictures on the internet so people can stop reposting all of your high school stuff. Also, you have nothing to worry about, I am on this, I'm representing you and I have a very good reputation, no one is going to take advantage of you or your earnings," she said calmly.

"Earnings?" Nova questioned her.

"Yes, the clothes you're wearing that you're going to introduce to your community are from brands who are paying you,"

"What? It's only been a few days, how are people paying me? Where is this money coming from? Who are the brands? I literally know nothing and yet my face and my image is supposed to be plastered everywhere?" she asked.

"Nova, these things are taken care of, I just need you to trust me. I've drafted the pertinent documents and sent them over to these brands, I'm working now to have your channel name trademarked. I didn't mention the money you were paid because the truth is it—it all goes right back into the legal fees for now. Once these things are taken care of, you will begin receiving checks and then it's onward and upward. But listen I have to go; I have a meeting. But I love you and please just stay calm and try to cooperate," Alex said and then came the dial tone. Donavan looking to Nova wondering if she was going to disclose the information she received from Alex, but Nova was in no mood, shimmying back up the stairs there she stood, arms extended just like when she was a teenager getting her measurements taken and clothing adjusted.

Hours passed and Nova did not shoot anything, rather spent the morning getting tailored, shouting to and from Agatha across the room requesting her approval to which she mindlessly gave. She was feeling tired, overworking and irritated, her crown angry as she could feel her scalp beginning to itch. Donavan seeing the restlessness on her face asked Agatha who remained energetic, showing no signs of slowing down,

"Hey, do you know when she'll start?" Agatha ignoring him, recognizing only one star in the room,

"My dearest Nova in about twenty minutes we are going to begin your brand photoshoot and our creative director will be here shortly, he was running some errands and finishing up with another client of mine. Surely, I do apologize for the long wait, but this is the price of fame," she said.

Nova knitting her brows, "Tuh, fame, no one knows me and I am not going to lie to people," she snarled. "I mean, I've checked my phone and in the past hour alone my commentators have been responded to and none of those responses are genuinely from me."

"My dear, in this life, this new world you're entering sadly you won't have the time to tend to the general public and the truth is, they don't care. They just want the content; they want the work you're producing. Having a relationship with you is not on the top of their to-do list. Maybe one day if you want to feed the pets a bit of your time then you may, but that's what we have the assistants and the interns for. They love doing it anyway," she said bellowing for a press release to an Ebony Magazine editor. Nova feeling chipper, shot Donavan a look, mocking Agatha,

"Okay it's showtime! Nova, please head over to the backdrop," Agatha said startling both Donavan and Nova. Nova wearing a knee-length dress made from sequins and a pair of heels from two fashion houses stationed in Los Angeles. Her makeup flawless and her hair uncombed as Nova would not allow anyone to touch it, she retired to the restroom where she began moisturizing and stretching her tight coils using water and a leave-in conditioner, she so heavily favored. Returning to the set twenty minutes later she was ready, Nova was feeling confident, stepping onto the beige backdrop, a man wearing an all-white suit entered inside, barging almost—Marcus Mann is his name and with little to no hesitation had a quick word with Agatha before heading over to Nova. Flamboyant and observant, Marcus whispering to the interns who quickly ran to Nova plucking loose threads from her clothes, re-sewing pieces of sequins which had fallen and another gentleman removing a piece of lint from the backdrop ensuring it was immaculate. Nova was impressed in only a matter of minutes after taking one look at the space around her, Marcus spotting the imperfections.

"I do not like it," he whispered to Agatha. "This is too commercialized." Walking over to Nova, Marcus extending his hand, asking, "Is this you? As in, is this what you want?" He smelled blissful and Nova feeling grateful that someone finally asked her, *what does she want?* With their hands interlocked Nova looking into his eyes, remained truthful,

"I have no clue what I want because I have no clue of what's happening," she said innocently. The laugh lines on his face palpable, Mr. Mann in his late forties, reminded Nova of her father, instantly making him intimidating to her.

"What is your story?" he then asked, his hands still firmly wrapped around hers. Looking to him Nova admitted,

"To grow my hair and show people how I do it. I only meant to introduce myself to whoever would listen just to provide a back story, but-but I'm just a girl who got her heartbroken and shaved her head, but I'm no relationship expert or revolutionist," she admitted. Marcus shaking his head in understanding, smiling as he turned to Agatha releasing his grip of Nova's hand.

"Did you hear this woman? Huh, she wants to grow her hair and now she has a following, why are there clothes here and no hair products for her to brand? Why are we shooting with a large beige, boring backdrop and her dress is red? Huh, why are we selling her to the designers and not to the hair product makers? I need answers Agatha; did you speak to this young lady? She is not your clothing guide; she is your product guide."

"This is fathomable and of course we will get to that, but she went viral for ranting about a man not ranting about her hair crème. We have to continue to give the people what they want and right now, they want a woman who they can relate to, a woman who looks like an expert in the field, carries herself as such and perhaps one day we can transition into product branding, but for now with thousands of dollars now riding on her, she has to push the clothing. I did not bring you here for your opinion on her brand Marcus, you do your job and let me do mine," she said audaciously.

Grabbing his coat Marcus handed Nova his business card, "When you are ready to brand your hair crème you come and find me," he smiled before boldly taking his leave. An annoyed Agatha clapping her hands, shouted,

"Okay please let's get to work!" Agatha, deciding to take control of the creative process, Nova took photos after photos, trading in one look for another, her business professional attire flawless. Skimming through the photos Nova was elated, seeing Agatha's vision for her come to life, she was branding her as a professional. Nova taking for the first time an appropriate headshot, her logo etched to the bottom digitally. She was now having the time of her life as the radio blared, the night air blew inside and Donavan continued patiently waiting for her to wrap up. A thirteen-hour day producing clothes, photos and logo design while assistants responded to Nova's fans was well worth it as she now felt like she was getting the hang of things.

Exchanging air kisses with Nova and her staff when the night wrapped up Agatha remained behind with the photographer editing photos for Nova's new Instagram account, and cards for YouTube promoting the clothing she was seen modeling today. Donavan outside waiting patiently, in front of the high rise building he was there to greet her,

"Well superstar, can a poor man like me take you out for dinner?" he asked playfully. Walking down the bustling city streets, Nova taking his arm, wrapping it around her shoulders both walking side by side their steps in unison, a happy Nova kissing him passionately on the lips.

Outside, Donavan walked Nova up to the front steps of her home. The time 10:16 p.m. and although Nova was exhausted a part of her did not want Donavan to leave. She remained hugging him, her arms outstretched, her eyes closed taking in the sweet smell of his cologne. Dinner was pleasant and for him Nova was thankful. Across the street Hunter removing the garbage from his house, spotting them, just under the shimmering light in front of the large house. Licking his lips, he lowered his eyes—feeling warped with envy.

Moments later Nova allowed Donavan to head home, inside the house was quiet, with Tucker spending time with Mrs. Higgins and Alex and Ryan tucked away in her bedroom, Nova made her way into the kitchen pouring herself a tall glass of Minute Maid fruit punch. Alex startling her,

"Hey there kiddo," Nova jumping in fear,

"Jesus," she said placing her hand on her chest, over her heart, "You scared me," she smiled. Unable to conceal her happiness.

"I wonder who has you glowing, your makeup looks amazing by the way," Alex said, resting her arms on the kitchen island grabbing an apple to eat.

"Auntie, I had an amazing time, oh and there was this guy named Marcus Mann, he's so awesome and kicks ass, he was like, '*what do you want?*' you know all firm and manly and stuff," Nova laughed, mocking him. Alex had not seen her this happy in a long time, she took pleasure in seeing her smile.

"You're very beautiful," Alex said doting at her.

"Thank you, so are you," Nova said laughing. She could not stop; she was feeling rather hyper and giddy.

"So I have some good news and greater news, the good news is, we have wire transfers from brands now sitting in an escrow account for you, not much, um, we're just starting so obviously that's going to take time to grow. But for now, um, it's about four thousand dollars," she said. Nova's eyes widening.

"Wait what? For what? Four grand for what?" she asked nervously.

"Those racks of clothes you saw in that studio today. Now the money is sitting there and that's not money that is going to be paid out to you right now. I have to get a financial advisor to help manage things and divvy out the proceeds, but just think in four days, you've potentially just made almost two thousand dollars." Nova still could not comprehend, a look of shock on her face,

"Wait what!" she said placing her hand on her head.

"Nova you are what most people would call an overnight success, it's not impossible, it happens. I just knew once that video went viral, I had to get the best and so I did, Agatha is that," Alex told her,

"But how am I paying them, how-how am I paying you?" she stammered.

"Don't worry about the public relations firm, I've paid that—"

"No, how much was it? Oh my God, you've already done so much. I could have done without all of this, I mean I don't have two nickels to rub together and if I knew this was going to be such an investment, I would not have asked for any of this, I mean technically I didn't. What if we just stopped uploading videos? I mean surely the buzz would die and—and we could go back to our normal lives, you know," Nova speaking quickly, feeling all too panicky.

"Hey! We are not going backward, the money is of no issue to me, you are my niece and we will see this through. What is for you, is for you and I will see to it that you get what is yours. I am happy for you and I will spend whatever money I have to, to see this monumental time of your life come to fruition," Alex said, Nova now drenched in tears,

"I used to hate you," she said laughing as she now sobbed.

"I know," Alex chuckled, making her way over to her, hugging her as tight as she could muster, "Oh and Ryan and I are trying to have a baby," she then smiled pushing away Nova, her hands gripped firmly on her shoulders. Nova leaping into the air,

"Yay! That is so awesome, you're going to love the smell of babies," she said continuing to hug Alex. Their night peaceful and filled with an immense amount of delight.

In her bedroom Nova could not sleep, again, another

sleepless night she remain awake, refreshing and scrolling through her YouTube channel, an email forwarded to her from Agatha by two in the morning advising of her new social media accounts all of which were heavily filled with content; behind the scenes videos very well put together, call to actions listed for her channel inviting others to subscribe and surprisingly so, many people did. Nova itching to reply to commentators, wondering if it would be a good idea as she now liked the idea of conversing with fans, but she immediately decided against it, fearing she would say the wrong thing undoing all of the hard work Agatha was putting in.

A fresh Instagram profile now showing over three-hundred followers and her photos impeccable. A part of Nova in disbelief that it was in fact her, the natural make up on her face looking all too smooth, but she could not help herself she wanted to knit pick her face, her hands, her feet, her nails, and her neck not matching the color of the rest of her skin.

Praying no one would notice she searched the comments, although few, they were polite, she continued refreshing. Her phone dings, it was Donavan calling, he and Nova speaking until finally, she closed her eyes, fading off into a deep slumber.

Tangles lead to breakage, which hinders growth.
Detangle regularly and gently,
using a wide-toothed comb on
damp hair (do not use a brush!)

The next morning Nova slept in, feeling too weak to get out of bed until the voice of Marian made its way to her ears. But before heading down the stairs she sat upright checking her social media channels, shrieking in excitement over the men and woman who were speaking so highly of her and the wonderful compliments she was receiving. Nova could not believe her eyes, finding it all to be astonishing. She stood, racing out of the bed wearing her cotton pajamas, finding her way downstairs where Marian was now in the foyer removing her light coat. Ecstatic, Nova leaped into the arms, the sisters falling to the floor.

The unprecedented joy she felt seeing her sister now for

the first time in months could not be explained. Nova feeling liberated, Marian having lost an abundance of weight, her hair longer, her face slimmer and her skin simply flawless. The braided mohawk she wore carrying a Louis Vuitton handbag wearing a pair of red bottom heels she looked fashionable and well-rested.

"My sister is famous!" she teased. Her bangles dangling, in the kitchen she removed a bottle of juice pouring herself a glass, Alex gone to run errands leaving the women alone in the house. Nova walking Marian into the living room where she explained all of the wonderful things that were now taking place, her first photoshoot to the origin of the video. Marian growing concerned that Terry was seeking full custody, but Nova did not want to focus her attention there, deciding it best to focus on the positive things that were happening and thinking now that with her new income there was no way a judge would seek to take Tucker away from her—he was happy with her after all.

Listening to how confident she remained Marian decided to digress, trusting her sister had the situation under control,

"So, tell me about you! How is the fashion stuff going?" Nova asked.

"It's going so amazingly well, but I mean I have had a few hiccups you know trying to get some backing for one of my ideas—The Dolls." Just then the front door opened, it was Alex returning with groceries and bags from boutiques. "Hola auntie!" Marian called to her, never moving from her seat. Alex unaware of Marian's arrival she greeted her before heading into the kitchen, a displeased look on her face. Alex was angry because when no one could reach Nova, they were contacting her, the ubiquitous questions from every member of Nova's team now growing frustrated that the twenty-four-year-old girl remained unresponsive. While Nova and Marian remained in the living room, Nova's phone dinged, messages, voicemails and conversations all happening without her present in a group chat she created with Agatha and one of her assistants. Having little to no time to rest, Agatha and her team were looking for the next content, the next story, the next video but this is all unbeknownst to Nova who was simply enjoying the moment by speaking highly of it.

But Nova simply wanted to enjoy her sisters' company, take a moment to bask in her new success, but with Alex now on the move there was no time to become complacent.

"Nova, can you call Agatha, she's been calling and texting me all morning?" Alex asked, annoyed. Alex only learning earlier that day that she had not yet conceived and although Nova was not the source for her frustrations, she was in no mood to be bothered or communicative. Nova standing, excusing herself from Marian's presence, walking upstairs, removing her phone which now happened to be ringing. It was Agatha speaking hurriedly explaining that she had only three hours to produce new content to submit to an editor. A shocked Nova could not believe her ears,

"Three hours?" she said.

"Yes, I have been calling all morning, had you answered then, maybe you would have had more time," the woman said, hanging up the phone. Nova standing in the middle of her bedroom contemplating what to do next. She so desperately wanted to spend time with her sister, but now she was in demand. Just then a text came to her phone; it was Hunter kindly reminding her to take her permit test; the road test is coming up shortly. This making Nova happy.

19

Week two and Nova was slowly coming into her own, her
headline, logo and story all promising viewers new content
weekly, and with her relationship going well, Nova began
feeling reluctant speaking so condescendingly about men and
her betrayal. The thought of reverting back to such a painful
time in her life making it almost hard for her to move on.
Tucker sensing her discomfort eventually grew tired of being
taken to his grandmother's house every weekend making him
restless. Any free time Nova had now was spent sleeping,
resting or engaging with her fans on social media.

Agatha keeping her word and value managed to book Nova
for three upcoming talk shows, but this was staggering to Nova
as she still did not receive any check or monies leading her to
question Alex's true intentions but never vocalizing it. She was
overworked in such a short period of time and felt by now she
should be compensated, even a portion of what she had
earned—but nothing. Taking a long sigh, she arose from bed on
a Friday, Tucker having left with Alex to be taken to his
grandmother, Nova needed to record, edit and upload yet
another video, feeling like the days were passing her by; a full-
time mother, managing social media, taking calls and answering

interview questions by way of email while cleaning, cooking and trying to keep her sanity was proving itself difficult. This was not the life Nova intended for herself or her son.

Tucker feeling neglected, she could hear it in his voice and see it in his eyes when he would arrive home from school asking his mother to assist him with homework only for her to very politely decline, turning him away citing how busy she was.

The house quiet Nova turned on the camcorder, voicing yet another one of her opinions on relationships, feeling like she was losing the core focus of her channel, the reason she wanted to begin video blogging in the first place—her crown. Rubbing her hands in her hair she stood, taking the camcorder with her deciding today would be wash day, she had nothing left to say about relationships, the topic truly proving itself to be mundane for her now. Nova sat, speaking into the lens,

"Hello crowns and thanks for tuning in this week. Today I want to discuss my natural hair routine, now I know some of you may be wondering, why are we talking about hair, where's the man slander? But truth be told, I have a lot more that I would like to share and besides, no matter what we say about our brothers loving Becky's will they ever truly change? The answer is no, so, let's get started," And just like that she began another taping. Heading into the shower Nova did not undress, rather massaging into her scalp a rich lather of shampoo, the water and suds dripping down her back as she closed her eyes, standing under the silver pipe, the water pressure heavy, minutes later her arms grew weary and after two shampoos and a conditioner she was out. Face dripping, clothes soaking wet she remained standing atop a towel she had tossed on the floor prior to stepping in the bathtub.

Rubbing her short hair strands Nova worked into her scalp a gentle scalp mask, placing a plastic shower cap over it, providing a step by step routine. With little hair to manage, she hadn't much else to do, leaving her to take a seat while the conditioner worked its way into her hair, and at this time for the next fifteen minutes decided to answer some of the commenters' questions—much of which spoke to her past relationship. Although nervous, Nova handled herself with poise, learning that the more she spoke about Terry, the easier it was becoming for her to come to grips with their marriage ending. Thinking of it, she was beginning to wonder when their divorce would be finalized, believing herself to be awful as she was feeling that she was still in fact a married woman, but dating Donavan and having slept with Charles. Temporarily Nova felt tainted as she vowed never to practice the act of infidelity but quickly, she resumed. Some of the questions bringing her to chuckle, astonished by how fast many of the subscribers felt closer to her, liking her and speaking to her as though they had been all been friends for years.; many of the women transparent, speaking to their own relationship dysfunctions and pitfalls, making Nova grateful that things were not worse.

Fifteen minutes later Nova returned to the shower where she rinsed her hair with lukewarm water, making mention of this in her video as well, afterward moisturizing and styling as usual. Moments later Nova returning the camera to the tripod, took a seat on her bed where she nervously gave a final speech to her crowns. Still finding this moment to be unbelievable— fans, she had fans. People who cared enough about the things she had to say and do, she was beginning to find her confidence again, smiling as she walked over to the recorder shutting down the light.

With Donavan by her side, Nova was now regaining her vitality, heading to events, meeting new people and mingling across town. After only three weeks, Nova gained over seven hundred new subscribers, and her social media following tripled. Agatha, although despising the fact that Nova wanted to speak primarily to hair care encouraged her to broaden her range, speaking both to hair and relationships, speaking to her brand of a man causing her so much stress that she inevitably needed to cut off her hair due to it falling out—which for Nova was completely accurate. But selfishly, she only wanted to now focus on the positive things going on in her life, never having to revert back to such a traumatic time. While she gained her self-confidence, her channel gained subscribers and her social media grew, Nova now only had one question,

"Why am I not being paid?" she wondered standing amidst a crowd of fellow YouTubers. Much of whom ignoring her, not yet thinking of her as one of their own, an insider if you will, she remained in isolation, off in the corner sipping champagne in the hotel ballroom. The night sky tranquil, her eyes darting, looking around for Donavan to make his appearance inviting him to join her as she did not want to attend the event alone. A star-struck Nova looking around the room watching the men and women who she drew inspiration—everyone so lavishly draped. Turning around Nova took notice of the sponsors and fashion powerhouses responsible for buying tables for their staff members and endorsed insiders. Locating the Dash Signature plum table cloth sent her heart racing. Shifting her eyes, a firm hand gripping her waist from behind,

"Sorry I'm late," he said, leaning down to kiss her. Donavan looking dangerously handsome and smelling of exquisite cologne, Nova could do nothing but smile, kissing him, promising him her love by the end of the night. Momentarily her mind forgetting about the sponsor table for her father, dreading she may see him, but knowing him as well as she thought she did, Nova only assumed such an event would be far too below his consequential status. The Grand Ballroom filled with over two hundred guests, mingling in their finest, Nova coming face to face with transgender men and women, Gay and Lesbian couples, the influencers she only heard of, media reporters, bloggers, and journalists all within the industry. She wondered how Agatha managed to get her an invite as she was not yet too well known—well not as much as everyone else anyway. Before the night was over Agatha and her assistants began making their appearance. Unbeknownst to Nova everyone and their publicist were there, managers and agents, escorting everyone along so the media would be given a chance to interview them all. Once her turn came around Nova remained still, the padded microphone shoved to her face, the Indian-American woman speaking quickly asking Nova a series of questions to which she could not respond. The loud conversations going on around her, distracting, Agatha pulling her along, making room for the next YouTuber,

"Nova you have to answer the questions you're asked, these people are going to be writing journals about you," Agatha snarled. But Nova could not concentrate, feeling nauseated, overwhelmed by the crowd, the expectations and the demands set forth—she hurled. The loud splatter heard over the blaring speakers, the flashing lights sparking attention her way, the huge gasps heard across the room bringing her to quiver. Agatha, realizing it was now time to do damage control, grabbing a hold of the microphone from one of the journalists she screamed, "What on earth did they put in the food?" The sound of Agatha's voice resonating throughout the hall; simultaneously everyone dropping their hors d'oeuvres, the waiters and waitresses outraged but such an assertion. Shortly, aiding Nova to stand straight, Donavan whisking her away outdoors allowing for the California breeze to blow gently across her face; Nova breathing heavily, her mind filled with regret and thoughts she ceases to control. Standing adjacent to her, Agatha stood with her arms folded and her back turned, dialing her communications department hoping they can diffuse the story before hitting major news outlets.

"She's new, people do not know her yet, this can't be the first thing they read," she quarreled. Nova standing, taking a long look at her, secretly hoping there was nothing that could have been done. This is not the career path she wanted for herself or her son, she just wanted to go home. But suddenly, Agatha turned to face her, a devilish smile stringed along her face, "I swear this girl is destined to be a star," she said to her assistant on the opposite line—Nova and Donavan both looking on, their eyebrows knit and their palms sweating, anxiously awaiting her response. "Kid, you're going to New York," she said.

Nova now terrified, feeling her legs begin to quiver, their moment of exchange awkward, she could not fathom the thought of going to New York, just then an image of Terry flashed through her mind, she was now beginning to miss him, thinking of him sentimentally while staring in to Donavan's eyes, she walks away. The heels from her shoes, bringing her feet to hurt, Agatha taking no notice to her discomfort, grinning like that of a malevolent mastermind.

"You leave in a week Nova! It's for a feature," she shouted to her as Nova made her way down the beige stairs, looking up to Donavan signaling for him to take her home. Nervously he bid Agatha a farewell. Their ride home silent—Nova taking in the view of the ocean they passed along the bridge heading back to the hills. Donavan beginning to feel uncertain of their relationship, asking her,

"Do you still miss him?" Nova turning to face him, worried that she did, but unable to bring herself to speak the truth and so, she lied,

"No." But Donavan is no fool as her reaction only told him otherwise. Nova and Terry had not spoken for some time, blocking him from that day in the park and asking only that he communicates with Tucker through his mother whenever Tucker was with her. An arrangement Nova made with Mrs. Higgins, confident she would pass along the message and from then on, Nova and Terry remained only distant strangers. Arriving home Donavan turning into the driveway, seeing Hunter seated on the step just outside under the darkness. Donavan and Nova exchanging a bewildered look, but Nova did not want any friction, asking politely that Donavan leave her to have a moment alone with Hunter to which he obliged. Feeling rather territorial Donavan leaned in, kissing Nova gently on the lips before unlocking the automatic doors granting her the ability to leave.

Lifting the gown from the pavement as it dragged slightly, the smell of puke making its way to her nostrils disgusting her, she took a deep breath making her way towards Hunter, who in all his days have never looked more tragic.

"Sorry to have just popped up like this," he said bashfully, his hands planted firmly in his front pant pockets, "Just wanted to tell you congratulations on all your success, you uh, definitely deserve it. I'm um, I'm moving, the truck comes in the morning," he said solemnly. Nova could not believe her ears, gasping frightfully, releasing her dress; she extends her arms, hugging him around the neck tightly,

"Oh my God, why?" she questioned, refusing to let him go. Nova was feeling confused, unable to label her emotions. Hunter did not reciprocate, only pushing her away by the torso, looking into her eyes, he said,

"Mom is pretty sick and I uh, I have some loose ends back home I need to tie up," he admitted. Nova fighting tears, her eyes beginning to well, she remained standing, Donavan parked under a tree not too far away, the black car camouflaged by the darkness. In that moment Nova knew, she was falling in love with a man but only afraid he was too perfect, so perfect in fact that she would once again be blindsided and in all her efforts to remain calm, she failed. Weeping.

"I don't know what to say," she said. Hunter grabbing her by the shoulders, kissing her softly on the forehead before walking away, Nova left standing, her dress flowing freely behind her, watching him walk away, his muscles protruded and before she could step inside, she heard her name called,

"Nova," it was Alex making her way across the lawn from Ryan's house, wearing a blouse and a pair of pants, "How did it go?" she questioned looking back at Hunter making his way home and then to Nova, whose tears were now coming into view. Alex wrapping her arm around her shoulder as they walked inside. However, Nova was in no mood to converse with Alex, she was far too angry with her, believing Alex to be withholding information, money and much more from an oblivious and naïve Nova.

"Hey, are you alright?" Alex asked sensing the tension. Nova stomping her way up the stairs, slamming the bedroom door behind her—inside of her room, she undressed, looking into her closet ripping clothes from hangers and tossing shoes into a black garbage bag she retrieved from the bottom of the bathroom sink. Overhearing the rattling Alex racing up the stairs, lifting the door handle, she entered inside. "Hey!" she screamed. An unresponsive Nova, appeared to be packing, "Nova, what the fuck is wrong with you?" Alex asked again, this time her voice elevated.

"You're robbing me!" Shouted Nova. Alex quickly stopping her, placing her hands above the bag as her eyes filled with water,

"Nova I would never ever, do anything like that to you, I swear. I literally have the money sitting in escrow, I am waiting for you to have a moment of free time so we can go and open a personal bank account for you. I mean, geez, how can you even think that of me?" Alex questioned. Nova thinking twice now, standing, looking in her eyes, wondering if she were overreacting, she had no idea where she was even headed, in her bra and panties, she dropped to the floor, her legs crossed,

"Auntie, this isn't the life for me, I feel like it's too much," she cried. Alex taking a seat by the edge of the bed, rubbing her head in dismay,

"I know Nova, it all just happened so quickly, so this is understandable, your fears, your anxiety, I get it. Would you like us to find you a therapist?" Alex asked with concern.

"No, I'm not going crazy I just—I just need some guidance. Agatha is all about results, videos, social media and never once does she ask if I'm tired or need a glass of water. It's logos, making the people happy, finding a cross between my videos and I know she hates the hair care routines I upload; I mean hates them. She doesn't believe in me, right now she's just milking me for what she can get," Nova sighed.

"Agatha will not be around long, it's just for right now, she's literally the best in the business and I knew once the video went viral, we would need only the best. She has an amazing track record, her clients almost always reach mainstream status, but Nova, nothing is more important to me than your safety and mental health and that of Tucker's. So, if you want to stop, then we can stop," Alex said reassuring her.

"Everything is just happening so fast; can I sleep on it?" she asked. Alex nodded. Nova feeling it best not to disclose her true feelings, thinking she would be seen as feeble with all things considered and Alex remained adamant that Nova should, in fact, be over Terry and accepting of his decision to leave. The fame was not the issue, the rise of her career, never an issue either, what Nova feared most now more than ever is looking foolish in the media in front of her estranged husband because she still cared about what he would think of her. Knowing this is why she can never be with Hunter; it simply would not be fair to him. Hours later dozing off to sleep Nova dreamt of a more pleasing affair, the one where she is introducing her sister's show to the world at Fashion Week, only this time she excels, the exaggerated round of applause bring a smile across her face, her eyes closed.

Deed Condition: 4C hair thrives
with weekly deep conditioning treatments.

Hunter scheduled Nova's road test weeks in advance and today is the big day, asking Alex to bring her down to the road-testing site, she arrived on time ready to go. In only a few minutes Nova passed her test making her now a licensed driver and she had no one else to thank but Hunter himself. But arriving back home, she noticed the curtains missing from his window and the car from the driveway absent, "*he's really gone*," she said thinking to herself. Alex ran inside retrieving some documents, advising Nova to remain outside, excited she made her way into the driver's seat, a terrified Alex settling into the passenger's seat upon her return,

"I need practice," Nova grinned. But Alex was feeling anything but pleasant, "You mess up my car then you really won't see a dime of your money. Let's go," she demanded. Nova taking her time, inching her way down the steep hill onto the main road, the ladies off to the bank where Nova would open her very first checking account depositing into it, a little over six thousand dollars.

Donavan did not contact Nova but she remained too busy to notice, excited now that she was making a living with her channel and although the money was no longer coming in, Nova had many obligations to fulfill and until then was not taking any more work. Brand market officials requiring her attendance for photoshoots, meetings with Agatha and her team to further outline the direction Nova and her channel would take. Nova now finally responding to commentators, leaving her phone in her hand constantly throughout the day, she was slowly losing focus of the extrinsic matters. With Alex and Ryan ensuring that Tucker make it to school and assisting him in the evenings along with Cassidy with their homework, left Nova more time to devote into her dialogue. In addition, Nova was learning, teaching herself the ins and outs of editing, product placement, marketing, and public relations and reaching out to product brands requesting placement onto their public relations list—many of which obliged.

Agatha was displeased, despising the fact that Nova was beginning to take matters into her own hands, but Nova did not fancy the conversations about relationships, she was no expert and hated having to remind Agatha of such on what felt like a daily basis. Alex withdrawing herself, only inserting when needed for legal matters in which case, Nova was thankful, feeling now for once she was given complete creative control over her channel and now her destiny. With Halloween nearing Nova was contemplating a Halloween themed video, with over twelve videos now successfully uploaded, eighteen thousand subscribers and over two hundred thousand video views for her feature and her viral video nearing one million she was well on her way. Commentators often times stopping by and with the transition from relationship to hair Nova feared she would lose many new fans, however the opposite occurred, women were pouring in, referring her channels and loving the journey she was taking them on as her hair now continued to grow. With over four inches added in six weeks, Nova was now able to brush her hair into a small afro, it was thick, healthy and jet black! Nova often times massaging her new growth while reading through articles online and gaining additional insight to the community.

Nova and Tucker were now growing distant; her bedroom filled with gifts from brands, new products for her to try and some she tried and hated having to often waste what remained. Nova was honest and her crown's loved it, brutally honest because she did not like the fact that many companies were offering her money to lie, some sending over half-filled products of placebos leaving her angry if not disappointed in them as business owners; Nova did not hold back, voicing it all, growing comfortable day by day and now on platforms such as Instagram Nova was received payments for advertisements starting at almost five hundred dollars per post. Residing with Alex she did not want nor need for anything allowing her to save drastically, and now Nova was closer than ever before to earning almost twenty thousand dollars in such a short period of time, the kind of money she only one day dreamed of having.

Nova so desperately wanting Agatha gone, finding her to be curt, at times verbally aggressive and condescending—she dialed Mr. Mann. Retaining his card for all this time Nova could think of no one else who could possibly respect her craft as much as he did, or even come close to appreciating it. Elated to hear her voice, he requested her presence for lunch to which Nova happily said yes. But Tucker was ready to work on his Halloween costume, Nova having promised him weeks ago, excited he made his way upstairs, watching by the door threshold Nova hurriedly ready herself.

"Mom, where are you going?" he asked angrily.

"Oh Tuck, mommy has a quick meeting, but I promise I will be back soon," she said squabbling around, whispering to herself places where her accessories could be hidden.

"But you promised," he whined. Nova ignoring him, finding herself growing impatient with his pestering,

"Tuck sweetie, please go find auntie and ask her to help you," she demanded. "I will be home in a few hours whatever you guys don't finish, I will help you with," Nova said, adding to her wrist her last bangle, her earrings now intact, her hair moisturized and her hands rubbing the top of his head before heading out of the room, down the stairs and out of the front door. Tucker remained standing, dropping to the floor his Superman costume and fabric for the cape he wanted handmade—a look of sadness wiped across his face.

Use conditioners to add slip
and help with the process.
When you find knots—don't yank—
use your fingers to gently pull
the hairs out of the knot.

Arriving at The Opal by way of taxi Nova could not help but bask in the California sunshine, waiting outside of the Tapas Bar for Mr. Mann to arrive she paced, kicking up light dirt with the front of her shoe. She decided against getting a table beginning to feel apprehensive that he would show up, but he did, wearing an all-white jumpsuit with a pair of beige Louis Vuitton five-inch heels, sunglasses decorating his face and over his shoulders a light trench. Elated to see him Nova gleaming with joy, Mr. Mann walking to her, his manicured nails pressed along her shoulders, air-kissing both her right and left cheek,

"Table?" he questioned but Nova remained awestruck,

"No," she said timidly. Raising his hand for one of the waiters who scurried over, Nova and Mr. Mann were seated only seconds later; their table nearest the water fountain, just under a large umbrella for shade. Setting his trench to the rear of his chair while the waiter filled their glasses, Mr. Mann wasted no time,

"You look quite famished," he said, his tone judgmental. Nova having no idea how to approach him, she only nodded her head in agreement, her legs trembling, "I've been watching your videos and um, what are you hoping to change?" he asked, Nova now taking a closer look at the lipstick he wore, his face clear of blemishes, he turned, crossing his legs, sunglasses still decorating his face, Nova staring at her reflection, thinking of a response that would make her sound somewhat intelligent,

"Um, I'm not sure I want to change anything, only grow I suppose—"

"Hmm," he said, the look in his eyes cynical, "You were lucky. A little young girl, with no knowledge, no style, no ambition merely screams at her little camera and overnight a plethora of people came knocking at your digital door, and here you sit in front of me, in front of the world, uncaring, nonchalant, not hungry, just complacent with what? With your nothing," he asked aggressively. "There are thousands of people who wish they could have the success you have, who work their asses off daily, invest money they will potentially never see again all on a dream and here you are ungrateful of all which you've acquired. You do not want change, then why am I here?" he asked.

Nervously she responded, the contents from the glass she held in her hand spilling from her minor trembling. "I—I um, I don't' know, I mean, I didn't ask for any of this. I am trying my best to fit in and attend the events I am told to, mingle, take pictures, but-but this isn't me. I am not meant for fame," she admitted.

"No one is not meant for fame and now you have it, so get with the program, because now that you have it the world is going to be scrutinizing you, the world is going to make you their bitch, but before they can do that, get something, milk the industry for the billions it has to offer, make a life for you and your kid and stop sitting here looking so shy and disastrous," he said, his tone scathing. Nova sitting up straight, her eyes widened, her lips pursed, taking it all in. Nova asked questions upon questions about the next move she should take. Mr. Mann happily agreeing to mentor her through the process, advising it best she does not fire her publicist given her extensive background and connections, she remains an asset to Nova. However apprehensive of Agatha, Nova did believe Mr. Mann and with an afternoon of conversation, learning and the knowledge bestowed upon her; he revealed a shocking truth,

"Personally, I hate your videos," he said, scooping a spoon full of the mock meat and brown rice he requested for his meal. By the late afternoon, Nova was engrossed in her new growing brand, learning new tactics to appeal to her audience, therefore broadening her outlook. The next day with her earnings Nova invested in better equipment, calling on Mr. Mann to assist, to which he happily agreed. Mr. Mann is a fan of tall heels although puzzling to Nova how he manages to walk so well in them.

Mr. Mann was stringent, advising Nova not to be frugal; she was, after all, investing in her career and the betterment of it. Listening, Nova now had a great deal of high-end equipment to work with from home, distracting her and working late at night she thought if a theme. Nova organized products and after reading through an abundance of blogs came to the conclusion that she too would seek to release a natural hair product, which was not far-fetched considering she now had a platform and people were eager to hear from her and interested in the things she began to promote.

The next morning Nova overslept, her alarm clock blaring, the room she occupied contained little to no space for movement. Caught between the bed and the nightstand Nova meticulously climbing down from her mattress landing her feet firmly on the plush carpets granting her legs and back a transient feeling of relief. The clock now reading 11:14 a.m. a thud came to greet her on the front of the door. Nova now brushing her teeth, curious to see who it was. The toothbrush settled to one side of her mouth, causing her left cheek to protrude, unclicking the lock on the door, Nova watched a panicked Alex on the other side, stark raving mad,

"You missed the court hearing!" she screamed. Nova remained stoic, unable to make out what her aunt was saying through the yelling, her words only slightly audible. But Nova is beginning to feel dizzy, lacking sleep and now mildly swaying, "Terry called me and said they've dismissed your case and now

Tucker needs to be packed by the end of the week. Nova!" Alex shouted again, snapping her fingers, watching as Nova now fall into a trance, incapable of moving, she was numb. "Nova I know you don't know what this means, but it means the court heard the case and they did not rule in your favor. I think in lieu of all of this stuff you have going on, he deemed you too busy and unfit to care for Tucker, not showing up only strengthen his claim. Get dressed and stop standing there looking lost, we have to get down to the courthouse and I need to find you a family attorney. Fuck!" Alex shouted as she walked away.

Alex disappearing downstairs Nova closed the door, removing the toothbrush from her mouth, rinsing and cleaning her face, calmly she maneuvered through the unopened boxes and equipment, walking over to her bed, she lie down, closing her eyes, bringing her knees to her chest, sobbing silently.

20

Forever indebted is how she felt—two days later Alex retained the best family attorney in the city, a close friend to Ryan, Nova relieved to learn she may very well still have a fighting chance of getting Tucker returned to her with the filing and approval for a modification petition. In the meantime, however, Tucker would soon seek to relocate to his father, leaving Nova without him and she could not be more distraught of the news outwardly. But her actions showing otherwise—thinking Nova would begin to slow down and hold herself accountable for such a frivolous mistake, Alex became appalled to learn she did no such thing. Almost cringing to witness, Nova remaining optimistic but elated that she now had to solely focus on her work.

With only a few days to prepare for a press run in New York City, Nova was not taking the news of traveling to the big city well. She was growing nauseous; spending more time hovered over the toilet vomiting from fear and nervousness. Unblocking Terry to arrange for Tucker's pickup was brief, discussing only the relevant details of her travels, for traveling with Tucker she knew the evitable would happen; coming face to face with Terry. The coincidence uncanny, Nova convincing herself that Terry and Tucker will only be a temporary change, she remained diligent in her work, now looking forward to working alongside her attorney and Agatha, she was not going to allow herself to fail.

Their relationship now strained, Tucker and Nova did not speak, Tucker spending most of his time downstairs in the living area playing on his video games or next door with Ryan and Cassidy. Initially, Nova never had a problem with this, but shortly found herself drenched in tears on the morning of their arrival to the airport. Los Angeles International, Monday morning stood Agatha, her assistant, Nova, Tucker and a strange man whom Nova had yet to meet but was happy was coming along—his bulging muscles making him appear forceful. Six hours and thirteen minutes later their plane landed, the sounds of the jet engines settling bringing her ears to pop—Nova gripping her son by his shirt, hugging him tightly, however, Tucker remained disinterested.

The economy flight packed with passengers, Nova wearing a pair of sunglasses, sweatsuit and sneakers spotted by a pair of teenage women hesitant to request a photo with her; their whispers heard in the distance. But Nova could not understand, telling herself she was not famous, she was not known and she simply was a woman with a few videos on YouTube and a meme of her circling with her tongue hanging lifelessly from her head—this Tucker found amusing although teased in school. Nova admiring him for his tenacity and sense of humor, regretful of her mistakes and seeking only to make things right she kissed him. Tucker hating this, feeling like he was too old for such public displays of affection. But Nova knew in order to do as Mr. Mann said she had to remain focused, and with Tucker now with Terry she could do just that. No longer subconsciously worrying or feeling guilt-ridden when not having the time to assist him with the simple things such as homework or sewing together a cape for Halloween trick or treating; a routine they practiced annually since Tucker was the age of five.

But it was the fear of never seeing her son again which terrified her, but assured by her attorney this could never be, he remained vague in advising of a time table for when Nova could even consider seeing her son unsupervised again. Purposefully, Nova withheld this information from her son, she could not bear to disclose to him that he would not be returning home with her, rather she left that to Terry, knowing just how inquisitive Tucker is, he is no doubt going to have to learn soon enough, but Nova remained too cowardly in speaking this truth. Once inside of the John F. Kennedy airport Nova despised the overcrowding and the rude individuals bumping into her and her son, never once apologizing. Moments later, they appeared, it was Terry and Laura standing downstairs by baggage claim, Nova waiting patiently to locate their luggage from the carousel.

Gripping Tucker and his t-shirt, Nova lost her footing once he shouted his father's name, in conjunction, a chill sent down her spine. Praying to locate her luggage quickly Nova was chilly, the November weather unpleasant, snowflakes appearing to fall outside. Racing into his arms, Tucker hugging his father firmly, Laura looking down on him smiling as they all now came face to face—a short Nova looking up to them; Terry and Laura taller than her, the height differential always aiding in making their conversations awkward. Nova stood,

"So I guess you and him can have a talk," she said to Terry never turning to face Laura although she could feel her eyes piercing through her, meanwhile Nova keeping a watchful eye on the carousel.

"Sure and uh, congrats you know, on um, all this stuff you have going on," Terry said, his tone calm and pleasant refraining from carrying on a conversation discussing the contents of her video for he did, in fact, watch it to its entirety. But Terry only felt the need to pity her and for once Nova did not feel shy or timid, she no longer loved him, which for her felt liberating. Lowering her eyes, she turned, locating Tucker nearest Agatha just on the other side waiting for the carousel to begin to grab a hold of his bags. Walking slowly to him, Nova kneeling, looking up to him, she fought the tears, having to tell her son goodbye was now setting in. Terry winning time and time again, this moment making her angry, her disdain and dissatisfaction heavily masked with a smile, she pulled him close kissing him on cheeks, whispering,

"Tuck, I love you so much and please remember that everything I do, I do it for us, I do it so that we can have a wonderful life one day," she now cried, unable to keep it together, Agatha witnessing this, placed a hand on her shoulder. Terry walking over to her, the buzzer now beeping indicating the carousel is to begin moving and it did. It plagued Nova that she was so tranquil, she wondered if her tears were for the loss of her son, or if she was crying because she felt free of him—the latter making her question herself as a person, a mother. But she remained truthful, unable to tell herself lies, her hubris never getting the best of her when it came time to indulge with her internal monologues.

Grabbing the red Spider-Man hard-shelled suitcase, Tucker ran to the door, holding onto Laura's cardigan as she aided him in locating a winter jacket from his personals, placing his hands gently inside the sleeves simultaneously filling her ears with stories about his classmates and his days at school, stories he wished he could have shared with his mother. Terry waving Nova goodbye only infuriating her, deciding not to bid him a farewell, her eyes fixated on them, her luggage passing her, Nova once again found herself in a trance, her eyes hanging low and her happiness taken from her. Realizing now to be a good time for a pep talk, Agatha turning to face her,

"This can only make you stronger. I know there is a lot going on right now, but you have to keep your head in this game to win. Tucker will be back in your arms before you know it, and by that time, you will have matured and will have worked hard enough for him have an exemplary life. But until then kid, let's kick some promotional ass," she said finally grabbing hold of Nova's suitcase to which Nova assisted.

Draped in winter jackets everyone retrieved from their luggage they made their way to the Holiday Inn on Schermerhorn in Brooklyn by way of a black town car. As a child, Nova would travel to the big city with her father, a teddy bear in hand and be taken on helicopter tours and enjoy fine dining with their mother and Marian. The car ride silent, Agatha shouting orders to her assistant, her hands moving quickly to take notes. Overlooking Brooklyn Bridge, they stood in the lobby of the Holiday Inn checking in, Nova grabbing her key card rolling her luggage up to the seventieth floor.

The room small, in it a queen-sized bed, desk, wardrobe,

chair, and television, immediately Nova looked to turn on the heater, Agatha later informing her of her call time, 5:45 a.m. Nova could not believe her ears thinking the time to be a tad bit too early, and so she decided to turn in after showering and making her way down the hall to grab ice for tea. Hours later unable to sleep, she turned to face the blinking alarm clock next to her, the time reading 3:14 a.m. with only an hour and forty-five minutes left to sleep Nova forced her eyes shut, but she remained restless, laying down, her eyes to the ceiling she pondered.

Touching and styling your hair
excessively can also cause breakage.
Explore styles that require
less styling products, or alternate
between high and low manipulation
styles to give your hair a break.

In California, midnight struck only fifteen minutes ago, and Alex along with Ryan remained awake discussing new ways to redecorate and plan for the newest addition to their family. Alex now learning she is in fact with child earlier that morning making them both thrilled. However, Alex chose not to share this news with Nova in light of recent events, believing the news to have been selfish given the timing. But she and Ryan remained celebratory, hating the fact that she now had to plan the rearrangement of Tucker's belongings making room for her own child.

"Do you think she's even going to continue staying here?" Ryan asked taking a seat on the plush carpet, Alex standing, her arms rested on the oak wardrobe inside of Tucker's bedroom. Shrugging her shoulders, she could not answer, fearing her response to be misleading and untrue. "I mean, she has money now, she is pretty popular, my guy says he can get her son back, but of course you know the courts will probably not find it in the child's best interest to be moving from state to state so frequently so one of them may have to relocate," he then added. Alex shot him a worrisome look.

"Can't they just get joint custody and Tucker visit his father in the summers?" she asked.

"Perhaps, I mean I don't know the law or how this family stuff works, but from what I gather, hearing his talks, it seems now the father is the custodial parent making Nova the one who may just have summer visits," Ryan said.

The New York weather winds brutal Nova awakens, staggering into the shower allowing the hot water to beat along her body and face. Exactly one hour later from when she had opened her eyes, unable to return to sleep and Agatha was ready, standing just outside her door completing an email and hitting send, alongside her the 6'3, muscular build security guard by the name of Horatio—banging the door now, Nova opening it, standing on the threshold, a towel hiding her naked body.

"I will be just a minute," she said.

"No, we have to be at the radio station in less than an hour," Agatha demanded. Nova hurrying, applying lotion to her skin, face and moisturizer to her hair she was ready in as little as ten minutes. The jeans and blouse she wore accompanied by a cardigan and a winter coat, bringing Agatha to cringe.

"Thank God we found you a wardrobe stylist," she snarled turning her back and making her way down the long corridor.

Inside the radio station was cold, freezing rather, Nova shivering as they all make their way up the elevator; in less than a day Nova despising the high-rise buildings, making their travels exceedingly long for no apparent reason. Entering into the room with the two-sided mirror, there was a large table, on it, four padded microphones, papers, bottles of alcohol and rolling chairs, one of which holding a pair of oversized headphones. Nova having no clue what to say or do, the urban hip-hop radio station presenters making their way inside, two males and one female, her heart sank. The sun had not yet risen, but there she was, sitting amongst what she perceived to be media vultures, ready to tear into her like a raw piece of salmon.

One of the presenters taking a seat, placing down a cup of coffee, adjusting his microphone, still no one spoke, the room still aside from the minor noises heard here and there from the grumbles and mumbles of the presenters. Nova did not recognize them; she only prayed the day would soon end.

Finally, after settling in, one of the gentlemen approached her, he was tall and slender, taller than Nova at least, his facial hair gray and his eyes a dark brown.

"Hey there, Monty," he said extending his hand, swinging in her chair, her feet dangling freely, Nova smiled reciprocating his acquaintance. Shortly thereafter the young woman approached, appearing to be in her early twenties, long flowing straight hair—a weave. Her eyes brown and tone masculine,

"What's up, I'm Candice, and this is Raymond," she said pointing to her co-host. Agatha appearing inside, smiling, cackling and making small-talk with the hosts, only minutes later politely asked to exit as they would soon look to begin. Nova remained smiling, although mentally she was no longer present. Staring off into space, she missed the moment the switches went on, and the *on-air* light shining,

"What's going on good people of New York? It's your boy Monty here and we have with us today the new and talented Nova." He said turning to face her, his mouth to the microphone, "You look very beautiful and well-rested. Thank you for coming on the show today,"

Sitting upright now, tossing the headphones over her ears as everyone else in the room did, Nova replied, nervously, "Oh no please thank you all so much for having me."

"No problem, no problem at all. So, I mean, we're going to dive right in here Ms. Cali living, I know this transition of weather must be killing you right now," he laughed looking to make light conversation while swerving in his chair, the others looking on patiently waiting for their moment to intercede. "Tell us, how did you come up with the name, *Even My Hair Is Mad TV?*" Nova now frozen, searching her mind for a clever response, she was not as quick on her feet as one would imagine considering she can speak for up to one hour on topics of interest to her. Surprisingly enough, she had a response in mind, thinking it best to be as straightforward and candid as possible.

"Wow," she chuckled, wiping her palms together, sweating now she removed her jacket, the vents on high. "I am a lover of my crown, I went natural only a few years ago and when I saw just how healthy my hair became, the length retention I was getting, body, I just came to realize that 4C hair is truly beautiful, however, it isn't without its downfall. I can very easily experience breakage, balding or something unpleasant when I'm either heavily stressed, neglectful of my crown all because I'm too busy, or I want to hide her under a wig for weeks. So, when my marriage ended, my crown, as I like to say it, became mad, she started falling out and I had bald spots. I was heartbroken during my trial separation and neglected both my hair and myself. So *Even My Hair Is Mad TV* is for women and men who are experiencing life-altering changes which undoubtedly affect their crowns, and learning new ways to regrow their hair and finding means of keeping it both happy and healthy," she smiled—Agatha tapping the glass behind her, shooting her a thumbs up, her face gleaming with happiness.

"That makes a lot of sense, so now your fans, you know they call themselves Nova's Crowns, how do you feel about that?" Candice asked, turning to face her. Nova feeling slightly claustrophobic, afraid of embarrassing herself, she spoke slowly, thinking of her response as the words left her mouth.

"I am shocked honestly, everything happened so quickly and you know my calling her my crown," she said pointing to her hair, "was just something I did effortlessly, I see myself now as a Nubian Queen so of course, my hair is my crown and to see people taking that and joining in on a community where crowns are uplifted is pleasant to see," she smiled, her confidence boosted. However, her comfort did not last long, when Raymond interjected, his tone condescending and curt.

"Overnight success stories can be hard to manage as they are often short-lived, tell me, Nova, how do you plan on staying relevant, keeping your crowns happy and balancing work and home?" he asked speaking from the furthest corner. Nova stopped swinging her chair, thinking of the family she allowed herself to lose and how at such an early start in her career she was already unbalanced. Agatha secretly praying she did not mention the child custody case believing it would surely do more harm than good to her reputation, especially as a woman, especially as a mother.

"Um, well Raymond to be quite honest I wish I was finding better ways to balance my growing career and family. It's been tough, but I think one day as long as I can make myself and my family happy everything else will fall into place—just can't lose focus on who this is all for—" she said. Candice interrupting, "Tell us Nova, who is this, all for?" she asked.

"My little boy, Tucker," she replied, her eyes hanging low, knowing she did fail as a parent but assured her failure only temporary. The hosts did exactly what she thought they would, they cooed. Inexperienced Nova is no fool, knowing that her brand could be tainted if ever she revealed her son had been taken from her due to a moment of weakness she endured. Wrapping up, the hosts played music intermittently, laughing and taking calls to which Nova was surprised to hear from the women behind the keyboards, the ones who were leaving her comments or following her on social media. Using her phone Agatha photographed Nova at the station, posting videos and asking her assistant to document their press run. Next, Nova was going to visit an urban podcast host where she was astonished to find a glam team awaiting her presence.

By noon Nova had been to three radio shows and sat with two talk show hosts conducting interviews—she was both exhausted and hungry. With only one day left in New York, she began to dread the idea of not being able to go site seeing. Agatha reminding her every few minutes, their trip was business only, nothing personal is to be conducted. Nova understood this, nodding as she sinks into the back seat of the town car, responding to commenters, winding up the black tinted windows ignoring the patrons, buildings, and high-life happening in the New York City streets.

"Is your father Dash Signature?' Agatha asked abruptly, hours later as the day began to wind down. Nova remained seated, silent.

"I'm sure you already knew that," Nova snapped.

"I did, but the information did not come from you, so I just wanted to act aloof. I have Essence and Forbes editors willing to do an article on you, but they want to include your father, believing the reach will be greater—and let's face it, it will. Do I have a green light from you to run it?" she asked, the look in her eyes devious. "Just know that once these articles make it to print, you will literally have the world in your back pockets. It's like having Karl Lagerfeld for a father, it's big news," she said. Looking to aggrandize her lineage to increase both wealth and media reach, Agatha had no plans on receiving Nova's permission to go forward with the articles, for she already accepted the offers, but could not resist seeing the expression on Nova's face once she asked, making her aware that soon the world would come to know of her family. Cunningly wicked, this move was, but Agatha having no true care for Nova only saw this moment as a glorious one.

"Don't run the articles, the last thing I need or want is people saying I am only here because of how privileged I am, or-or because of my father. Especially when they don't know the half of it," she said angrily. But remained distrustful of Agatha, texting Alex a rather lengthy deposition. "Before we leave on Monday, I need to see Tucker," she pleaded lifting her head from the phone. Agatha looking to her,

"No, you've already had one personal moment, this trip is business only. You have meetings and then we leave. Your accommodations were sponsored, we have to abide by the rules set forth or we can be sued or worse, blackballed," she said— Nova letting out a long sigh, placing the hood from her jacket comfortably atop her head, the remainder of their car ride unpleasant.

Inside her hotel room Nova paced, shouting to Alex, who was on the other side of her cellular phone, online shopping and taking the day easy.

"...Agatha's flagrant disregard for my authority is completely unacceptable auntie. The look in her eyes told me, her eyes told me that she approved the article," Nova said, her tone accusatory.

"Nova calm down, you don't know that, and I never told her you were Dash's daughter. She isn't stupid, I would hope, so I guess she figured it out. She knows of my relation to Dash, relation to you, so I mean, it makes sense, I'm guessing that's why she was so eager to work with you," Alex confirmed. An angry Nova ending their call, deciding to go for a walk, but forgetting how terrible the weather was she made her way down to the lobby locating a bar inside where she climbed atop the stool, browsing the menu ordering a cosmopolitan. Seconds later a voice behind her said,

"Hey there."

Although familiar she could not make out who it was, and so she remained staring into the menu, only safely assuming the stranger was not speaking to her, when in fact, he was. Feeling a light tap to her shoulder startling her, she turned; it was Donavan, a lighter-skinned woman hanging from his arms. "Um hey, you look nice," he said stammering, but Nova paying him no mind could not keep her eyes off of the woman, bewildered by the fact that he would even approach her, both of the ladies appeared perturbed by this very insensitive reunion. Noticing the silence, Donavan spoke, "This is Andrea, um, my ex-girlfriend, turned new girlfriend, I think that's how it goes," he said laughing. "We're here for Thanksgiving at her mom's house—" Fighting the urge to dismiss them both, cursing them in her mind, Nova smiled, extending her hand, faking a pleasantry,

"Nova," she said.

"Definitely a pleasure to meet you, I've heard a lot," the young woman said nicely. Andrea is twenty-two with a beautiful smile, long curly brunette hair and dashing eyes. Appalled, Nova felt it best she turns away, sensing her distance, Donavan bid her farewell, "Well, I mean, hopefully, I see you and Tuck around when we get home," he said tossing his arm around Andreas' shoulder walking away. Still piecing together, the events which just took place Nova wanted to scream, she had no clue Donavan was over her, it was not that long since they had last spoken.

Receiving her meal and sipping the last of her cocktail, Nova purchased an overpriced bottle of wine from the hotel gift shop, heading back upstairs where she penned her frustrations. Promising she would not return to male-bashing sexist videos she could not resist. Although she was not in love with Donavan, a part of her still felt betrayed, mislead somehow and with no further warning, she began to record, only this time on her cellular phone, speaking carelessly of the ways in which a man can move on so hurriedly. Or return to an ex-lover, back to what's familiar, back to what's easy, rather than working hard to pursue someone else who may be worth it. But then again Nova felt there was no way Donavan could have been truly invested or interested, when she withdrew, he allowed her to— which only spoke volumes.

Heavily disappointed in herself for not seeing the signs, Nova voiced her qualms, uploading the video to social media, and although it was without editing, failing in the superb quality department she hit share. Sending her anger to the internet, the Wi-Fi connecting her to the thousands of people who shared her network, making her instantly receive notifications from women agreeing and men arguing in the comments section of her Instagram account. Nova sat, twisting the cap from the cheap wine, taking the bottle to the head, she re-watched her video, her makeup and hair still applied from her interviews earlier that day,

"Interesting, how a man can claim to like you, want to date you and the second you can't find some time to respond to a message, he moves on! Or—or moves backward. Ladies, most if not all the time, if he comes back it isn't truly because he cares, no, it's because you're easy to access, courting you is done, the hard part in obtaining you is done and so, there he goes, showing his face again. Wrapping you around his little finger; surely I hope women can be wiser than this, he doesn't love you, he loves the access he has to you,"

Many men and women agreeing leaving her video without fail, another short success. Agatha soon sending over a text message,

"Saw the vid, good job kid; call time, 6:45 a.m." Rolling her eyes, Nova wondered how her anger was translating into a payday for such a vile human being, the thought making her skin crawl. She took another large gulp of wine massaging her hands into her scalp, the oils seeping down her fingernails, blackening them underneath,

"I totally need to wash my hair," she sighed, falling backward onto the mattress. And then her phone dinged, it was Donavan,

"I can't believe you posted that, listen, I did not stop speaking to you, it was the other way around. Now if you have an issue you could have been woman enough to simply say so, not rant on social media like a child. What we had was cool, which is why I was taken aback that you so abruptly stop speaking to me, but please don't judge what you do not know. I wish you the best of luck and as your child's teacher, I do hope we can remain amicable, at least for his sake," Donavan wrote. Reading his statement did not matter to her, she was now missing her son, thinking of contacting Terry so she may speak with Tucker. Nervous as the phone rang, praying he would answer,

"Nova!" he said, sounding shocked. Clearing her throat, she said, "Yes, um, can I talk to Tucker? Is he sleeping? Is—is everything alright?" she asked. Terry taking a deep breath,

"Yep, things are excellent. Nova I didn't want any of this, I mean at first I did but, now I don't want you to feel like I'm doing all of this to spite you or-or hurt you. You're the mother of my son, my firstborn, so I will always have a great deal of care for you, okay. If you want, I can have Tucker call you in the morning, I think he's just about turned in for the night," he said nicely. Nova unable to believe her ears, she let a tear fall, she was missing him, missing his touch, missing their family, missing her happiness. Now nothing will ever be the same.

"Thanks," she said before hanging up.

The next day Nova opened her eyes feeling heavily exhausted having spent the night before scrolling through social media contemplating whether she would delete her video. With the promotion of her channel she was growing more excited and warming up to the idea of having a fan base. Heading back to Los Angeles she was happy, despising the New York weather and the rude individuals she encountered along the way, although her time there short. Agatha spending most of her time cellular phone diving, prepping Nova for one more press run upon landing and sleeping intermittently during their flight.

Nova having little-to-no time to speak with Tucker, she exits the airport, packing her luggage into the backseat of yet another black town car. Agatha advising her to fix her makeup, and change her clothes whilst they drive—this task almost unbearable, her head hitting the ceiling numerous times almost causing a concussion and with only twenty-five minutes to spare they were pulling up to a warehouse in Hollywood square, where Nova stepped out zipping the back of her dress, rubbing her hands into her hair, creating an array of kinky curls. Barely standing Agatha ordered her assistant to fetch Nova a cup of coffee, she moved with haste.

"Who is this?" Nova asked, wondering who would be

interviewing her, but Agatha remained quiet. Walking past the entrance and the gates, showing her media pass to the guard and another security only a few feet away they entered into a studio. Nova turning to face her, her eyes filled with anguish, "Oh my God, no, look at me, I do not look groomed enough for a television sit down," she said. A strange woman walking up to her, her hair a flaming red,

"Nova," she asked nicely. The Caucasian woman extending her hand to greet Nova who was feeling unconfident, her sureness rattled, her eyes glistening with fear in conjunction with her nervousness. The woman realizing this, assured Nova, "No need to be nervous, we aren't going live, just going to interview you here in the back for the article I am producing tomorrow," she said.

"Oh okay," Nova said sounding relieved. "What publication is the article for?" she then asked, the woman smiling,

"Forbes, you're quite lucky to be the daughter of the legendary Mr. Signature himself," she said. Nova turning her head to locate Agatha who disappeared from view, she was infuriated, her eyes filling with rage, knowing there was nothing she could do she followed slowly behind the kind lady. Leading her to the rear stepping by the vanity climbing into the director's chair where she fixed her garments, tugging on her pencil skirt, the bright lights shining in her face causing her eyes to burn, the assistant making their way over to her, in his hand a cup of coffee—black. Members of the crew making their way over, etching a small microphone onto her clothing and that of her peer. Nova taking slow sips, readying herself for an awkward conversation.

The woman sitting across from her, legs folded she held in her hand a notepad and piece of paper.

"So, Nova, first and foremost, congratulations on all of your success! My name is Andrea Barnes, but my friends call me Andy. Now tell me, how does it feel being the daughter to Mr. Dash Signature himself?" she smiled, her eyes widened in excitement. She was no doubt star struck, but Nova could not comprehend, she remained seated, her eyes in search of Agatha. Feeling disheartened that she could not forfeit this opportunity.

21

One-week later Nova was feeling anxious, her nightly teeth grinding getting worse. All she could think about and care for is her brand, her business, her channel and with all the promotion she did she was growing impatient waiting for them to air or become publicized. Pacing in the living room she turned the television onto E! Television, a network known for their up to date celebrity gossip and information, and there it was, a photo of her flashed across the television screen, the host speaking of her as though she were of significance. Nova stood, screaming to the top of her lungs, bellowing for Alex to join her. Immediately she turned the program up higher, the volume exceedingly loud as the young woman said,

"Ladies and gentlemen, my name is Alissa Shaw and welcome back to Entertainment Tonight! Just last week Forbes Women released their article entitled: Powerful Women From The Family Powerhouse," Nova turning to face Alex, perplexed as she did not receive the article or any linkbacks to its publication online, leading her to worry, but Alex hushing her, eager to hear the woman from the television speak, she stood, her hands placed atop her hip cradling the oversized shirt she wore.

"...and in it, they gave us some startling news. The fabulous Fashion Designer Mr. Dash Signature is the father of two! Yep, two now adult daughters—Nova Signature and Marian Signature," the women gasping in unison, Nova disappointingly taking a seat, readying her phone to contact Agatha to whom she had not spoken in days. Her nose flaring as she grew angry, "The ladies have been pretty well hidden up until recently, considering no one knew of the legends offspring for the past twenty years he's remained in the industry. But don't you go thinking one of these ladies is using her last name as her claim to fame. Nova, the curator to *Even My Hair Is Mad TV* becoming an overnight success only seven weeks ago—with over half a million views on multiple YouTube videos in just two days from her famous rant calling out her now estranged ex-husband. The Signatures sure are a talented bunch," Nova stood turning off the television.

"I'm never going outside again," she mumbled. Alex sighing,

"You're over-reacting, this is not a bad thing," she said.

"What! This is the epitome of bad, I never wanted to live in his shadow. I never wanted anything from him. He threw me out, pregnant and has never called, text or even paid a visit," she sobbed, embarrassed to be crying. Alex consoling her, her stiff abdomen rubbing against Nova's arms, she pulled away, drying her eyes as she looked Alex up and down,

"Is there something you're not telling me?" she gasped. Alex, shaking her head no, believing once again now was not the time to reveal such news. Sensing her hesitation, Nova asked, "Are you pregnant?" changing positions now, her legs crossed, her facial expression immensely joyful. She placed her hands over her lips, looking to cry once more only this time tears of joy. Alex scoffing,

"Yep," she whispered. An ecstatic Nova jumping atop her, although gentle, laughing as she kissed her cheeks, she could feel nothing but delight for her aunt, knowing she would one day make an impeccable mother.

"Why on earth didn't you tell me?" Nova questioned returning to her seat, thinking momentarily of what her response would be, just then her phone rang, on the other end is a furious Marian—feeling completely blindsided and

outraged. Alex encouraging her to answer,
"Marian,"
"Nova, what the fuck! Why would you do this? Why on
earth didn't you prepare me for this? My social media is in a
frenzy. Our photos are plastered everywhere, none of mine are
even professional, next to you I look like the adopted sister!"
she beckoned. Nova taking a deep breath,
"Marian, that was totally a setup and I am so sorry. But
Auntie is pregnant," she said quickly, arm wrestling Alex who
fought to remove the phone from her ear, turning to face her,
shocked, mouthing the word *no* to her niece. Praying she
would speak no further, but Nova hated it when Marian was
upset with her and now, she needed a cushion, something to
soften the blow and that did it. Immediately Marian was
soothed, begging to speak with her aunt, congratulating her.
Nova felt relieved. Her eyes lowered, shrugging her shoulders,
she proceeded to rub Alex's lower stomach feeling how stiff it
is, she lifted her sweater, seeing now for the first time a growing
belly.

That evening Nova and Alex, stayed up until the late hours
of the night, speaking, laughing, eating popcorn, and watching
reruns of *The Fresh Prince of Bel-Air*. Nova still having not
contacted Tucker, unable to determine why she was feeling
relinquished of her parental rights and free, she decided to
work on producing more quality work. Following the news of
her kinship her social media grew exponentially, she was now
showing sixty-eight thousand followers on Instagram and
seventy-two thousand subscribers on YouTube, her
engagement high averaging no less than twelve thousand
comments per photo. And now with people knowing the truth
Nova found links to her father, articles of him receiving the
Council of Fashion Designers of America award only just last
month. Photos of her father looking amazing, still draped in his
signature colors.

Drawing a long sigh, it no longer bothered her that people
knew, Nova was feeling forgiving, missing him-almost. By
morning another generous deposit was wired to her bank
account, Nova now being called upon to post photos on social
media in exchange for currency. Agatha's assistant handling

these transactions, and now Nova began contemplating the idea of moving. By morning she headed downstairs for breakfast making the conscious effort not to check her phone or social media, no matter how tempting. Watching Ryan maneuver in the kitchen fixing Alex a wonderful breakfast she decided now, getting to know him was essential. Biting into a hard apple she removed from the glass fruit bowl she said,

"So, you're having a baby, well another one."

"That I am," he said resting his hands on the marble countertops.

"Are you moving in here?" she questioned.

"Cassidy and I will be moving in, yes, by the end of this month actually. I thought um, Alex was going to speak to you about that," he said removing his hands now. He did not want to risk speaking too much, in case Alex had yet to disclose the news and judging by the look on Nova's face, this was the case.

"No, auntie did not tell me that, but no worries, I'm thinking of getting out of your hair fairly soon. Tucker and I will need a new house, so he can have some stability," she said. Ryan turning to face her,

"You've spoken to the lawyer?" he asked, flipping the eggs, loading the center with tomatoes, meats, and seasonings for the omelets.

"Um, no, but I will. I mean, I don't think it will be that bad," she chuckled nervously. Ryan sneered.

"I see." But Nova missing this reaction, stood, walking out of the kitchen making her way back up the stairs. Her phone blaring uncontrollably on her bed, Agatha demanding her presence for another press run—an abrupt run in lieu of the recent discovery of her lineage. Feeling a tad bit excited, she showered, dressed, and exited the townhouse calling for a taxi.

In downtown Los Angeles Nova was sitting in the glass building accompanied by Agatha and Horatio. Confused on what was taking place, she remained seated, taking in the beautiful view around her. Moments later, after a fair amount of waiting, two gentlemen draped in black three-piece suits made their appearance, everyone in the room exchanging a handshake before taking their seats once again.

The shorter pudgy gentlemen began sitting across the oversized conference room table, his hands folded,

"Ms. Signature," he smiled, but quickly Nova corrected him, her and Agatha speaking in unison.

"Nova." The sounds of their voice forceful.

"My apologies, Nova. We are a Fortune 500 company and we would like to hire you as our new brand ambassador. I want to tell you a little bit more about our brand, of course. So, we made our way into the homes of Americans in 1968 and have since then been providing a wonderful hair product to the citizens of America called Brawns Moisture. We have a series of products from leave-in conditioners to hair oils and all the essentials, but our issue right now is reaching the African-American demographic. You see, our product is a leading brand, we are one hundred percent sure that our line is safe and can be used on all hair textures, no matter race or color—"

Agatha growing seemingly impatient, interrupting him, "What are the rates?" she asked, leaning forward, their eyes now interlocking. The gentleman smiling fretfully, flipping open a catalog, removing from it a piece of paper, scribbling a number he slid it across the table, Agatha looking first, handing it over to Nova, the number reading, eight million dollars. Nova gagging.

"Wait, what!" she said aloud. Agatha speaking, "This number looks good." But Nova was not sold.

"Is there a way I can test the product? I mean before I start peddling it to my crowns." It was in that moment Nova realized her importance, her worth, and just how caring she indeed is. People loved her, people were rooting for her, and that meant more to her than a product that would require her to simply sell blindly while still reaping in a cash reward.

"Nova, please we assure you no sample testing is necessary. This product will for sure work for all races and all hair textures. Nappy hair included," he said innocently.

"Napp—" Nova stuttered, "Get me out of here before I embarrass them!" she screamed to Agatha who begged the gentlemen to give her and Nova a moment. The men immediately exited, promising their return in a matter of minutes. The door closing behind them, Nova began her badgering,

"These people are racist!" she shouted, "Nappy?"

"Lower your voice, look, this is the industry. No one, and let me repeat, no one this early in their career are seeing numbers like this. Your father is a very prominent public figure and so, you're getting some favoritism here. You don't have to use the product Nova, you simply wave it in some videos, make believe you're using it, sell it, and collect your check. Who cares what happens to the buyers? Not everyone is going to experience any issues, some of your fans, followers, devoted crowns are Caucasian women, they may find this to be the best product they've ever used," Agatha said.

"What about my sisters? What about the women with the same hair type as mine? How can you ask me to sell out like this? For a check, send my sisters down balding road so the Caucasian women can continue to have long, flowing hair down their backs, as if that's ever been hard for them to acquire before. Get me a different deal, I am not selling out." She demanded, standing and walking away, Horatio following behind her. Agatha spent her morning sending detailed reports to news outlets, hoping for coverage, knowing now that the world was ready to see the daughter of Mr. Dash Signature himself, nothing could have prepared Nova for what she was to experience next. Walking down to the lobby she heard it, the sound of a camera snapping, then another and then another, fearing for her safety she turned, making eye contact with Horatio as she now made her way around the corner to see standing outside a crowd filled with men and women, reporters, paparazzi all hailing their name, but they were not calling for her, they were calling for someone else,

"Is Dash Signature with you?" One guy inquired.

"Nova Signature may we have a word?" A woman beckoned loudly. The cameras and microphones shoving their way towards the glass, but no one entered, knowing they would be considered trespassing. Nova feared going outside. Looking for Agatha who had yet to make an appearance, she was doing the unthinkable, promising Nova's cooperation for a deal she was previously vocal about not taking. Agatha knowing just how persuasive she could be, remained confident that she could, in fact, get Nova to sell the products, and so, she rustled up her documents, shoving the leather binder under her arms, shaking the hands of the brand owners and making her way down to the lobby where she spotted Nova and Horatio standing inside. Agatha moving swiftly, grabbing Nova by the arm, she instructed Horatio to walk first, the black town car awaiting them just outside the building, pushing the doors open, Nova felt it for the first time—attention. The men and women screaming to her, the cameras flashing, she held her head down low, looking to the ground, everyone beginning to close in on her, she was feeling trapped, pushed left and right, Horatio pushing his way through, guiding them both until finally, they made it, seated to the rear of the car, Nova watched the women beating the tinted glass shouting to her for an interview. Her breathing heavily, her hands trembling,

"How on earth did they know I would be here?" she questioned.

"I called," admitted Agatha, her lips pursed she handed Nova the black binder. "You have two days to sleep on this, I want a yes response, so if you have to confide in your aunt or your friends, or whomever, then do so, but we aren't turning down this deal," she demanded. Their ride silent.

With Nova growing stronger day by day she was slowly becoming acclimated to her lifestyle, the demands that came with the work. Watching her social media channels flooded with commenters and lovers of her craft, Nova refused to sell out, deciding to record another video where she completed a thorough hair routine, styling for short hair while speaking candidly about her new unjust opportunities. This did not go over well once she concluded, using the desktop in the living room to edit her sixteen-minute video and add her cards and cover art, she hit the share button. In a matter of minutes her phone began to blare,

"This is defamation!" Agatha screamed—Nova turning to the channel, looking over the video where she very openly spoke about the industries seeking to peddle un-savory products to consumers using influencers who will conform for a payout. Agatha felt mocked like her authority was being challenged, listening to her rant, Nova remained stoic,

"You work for me, not the other way around. I am not taking the deal, and now, after they see this, they won't want me to. Either get me a better deal or I will find someone who can," she said hanging up the phone, reclining in her seat and admiring how beautiful she looked. Her chocolate skin shimmering in the light, the equipment she invested in all worth it as she re-watched the video, refreshing the page and watching the numbers increase minute-by-minute.

Standing in her downtown office overlooking the patrons and the business owners just outside on Hollywood Boulevard, Agatha was feeling inferior, a feeling she heavily despised. This was not her usual client, thinking for a moment that a timid Nova would be easy to control, her plan backfiring. She was now far more assertive, quiet, yet devious, making her dangerous in her eyes. Contemplating now, she called on the one person she knew could help, Mr. Mann. Although they had not seen eye-to-eye before, he remains to be her go-to for client damage control.

With a full down payment for a home, Nova began making phone calls, wanting a home for herself she knew the process would be long, but now she was trending, her, Marian and their father, the general public eager to see who she is, emails coming in from everywhere, makeup artists, hairstylists, doctors all reaching out for a cash grab, mention, just anything to be in her presence. Marian receiving the same attention, only minimal, Joanna finding this to be a distraction for her, not fond of the publics' sudden interest in her intern. Things now smooth, peaceful, still, however, their father never reaching out to make contact. Nova toggling with the idea of reaching out to him, his public relations team easy enough to locate online, but she refrained, reminding herself why their relationship became obsolete in the first place. But Marian feeling otherwise, contacted her father, believing it was time. This, Nova was not privy to.

In a matter of days her attorney called, delivering the news which made Nova rise from her bed, slide her feet into shoes and race downstairs to locate Alex. She was told the motion was approved and a re-trial was scheduled for one week from today. This was excellent, she could not wait to see her son again, hug him and hear his voice, but she was not entirely happy. Almost immediately reverting now to that indecisive state of mind, thinking she could not find time to work as much if she did indeed have Tucker primarily in her care. Her conscience making her aggravated, telling her to be a better person, change her thought patterns, feeling coerced almost into motherhood. Enlisting Alex's help, Nova found a realtor. Alex recommending a small home to start, something where the mortgage did not exceed six thousand dollars, Nova concurring. She found house hunting to be pleasant. Three days a week she was visiting potential properties, fighting the urge to cry, her life turning around for the better, but a part of her could not help but feel like it was not earned.

Deals to Agatha now swarming into her office, knowing how elusive and disengaged her father was, his status outranking that of many companies now willing to pay millions for even the slightest affiliation to his name—his children. The month of December Nova worked on improving her channel's presence, uploading quality videos only approved by Mr. Mann himself. Attending photoshoots and now renting out a studio twice a week with glam on call. Nova was beginning to feel somewhat tranquil. Old friends from high school reaching out to contact her, hoping for a moment of her time in which she did not engage them. Marian taking frequent trips back to Los Angeles, her touring with Joanna almost complete and she too began receiving deals for working and promotion. But Marian did not take them, promising herself that all the hard work she placed into earning her education was not going to go to waste— her dream is to pursue fashion and that is what she plans to do.

Feeling proud of her sister for not allowing herself to be bought and sold, Nova begged Marian for a sibling photoshoot where they would cover Essence Magazine, making their formal introduction to the world. Nova had yet to communicate with her father, but with a new deal on the table she feared that soon may change. Sitting in Alex's kitchen staring out of the window, taking in the beautiful landscaping of the backyard Nova and Marian conversing over the telephone,

"I can be there in about a week for the shoot. What day is it?" Marian asked.

"Tuesday," Nova replied, picking a scab on her left hand. "When is your show?" Marian now began preparing for her own introduction, working diligently on a few pieces of clothing for her line, inviting her father and Nova to the show in Los

Angeles, neither of them knowing of the other's presence. Although Marian is preparing for the worse, she remains hopeful for the best possible outcome, that her sister and father can reunite, make amends and they all move on to becoming an influential family, leaving their mark in history.

Style with shrinkage in mind.
Shrinkage can be frustrating
because it keeps you from seeing
growth and it can make your hair
more susceptible to tangles
and single strand knots.

Terry now receiving the news of a re-trial traveled to Los Angeles, leaving Tucker home with both Laura and their growing daughter. Landing into Los Angeles International Airport, he headed to his mother's home where he and Mrs. Higgins had a transparent talk regarding his emotions and the shocking revelation that he was unsure of how to face. With their divorce now only days from being finalized, a new hearing for Tucker underway, he was sure that a life with Nova was exactly what he wanted. Feeling like he was too young to have gotten married he explained himself to his mother, hoping for her understanding to which she did supply, wishing him nothing but happiness, knowing now that he was going to pursue Nova, Terry spent days wondering how to execute his return back into her life.

Keeping this part of her life private remained crucial, heading to the courthouse for the re-trial meant hearing the possibility that the judge's decision would not be overturned, something her attorney remained very transparent of when informing Nova. With only less than five percent of cases ever receiving an overturn, Nova did remain optimistic, walking up the stone steps, she spotted Terry staring lovingly into her eyes, a look she had long soon forgotten. She turned away, stepping into the courthouse and making her way down the chilly hallway—the attorney, Daniel Christopher next to her. The appellate court felt different; the room smaller—dreary.

Nova remained unaware of the reason her appeal was approved, walking inside she held her head high, watching as

Terry sauntered in slowly after her, unaccompanied by anyone; Daniel Christopher stood beside Nova buttoning his blazer, waiting patiently for the judge to enter. Believing the damage to have already been done, Daniel was not sure he could help Nova, but researched long enough to learn there was only one solution—the judge now entering, everyone remained standing as she took a seat.

"Mr. Higgins, I came here this morning with one thing on my mind, to reprimand you for your misuse of our justice system. This is not a game, falsely accusing your spouse of neglect, amongst other horrors; I have read your letter and your call for the misapplication of the law. In which case, I am not going to reprimand you, only demand that this never happens again. You have stated that the defendant is an amazing, attentive mother to whom you apologize for misjudging and tainting her name in the court of law. Knowing this, I am moving for joint custody between the two of you," Listening to her speak, Nova could not retain her happiness, shrieking in joy she covered her mouth, the judge turning to face her, "Ma'am, please mind your decorum in my courtroom," she said sternly.

"I am so sorry," she mumbled.

"Joint custody and we will revisit in two months for further discussing of visitations, if needed, and the best interest for the child. In the meantime, ma'am you are free to see your son, I believe now he is school Mr. Higgins?" she questioned.

"Yes, your honor," Terry said, his hands placed behind his back.

"Good, he will complete the school year. Case dismissed," she said banging her gavel. Nova jumping joyously, her heart falling to her ankles. Terry made his way through the brown doors; ecstatically she raced behind him, hugging him from behind. Surprised by her actions he turned as Nova's eyes began to well.

"Oh my God, thank you so much for that, so—so much!" she smiled, her cheeks beginning to hurt. Terry staring at her with admiration, her hair now long enough to wear Bantu knots, her face clean, her smile perfect, he could not take his eyes away from her. "Where—where's Tuck, did you bring him? Is he with your mom? Can—can I see him? She asked. Daniel Christopher walking up to her, standing; tapping her shoulders, nodding his head to Terry as if to indicate his appreciation.

"He's in New York, um, I was wondering if we could talk, you and I, alone?" Terry stuttered, lifting his head to face Daniel, who was ready to take his leave. Nova shook his hand, thanking him for his time. Watching him walk away she felt strange, as though there was more bad news that is going to be bestowed upon her, fearing it was something relating to Tucker, she stepped aside, closest to the walls, away from the crowd so she can hear him clearly.

"Um, sure," Terry took a long pause, squeezing his hands together,

"Okay, so, this isn't easy but um, I've been thinking a lot and I just want you to know that I know that I've made some mistakes, a lot of mistakes, um, unforgivable mistakes, but I am very sorry. I want us to work Nova. Like, I know our divorce is almost finalized, but-but I want us back together. Everything with Laura I will figure it out, I promise and things with you and I can be smooth again, happy—I really miss you," he said. Nova remained standing in silence, looking into his eyes, speechless for a moment; her mind drawing a blank. Finally, she said,

"You taught me how to live without you by leaving me and ignoring me. Now I am accustomed to life without you. Also, when I wanted to fix things you didn't, when I cared just an ounce, you didn't. You have single-handedly taught me how to stop loving you because you were incapable of reciprocating it, thinking the grass was greener on the other side, Terry. I feel for you, I do, but I have nothing left for you, I don't share your feelings and—make no mistake, I want us to be as kind to one another as much as we possibly can, but Laura and the baby, that's your new life now, Tucker is my life and I just want to focus on him and I," she said. As the words left her mouth, she felt extricated, powerful even, and without a doubt, grateful for all that she had come to experience. Terry teaching her how to fend for herself, leaving her stranded, only awakening the true power she had inside, and this was by far the best feeling she could have ever experienced. Hugging him she asked politely that once the school year ended that she be allowed to pick up

Tucker from New York, surprising him, and now that she was planning on buying a home, she couldn't wait to see his reaction. Terry agreeing, feeling proud of her, kissing her forehead preparing to walk away. He soon thereafter, disappeared into the thick crowd.

Slamming the door Nova stood in the foyer of Alex's house, feeling redeemed of her faults. Her cellular phone dings, Agatha requesting her presence for yet another meeting, this time Nova feeling more confident in refusing if she did not find the deal to be fitting. Dialing Mr. Mann, Nova requesting his attendance this time, hoping he would say yes, and he did— moments later a stretch limo arriving to bring her to a warehouse. Mr. Mann being quite secretive, he did not announce to Nova the plans he and Agatha had in store for her. Feeling quite confident in his agreement to participate, they drove, the ride filled with laughter while Mr. Mann teased Nova on her choice of clothing, bewildered by the fact that her father is a high-end fashion designer, and yet, her rags always appearing to make her look destitute.

The large warehouse with pink brick walls, just on the border of San Francisco valley on a desolate road, was quite eerie. Feeling a bit taken aback she took a deep breath before climbing out of the back seat to stand next to Mr. Mann who wore a gown and a pair of Giuseppe Zanotti slippers. Inside of the warehouse were machines, supplies, men and women working in uniform, their name tags reading Brawns Moisture, Nova's anger imminent,

"Why am I here?" she bellowed in disgust.

"Down girl," Mr. Mann replied. An elderly gentleman was making his way to them, he wore a pair of Dickie work pants, a button-down shirt, and a construction workers hard hat. Removing it, he extended his hand to greet her,

"Pleasure to meet your acquaintance. My name is Maurice Dyson, Product Management Director for Brawns Moisture," Nova shaking his hand, sliding hers from his gently, folding her arms. "Please, let's head up to my office," he instructed leading them up the horizontal iron stairs. Inside of his office, high enough to overlook the complete laboratory; he instructed both Nova and Mr. Mann to take a seat, they did. "I am aware that you had a meeting with our company's CEO a few days ago, but you did not fancy the offer on the table. So, Mr. Mann here, your publicist, and I, well, we've thought of something we think may appease you. Because of your status and the strong appeal you have to men and women in the urban communities, we would like to offer you a partnership, your own line of products, as an extension of our brand. For starters, we will look to produce what will be known as *The Even My Hair Is Mad* leave-in-conditioner," he said, his tone comforting.

"You will have full creative control of the contents, the texture, the smell, pretty much everything you think is going to be beneficial to appeal to the African-American demographic. Your affiliation with us will be longstanding and we are offering seventeen million dollars for upfront costs, covering manufacturing and a generous percentage to you of course for all items sold. I was instructed to send over this information to your attorney, a Ms. Alexandria Howard?" he asked seeking her approval. Nova nodded, looking to Mr. Mann and fighting the urge to hug him, feeling within her heart that he is responsible for formulating such a deal. The wink he gave her confirming this. To further corroborate this theory, he stood, shaking the hand of Mr. Dyson who very generously thanked him for bringing Nova along. Nova was on board, guaranteeing her services once Alex would approve their contract. The meeting ending in happiness and complete satisfaction. Outside, Nova hugged Mr. Mann, who then whispered,

"Get the millions while you can."

> You can explore heat-free styles that
> stretch your hair, such as twist outs,
> braid outs, and Bantu knots.

One-month later Nova was visiting the factory every single day, meeting with marketers, product specialists, and creating something she would have never dreamed could happen for her. Feeling for textures and ensuring her products remained free of unsafe ingredients were her primary concern. Sulfates, toluene, triclosan and a long list of others Nova derived from the internet, although far costlier, she was determined to make a quality product, never selling her soul for money. She remained true to her beliefs and the happiness of her crowns, which always remained her top priority when recommending new products. With the promise of her own hairline, the crowns were elated, waiting patiently, and Nova herself could not wait, learning it would be almost a year before the product could hit the market, but she did not mind. In the interim she was planning other ventures and soon learning the closing on her house took place—Nova is now officially a homeowner to the three bedrooms, two-bathroom bel-air house.

With things going smoothly in her career and personal life, Nova remained focused. Speaking to Tucker on many days, but she was saddened to hear how happy he was, almost too busy to have a conversation with her. She was learning the hard way that he was now favoring the time he was spending with his father, making her feel almost non-existent. Their conversations often brief, but hearing the good news about their home, Nova could not wait. She dialed, Terry asking to speak with Tucker on a Saturday afternoon. Her son, answering, his tone mundane,

"Hi mom,"

Nova shouting in excitement,

"Tuck, mommy got the house! We're going to live in a house! And it's so big, you have a huge room and we're going to have Superman decorations everywhere, I can't wait for you to see it, sweetie, plus we have to start planning your birthday," she said.

"Oh okay," he said, handing the phone off to Terry, taking Nova by surprise.

"Hey there," Terry said. Nova's joy removed almost instantly,

"What's wrong with him? I mean, it's like he doesn't love me anymore," she said, her voice shaking.

"No, I mean, he just feels like he's having fun here, um, he told me yesterday he doesn't want to leave," Terry said. "I uh, have no plans on making this a court issue, at all, I think if he decides to come home, then, we can most certainly arrange for that. But for now, it seems he wants to stay," Terry said. Nova was finding this news difficult to take in, but she trusted Terry, knowing now he had no reason to lie. The news, however devastating, was not going to allow Nova to give up on her son. Ending their call, Nova sat in the foyer, by the bottom of the stairs, staring off into space.

22

The one thousand, two hundred and twenty-five hundred square foot home now hers. Signing the contract over a week ago enabled Nova to acquire the keys and begin moving her things, the moment felt surreal. Perfectly positioned to feature an amazing panoramic sunrise to sunset views, she stood walking around the ground floor, drawing back the shades overlooking the mountains. The house, accompanied by a private courtyard entry and an open flowing floorplan to a large living room with a fireplace and bar leading out to the pool yard. The enormous living space perfect for entertaining, but Nova knew she was not going to be spending much time home due to her ever-growing busy schedule and the website designers contacting her around the clock forcing her to take matters into her own hands.

Inside the kitchen Nova entered, sliding her hands gently across the stainless-steel appliances with a commercial Wolf range oven, a sub-zero fridge and a wine cooler—her new home also having a formal dining room, office, and a large den with built-ins, perfect for additional living space or a media room. Nova's master bedroom equipped with a walk-in closet and an updated master spa-like bathroom. Centrally located with an easy drive to either side of the hill and easy access to the interstate, and although she had her license, Nova had no desire to buy a car, deciding to utilize the town cars bringing her from one place to the next; a luxury she now came to appreciate. The house only slightly larger than Alex's home, Nova feared to spend the night alone. With the sun going down and her home still empty, she taxied her way back to Alex's where she packed, showered, and logged into social media, going live with her fan-base. She could never have imagined that at this time in her life she would be this popular, well-loved and appreciated by so many strangers. But lest she complains, she was having the time of her life and with their patronage, support, and constant admiration for all of her hard work she was no doubt going to reciprocate, ensuring her products to be authentic and affordable, yet affluent in nature.

Alex and Ryan now residing together, his daughter Cassidy well-mannered and kind, bringing Nova to miss Tucker, regretting past behaviors, but with cognitive dissonance believing it still all to have been worth it. Marian speaking to Nova daily, having now landed in Los Angeles heading back to her own apartment on the beach, she called to invite her sister to join her. Since her home had been uninhabited, she walks inside, illuminating the rooms as she entered, placing her bags down, and walking to the patio to overlook the beach and take in the sunset. With her internship now ended, she was thinking of ways to begin her new journey, the connections she made profound and with the media now knowledgeable of her relation to Dash, she is now the most anticipated fashion designer to watch according to Entertainment Tonight.

Feeling the pressure to live up to her father's legacy Marian is now ready to drown her anxiety in a pitcher of margaritas. The Essence Magazine photoshoot taking place in the morning, she remained mindful not to become inebriated. There is a faint knock on the door. It is Nova. She arrived in one of the town cars which serves as her new mode of transportation. In her hand is a bottle of dark Jose Cuervo and a small bag containing a celebratory gift. Marian, elated to see her little sister, squeezing her tightly as she hugged her, thanking her for taking the time to join her. Nova entered inside, removing her shoes and she proceeds to mix the drinks, thinking she was the

far more skilled barista. Marian peeks into the bag, smiling,
"Open it," Nova says, laughing at her sister's impatience.
Marian, moving quickly, thrusts her hand inside, removing the
Cartier box. Inside is a rose gold bracelet engraved with the
words, *My Sisters Keeper.* Her face blushing, she leaps up,
hugging Nova and thanking her, she was essentially grateful,
and happy that Nova was now so abundantly blessed. As the
blender roared and cool breeze now made its way inside, the
ladies poured their glasses and headed outside. Their night is
peaceful, filled with laughter and confessions of untold
childhood truths, and a shocking update from Nova to Marian
in regard to Terry leaving her speechless.

Arriving on the set of a magazine cover photoshoot for the
first time in her life, Nova stood in awe—taking it all in for the
moment, the men and woman moving with a purpose, her face
bare, along with Marian trotting behind her; a crumcake falling
from her lips, its tiny details decorating her short-sleeved top.
The creative director greeted them, Paula Buck, a short
African-American woman with her hair slightly greyed. Next to
her is a Hispanic gentleman, painstakingly handsome, with a
bald head and full beard, standing at 6'4, muscular build—the
photographer, a Nikon z6 hanging from his neck, extended his
hand to her. Nova, remain standing, her feet planted firmly
onto the ground, impressed by his beauty,

"Nova," Marian whispered. "Now I know he looks good,
but tread carefully dating outside of your race when you're out
here preaching about black men finding them some Becky's,"
Marian said smirking; Nova, rolling her eyes, sarcastically
thanking Marian for her unwanted input. With the sun yet to
wake, it is pitch black outside. The women prepared, heading
into hair and makeup, their looks urban style inspired—
cropped top, baggy pants, and oversized jackets with wet hair
and natural foundation with a smoky eye. The February issue,
set to hit stands and introducing the ladies for the upcoming
holiday, Agatha showing up over an hour late, completely
apologetic, thanking her friends for the favor of placing Nova
and Marian on the cover.

Agatha knowing the benefit was more for the magazine, but
to remain in the good graces of the editor and creative director,

she mastered the art of pseudo ass-kissing. The photoshoot lasting for hours, and as always Nova clueless on how to perform. Marian, however, looking flawless, maneuvering like a professional, emulating the models she had seen during her time traveling and working for Joanna. Paula, facing Agatha behind the camera, whispers to her as she watches the stills,

"Such beautiful, graceful women, who would you say is their celebrity twins?" she asked. Agatha looking closely, thinking,

"Well, I can see that woman, the one from Boomerang in Marian, the older sister,"

"Ah, Robyn, yes, of course and Nova,"

"Brenda Sykes," they both said in unison.

"A young Brenda, completely gorgeous," Paul confirmed before yelling, "headshots Ramon," she instructed him from behind the camera and away from the backdrop. By noon the women were feeling exhausted, overworked and their eyes heavy from the false lashes. Nova so desperately wanted to remove them having never been a fan of wearing an excessive amount of makeup, she was finding this look to be rather arduous to upkeep. Ramon laughing, once he bellowed the words, "It's a wrap," Nova unlacing the corset from around her waist, the one used to take in her stubborn belly fat, she let out a long sigh of relief. Although petite, she began realizing that to exist in their world, however ambiguous, she would have to be mindful of her diet. Draped in white robes, left on their own as the crew went to work dismantling the equipment, Ramon making his way to Nova hoping to have a moment alone with the YouTube Signature as he referred to her whenever not in her presence.

"Hey," he said breathing shakily.

"Hey yourself," Nova turned, facing him, a wipe in her hand cleaning the makeup from her face and around her eyes. Distracted, Marian simply sought to take selfies, uploading them to her social media learning that she soon had a growing and engaged fanbase which she loved to entertain.

"I was wondering if maybe we can have dinner some time," he said. Nova nodding, looking around the room suspiciously, praying no one would notice. She was feeling guilty. "Good, so tonight I can pick you up around eight?" Nova handing him a piece of paper, using his arm for a place to press, she removed an eyebrow pencil from the wide vanity, scribbling her new address. Pleased, Ramon tilting his head, walking away feeling exhilarated. Marian tapping her sister on the right shoulder, shaking her head in disappointment.

"Oh hush," Nova replied. Their morning-turned-afternoon coming to an abrupt end when the women bid everyone a farewell, climbing into the backseat of a town car, along with Agatha and Horatio. Nova, having no desire to work any further, suggested a trip to 'In and Out Burger' before heading to Alex's where she spent her afternoon packing and boxing up the little belongings she had there, and then off she went to the furniture store accompanied by her sister.

Rummaging around the new house, Nova could not find anything. After a long day of shopping for both clothes and furniture she was happy to begin packing away the china and glasses, Marian assisting before departing early, learning of Nova's date night with the photographer—in which case she still did not approve. Her phone rang. It was Tucker, calling from his father's phone hoping to wish his mother a good night because after a very lengthy conversation with his father learned that his mother was feeling like a pariah. Although he could not comprehend the meaning behind her emotions, he knew his mother was feeling unwanted and that was enough to make him sad, and so, he called. But Nova remained wrapped up in her new life and now finding something to wear while twisting out her hair she could not take the call, deciding tomorrow would be better.

Nova loved date night in Los Angeles. The options are always limitless, and tonight Ramon is taking Nova to a Tuscan cooking class, their menu; crostini with roasted eggplant, bistecca alla Fiorentina and Pollo alla Toscana. Ramon was driving fast, with the engine roaring and the tires smelling of burnt rubber along the interstate, a timid Nova asking him to slow down.

"You look very beautiful. I love that color against your skin," he said, intermittently looking to her, as he kept his eyes on the road, one hand on the steering wheel. Nova thanking him, hoping he would, in fact, take notice. She wore a tangerine-colored blazer, with a white blouse and white flare pants with a pair of yellow strapped sandals. Her toes painted white, and her manicured nails as well. She looked very sophisticated, a new style for her, but one she no doubt has loved ever since her first photoshoot, and taking the advice of Mr. Mann on the improvement of her wardrobe. Nova no longer finding it appealing to carry herself like that of a young teenage girl, she is grown after all.

Arriving at the restaurant, Ramon parked his car, assisting Nova out of the passenger seat, taking her by the hand, his fingers interlocking with hers. The glass building opulent, a concierge opening the doors, allowing them access, upstairs, a large room filled with appliances, an open space, two chefs, a tiny table, and three bottles of wine chilling off to the side. Nova looking up to Ramon, impressed by him as he hands her a bouquet of white roses,

"Matches your outfit," he said. Nova, blushing, resisting the urge to kiss him. Their evening whimsical, Nova eventually removing her blazer when the cooking began and a few glasses of wine made its way into her veins. Laughter expelling from the room once they concluded, a smile she thought she had lost plastered across her face, feeling almost permanent; her cheeks beginning to hurt. Seated on top of the counter, her shoes now on the ground, and hours later, the pair was conversing, comfortable, Ramon loosening his tie and Nova swinging her legs in the air, inebriated, pouring her glass, tipping it almost. Speaking to Ramon came easy, so easy in fact Nova found herself retelling her past as though it were yesterday, speaking candidly of her stupidity, vowing to never make the same mistake again.

Ramon appearing perfect, too perfect, replied to Nova while listening keenly to her qualms.

"I could never do anything like that to hurt you," he said, tilting his head, kissing her plump lips, the sounds of their wet kiss echoing throughout the room, Nova sitting upright to balance herself and to keep from falling.

Ramon, realizing Nova to be impaired, drove the young woman home around 2 a.m. assisting her inside, up the stairs and into bed where she slept soundly. The next morning Nova awoke on the air mattress found in the center of her master bedroom, unable to recall the events from the night before, her headache excruciating. With her phone having lost its charge Nova woke staring at the dark screen pondering who could have been seeking to contact her, stretching her torso across the room she was able to locate a phone charger, plugging her phone she made her way downstairs, unpacking her video equipment and setting it up meticulously in the media room.

Ten minutes later while wandering the ground floor and utilizing the half bathroom to freshen up and re-twist her hair Nova heard the loud buzzing of her cellular phone upstairs. Retrieving it, she bypasses the countless text messages from Terry and missed calls from Tucker. She could not find the time to respond, gathering her things hurriedly she made her way across town, draped in a pair of pants, a button-down and a cardigan. Feeling unclean from a lack of shower she walked away from her peers, standing and conversing as normal as possible. Her eyes hanging low she arrived at Agatha's office where a reporter awaited her by the name of Allie Cristian. Agatha had yet to arrive. But Allie had other appointments, kindly requesting that Nova allow the interview without her publicist present.

Barely able to comprehend the Caucasian woman due to her hangover, she nodded in agreement. A newly bombast Nova speaking confidently, never processing the questions,

"Are you dating anyone?" asked Allie, ten minutes and eight questions later, Nova reverting back to Ramon, speaking without thought, she said,

"Yes, Ramon,"

"Ramon? Is this an African-American man? How did this come about?" Nova blushing, praying she could keep it together long enough to conduct herself properly,

"Hispanic," as the words left her mouth, she watched the facial expression of a dear Allie change from mellow to dramatically charged.

"Oh," she said, her head pulling backward. Nova feeling far worse now, dizzy, thinking to herself she is far too old to be living life on the wild side. With barely any sleep, the time now reading 6:14 a.m. she could understand why her body was giving her such a hard time—rebelling. Under her buttocks

Nova could feel the sweat building, her body warm and her hands trembling, she desperately needed a bed, to sleep. Wondering why she was not feeling this terrible when she was home in the media room, but something about being outside was making her disengaged. Allie wrapping things up, stood from the cushioned bench, extending her hand to Nova who meekly reciprocated. Watching as Allie exit, Nova shifting her body fell into a deep slumber, her head placed atop her cached arm, right there in the lobby of a thirty-six-floor high rise building in Los Angeles.

The sun greeting them by 9 a.m. Agatha stood watching a sleeping Nova in the lobby, guests making their way past her whispering in worry. Shaking her, she said,

"Hey, wake up!" Agatha demanded. Nova's eyes shuttering open. Gasping she looked around, flabbergasted, wiping the drool from her mouth,

"Oh geez," she cried. Agatha appearing to be angry, dragging Nova along onto the elevator until reaching the safety of her office. Tossing before her a magazine, Agatha calling to her assistant to bring tea for Nova.

"What is this?" Nova asked, slowly coming to.

"Paparazzi photos of you last night with some Spanish guy," she said. But Nova was not following,

"Okay so, I went on a date, what's the issue?" she asked reclining in the leather Herman Miller lounge chair found in Agatha's office.

"People are pissed, your crown's. I mean, have you even been on social media? I had to spend my morning in a meeting trying to conjure up a plan to get you out of this! At least the editors were nice enough to shoot me a heads up before they ran the story, but this cannot be publicized. He is a fling, and you're going to tell him it's over," Agatha warned. Nova shot upright, turning to face Agatha's assistant who was now delivering a steaming hot cup of tea,

"You don't get to tell me who I can and cannot date. Like, what is this?" she scoffed sipping slowly.

"This—this is fame! You are not some raggedy little girl living on the wrong side of the tracks because she got pregnant as a teenager anymore. You now belong to the public and when you go on rants telling women and men that their own preferences to date outside of their race is a form of self-hate and then go around practicing it, you're diminishing your credibility," Agatha screamed. Nova placing her hand on her head, thinking,

"I mean, I was angry when I made those videos and they usually stemmed from some bad experience with a guy, but I don't feel that way anymore. I really like Ramon; I'm not going to just dismiss him—"

"Yes, you are." After her tyrant and calming down, Agatha asked, "Did the reporter come this morning? Did you speak with her?"

"Yes, I told her about Ramon," Nova whispered in shame. Agatha shouting obscenities towards her window, sifting through her Rolodex where she located the number for Allie, dialing her. While the phone rang Nova remained perturbed, unsure of how things were going to unfold, she removed her phone from her back pocket, opening Instagram, her tags almost doubled with photos of her and Ramon sitting in the car pulling up to the venue and taking steps inside, there was even a photo up close of them holding hands, only further strengthening the speculation that Nova, is now, in fact, dating a man outside of her race.

"I knew this would happen which is why I did not want to take this route, there are people calling me names, a phony, a hypocrite, a liar; I mean Jesus. I just wanted to upload hair tutorials," she screamed. With no success of reaching Allie, Agatha slamming her phone down on the receiver,

"You spoke about Becky's and Afro-Latinas and how they are a primary preference amidst the men in the African-American communities, Nova and then related your own experience and tied it into a catchy name, Even My Hair Is Mad. But no matter how much you try to differentiate between the two: hair tutorials and relationship advice, it will never happen. These people are now out for blood, you don't backpedal in this industry, it's a sure way to get the media to end the very career they gave you," Agatha said sternly.

"It was one date," she said disappointingly.

"Sometimes that's all it takes."

23

That evening Nova did the only thing she knew she could do, she turned to the very platform that gave her a voice. YouTube. After a dashing shower and a few moments to gather her thoughts and avoiding the comments section like a plague she arrived in her media room. The room housing a solid white backdrop she set up her equipment, the tripod from Alex's house still with her, holding strong. Twisting out her hair after having it heavily moisturized, she decided against makeup or anything which could serve as a distraction to her audience, therefore taking away from her message.

Nova spoke explaining herself in detail speaking into the red light she had come to favor, taking a seat on a small bench.

"...and I never want men or women to feel like they are not allowed to be happy with the people they prefer to date. However, I believe my comments may have been misconstrued. I think it is important that we give our culture, our own kings and queens a fighting chance for our love and long-term commitment before making the decision to date outside of our race. With that being said, I am dating someone, who is Hispanic-American and he is by far very kind, and attentive, however, I am not sure whether or not we will last, what I am sure of though, one hundred percent, is that no matter where life takes me I will not make the conscious decision to primarily date outside of my race believing any other race to be superior to my own," she said. Nova now feeling relieved as she sat down to edit the fifty-three-minute video, hoping to get it down to only twenty minutes. Afterward, sitting alone in the pitch-black house, the media room illuminated she completed what was to her, a moment of truth, hitting the share button she waits. Staring at the computer screen, refreshing the page every now and then, Alex called, her phone buzzing next to her,

"Hey Auntie," she said peacefully.

"Nova, why haven't you called Tucker? He called me today worried about you, saying he hasn't heard from you," Alex said sitting in her home, her feet elevated to relieve her edema. Nova taking a long sigh, feeling annoyed,

"I will call him," she said lying, distracted now as the commentators began pouring in, before she knew it fifty-three comments and she was dying to read them. "Auntie, I have to go," she said hanging up the phone. Reading through Nova felt relieved, somewhat. People were citing their understanding, advocating their want for another hair video as her private romantic life is none of their business. This making Nova happy, she took to her phone dialing Agatha, who sent her through to voicemail. Nova hanging up wondering if Agatha was still angry and whether she had seen her new video, believing if she did, all would be well. That night Nova dialed Ramon exchanging a wonderful conversation, he was astonished to learn of how quickly he was catapulted into the spotlight after only a few hours. Nova discovering how worried he was for her when she did not respond to his messages or calls throughout the day, but she was happy he understood.

The next few days furniture began arriving and Nova now heavily busy, previous engagements from functions to photoshoots, and interviews, all piled onto her calendar and now Ramon spending more time with her, carefully making his way to her home where they would stay up watching television, Nova never feeling pressured to be intimate. Her life felt perfect, if only for a moment. She was smiling more, poised and with her hair now reaching her earlobes, Nova was doing more styles making her look exotic and bringing about a new feeling she never thought she could feel again—cherished.

Nova and Marian rarely speaking, Marian deciding it was time to enlist Nova's assistance with her show and so Nova arrived, one week later in the calm of the storm and her paparazzi scare was beginning to blow over. Inside of the large auditorium they stood, taking it all in, Marian to her left,

"I can't believe it's going to happen." She said. Nova wrapping her arms around her. The theater large enough to fill over two hundred people and Marian now expecting press, patrons and family she could not bring herself to fall short, not even in the slightest. "The show is going to be epic," she told her sister. "I have performers coming in and I'm collaborating with other up and coming designers who paid me to be in the show, can you believe that?" she grinned.

"Of course I can, you have status now, so I would hope you're letting people pay you to be a part of your show," Nova said.

"We didn't always have this, especially when we made the decision to sever ties with daddy Nova. So, I still think we should remain humble and grateful," Marian said kindly.

"My esoteric past can only be understood by a few people, yourself included Marian, I am humble, but I always do take credit for my hard work as well, and all of the sacrifices I've made—"

"Do you mean Tucker? That sacrifice? Auntie told me you haven't spoken to him," Marian said, twiddling her thumbs,

Nova sighing, "I am so tired of this, why is everyone making such a big deal about Tucker, he will be here soon, and I'll have to speak to him every single day."

"You make it sound like a chore."

"No, but he's my son, and the way everyone is speaking it's almost like its being implied that I'm neglecting him, which isn't the case."

"No, but I know you and now that your life is changing, I think you want to be free, but Nova, don't make the same mistakes our father made with us and have your son resent you, because that's the worst thing you can do," Marian said, walking away towards the entrance to greet the models who were now making their way inside for dress rehearsal. Taking a seat in the third row, centered, Nova, thinking long and hard, wondering if she was, in fact, making a mistake and should begin to slow down, she moved to send her son a message by way to contacting Terry, "Please tell Tucker I love him and I will call him in twenty minutes," it read. Nova meant every word. Thankful for her sister and her kind words she sat. watching Marian take charge, dictating, sewing, and walking her models through rehearsal. The drummers present, and performers all appearing for their walkthrough, the show only a few nights away. Looking up to the stage, Nova allowing herself to cry silently—feeling proud.

Don't forget to embrace and
celebrate shrinkage,
and have fun with your
natural hair!

The night still, Marian draped in one of her designs, taking the same approach their father did—creating for herself a color signature. An idea in which many designers still did not agree, believing it to be non-daring and easily mundane. Dash Signature the only man of his time to successfully accomplish this, patenting his signature color leading his brand to be instantly recognizable in every part of the world. While others have letters and logo, Marian had color patterns and signature fabrics like that of her father. An instant comparison made by members of the press who managed to catch a glimpse of the young woman.

The crowd pouring in, members of the media beginning to arrive, Nova and Ramon making their way backstage to greet Marian who wore a pantsuit, her Pantone colored monochromatic look featuring a blouse and a fitted bell bottom with a crimson turban wrap and hooped earrings. Her accessories minimal. Marian and Nova exchanging a long hug, her sister feeling tense, Nova offering her words of encouragement, the theater now packed to capacity, the lights falling, creating a pitch-black room. Everyone noticeable from the stage—some of which Nova immediately recognized peeking through the curtains and there he was, sitting to the rear, surrounded by a group of men standing before him, four rows and twenty chairs allocated to Mr. Dash Signature himself. For a brief moment, Nova could not breathe, paparazzi and media outlets photographing him, ready to run their story. Her father appears to have lost an abundance of weight, his face slimmer, he continued to sit, patiently waiting. Nova could not believe her eyes, gripping the curtains tightly, she struggled, torn between wanting to embrace her father or scold him for abandoning her, she did neither. Catching a hold of herself, she let it go, allowing the curtains to fall as she sauntered down to her seat in the first row. Now unable to concentrate, her mind elsewhere, creating scenarios in her head where she comes face-to-face with him, and then she doesn't. Seconds later her phone rings, it is Terry letting her know that both he and Tucker had arrived, seated in the fifth row, Nova standing, looking over the crowd for him, her son, her baby boy, and try as she may she could not look anywhere but to the rear of the room, at the nineteen empty seats and her father draped in Iris colored fabric, with snakeskin shoes and a pair of Santos de Cartier sunglasses that he wore inside, drawing even more attention to himself.

Distracted by his presence and the remembrance of her childhood Nova had not taken notice to the start of the show. A strange man taking center stage, into the microphone he sang, the tone of his voice divine, harmonizing a slave hymnal, bringing those in the audience to be moved with tears. Immersed in African-American studies, Marian could not allow this moment of homage to pass her by and so, she opened with the first view, a re-enactment of the mass suicide of the IGBO landing of 1803. Several women walking down the runway tethered to one another, their hands placed together in that of a prayer, their fabric light garnet colored, barefoot, with gold plated face veils, Nova sitting upright, her tears dry, her eyes widened as with the other members of the audience. Marian opting out of the traditional upbeat tempo of popular culture music to African drums played in traditional African folk music bringing some members of the crowd to their feet as the models danced while simultaneously showing their pieces and taking moments for poses amidst routines—a first to be done.

The African drummers all lined to the rear of the stage, shirtless and barefoot. They played. Marian was beginning to make history, one reporter racing through the back doors, requesting permission to run his story before the end of the night, as did many reporters beginning to follow suit.

By the end of the show, two hours later, Marian was receiving a standing ovation. Her depiction of African slavery translated to the fashion runway remarkably and tastefully done, the applause extending well over five minutes, respect filling the room. Marian looking down to Nova motioning for her to join her on stage as she prepares to take her bow, Nova, hesitant at first, but then making her way past Ramon entering stage right. Grabbing a hold of her sisters' hand, they bowed, members of the crowd whistling and screaming their names as the lights shone down on them. Marian and Nova hugging one another before exiting.

Racing from the stage Nova locates Tucker, falling to her knees she hugs him, kissing him, guests stepping over her, she was filled with regret, her eyes watering, looking into his eyes she apologized, Terry looking down on her,

"The show was really good!" he emphasized, still looking upon the stage in awe. Nova ignoring him as she continues to hug Tucker, looking around now amongst the murmurs and the large crowd she found Ramon, calling to him, all making their way towards the back, Nova holding onto Tucker's hand gripping him firmly so she does not lose him. Outside as the crowds diminish into the darkness, Nova stood patiently waiting for her sister, her mind no longer thinking of her father, until people began screaming his name from the distance, even strangers from outside of the theater who only merely glimpsed the color and fabric of his clothes, recognizing him. He remained seated, armed security heavily surrounding him. Nova could not see him any longer as he went out of view, but then Marian appeared, sweating as she ran from the stage to the rear of the theater, begging Nova to stick around until the theater cleared, Nova was nervous, her heart beating excessively. She just knew Marian was going to bring their father over, and the anticipation was killing her. Alex and Ryan are seated with Dash now, conversing casually. Guards ensuring the theater was free of patrons now instructing Dash to exit through the rear of the building just under the stage, with the paparazzi now swarming outside awaiting his arrival, Marian pushing Nova down towards him, the guards all walking menacingly behind him.

Down under the stage floors, Nova stood, Dash appearing behind her, intimidating Tucker with the look of fury wiped across his face, her son squeezing her tightly, Nova turning to face him, her heart beating rapidly.

"It's been some time," Dash said to his daughter. Nova remained speechless, everyone looking on in anticipation. Marian praying internally for things to go well. "You've both made me very proud," he said. His voice groggy, Nova remained standing looking up into his eyes, fighting to breathe, questioning whether or not she should hug him. She remained hesitant, seeing the fear in her eyes, bringing her closer to him, Nova sobbed, the tears falling as Dash took her hand, pulling her, Nova tripping over her feet, Alex and Marian sobbing behind them, quietly. Nova falling into his chest, releasing Tucker from her grip, closing her eyes, she envisioned those days when she was just a child and her father would play teapot or cook her a late-night snack careful not to awaken her mother for, they knew she would waste no time scolding them. She had to be no more than six years old, at this moment she knew, she had a father. Empathizing with him now having almost did the same to her own child, Nova only wanting change. There they stood, Dash feeling complete, missing his children, he extended his hand, pulling Marian to him—kissing them tenderly atop the head.

One year later...

December 2017, now one-hundred and two videos uploaded to
YouTube, a millionaire and social media phenomena, Nova
wandered through her empty home taking the time to say
goodbye. Tucker, grabbing his toys and book bag, meeting her
by the front door. Nova tossing the keys in the air catching
them, shutting the door behind her as she headed out to her
car, Tucker climbing in the back seat,
    "Put on your seatbelt," she said shifting the car into drive.
Making her way down the interstate in the direction of her
aunt's house Nova pulling into the driveway, removing a gift,
slamming the door, instructing Tucker to remain inside.
Ringing the doorbell Nova felt like she was heading to an
unfamiliar place, opening the door to greet her was Ryan,
holding baby Rory who was cooing and having a bottle. "I just
wanted to drop off this gift for you guys, in person. I know I'm
a few months late, but things are dying down now," Nova said.
Ryan smiling,
    "Hey, it's perfectly fine, just make sure you're back next
month for the wedding," he smiled. "Alex is in the gym
downstairs, you can uh, let her know you're leaving," he said
moving out of the way so Nova could enter, but first she
motioned for Tucker to now join her. In the basement Alex is
hard at work, sweating on the echo bike wind guard,
determined to lose at least fourteen more pounds before her
wedding day. Nova heaving as she laughed,
    "Don't laugh, we all don't have a fast metabolism like you
or can magically shrink back down to a size two after giving
birth," Alex said, her breathing stagnant.
    "Ha! Is that what it is," Nova said playfully. Alex remaining
hard at work, she could not believe Nova was leaving, heading
to New York to be closer to Terry and his children, hoping
Tucker can have a normal parental life.
    "I can't even believe you're doing this," Alex said, slowing
down her routine for a drink of water. Nova watching her,
Tucker taking a seat on the concrete steps.
    "Yep, I mean, I have some deals lined up in the city so I
doubt it will be that bad. Plus, I'll be in New Jersey, not
necessarily New York, but close enough so Tucker and his

277

siblings can have a better relationship," said Nova.

"Tuh, still can't believe they've had another kid," she said.

"Oh yes and getting married, did I tell you, they've invited me to the wedding?" Nova scoffed; her hands folded.

"Wow, two weddings this year. I wonder when you'll be attending your own, "she smirked.

"Hmm, I have no clue what the Lord has in store for me. But I am happy now and with Ramon, who would have thought huh, he wants to marry his own, after I almost lost my career for that fool," she laughed.

"Well, you've moved on, you're growing and glowing, and like you said, we have no clue what the Lord has in store. Just travel safely and I love you," Alex said deciding not to hug Nova while drenched in sweat. Nova laughing, providing her aunt with an air kiss.

"Bye Tuck," Alex bellowed watching them walk through the door. As Nova drove and made her way to the airport, she and Tucker parking her car for transport the next morning before heading down to the gate where they were to catch their flight.

In New York Marian flooded the news channels, the Megatron televisions and newsstand, she was now a household name. Nova having hired new management and a new public relations team explaining to them the importance of family and her strict 9-5 schedule she was on her way to the office she rented down in Times Square—headquarters to *Even My Hair Is Mad* products and television. Agatha losing faith in Nova during that brief moment of mild destruction made Nova leery of her, eventually firing her and deciding to move forward. With her leave-in conditioner set to hit shelves shortly, Nova was loving the new product, using testers weekly on her crown which was now reaching her shoulders.

Pushing through the doors she was greeted with esteem. Her employees speaking candidly to her, walking into the large conference room she saw a man awaiting her, his suit heavily pressed, promising not to stay long as she and Tucker were headed to their new home, but she had to meet with one individual, recommended to her by a friend of Marian's, Nova was hoping he would impress her and he would not be there to waste her time as many others have proven themselves to do.

Remaining bi-coastal for the past year was strenuous, and now she was happy to have chosen a destination.

"Hello ma'am, nice to finally meet you," he said, standing. "My name is Kenneth Anderson." Impressed by his mannerisms, Nova taking a seat at the head of the table, 2 p.m. and she was still energetic, having a positive feeling now about this guy,

"Pleasure to finally meet you," she smiled.

Works Cited

Blogs, N. C. (2018, May 22). *Naturall Club Blogs*. Retrieved
from www.naturallclub.com:
https://naturallclub.com/blogs/the-naturall-club-blog/7-
tips-to-maintain-grow-and-care-for-4c-hair

Thank you to the Naturall Club Blog for their wonderful haircare tips found throughout this novel.

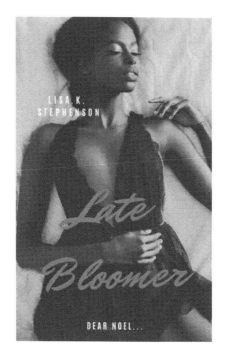

Late Bloomer
Available Everywhere Books Are Sold

CHAPTER ONE

Present Day

Noel pondered, listening keenly to the pugnacious woman outlining the play-by-play details of the affair she could figure was nothing short of karma.

He was successful, he was exhilarating, and he was married. Married to a woman who had made her way onto this excursion, tagging along with her a bitter and unpleasant revelation. With the truth stabbing like a thousand knives, Noel could do nothing but embrace the blessing she had growing inside of her.

Four weeks, six days, and eleven hours had her experiencing nausea, intense migraines, and insomnia to which Frances had yet to have taken notice. She was dozing off, misleading the woman who sat adjacent her into thinking she was listening.

Alicia was her name. Latina-American, five-foot-nine with long, flowing, straight brunette hair. Although she was beautiful and her tone soft, the words that left her mouth made her presence unflattering.

The story went on, but there was nothing she could do, no defense she could make. Everyone gathered around, confused on whether they were to console the wife, scold her, or rid themselves of her toxic company.

The room felt dark, and with little to no resolution, the ladies decided it was time, time to intervene the only way they knew how; turning to face Alicia, Frances said, "I think it best you leave."

Noel's best friend spoke as though she and Alicia had now become imminent strangers. The joy had been taken out of the room, the air now brisk as Alicia prepared to take her leave, the other women staring at her—their eyes glowing with malice. But it was not her they wished to have removed from their presence, despite her ongoing conversation; interrupting, Frances spoke with assertion,

"No, married lady! You need to leave."

It was at that moment Noel realized, despite this low point in her life, she could count on her friends to remain by her side. The thumping in her heart meant her anxiety was beginning to flare, and without so much of a second thought, as Alicia began to gather her belongings and roll her suitcase through the front door to await her driver, Noel said the words she knew was going to be enough to change both their lives forever.

Peacefully she said, "Alicia, please tell Nathan that I am pregnant."

Flashback

Seattle was cold in the winter, colder than she could have ever imagined. Walking around outdoors had become familiar whenever her parents quarreled. A perfunctory ritual, almost subconscious. Their voices would rise, and without realizing it, she would begin to dress in her day's ensemble to head outside and face the brutal winds that a city like Seattle could offer.

A young woman coming into her own, now twenty-six years of age, preparing to face the world, though her mother may not approve. Relieved by the fact that she had now escaped the den of parental disagreement, she found herself parked at a bench just five miles up from a creek across from the elementary school she attended. Mr. Kwon left to reason on her behalf, convincing his wife that the move would do her good, considering that one day the children would all have to leave the nest. Noel-Lee, Xavier, and their youngest, Daniel—who by now had learned the hard way that no one, absolutely no one, wins a verbal argument against Mom.

Noel was stumped, torn almost, as she watched the squirrels frolic around on the grass, playing, searching for food, looking as though they were having the time of their lives. Envious, she could not bring herself to admit that she had come to despise her mother. She loathed her for allowing her to grow up so sheltered all her life. She felt inexperienced, terrified to even consider going out on her own, to relocate and begin fending for herself.

But there was something telling her to do just that, something pulling her away from them, away from family, away from Seattle.

As the sun began to set, she continued to warm the park bench. Dear Noel, she thought to herself as she had many times, it is time to set yourself free.

Her eyes fell to the ground in devastation as she arose; she knew it was time to face the only person holding her back: her mother. Once home, she entered, shutting the door quietly behind her. It was half-past nine, and she wondered to herself how she had not yet gone mad. Half past nine on a Friday night and the house was so quiet you could hear a pin drop; everyone had gone to bed. Standing downstairs in the foyer of their Victorian home, surrounded by five thousand square feet, much of which she still could not account for, it dawned on her: this was her only chance.

Stepping lightly up the carpeted stairs, she realized she had to act quickly.

She entered her room. Closing the door behind her, she threw the closet door open and retrieved her suitcase, thrusting it onto her bed with the pink bedspreads. She began to throw clothes inside.

Ripping clothes from hangers, angry, her tears beginning to flow freely down her cheeks. She shoved her hair away from her face. As Noel looked at the clothes she found herself willing to travel with, she saw they were adolescent in nature. A tank top here, an oversized, homemade knitted sweater her grandmother had given her, jeans that were two sizes too small, and hats and gloves accompanied by overalls.

Noel halted. Taking a few steps back, she took a long look into her standing mirror, the one annexed to the back of her bedroom door. She felt trapped.

Placing her hands on her head, she felt bamboozled, tricked into a life she wished greatly she had avoided. Her eldest brother, Xavier, was thirty-three, living down the hall from her, and all she could think about was how one day she, too, would be just like him. No goals, no family, no ambition, just Mom and Dad and two brothers, the American family way as she had always been taught.

Sitting on the edge of her full-sized bed, she stared ferociously at the stuffed animals, throw pillows, and ornate pink comforter that her mother had purchased for her. She was ashamed to know she had gone through a portion of her adult life living like a child. Deciding to wallow no more, Noel changed her clothes. A tracksuit is fitting, she thought. Just then a faint knock came to her door.

Hesitant, she responded, "Who is it?"

"Daniel," the voice whispered. She loved her youngest brother; he was charming, intellectual, and welcoming—a heart of gold was what he had. Opening the door, she extended her arms hugging him tightly for she knew this was going to be it. The last time she would hold him for a long time.

Daniel remained clueless, and then it hit her: she needed his help. He was stealthy and could get her exactly what she needed to begin her new life.

She whispered in his ear, "Can you bring me the keys to the truck?"

Daniel was appalled. "Wherever you're going, take me with you!" he said. His eyes widened, "Take me with you, or I tell."

Daniel now peeked into the bedroom: He was no fool; he knew she was heading somewhere, anyplace but there.

Taking a long sigh, she said, "Daniel, no. Mom would kill me, and I have to do this alone." Gripping his shoulders, she knew he was not going to allow her to leave in peace.

"Fine," he snarled, removing her grip. "I am going to tell mother now."

She had never felt more afraid than she did now. His tone was calm yet frightening, but she felt he was bluffing until he was on the move. Making his way down the long corridor to the master's bedroom, he found himself face to face with the entrance to hell; at least that's what they had come to know it as.

"Please, please, please I am begging you! Do not tell Mom. Daniel, please," she whispered, her palms pinned together as she pleaded for what felt like her life. She knew if their mother became aware of her intentions, there would be no rest in their home ever again.

"Mom is a light sleeper; one knock and she will wake up!" he warned, balling his right fist as he prepared to thump.

"Stop! No, I will take you!" she lied. "I have no idea where I am going, but I will take you. You just have to pack, Danny," she said, feeling aggravated. She had hoped things would have gone smoother.

Daniel must have seen through her lies, as he began to bang on the bedroom door aggressively until their father came to greet them, erasing the sleep from his eyes.

Noel remained stationary, unafraid; despite what she'd thought she would have felt, she was relieved. Her mind was made up, and there was nothing anyone could do about it. Mr. Kwon, better known as Jin, faced his children, startled.

"What on earth are you two doing up?" he asked pushing his way between them, walking downstairs, begging for their silence.

"Please do not wake your mother. Noey, will you close the door? We can talk down here." Jin was a wise man; owner of three factories across the globe, he made a fortune from his candle corporation.

Slamming the refrigerator door, both Noel and Daniel sat at the kitchen island where they waited for their father to begin scolding them, which to their surprise he did not.

"Dad—" Noel decided it best to speak first. Jin lifted his left hand, palm open as he took a huge gulp of the Coca-Cola he had hidden to the rear of the refrigerator.

Sarcastically, Daniel said, "I guess everyone just wants to break the rules tonight, huh?" he scoffed.

"I haven't had one of these in seventeen years," Jin told his children as he took his first sip. "I know what this is about," he continued.

"Noel wants to leave, and if she goes, I go!" Daniel said.

Noel just listened, ashamed.

"You will go nowhere, and do not let me ever hear you speak like that again!" Jin scolded his son. "You are eleven years and will continue to stay under this roof until your mother and I see fit. Do you understand?" he asked.

Nodding his head in disappointment, Daniel reluctantly agreed. "But what about Noel? Why does she get to leave?" he asked. Turning to face her, Jin and Noel exchanged a look of understanding.

"My dearest daughter, you are my only daughter, but I know you have your need for space and companionship. There is a world bigger than our home that you wish to experience, and I for one cannot stop you." Jin could tell his daughter had been crying. Her sweet caramel complexion, dark brown eyes, and dark brown hair made him stare at her longer than usual. She had become a woman right before his eyes, and he could not bear to let her go. He understood this to be true of his wife as well, but knew it was simply selfish of them to deprive her of living her life on her own terms any longer.

"I will get your accounts set up first thing in the morning, and I will hand you the keys to the truck as well. Where exactly will you be driving to, my dear?" Jin asked.

Taking a long, deep breath, Noel could not believe her ears.

Envious now, Daniel said, "What! I hope when I reach my mid-mid-midlife crisis you and Mom are this generous with me!" he sneered.

"Oh, hush, young man," Jin playfully responded. "Your— your sister has not been happy for years! Have you Noey?" he asked, concerned.

"No," she said, tense now as she began to wonder if this was all some ploy. Hopelessly she said, "How will you get things going tomorrow? If Mom finds out she will not allow me to leave."

Jin took his Coca-Cola can and threw it into the garbage bin, where he then took out the bag, tying it tightly at the top.

"I am still the man of this house. Also, neither of you will speak a word of this to your mother! This includes my little drink," he demanded, and just like that, he began sliding his slippers across the elegant wooden floorboards back up to his master bedroom, where he closed the door ever-so-gently behind him. In a room where the lights were off and the street lights were beaming outside, Mrs. Kwon lay awake on her right side facing their nightstand, a tear falling from her eye.

Noel decided against sleeping in her bedroom that night; she awoke on the prime stone Ainsley sofa which faced closest to the den door. That piece of a three-sofa set was only a small piece of décor that made up their affluent living area. That morning, the malodorous scent of her clothing turned her face a blushing red. She needed a shower but decided against it as she could not stand the thought of stepping foot into her room ever again. The idea of Hello Kitty smiling on the back of her underwear repulsed her; what sickened her, even more, was that she had no other options.

"Breakfast is ready!" her mother bellowed.

The Seattle sun was now being generous, greeting them with natural light and bright-green, fresh cut grass. Making her way down the long corridor into the kitchen, she found what appeared to be a buffet-style, gourmet breakfast fit for any king or queen.

That morning, Jennifer had prepared waffles, oatmeal, sliced strawberries, strawberry pancakes, diced bananas, turkey bacon glazed with melted honey, freshly squeezed orange juice, and scrambled eggs. There was enough food to feed an army. Stepping into the kitchen and taking a seat at the kitchen island on the reupholstered stool, she realized what she would be missing.

As she reached in to grab a plate, her mother said, "Oh no, no, you are an adult and want your independence, remember? So, breakfast is not served for you until you cook it!" she said too politely. Noel was astonished as she listened to her brothers cackling from the dining room. Xavier had his mouth full, a complete disgrace in her mind.

"Where is Dad?" she inquired as she didn't give her mother's remarks a second thought; she was right after-all; Noel was moving out and therefore moving on to the real world.

Taken aback by Noel's lack of response, her mother was astounded, "You—you aren't hungry?" she asked, obviously disappointed to know her daughter was not seeking to grovel at her feet for the chance to indulge in the most important meal of the day.

Noel paced, frantically asking again,

"Mom, where is Da—" Just then, a horn began to honk outside. Immediately, the boys and their mother made their way outside onto the front porch. Their father was making his way up the winding stone driveway, the gates closing behind him as he pulled up to the front of the house driving a grey 2013 Land Rover.

Hopping out of the driver's seat, he shouted, "Surprise!" shaking his hands above his head in excitement, but Noel was not surprised. She once again felt coddled, deceived.

"What is this?" she questioned.

Her mother turned to face her. "This is your long overdue graduation gift. No more asking Dad for the car keys or bribing your brother into stealing them. This here is your very own car."

She was outraged.

"Dad?" she shouted as she turned to face him, no longer interested in what her mother had to say because, by now, she knew she was only hovering. "You promised me!" she said.

"Yes, I know, and then I spoke with your mother, darling, and you should have seen the look on her face—" Jin pleaded as he made his way up to the porch. But Noel was not happy.

"No, you both just want to keep me locked up here like some prisoner. Mom, you wouldn't even feed me this morning because you said I was independent now or whatever; I honestly thought you two had gotten it. But no, it seems neither of you do!" she argued.

"We get it! We get it!" her mother said.

Crying now, Noel turned to face her. "If you get it, then what is all of this?" she said, motioning to the car and her siblings.

"These things were wrong of your dad and I; we wanted to keep you here, and we thought that something materialistic would do the trick. But we were wrong, and we apologize," her mother said solemnly.

Xavier and Daniel both interrupted, "We all just want you to be happy, Noey," Daniel said.

"Yeah, we do," said Xavier.

"Xavier why are you still here?" she asked. "What—what makes you think being here is healthy or even somewhat attractive?" she continued.

"The truth is, I'm not as brave as you," he nonchalantly replied.

"That's just it though. I am not brave; I am scared as hell! But we must face our fears one day. You don't have to be brave, but goddammit, at least stop being such a coward," she scolded, making her way back inside.

Her parents asked to be alone. They were saddened by what they knew would have to come next. Wrapping her cardigan around her torso and throwing the front around her shoulders, Mrs. Kwon took a seat on the tiled porch step. Jin accompanied her. The cool breeze felt delightful; the weather perfect.

"We raised a smart girl," Jin said. His wife nodded in agreeance. Jennifer Jefferson-Kwon was born an African-American woman to her parents Mitch and Joanna Jefferson. A surge of nostalgia overcame her as she reminisced back to when she realized it was time to leave the nest. She was sitting adjacent to her mother, her father sitting to the right of her at their small wooden table one evening during dinner. Jennifer then politely told her parents that a cab would be arriving for her shortly, thereafter taking her to a hotel where she would be staying for a little while with her boyfriend until they found a place of their own. Of course, her parents were outraged, questioning whether or not she was pregnant. She was, but lied to avoid worrying them.

There she was, twenty-two years old, pregnant by a man she had barely known, Bryan Waters, who promised the world for both her and their unborn child.

Later that day, her father Mitch demanded to know where she was going and with whom, to which she later complied, telling them everything, from her pregnancy to her relationship to the possibility of her living with a man without having so much as a steady job. But she fought the urge to tell her parents the entire truth; Bryan was in his forties, a divorcee with two children from his previous marriage.

When Jennifer made the decision to leave, her parents did not quarrel. They simply expressed that she do whatever made her happy, and at the time, Bryan made her happy.

Once she and Bryan moved out on their own, things took a turn for the worse: infidelity, miscarriages, dishonesty, and domestic violence. It was single-handedly the worst time in her life; Jennifer swore from the day she left Bryan that should she ever have children, they would never suffer the same fate. They would be loved unconditionally and without question, never feel they were not welcomed home. She thought that was best.

"Honey, we have to let her go. She wants to experience the world," said Jin as he watched his wife's mind begin to wander, the expression leaving her face. He could tell she was afraid,

"What is wrong?" Jin asked as he consoled her.

"She can't go," Jennifer cried.

"Ah baby, she has to. We must let her go. Xavier too, he needs the boot! When they're gone, we can travel the world. Plus, Daniel is old enough to no longer need a sitter, and he'll be off to high school soon. We have to allow the children to grow up, sweetheart."

After a few hours, Jin managed to help his wife see things differently, Jennifer stopped sobbing now, thinking: a life without kids; at first, this seemed almost foreign, considering a child was beaten out of her, but now, she had no worries for she had a man who had been by her side for three decades and they too deserved a chance to experience their own freedom.

Stepping inside of her Victorian home, Jennifer had now turned a new leaf; having a new outlook, it was time she began living and learn to let go.

"Noel!" she shouted.

Made in the
USA
Middletown, DE